LOST IN MAGADAN

Extraterrestrials on Earth

A Science Fiction Novel

William Lee

Lost in Magadan: Extraterrestrials on Earth by William Lee
Published by: William Lee
© 2017 William Lee. All rights reserved. No part of this eBook or book may be repro-
duced or transmitted in any form or by any means, electronic or mechanical, including photocopying, recording or by any information storage and retrieval system,
without written permission from the author, except as otherwise permitted by US
Copyright law. For permissions, contact:
WilliamLee73@gmx.com
This is a work of fiction. While some of the places, agencies, institutions, organizations and historical events are well known; any names or characters, businesses,
events or incidents, and conversations between characters, are completely fictitious.
Characters interactions with historically significant persons, such as Stalin and Hitler,
are completely fictional as imagined by the author. Any resemblance to actual persons
or actual events is purely coincidental. The opinions and beliefs expressed by the
characters belong to them alone, and not the author.
Editing by Shanna Harris.
Cover Design by James, GoOnWrite.com
ISBN: 9780999531303
ISBN: 0999531301

CHAPTER ONE

Central Virginia
Last Summer

Snap felt a bit of nostalgia as he drove through the rolling hills of Route 29, an endless army of trees lined the highway; their ranks broken only by an occasional country store. In the distance, stood the Blue Ridge Mountains and a clear blue summer sky. Despite it being a warm day, Snap was wearing a pair of blue jeans and a green t-shirt. His black ball cap simply read: DELTA. Turning off the main State highway, he drove for several miles down unmarked winding roads, passing the occasional barn and field of corn.

Snap drove down the long dirt driveway leading to the old farm house. The unyielding summer sun caused him to squint to navigate the once familiar turn that led up to where the dense trees opened into a small field. The field, which once yielded crops, was now overrun with weeds and encroaching saplings. As the house came into view, he noticed the roof and shudders were in disrepair. A feeling of Deja vu washed over him as remembered playing on a tire swing and drinking lemonade near the large old tree in the front yard.

Dust swirled around the Dodge Challenger as it ground to a stop before the large covered porch that surrounded the two-story home. As he approached the deck, an old man struggled to stand, leaning on a wooden cane.

"Sit down, Pops," Snap hollered as he sprinted up the steps, removing his aviator style sunglasses as he approached the shade.

"I thought that was you, Morgan," the weak voice responded with a chuckle; "You got yourself a fancy new car, I see. A real panty dropper, hey?"

"I don't need any help dropping panties, Pop. That's just an added benefit," Snap said as he hugged his grandfather.

"I see you are wearing your old Army cap?" Snap asked in jest; "I thought you were an Air Force man." Snap gently push down the brim of his grandfather's tattered black ball cap which proudly displayed the slogan 'Army Strong.'

"It reminds me of a simpler time. When good guys were good guys, and bad guys got shot."

"I know Pops, do you ever wear your Air Force cap?"

"Sure do, if it weren't for the Air Force, I wouldn't be a triple dipper," the old man said with a grin.

Snap laughed; "That's something I'll never see."

"It's good to see you, Morgan. What brings you to this part of the country? Aren't you stationed in Utah?"

"I'm at Hill Air Force Base."

"I thought you were Delta?"

"I am. Just on loan to the Air Force."

"So, what they got you doing for the Fly Boys?"

"I'm part of a special unit, testing new battle armor and weaponry."

"Interesting, can you tell me about it?"

"It's mostly classified, but I know you can keep a secret. I'm testing a new combat armor called FALOS. It stands for Fusion-powered Armor Light Operator System. Basically, it's full body armor supported by a titanium exoskeleton. The built-in fusion reactor powers a 100-kilo-watt laser rifle, also referred to as a DE Rifle."

"Wow. It's come a long way since I was in the service. Guess you will be getting an Air Force cap soon too, eh?" The old man said with a grin.

"Anything seem off to you about the new equipment? Like something just doesn't seem right about it?" Pops asked.

Snap pondered for a minute, thinking that was an odd question for his grandfather to ask. "No, not really. I can't really say anything else, you know, national security stuff."

"So, what brings you all the way out to Nelson County?" Pops asked, obviously changing the subject.

"I'm in DC for a few days, Pentagon stuff. So, I thought I would come by and visit. Say, what's wrong with your phone?"

"Got a new provider. Now, I hardly get any service out here in the sticks. Think I need to switch back."

"Yeah. I've tried calling you several times. At your age, living alone, you need a phone that works all the time."

"Roger that Major," The old man gave a half-ass salute to his grandson.

"Pops, you know Mom and I worry about you. Out here alone on the farm."

"Speaking of my daughter, how's your Mom doing. I haven't heard from her in a while."

"Well, maybe if you had a . . ."

"Don't be a smart ass to an old man," Pops cut him off with a twinkle in his eye.

"No seriously, Mom is doing fine. She moved to Florida a while back."

"She found a new man, yet?" Pops asked.

"I don't think so. She hasn't said anything."

"Ever since your father died, when you were knee high to a grasshopper, I been telling her to find a new man – get married."

"She would probably be happier," Snap agreed. "But after all these years, I don't think it's going to happen."

The rocking chair squeaked against the uneven floor boards. White paint was peeling across the exterior of the house. Snap knew his grandfather did not have the strength or energy to keep up this house from a bygone era.

"Could I get you something to eat, a sandwich or lemonade?"

"Do you still have that homemade root beer?" Snap asked.

The old man chuckled and said, "I don't make it myself anymore, but my neighbor brings me some every now and then. Got some in the fridge."

"I'll get it," Snap said as he leapt from the rocking chair. For a moment, Snap felt like he was five years old again. "Do you want one?"

"Sure, I'd love to share a beer with my only grandson."

Snap walked into the old farmhouse. It was much like he remembered, except messier. How long had it been since grandma died? Was it ten years? Longer? As he rounded into the kitchen, he noticed the dining table was buried beneath hundreds of papers, documents, files, and books. The hand-bottled root beer stood in the old-fashioned refrigerator, ice cold. Snap returned to the porch; a cool breeze pushed through the worn screens. Pops was reading a hand-written leather-bound journal.

"What you got there, Pops?" Snap asked, as he set the brown, glass bottle down on the small table.

Pops leaned back in his chair and took a sip from the bottle. He appeared to be in deep thought. Pops said, "You know I won't be here much longer."

"Come on, Pops. You're in great health," Snap protested.

"No really, I'm ninety-five; every day I wake up is a surprise. Seriously, I have something important to say. So, listen."

Snap shrugged and said, "Sure, Pops, anything you want."

Pops took another sip of the sweet root beer and said, "I'm not the man you think I am. I've done a lot, seen a lot. Everything is recorded, right here in this journal. When I die, you need to come back to the farm and retrieve this journal. It will be here, waiting for you."

"I may not be able to, I could be deployed to the other side of the world."

"Doesn't matter. This house will still be here. It's not in my name; a corporate trust pays the taxes on it. When you get back, the journal will be here, hidden. It won't be easy to find."

"Why hide it?"

"When I'm gone, people, lots of people, will be looking for my papers. It will take them a while to find this place; it is well hidden in shell companies. But they will find it, given enough time."

"What's in the journal, Pops?"

"All the secrets." The old man smiled. "I was in the Air Force, in the beginning, when it all started." The old man smiled as he gently closed the leather-bound journal and patted it with his crippled hand. Snap was sure he saw a twinkle in the old man's eye.

"So, I hate talking about this, but it's obviously important to you. How will I find the journal if it's hidden?"

Pops grinned, "You know how people say, 'if these walls could talk.'"

"Sure Pops."

"Well, mine actually do. You still like plinking cans?"

Snap shook his head and laughed. "Of course."

"Well, why don't you go set some up under that shade tree," Pops said, pointing to a tree about sixty-five yards away from the house.

"Just like when I was a kid."

"Yes sir. Except this time, we don't have no woman folk to tell us we can't shoot from the porch."

When Snap got back from setting up the rusty old tin coffee cans, the leather journal was gone from the table and had been replaced by an old pump-action twenty-two rifle.

The afternoon flew by and Snap had to head back to Washington DC. As he was driving back down the long dirt driveway, he wondered, had just seen his grandfather for the last time?

CHAPTER TWO

Present Day
Milky Way Galaxy

Commander Forte coughed and gasped for air. He tried to focus on the objects in front of him. Slowly, his vison adjusted, and the cold, gray, sterile environment came into focus momentarily. He was shivering, cold, and naked. Hordes of tiny goosebumps lined his body, and he coughed up a pink, slimy, liquid substance; his lungs frantically grasped for air, until the fluid was expelled from his system and he could breathe normally. His thoughts began to sharpen, his legs gave out below him and he fell to the metal floor. He looked up and saw an attractive blond rushing his way.

"Commander, I'm so sorry. We have so much going on; you woke up before I expected." Forte stood up, twisted his head from side to side, stretched his aching neck, he was not shy about being naked in front of the female medical officer. Standing six-foot-two, with a slightly graying beard, he was well-proportioned and fit. Unfortunately for him, it did not help with the ladies because every member of his crew was genetically predisposed to being nearly perfect.

"No problem, Officer Telnecki, what's our situation?" Forte asked, as he cleared his throat of the last bit of pink slime.

"We just came out of the time-space bubble a few hours ago; I am working on getting the crew out of LTS mode," Telnecki responded, turning towards another *Long-Term-Sleep* unit to release the next crew member.

Forte had entered the coffin-shaped, metallic container 300 days earlier when his last duty had ended. Each of the crew served two-month shifts, monitoring the ship's functions, before returning to the LTS unit. The journey through space lasted thirty years, but the crew slept through most of the trip, only waking to serve their watch. Forte stretched one more time, listened to his joints crack and pop, and walked into the shower room. The LTS chamber was large, it housed over 100 units standing against the walls facing each other. Medical Officer Telnecki had only opened ten LTS units so far; each LTS unit stood against the wall with a door facing the middle of the room. As Forte walked past the units, he recognized almost all the crewmembers' sleeping faces.

Passing through the LTS chamber, into the shower room, he noticed two men and one woman showering off the slimy residue in which they had just been submerged. The shower room was one large open space with shower heads protruding from the walls. All three of the crew members in the shower room were tall with blonde hair.

"Good morning, Commander," said one of the showering men, as he wiped the soap from his eyes. Of course, they all knew it was not morning, but it was common for crew to greet each other by saying good morning after waking from a long sleep.

"Morning, Lieutenant. Did you sleep well?" asked Forte, smiling, as he was becoming more like himself by the minute.

"Yes, Commander."

Forte lingered under the hot water for ten minutes, thinking about the many tasks that would have to be completed in the upcoming days.

Commander Forte, while having the appearance of a human, was not from Earth. His planet, Vitahic, circles a star located in the Cygnus Constellation – 620 light years from Earth.

Forte finished showering and headed into the dressing room, where there were several officers putting on their utilitarian uniforms. The navy-blue uniform was a synthetic, form-fitting material, thicker than spandex, which protected the crew member from extreme weather conditions. The uniform contained millions of nanobots that would activate to protect the crewmember in hazardous situations, and it was capable of being powered by multiple sources, including solar, kinetic and thermal energy. The uniform was made from a ballistics resistant boron carbide fiber, and had a built-in forearm display that allowed the crew to communicate and remotely access critical data.

As Forte finished putting on his uniform, he attached the small star-shaped pin over his heart – one of only two distinctions between his uniform and the other officers'. The other difference was that commanding officers were to wear a holstered, laser pistol. The laser pistol, while fully functional, was mainly symbolic, as no commander in recent memory had found cause to use it. At one point, Fleet Command had even discussed discontinuing the practice of commanding officers carrying side arms.

Much like humans, Vitahicians were hungry after sleeping for long periods; so Forte decided to walk to the galley in search of food. As he left the LTS chamber, he noticed that more of the crew were stumbling out of the LTS units with the assistance of Officer Telnecki.

CHAPTER THREE

Forte stepped into the elevator, and it smoothly glided along an electromagnetic force field, up five levels, to the Galley. In the dining facility, Forte walked up to three officers sitting at a round table.

"Good Morning, Commander," blurted one of the younger officers.

He could not remember the officer's name, as he was the newest edition to the ship. Forte forgave himself for not knowing his name, after all, he had been asleep for most of the last decade.

"Good morning," responded Forte, hoping one of the seasoned officers would use the kid's name.

"Yes Sir, I'm ready to get back to work. I feel like a slacker having slept for all those years and not even producing a dream."

Captain Cordatus, a veteran officer grumbled, "You get used to it after a few centuries."

"You must feel like Rip Van Winkle, you know, the character from that human story where the guy slept. . ."

Cordatus cut off the young officer, "Stop talking about human fairy tales. The rest of us don't care about their fiction," Cordatus snarled, with a scowl on his face.

The young officer, not picking up on Cordatus' lack of amusement, insisted, "We need to understand humans as much as possible, we are going to be living among them soon."

Cordatus glanced over at Forte and said, "We need to understand their technology, physiology, languages, strengths, and weaknesses, both mental and physical, we don't need to know their fairy tales!"

Forte inserted, "As one of the few members of this crew that have actually been to Earth, both of you are correct. Humans, unlike us, are very emotional creatures that make many of their decisions based on feelings and chemical imbalances in their brains. Very few, their leaders, sometimes, will use logic and strategy, but, all too often, the ones with higher intelligence make decisions based on greed."

Cordatus smiled and said, "You just proved my point, that we do not need to know their fairy tales."

Forte shook his head in disagreement. "Think about it. Humans make decisions based on emotions; they tend to rely very heavily on their fictional characters to help form opinions on important and complex subjects. I read in a report that many humans determine who will rule their planet based on the opinions of their comedians."

The young officer smiled and said triumphantly. "That's why it is so important that we understand their fiction." He jabbed his index finger at the table to make a point, "because humans use it to make important decisions."

Cordatus rolled his eyes and scoffed, "I don't need to know why a dog chases a bone, only that he does."

Forte grinned and said, "One thing those humans got right – coffee. I wish we had some here."

"Coffee, Sir?" The young officer looked puzzled.

"Humans have a hot drink, they call it coffee. I had some the last time I was on earth," Forte said.

"Is it safe for us to drink?" Lieutenant Brevis asked, now joining the conversation. He had been patiently waiting, in silent amusement, for the discussion to flow into a less heated topic.

Cordatus leaned forward. "Like most human food, we can digest it in small quantities. However, normally we should make sure the food we eat goes through a sterilization process. Your Commander here, drank a little too much the last time he was on Earth."

"Hey, we don't need to tell that story," Forte cut him off.

The young officer hustled across the room and then returned with two cups of *limpicom*, "Here you are, Sir."

Limpicom was a thick liquid that contained many of the calories and vitamins needed for a healthy diet; it was perfectly balanced, with no unhealthy side effects. Vitahicians were stronger, smarter, and faster than humans, but not immortal. Centuries of genetic planning and manipulation had increased the average Vitahician's life span to 325 years.

Forte turned to Cordatus and asked, "So, are you going to miss Vitahic?"

Cordatus sat back in his chair and stared out the portal. "I have been on this ship for almost 150 years – nearly half my life. I have no family back home. I'm looking forward to settling down on Earth. What do you think about decommissioning the ship on Earth, Commander?"

Forte took a sip of his tasteless limpicom. "It's about time. This ship is nearly 600 years old. As far as giving it to the humans, I think it will go a long way in maintaining our alliance with them. This old cargo ship may not have much value to our people, but, to the humans, it's extremely valuable. Besides, it will be stripped of any advanced technology before we give it to them."

Cordatus was familiar with Vitahician trade policies, but asked anyway, "What tech are we going to let them have?"

Forte said, "After unloading the cargo, we are going to remove the electromagnetic pulse drive and land the ship next to their current moon base. They will use the ship's super structure to expand that. We will leave the old antimatter nuclear fusion reactors in place, but they won't be used for space travel anymore, just to power the new space station."

Lieutenant Brevis inserted, "We don't want them to obtain faster-than-light technology from our electromagnetic pulse drive, right?"

Forte confirmed, "That's right, we may be joining forces, but we still want to maintain the upper hand. They already have reverse engineered our antimatter fusion reactors, which gives them enough juice to travel within their own solar system. That is all they need to know, for now."

"Commander, what's it like on Earth?" The young officer asked.

"I know it's not healthy, but I wish I had some of that coffee, the humans drink," Forte said shaking his head. "The main thing to remember about Earth is that, out of its seven billion people, less than fifty thousand even know of our existence. Most of our contact with humans will be limited to the government agents with whom we work. We will be allowed out into the world to interact with the public on a very limited basis and only under strict protocols. The penalty for revealing our identity to unauthorized humans is death." Forte gathered his thoughts for a moment. "The last time I was on Earth, Harry Truman was President of the United States of America. They had just developed the atom bomb and could barely achieve flight within their own atmosphere. Since then, with our assistance, they have developed antimatter reactors, invisibility cloaks, and space flight within their own solar system. The Earth we see in a few days will be very different than the one I left."

Cordatus interjected, "Most of that advancement is due to the teams of scientists we left there. Why do only a few humans share in the technology we give them?"

"That's not exactly true. Most humans have benefited from the technology we help them engineer; and they just don't know it came from us. Most humans believe that their technological advances come from the work of human scientists," Forte corrected him.

"This is a great breakfast," the baby-faced Officer interjected, "it feels like I haven't eaten in years."

Cordatus chuckled. "That never gets old. I will have to thank the cooks for doing a great job this morning. Hey kid, do you even have to shave yet?"

The young man looked a little embarrassed. "No, I'm only sixty years old; this is my first assignment."

Cordatus lifted his mug, as if to toast: "I would give anything to be sixty again - with my whole life ahead of me."

Commander Forte said, "I'm glad we wake up the cooks first." As the four finished off their breakfast, the galley was filling with newly awakened crew members.

"Shall we head up to the helm and relieve the crew. They have been standing watch for quite a while," asked Forte, as he pushed himself away from the table.

Cordatus stood up and said, "Time to get to work."

After thanking the cooks for the healthy breakfast, the men walked through the corridor that lead to the elevators., filed in, and headed up five levels to the command center located near the top of the ten-story tower at the stern of the ship.

CHAPTER FOUR

The *Impegi* was nearly 600 years old and had been transporting cargo in outer space for 570 of those years. The super structure was 1,700 feet long, 200 hundred feet wide, 300 feet high and could carry more than 270,000 tons. The *Impegi* was a *Gerulus* class vessel which meant its primary function was to transport large amounts of materials to distant planets, whether for colonization or trade. The ship had a long cigar-like shape and closely resembled an ocean going super container ship. The ten-story tower at the stern of the ship, housed the crew's quarters, the LTS chamber, communications equipment, and the command center.

Even though it was designed primarily for transporting cargo, it was equipped with a modest arsenal of defensive weapons. The *Impegi* was equipped with one hundred positron torpedoes and an antiproton electromagnetic pulse weapon, which was capable for firing over 70,000 high intensity energy bolts per second. Not enough to wage war, but enough to defend against pirates or lesser developed species, like humans.

The *Impegi* was designed to operate with as few as fifty crewmen, but could comfortably house over 100 without retrofitting any sections of the ship. Since it was designed for long distance travel, and many of its destinations took over twenty years to reach, the ship was outfitted with LTS chambers, or long-term-sleep chambers. These chambers would slow the crewman's metabolism and place him in a deep, dreamless sleep for years at a time. While sleeping in the chamber, the crewman would age at a fifty percent slower rate. The Vitahician scientists were working on a way to completely stop the aging process during LTS, but had not yet achieved success on that front. Once they could calibrate the LTS to slow the aging process down to zero, then they could attempt to send a ship to another galaxy.

On a typical voyage, the crew would take shifts operating the ship, while the rest were in the LTS chambers. Ten crew members would stand watch and monitor the ships functions for any problems. If there was a serious issue, they would pull the Commander out of LTS; otherwise, they were capable of handling most routine tasks. There was very little for the ten on-duty crewmen to do, as the *Impegi's* computer did all the calculations. The ship was essentially on autopilot while traveling at FTL speed. With a crew of fifty, each crew member would sleep for several years and then serve a few months on duty; this cycle would continue until they reached their destination.

The most impressive bit of armament was not the pulse weapon or the torpedoes, but the nanobot reinforced plasma shield. The plasma shield would protect the vessel from attacking pirates or, more likely, an unidentified asteroid or space debris. Not even the advanced minds of the Vitahicians could accurately plot a collision-free course through space at twenty times the speed of light, taking into account the stars, planets, asteroids and space debris. It would be nearly impossible to navigate around these things at such speeds. The ship's computer would calculate and recalculate the trajectories of all celestial bodies while they were traveling, but inevitably some small objects would be missed. If the *Impegi* were to run into a small asteroid or space debris while traveling, the plasma shield would repel the foreign object. If the object were to pass through the plasma shield, within a fraction of a millisecond, billions of nanobots would be shot at the object. The nanobots were designed to interact with and dissolve the object into a fine mist. Finally, the *Impegi* was equipped with an outdated optical stealth shield which would cloak the ship from the naked eye and radar. The optical shield was original to the ship; even though there had been numerous advances to the optical technology, there had never been any reason to update it on this ship.

The *Impegi* was powered by six antimatter injected nuclear fusion reactors that powered local propulsion and an electromagnetic propulsion drive. This would bend space and time around the ship, allowing it to reach speeds of up to twenty times the speed of light. The ship itself did not travel faster-than-light; it existed within a bubble that compressed time and space directly in front of the ship and expanded it behind the ship. While traveling at FTL speeds, the crew would not experience time differently than normal; however, people on their home world would seem to age more quickly. When the ship was not traveling in excess of the speed of light, the antimatter reactors would simply power the thrusters, which could bring the ship to speeds over 450,000 miles per hour.

The ship had 100 crew and passengers on board for its final mission. All crew members had volunteered knowing that they would likely never return home.

Commander Forte, and the three other officers stepped out of the elevator onto the ship's helm. The helm was sixty feet long and forty feet deep. The entire length of the command center was transparent so that officers at the helm could get a panoramic view of space. When traveling at light speed, or while under attack, an armored shield would slide down over the window for additional protection. The shield was not currently in use, so all those at the helm could see the infinite sea of stars before them. The helm had numerous large display monitors that tracked everything from positioning, course plotting, fuel consumption, life support, systems analysis, cargo holds, and reactor performance.

"Good morning, Commander, welcome back to the helm," exclaimed Captain Pilosus, with the standard Vitahician salute.

"Glad to be back, Captain," responded Forte. Forte was genuinely happy to be back on the helm. Even though time passes very quickly in the LTS chamber, Forte was eager to get to Earth and begin the next chapter in his life. "Anything interesting happen since I was last at the helm?"

"Not really, we had a close call with an asteroid, and there was an incident with a small craft," Pilosus answered.

"What small craft?" Forte looked surprised. If they had an unscheduled contact with another vessel, he should have been woken. It's not common to have contact with another vessel while traveling at FTL speeds.

"It was a burnt-out hulk of a small craft, could not have carried more than ten humanoids at full capacity. It was not listed on any of our charts and did not show up on our sensors - until it was too late," clarified Captain Pilosus.

"Okay, was there any damage?" Forte sounded relieved.

"None for us. The plasma shield repelled it quickly. Nanobots were dispatched, but I don't think they were even necessary. The small craft appeared to have been abandoned for years, maybe centuries. No way it got that far out into space on its own power. Must have been dispatched from a larger ship, and something happened to it," assured Pilosus.

"Good. Anything else to report, Captain?" Asked Forte.

"No Sir, only that we will be arriving at Earth's Moon Base in five days," replied Pilosus.

"Thank you for the report, Captain. I will take the helm from here. You're dismissed."

"Thank You, Sir," Pilosus turned and walked toward the elevators.

After greeting the rest of the helm's crew, Commander Forte took his position in the command center. His large chair sat on a slightly elevated platform, in the center of the room, where he could easily oversee the rest of the crew. In front of his chair was a holographic display, from which he could monitor and control all ship functions. After taking a few minutes to verify all systems were functioning properly, he decided to send a message to Earth's Moon Base.

Earth was in a remote, mostly uninhabited section of the galaxy; therefore, it was unlikely anyone was listening to his transmissions. Vitahicians and their allies on Earth had established an ultra-dimensional communication system secured enough to withstand any enemy infiltration so far. The very useful byproduct of the Vitahician's failed attempts at ultra-dimensional travel, was the ability to send and receive radio transmissions through alternate dimensions.

Forte spoke into the holographic display directly before him, "Earth Moon Base, this is the *Impegi*."

Instantaneously, a crystal clear male voice was heard, "This is Moon Base, *Impegi*. Switch to UDC 12."

Forte understood that UDC meant ultra-dimensional channel, and he made the adjustment, "We are five days away from you, traveling at 450,000 miles per hour."

"This is General Stone Byrd of Space Command. We just detected you on radar," replied the disembodied voice. "Please switch to optical stealth. We don't want to frighten any human star gazers."

"Done," Forte replied. Forte understood the need to keep their presence from being known by the public and potential enemies.

The fewer humans that knew of their existence, the fewer problems they may encounter.

"Everyone here on Moon Base is excited about your arrival. How long has it been since you were on Earth?" asked General Stone Byrd.

"Sixty-one years since this ship was last seen on Earth, and this time it's here to stay," Forte responded.

"We are all very excited to see the *Impegi*. No one on Moon Base has ever seen a ship arrive from Vitahic, and most folks that were alive the last time you were here are retired or dead."

"Copy that, we are anxious to arrive. I will make contact again when we reach our destination," Forte said.

"Copy that, *Impegi*."

CHAPTER FIVE

Commander Forte and Captain Stella stepped out of the elevator onto the hanger bay, where twelve jump shuttles stood; each facing toward a closed hanger bay door leading into space. Each of the jump shuttles stood with their stern facing a center aisle, like cannons facing outwards on an old ship-of-the-line sailing vessel. The hanger bay was in the super structure of the *Impegi*, directly below the ten-story tower.

Each of the shuttles were approximately the size of a school bus, and could comfortably seat ten crewmen and 10,000 pounds of cargo. The jump shuttle was designed to carry crew and cargo from an orbital position to the planet. The jump shuttle was not the primary means by which cargo would be off-loaded, nor was it designed for combat. They did not have any armor and had a maximum range of three thousand miles under ideal conditions. An optical stealth shield was the only defensive technology on the shuttle.

Captain Stella was the chief navigation officer and had been aboard the *Impegi* with Forte on their previous mission to Earth.

On that trip, they had assisted the Vitahician leaders in nego-tiating a treaty with the American government. They left 2,500 Vitahicians on Earth with enough supplies to last several decades. The purpose of this mission was to resupply the Vitahicians with materials that were not readily available on Earth.

On the previous trip to Earth, Forte and Stella had stood watch together early in the mission. While most of the crew slept in their LTS chambers, Stella and Forte got to know each other. There were eight other crew members awake and standing watch, but Stella and Forte were the two highest ranking officers awake at the time. It did not take them long to figure out how to entertain themselves. Ever since that first watch on the *Impegi,* many decades ago, Forte and Stella would always schedule their watches for the same time.

The hanger bay was 200 feet wide, the entire width of the *Impegi.* The jump shuttles were 40 feet long, leaving a center aisle of 120 feet for them to walk between the rears of the jump shuttles. Neatly lined up along the center aisle were numerous metal lockers full of tools and equipment. There were also large dollies that could carry tons of equipment and cargo from the cargo holds to the jump shuttles. Each jump shuttle was enclosed in its own chamber. The walls of the chamber were made of a thick, shock-resistant, transparent material so that when the door opened to release a shuttle, the entire hanger bay would not vent atmosphere and depressurize. After a jump shuttle was prepared to launch, the transparent, blast door would close be-hind the shuttle.

The shuttles did not "take off" so much as they were catapult-ed along a very short track. After being ejected from the hanger, the shuttle would travel under its own power. As Stella and Forte walked down the center aisle, they saw a man crawling out from be-neath one of the jump shuttles. Stella instantly recognized the man as Chief Belois. Belois stood up, his dark blue uniform, face and hands covered in a black tar like substance. As he walked from the front of the shuttle towards Stella and Forte he said, "Commander Forte and Captain Stella, I was not expecting you for another two hours."

Forte Smiled, "No problem, Chief. We are a little ahead of schedule on the pre-entry systems check."

The Chief, whose primary responsibility was to maintain the jump shuttles and hanger bay, shook his head in disgust, "I got three jump shuttles that won't clear the hanger."

Captain Stella asked, "What seems to be the problem? Will the hanger bay doors not open or the blast shields not close?"

Chief shook his head, "No, No, nothing as simple as that. The jump shuttles are not lined up on the tracks properly. If launched, the shuttle would get hung up on the track and not clear the hanger."

Stella looked puzzled, "So they would launch half way and get stuck. How would we retrieve the crew and cargo with the hanger bay door open and the shuttle stuck partially out in space?"

Forte interjected, "We would have to send several crewmen out in space suits; it would take hours to retrieve the crew from a failed launch, as Chief describes."

Chief said, "I don't think we can fix it before we reach Earth."

"Do your best to get the shuttles back on track, I'm sure it won't matter. I don't think there has ever been a time when we deployed all the shuttles at once. Anything else to report?"

"No Sir!" The Chief snapped to attention and placed his hand over his chest, the equivalent of a military salute on Earth.

Forte moved his hand to his chest and nodded at the Chief, the Chief disappeared beneath the jump shuttle to continue his work.

Stella touched Forte's elbow and smiled, as if to steer him further down the aisle of jump shuttles. Normally, she would not show that much affectation in an open space, but she knew no one else would be in the hanger bay. "Shall we continue our pre-entry inspections?"

Forte grinned, relationships were not illegal aboard long-distance cargo ships like the *Impegi*, but there still had to be a decorum. They had to avoid the appearance of impropriety. Forte believed that most of the crew was oblivious to their relationship; at least, he had never mentioned it to anyone. "Shall we move along to the antimatter reactors?"

"We shall, Commander," she drew out the word commander and intentionally twirled her long silky blonde hair.

Forte knew what tonight's activities would consist of, but for now, there was work. "Shall we take the stairs down to the reactors?"

Forte and Stella walked to the other end of the hanger bay, past the shuttles, and entered the stairwell, which they knew would be empty. Two levels down, not even half way to the reactors, Forte grabbed Stella by the arm and twirled her around. With his left hand he pushed her back up against the metallic wall of the stairwell. He moved in close, dropping his hand towards her waist, tracing her curves and cupping her ass as he pressed his lips against hers. She relaxed, placed her arms around his broad shoulders and slid her tongue into his mouth. They continued to kiss for a few minutes, until Forte pulled away.

"What was that for?" Stella asked, with a smile.

"Just a preview of what's to come," Forte glanced down at her form-fitting uniform. Even after 70 years he still enjoyed spending time with Stella. To be fair, many of those years were spent in an LTS chamber. He wondered if he would feel differently if he had been with her for all those years. Vitahicians liked to think they were greatly superior to humans, and in many ways, they were. Yet, Vitahicians, like humans, have emotions. They feel, to a lesser degree, emotions like love, hate, desire, and greed.

"I can't wait," Stella smiled as she shook her mane of blonde hair and adjusted herself, "have to keep up appearances." She winked at Forte.

Forte and Stella continued down the gray, dimly lit stairwell until they came to the reactor level. As they approached the thick, metal door that lead to the reactors, it slid open with a faint, soft whirring sound.

The reactor room was one of the largest spaces on the *Impegi*, second only to the massive cargo hold. The cavernous space housed six antimatter-injected nuclear fusion reactors. The six reactors were stationed three on each side of the large room. Each power plant was the size of a large house. There was a metal deck running down the middle, separating the two rows of reactors. Beside each reactor was a smaller antimatter container that was about the size of a travel trailer. The entire reactor room was pristine, not a speck of dust or smudge of grease. A stark contrast to the rest of the *Impegi*, which was a cloudy gray color, the reactor room was bright white.

Stella and Forte meandered down the center aisle and walked up to the display monitor in front of the reactor on their right. Neither of them were physicists or nuclear engineers, but they each had sufficient training to read the display well enough to be able tell if there was a problem. The sensors were indicating that all systems were operating within allowable tolerances.

"Hello, Commander. Hello, Captain Stella," a voice cheerfully echoed from directly behind them.

Forte immediately spun around, startled by the intruder that had so quietly approached them. He instantly recognized Commander Furier, the ship's quartermaster. On a cargo vessel, as large as the *Impegi*, it was common to have a quartermaster that was responsible for keeping track of the 270,000 tons of materials and supplies. The materials contained in the cargo bay would be worth trillions of dollars on Earth. "Commander Furier, what brings you to the reactor room?" Forte inquired.

"I'm just checking up on Captain Manabus," Furier replied. Standing at five feet eight inches, Furier was short for a Vitahician female. She had shoulder length, straw-colored, curly hair with natural streaks of platinum blonde. Manabus was the *Impegi's* Chief engineer, who should be somewhere in the cavernous reactor room.

"I just came from medical, and they told me that Manabus had not yet received his stage three vaccination," she continued.

Forte frowned, "That's not like him. I wonder what's holding him up."

Manabus appeared from behind one of the house-sized reactors waiving a sensor devise in one hand and small display screen in the other. "I've been busy down here reviewing the antimatter containment system. It seems we have a weakness in one of the containers."

"How bad is it?" asked Furier.

"Not bad, looks like the container is holding at thirty percent strength."

"Thirty percent? That does not sound good," Stella remarked.

"It would be concerning, if we were just starting our journey, but we only have three days until we arrive. The reactors and containment fields will receive a complete overhaul before being reassigned to the far less strenuous duty of maintaining a stationary moon base. I will continue to monitor it," said Manabus.

"First, you need to go up to medical and get your last vaccination," Forte insisted.

"Okay. I'm going now," Manabus said dramatically, and headed towards the elevator that would lead up twenty-two levels to medical. Manabus understood the importance of getting the vaccine. Without it, the Vitahicians would be susceptible to all kinds of Earth-borne diseases and illnesses that humans had developed immunity to over the last several thousand years. However, stage three of the vaccine was to protect the humans from diseases that the Vitahicians could carry, to which humans had no natural immunity.

CHAPTER SIX

Commander Forte stood in the center the helm with Captain Cordatus and Captain Pilosus. There were a dozen officers and crewmen at the helm, all at their stations processing data and working together for the final minutes before arriving. The plan was to bring the *Impegi* into a geosynchronous orbit with Earth and then allow smaller ships to dock and offload the cargo. After all the cargo was offloaded, then the *Impegi* would land on the dark side of the moon, where it would be repurposed as a Moon Base.

Commander Forte and the others stared out of the helm's panoramic window; they were approaching Earth at 400,000 miles-per-hour.

Captain Pilosus said, "Look, there is Earth's moon," as he pointed at the window. Captain Pilosus was the oldest officer at the helm. With over 200 years under his belt, he could have easily served as the commanding officer. Pilosus stood six feet nine, and the only hint of his age was a few specs of gray hair and crow's feet creeping up in the corners of his eyes.

Commander Forte nodded and replied, "Yes. For many of us, that will be our new home."

Captain Cordatus said, "We should slow down. We are on a direct intercept course with Earth."

Commander Forte called out, "Reduce speed to 40,000 miles per hour, relative to Earth's speed."

"Yes Sir!" Forte heard the eager reply of the young officer he'd met earlier. The lad was clearly motivated to do good work and wanted to make a positive impression on the more experienced officers. It was too early to tell whether he would be successful.

"Bring us into a geosynchronous low Earth orbit," instructed Forte.

A few minutes later, Captain Stella, having returned to her post as chief navigational officer, announced, "We are approaching a geosynchronous orbit."

Suddenly, a deafening explosion rocked the *Impegi* throwing everyone to the deck. Forte's ears were ringing as his eyes darted around the helm. Crewmen were sprawled all over the large command center as if they had been tossed about like rag dolls.

Forte yelled out, "Report, report! What just happened?"

Officer Caelum was crawling back up to his station and frantically operating the display monitor. "It appears that one of the antimatter reactors failed!"

"How is that possible? If an antimatter reactor failed it should have vaporized the entire ship," Forte questioned.

Pilosus was just standing to his feet as he responded, "No, this was a one-way mission. There was only enough antimatter to get to Earth. We had nearly depleted out antimatter reserves."

Forte yelled out, "I need a damage report now."

Lieutenant Mare, who had a bloody gash on the right side of his forehead, said, "It looks like we are venting atmosphere from fifteen decks."

Captain Stella interrupted, "We have a 275-foot-long breach on the starboard side."

At that moment, the ship shuttered, violently thrusting half the crew back to the floor.

Cordatus said with confidence, "That was the remaining antimatter reactors being jettisoned from the ship." Forte knew that in the event one antimatter reactor had a catastrophic failure, the others would be expelled from the ship. He had never heard of it happening, though. He guessed no one had ever survived the first reactor exploding. The theory was, if one reactor explodes, jettison the others so you don't have a chain reaction and can possibly save the vessel.

"Commander, without the antimatter reactors we have no propulsion, no thrust," shouted Captain Stella over the rising noise of frantic crewmen.

"It gets worse, we were approaching a low Earth orbit when the reactor blew. The explosion pushed us out of orbit, and we are losing altitude," insisted Lieutenant Mare. "At our present trajectory, we will crash in eight minutes."

"Eight minutes?" Asked Forte. "Is that right?"

"Eight, maybe nine," answered Captain Stella. "But, we don't even have that much time. Once our orbit deteriorates to the point that we are in free fall, we will no longer be able to launch the jump shuttles."

Officer Caelum, who was now wiping blood from his eyes, said, "We have three minutes of power left in the reserve batteries."

Captain Stella objected, "True, but without the reactors we have no propulsion; we cannot steer the ship."

"But, we could use the three minutes of reserve power to activate the antigravity field," Forte suggested.

"What? Who cares? We have an eight-minute fall. What good is three minutes of antigravity going to do?" Shouted a panicked Stella.

Ignoring her, Caelum added, "We can also use the three minutes to power the plasma shield. It won't save us, but it will greatly lessen the impact so that some of the cargo could be recovered by the humans."

Forte was reminded that he was lucky to have a team of such clever officers. Now all he had to do was make a decision, for better or worse, he started barking orders over the chaos, "Commander Furier, send a message to the Moon Base advising them of the situation; then, get to the shuttle bay. Stella, divert all helm's command and control to Jump Shuttle 135, where all commanding officers will gather. Captain Cordatus, make an announcement to the crew that we are abandoning ship and to rush to the shuttle bay. Everyone else evacuate, leave now!"

Just as he finished shouting orders, a warning light materialized on his display: Optical Stealth mode had failed, they were now visible to anyone on Earth that wanted to look up into the sky.

"Life support and ship functions are still online. Everyone board the elevator to the shuttle bay," Cordatus commanded, stepping up to lead the evocation efforts.

Forte knew that life support, lights, ships artificial gravity, communications, radar, LTS chambers, hanger bay doors, and the Jump Shuttles all ran off a different power source and would continue to function for hours after loss of the reactors. Still, it did not seem prudent to take the elevator. "Are you sure about the elevators?"

Cordatus replied, "We don't have time to run down twelve flights of stairs and launch the shuttles. We have to risk it."

Forte knew he was right. They had to risk it. As the elevator whizzed down twelve levels to the hanger bay, Forte thought to himself, "Well, this really changes my plans - for the rest of my life."

No time for mourning the death of his future dreams of constructing an annex Moon Base, work had to be done. As he entered the hanger bay, it was complete pandemonium. Crewmen were rushing back and forth between the jump shuttles making sure they were all ready for launch. Others were running around trying to load up equipment and boarding shuttles. Commander Furier was directing her crew to load important cargo onto the jump shuttle's small cargo holds.

"All command officers on jump shuttle 135, we are two minutes to launch," yelled Forte into the crowd of crew frantically running from place-to-place. "Everyone else, get into a jump shuttle now. Now, now!"

Forte ran up to quartermaster Furier and shouted above the deafening sound of the ship tearing through Earth's atmosphere, "What are you doing?"

"I'm the quartermaster, and the ship is going to be obliterated! I'm trying to salvage as much of the cargo as possible!"

"You have forty seconds to secure your cargo on the jump shuttles; then they all launch!" Forte screamed over the roaring noise ripping through the ship.

Forte ran through the center aisle, shouting the count down and telling people to secure themselves in the jump shuttles. As he reached shuttle 135, he climbed aboard from the rear, all command officers were present except Furier. "Everyone buckle up, this is going to be a bumpy ride. Transfer control of the helm to me, Pilosus."

"Yes Sir," Pilosus complied with the order. "Ship's command is on your display."

Forte made the appropriate adjustments and brought up the helm and hanger bay on his handheld display tablet. Looking across the hanger bay through the open rear hatch, he saw most everyone was settled in to their shuttles. Furier had just secured the last load in shuttle 135 and was climbing in to sit next to Captain Stella. Forte peered out the hanger and all the shuttles' entry hatches were closed. Forte slammed the lever that brought the hatch down on the rear compartment of his shuttle.

Taking a deep breath, he entered the command code to open all the hanger bay doors. What if they did not open? What if there was a power failure right at this moment? It would not be hard to fathom such a failure, seeing that the ship was plummeting to Earth at over 10,000 miles per hour. All twelve hanger bay doors slid open; Earth's atmosphere crashed into the hanger bay with a deafening roar.

Forte did not want to launch all the jump shuttles at once, for fear that they would slam into one another upon exiting the hanger bay. They were not designed to be ejected while free falling through atmosphere. Forte pressed the button on his display screen that would launch two shuttles that were on opposite sides of the ship. Immediately, his hand-held display monitor flashed an ominous read caution light. He looked around and noticed the shuttle next to his only partially launched and was stuck halfway out. The wind was exerting tremendous pressure on the front portion of the shuttle that was extended beyond the super structure of the Impegi. Immediately, Forte remembered the Chief's words: 'I don't think we can fix them before we arrive at Earth.'

Forte had a sinking feeling in his stomach, there were two more shuttles full of people that were going to fail to launch. Forte looked over at the shuttle next to him, they were freaking out. He saw though one of the portal windows, it was the eager young officer, he was sitting still as a stone with a blank stare on is face. Forte knew this was his fault. In the pandemonium, he had forgotten that three shuttles had malfunctioning tracks. Thirty people would die for his carelessness.

"We have to launch the other ships now! there is nothing we can do; five minutes to impact," Cordatus urged him.

Forte knew Cordatus was right. What if launching his own shuttle was futile? Maybe the next button he pushed would be killing him and the others in his shuttle. It would be what he deserved, punishment for his sin of neglect. Forte launched two more shuttles from opposite sides of the ship. No red lights. Both successfully launched.

Then two more successfully launched. Six in total, only one got hung up on the tracks. Six more to go, two of which would lead to certain death for its occupants. Forte smashed the button again; this time the red light blazed on his display. The shuttle that failed to launch was not within his field of vision, Forte timidly spared a second glance at the failed shuttle next to him, somber eyes stared out the window, wondering if anyone was going to come and save them. Wind was flashing around the stranded shuttle. It was starting to glow a faint red from the friction and pieces of it were starting to break away. While the super structure of the *Impegi* was built to withstand extreme heat and conditions, the jump shuttles were not so stoic. Under normal conditions, the jump shuttles would employ their heat shield upon atmosphere reentry, but it could not be activated while stuck on the track. Forte took little solace in the knowledge that it's occupants would be burned to a cinder long before the *Impegi* slammed into the Earth's surface.

Four shuttles remaining to launch. One will end in a fiery death for its unsuspecting passengers. Forte smashed the button again. This time, both shuttles shot out from the *Impegi's* super-structure. Two shuttles left, one with occupants that were doomed. Could Forte have condemned himself, and his command officers, to death by choosing this shuttle? He had a fifty-fifty chance. He pushed the button. His shuttle leapt forward and was free of the *Impegi*. For a moment, he was relieved to feel the freedom of a second of weightlessness, then the substantial guilt sank his heart. The launch of his shuttle meant the deaths of ten crewman. Had he remembered, he could have crammed those thirty crewmembers onto the nine shuttles with proper launch equipment. Better to sit in the pressurized cargo hold than be burned to death as the ship plummeted to Earth.

Yet, Forte could not afford to think about the dead, he still had work to do, and it had to be done fast. Four minutes to impact. Forte had the *Impegi's* flight control on his hand-held display. One minute until he had to activate the antigravity field around the *Impegi*. He glanced up at the stone-faced Pilosus – unsure if Pilosus knew why the three shuttles had failed to launch.

Forte pulled against his harness restraints to get a better look at the *Impegi;* it was far below them, freefalling towards the rocky surface. Forte's jump shuttle had engaged its fusion reactor and was approaching Earth in a controlled dissent.

Captain Stella was at the shuttles helm, "Where should I take her down?"

Forte replied, "About a mile from the impact crater; find a place that gives us cover. We don't know who will be there to greet us."

"Yes Sir," Stella muttered, putting on the jump shuttles helmet and focusing on the controls that lit up across the visors screen. The jump shuttle was controlled by a hybrid of handheld steering and neural signals received through the helmet.

Forte's plan, for better or worse, not that he had time to carefully consider it, was to activate the antigravity field around the ship three minutes from impact. The antigravity field would eliminate the force of gravity on the ship. Forte hoped that by activating the force field, the gravitational pull would be lessened, and the ship's speed would be reduced.

Forte activated the antigravity force field, and, as expected, the *Impegi's* speed stabilized. Still not enough for a survivable crash, but perhaps enough to salvage some of the cargo.

"Commander, two jump shuttles just lost power; they are in freefall," Stella shouted.

Forte shook his head, "Do we know why, what happened?"

"No radio contact," answered Stella, "their optical stealth shields are not functioning; humans on the ground can clearly see the shuttles."

The *Impegi* had three minutes of reserve power. Forte planned to use two minutes and fifty seconds of that power in the last minutes of the fall to minimize the planet's gravitational pull. The final ten seconds were to be used to power the plasma shields. Forte could see on his display that the *Impegi* was essentially in a nose dive toward Earth. Forte rerouted eighty percent of the shield's power to the bow. It made sense to divert the little remaining power to the section that would receive the brunt of the impact.

Ten seconds from impact. Forte pressed the button on the display to divert all power from antigravity to plasma shield. The *Impegi* smashed into the cold, hard rock that made up the surface of Far East Russia. The plasma force field, which was designed to withstand impacts of up to 25,000 miles-per-hour, shuddered, as the force field drove deep into the barren surface. The billions of nanobots that were directly behind the shield reacted with the rock as they came into contact, turning unforgiving rock into a sand-like powder, until the nanobots were completely depleted. The superstructure of the ship, which was designed to withstand temperatures of more than 10,000 degrees and impacts of comets and small asteroids, crumbled and broke.

There was no hope for the thirty passengers stuck in the jump shuttles that failed to launch. Any ship made from human technology would have been vaporized upon impact. The *Impegi*, laying in a crater that was created upon impact, was broken into several large pieces.

Commander Forte watched as his ship, and dreams of expanding a Moon Base, disappeared into an ever-rising pillar of dust and debris. Having been singularly focused on the plummeting space craft for the last seven minutes, Forte, now accessed the ultra-dimensional channel 12 to the moon base, "Moon Base, do you copy?"

"This is Moon Base, we thought we had lost you. Commander Forte, it is important for you to understand, you have crashed into territory that is under enemy control. We have no forces in the area. Any contact will be hostile," General Byrd warned.

Sighing, Forte said, "As if this day could get any worse. When will we have an extraction?"

"Negative Commander, as of this moment, there is no extraction plan in place."

"No extraction? We are not soldiers, we can't defend this crash site. What is the technology level of the indigenous population?"

"They have advanced human technology. Including jet planes, helicopters, organized military forces with high command-and-control, oh, and nuclear capabilities," General Stone Byrd replied.

"Great, what's the enemies ETA?" Forte asked.

"Fortunately, the *Impegi* crashed in a remote area. It will take several hours for first responders to arrive, and days before serious ground reinforcements can arrive. Commander, what's your situation?"

"We lost three jump shuttles upon launch and two more in dissent, all crew presumed dead. Seven jump shuttles have survived. That's about seventy survivors. Most of the command officers survived. Beyond that, I still don't know the condition of the surviving crew," Forte replied.

"Sir, was Commander Furier able to salvage any of the Element 115?"

Forte bristled at the question. He was aware the ship was carrying Element 115 and that it was valuable, but above all else?

Forte replied, "I believe so, but I don't know how much was lost in the crashed jump shuttles." He glanced over at Commander Furier with a wrinkled brow, as if to say 'I know there's something you're no telling me'.

"Commander," General Byrd directed, "your mission at this point is to preserve the Element 115 you have aboard the remaining jump shuttles. You must not let it fall into enemy hands. You need to evade and elude the enemy long enough for us to devise an evacuation plan. You need to find a place to hide and sit tight. Moon Base out."

"Stella, change course. Our mission is not to preserve the *Impegi*. We have been instructed to find deep cover and hide from the Russians," Forte ordered.

Stella glanced back at Forte, "Aye, Commander."

Stella informed the other six jump shuttles that they were to remain in optical stealth mode and seek cover.

Commander Forte and the other officers had taken off their harness restraints. The jump shuttle was flying at about 300 miles-per-hour, a hundred feet above the ground. The officers were looking out the portal windows for a good hiding place for all seven jump shuttles. The jump shuttles had plenty of fuel for local movements, but could not cross the Pacific Ocean fully loaded with passengers and cargo.

The jump shuttles were equipped with optical stealth, but if used constantly, it would drain the fuel supply. Forte wanted to find cover where they would not have to constantly keep the jump shuttle consuming fuel to remain hidden. An hour spent looking for the right cover could conserve their fuel for a week.

"Stella, do we have ground penetrating radar? Can we scan for caves? I'm looking for a place to set down that won't be spotted from the air?" Forte asked.

"Yes Sir," Stella replied.

Commander Furier, who was sitting next to Stella in the co-pilot's seat, started pressing buttons on the display. "Sensors indicate we are rapidly approaching a mountain range; the humans call it Chersky. It is about 900 miles long and the highest peak is 10,000 feet."

Captain Pilosus, looking at his hand-held display, added, "The Chersky mountain range is essentially uninhabited. There is little chance of detection, but we would be close enough to the crash site, if we are careful."

CHAPTER SEVEN

Present Day
Moon Base

Major Tom woke up at six am, just as he did every day, without the benefit of an alarm clock. He was sleeping in his twin bed; his personal quarters were smaller than a standard hotel room, as space was at a premium on the Moon Base. At least he had his own quarters; many of the lower ranking officers had roommates. As he unraveled from his twisted gray sheets, he stretched his arms and glanced out the small portal that stood watch over his bed. He was thankful for the window; not everyone had a view of the rocky moon surface. In the six months, that he had been stationed on the Moon, he had never left the confines of the base. His position did not require him to go outside the base's ten-story structure.

The Moon Base had an enormous footprint, larger than any Earthly shopping mall. The ground level of the base was a large open area used to store space craft and vehicles that could be used to explore the rocky surface. Space craft could land directly next to the large hanger and be transported into the bay through a series of air locks. From the base's command center, they could monitor all Earthly communications, travel, and dangers lurking in deep space. The level directly below the command center was the human crew's quarters and DFAC. The Vitahicians, often referred to as Nordics, worked side-by-side with humans, but preferred their own separate crew's quarters.

Levels three and four, above the hanger bay, were off limits to all humans. In those levels, the Nordics had complete autonomy to do whatever they wanted, away from prying eyes. It was sovereign Vitahician territory. That was the deal struck between Americans and Vitahicians decades earlier. In exchange for greatly advanced technology, the Americans agreed to give the Nordics their own sovereign territory, on Earth and the Moon Base.

Major Tom stood a slight five and a half feet tall, had strong jaw, and light brown, closely cropped, hair. Upon graduating from MIT at the top of his class, with an advanced astrophysics degree, he was courted by the top global corporations. He was offered signing bonuses large enough to pay off his student loans and buy a house in the suburbs. He never intended to go into the military; the idea never even crossed his mind. He always thought he would get a job working for a big corporation earning three to four hundred thousand a year, and maybe settle down and marry a smoking-hot chick and have some kids. That was not to be.

His whole life changed when, shortly before graduation, he was contacted by an Air Force recruiter. At first, he blew him off, but the recruiter persisted. Tom finally ceded agreed to do one interview. The recruiter met him at his apartment on a Friday morning and told Tom that he had to sign a confidentially agreement before even moving forward on the interview. Tom begrudgingly signed it and was told that if he spoke to anyone about what he saw, he would be thrown into an off-shore detention center for the rest of his life – no lawyer, no trial. By the look on the recruiter's face,

Tom knew he was telling the truth. He and the recruiter drove to the nearest Air Force Base and into an unmarked hanger.

There, Tom was introduced to an Air Force pilot who was standing in front of an unrecognizable plane. The recruiter explained to Tom that while NASA was reporting to the public about rovers being sent to Mars, the Air Force had been landing humans on both the Moon and Mars for decades. He went on to explain that they had a space ship that could carry people to Jupiter and back in a matter of a few days. The pilot explained that the antigravity plane behind him was capable of speeds up to Mach 6 and could travel around the globe in a few hours. The most impressive part was that the Mach 6 plane was over 20 years old.

The recruiter boasted that the technology Tom was being shown was nothing compared to what the Air Force truly had to offer. After taking a ride in the Mach 6 plane, Tom was beyond convinced, he was captivated. After signing numerous non-disclosure agreements, the Air Force gave him a measly signing bonus and sent him to officer's training school. Over the next several months, Tom learned about the existence of alien technology, treaties with other worlds, and the Moon Base. He was surprised to learn that the penalty for unauthorized disclosure of classified alien technology was not imprisonment - but death.

Like all other officers on the base, he had to follow a strict code of silence. There was absolutely no communication with Earth, other than official military business. Moon Base personnel were not allowed to return home prior to their leave for any reason, not for car accidents, holidays, or even family deaths. There was no email or video conferencing with people back on Earth. Most of the men on the base were single.

As Major Tom put on his clothes and made his bed, he thought about Marie, his girlfriend. 'Girlfriend' may be overstating it. She was a girl back in San Diego that he used for sex. He wanted more; he really liked her, but she could not wrap her head around him being gone for six months at a time with no communication. She protested that other military personnel could email and skype while they were deployed. It frustrated him that he could not tell her what he did.

He stepped out into a long hallway that contained dozens of doors. Each door led to crew's sleeping quarters. On the same level as the crew's quarters was the Dining Facility and recreational facilities. Tom had fifteen minutes before he had to be at his post; so, he stopped at the DFAC to grab a banana and cup of coffee.

"Good morning, Major Tom." The greeting came from one of the eight full time cooks that worked in the DFAC. Archie was Tom's favorite cook.

"Can I scramble you up some eggs, Major Tom? Or how about some grits and bacon?" Archie sounded even more cheerful than normal.

"No thanks, Archie, not today. I'm just going to get some coffee and a banana," Tom replied as he filled up a mug and pointed to a basket full of fruit.

"Big day, huh," Archie nodded his head as if to say he already knew. Even though he was a chef, Archie held a security clearance comparable to the President of the United States. Still, he should not have known what was happening today – compartmentalization at its finest.

"Don't know what you are talking about Archie," Major Tom smiled, security was not his department. Of course, on a base where everyone knew everyone else, the favorite chef is going to overhear conversations.

Archie chuckled. Archie was one of the few African American crew. In his late fifties, he had a pot belly and would normally never meet the physical qualification to be in the Air Force. Space Command was different. In addition to being an excellent Chef, prior to his first retirement, Archie had been a test pilot for experimental antigravity planes. Since Space Command wanted as few people to know about aliens and moon bases as possible, it made sense to recycle people that already had the knowledge rather than train new ones. Throughout Space Command, you would find seemingly entry level positions, cooks and janitors, filled with persons of incredible talent. It was commonplace to meet a maintenance technician that, in his first career, had been a test pilot or assassin. Space Command paid otherwise lower-skilled workers incredible salaries due to the top-secret nature of the things they may hear or see. It's hard to convince an eighteen-year-old high school graduate that's flipping burgers to keep his mouth shut about an interstellar space ship.

Tom walked to the elevator and pressed the button for the sixth floor where he worked most of the time. His team was developing a low yield antiproton ultra-dimensional missile to fire from the Moon Base at another planet. The missile would be completely undetectable to any radar because it would phase out into another dimension during travel time and only reappear in target dimension seconds before impact. Upon impact, the antiproton, a form of antimatter, would react with actual matter, creating an explosion equal to a 1,000-megaton bomb, yielding little to no long-term radiation. When the project was completed, the 1,000-megaton bomb would be capable of cracking the Earth's surface and lighting the atmosphere on fire for 100 years. The ultra-dimensional aspects of this weapon were still in the experimental stages, but the antiproton missile was operational. Major Tom could not figure out why Space Command would want a missile that would break open the Earth like a child breaks open a piñata at a birthday party.

He and his team had just finished the final testing phase of another, more useful project. They had developed a *Low Yield Tactical Earth Penetrating Nuke with Optical Stealth*, or TEPNOS for short. The TEPNOS could be fired from the Moon Base and penetrate deep into the ground before detonation on a time delay set by a controller. The TEPNOS also had a variable yield aspect, allowing the controller to adjust the nuclear yield after launching the missile. The primary purpose of this weapon was to take out deep underground military bases and terrorists hiding in caves. This weapon would cause all the devastation of a nuclear blast with none of the long-term radiation issues. This was a relatively small nuclear missile and the variable yield could be anywhere from two kilotons to fifteen kilotons depending on the target and objective.

General Stone Byrd of United States Space Command, a division of the United States Air Force, stood in the command center of the Moon Base overlooking dozens of officers seated at their work stations. Unlike the FBI, CIA, ATF, DHS and any number of other government agencies that had compartmentalized data, the NSA and Space Command had real time access to all computer systems and the authority to step in and assume control of any operation. The President of the United States was on a need to know basis, but was briefed, upon taking office, to whom he would be receiving orders from should the need arise. Day-to-day military operations and political bickering was handled by the President, but all strategic decisions were made by General Byrd.

General Byrd was arguably one of the most powerful men in the world. He was one of twelve people chosen to handle all issues regarding planetary defense. President Harry Truman had decided that interplanetary representation and defense was too important an issue to leave to petty politicians and political whims. Truman established the Air Force, NSC, CIA, NSA, and, perhaps, most importantly, the Majestic Twelve. These organizations, each operating in secrecy, would handle all issues pertaining to interplanetary negotiations, trade, and defense. When Truman handed the reigns to Eisenhower, he explained the situation, and Ike continued the policy through his eight years in office. After ten years of building the military industrial complex, Majestic Twelve became a force so powerful that even the U.S. President could not remove them.

General Byrd was second generation MJ-12. At sixty-five years old, he was the most senior member. General Byrd's title within the Majestic community was MJ-1. However, even he had to yield his considerable power to an MJ-12 vote of all members. All members of MJ-12 had above top-secret clearance. General Byrd knew he held the fate of the world in his hands; billions of souls depended on his decisions, and most of them did not even know he existed. Nor would they. The Moon Base, aliens, technology, alien wars and space craft were all above top secret and would never be revealed to the public. While NASA was still sending rovers to Mars, they were sending manned space craft to Neptune. During the 1950s and 1960s, the Air Force had toyed with the idea of disclosure. Project Grudge and Operation Blue Book were attempts to gradually reveal information to the public, but those plans were canceled in favor of deception. Some of his fellow MJ-12 members were responsible for manipulating the media into portraying those who believe aliens exist as unhinged, conspiracy theorists. There was an entire division at the CIA whose sole function was to discredit and destroy the character of anyone claiming to believe in aliens, but that was not his department.

Today was quite possibly the biggest day in General Byrd's long career. During his tenure, he had worked side by side with hundreds of Vitahician aliens, personally flown a space ship to Neptune, oversaw the development of Mach 6 AG Fighters, and even executed a few Large Gray aliens when the opportunity arose. But today would be a first, and based on his age, most likely his last first. Today, he would witness an event that had not happened in over seventy years.

"Good morning, General Byrd," said General Johnson as he joined him in the back of the command center. General Johnson was tall, lanky, and had thinning gray hair. The men had grown close. After all, the circle of men that could relate to their activities was extraordinarily limited.

"Morning, General, are you ready for the big event?" Byrd asked as he sipped on his black coffee.

"Been ready for twenty years, Sir," Johnson replied.

"*Impegi* is approaching low Earth orbit," one of the junior officers called out.

Two huge thirty-foot display panels in the front of the command center showed the *Impegi* approaching a low Earth orbit. Every eye that was not staring down at their own display panel was trained on the big screen in the front of the large room. Just as the *Impegi* was reaching an orbital speed, the unthinkable happened; a fireball shot out of her side like a volcano erupting.

"What in the fuck was that?" General Byrd barked at the officers nearest to him while spilling some of the coffee out of his white ceramic mug.

For a moment, Byrd could not process what he was seeing. It was so unexpected and unimaginable.

"Looks like an explosion," said one young officer.

"The antimatter reactor just exploded," said Mudar, one of the Nordic officers. Mudar had been on the Moon Base since it was first commissioned in 1987.

"What can we do?" Byrd asked, deferring to the alien's centuries of experience.

"Nothing, all is lost," Mudar flatly stated, "The other antimatter reactors will be vaulted out of the ship. At this orbit, the ship will crash to Earth before we can reach it."

"How long to impact?" Stone Byrd called out to the command center.

"Eight minutes, tops."

"Where will the ship crash?" Byrd asked.

"All trajectories point to Siberia - Russia."

"Will the cargo survive?"

"No way to tell, depends on the skill of the Captain," the Nordic responded.

Byrd looked at General Johnson, "What can we do to help? Those damn Russians will be all over our cargo like stink on shit."

Johnson shrugged and said, "We can give them cover."

"How?" Byrd questioned.

"As it stands now, the Russians can clearly see our cargo ship crashing into Siberia. They have very limited military resources in Siberia since they moved most of their military to the Ukraine border. If we gave them more targets to track, it would dilute their fighting force, giving our guys a chance to escape or recover cargo," Johnson quietly explained.

"Brilliant!" Byrd exclaimed. "All we have to do is nuke Russia."

"Get Major Tom up here now!" General Byrd commanded, with a slight grin on his face. This was the perfect opportunity to test out his new missiles.

CHAPTER EIGHT

"Never let a good crisis go to waste," Byrd thought to himself with a smile.

One minute later, Major Tom was snapping to attention before him with a slightly confused look on his face. "You requested my presence, Sir?"

"At ease, officer. What is the status of the ultra-dimensional missiles?" Byrd barked.

Major Tom, not at ease in the slightest, replied, "Months away from testing."

"What do we have ready now? That we can launch at this very moment?" Byrd insisted.

"I have ten TEPNOS missiles ready to launch," Major Tom offered.

"What's their yield and blast radius?"

"They are variable yield, Sir. We could set a blast radius of one mile, or up to 17 miles. We can also dial back the long term radioactive effects to nearly zero," answered Tom, somewhat proud that his invention might actually be used.

"I want six TEPNOS missiles launched at Russia right now!" Byrd called out to his command center. "We need to create a diversion, so the Russians will have something else to worry about besides our cargo ship."

The special weapons targeting officer, sitting near the front of the command center asked, "Target locations?"

"I want each missile to strike between two and five hundred miles of the *Impegi's* projected crash site," Byrd replied, "Don't let those missiles get so close to the *Impegi* that it will harm the ship, but they need to be close enough that the Russians won't know which site to investigate first, giving our guys a chance. If you can place the missile in uninhabited zones, then do so, if not. . ." The General's voice trailed off. Everyone understood.

Officer Denny called out, "*Impegi's* projected crash site in in the middle of the Magadan district in Far East Russia, north west of the Okhotsk Sea, at the foot of the Chersky mountain range."

Byrd mumbled, "Good, at least I won't be responsible for killing thousands of people today. Launch the optical stealth missiles, have them targeted in a star burst pattern around the *Impegi*, two hundred to five hundred miles apart."

The Magadan district of Russia had less than 160,000 people inhabiting over 178,000 square miles of land, most of whom lived in the port city of Magadan. With an average of less than one person per square mile, there was a good chance collateral damage could be kept to a minimum.

Byrd asked, "How long do we control the trajectory of these missiles?"

Major Tom responded, "Impact will be in six minutes. We will have flight control for the next five minutes, and we can choose to disarm any time before impact."

Tom knew the order to disarm would not be given. The thought of his team's creation being the cause of a major war was unsettling.

"I want a population map up on the display now. Guide these missiles to low density population areas, avoid all cities and towns. They are meant to be a distraction, to give the Russians something to investigate besides my space ship. If we can do this with no collateral damage, then let's make that happen," Byrd ordered.

"Three minutes to impact," officer Denny called out. "Final targeting solutions acquired, projected death toll - under two hundred."

"Just how stealth are these things? I can't have a trail of bread crumbs pointing back to our secret Moon Base," Byrd asked.

"In all the tests, they were never detected by any radar or sensors, not even our advanced stuff. It's highly unlikely that the Russians will be able to detect these prior to impact. Upon impact, they will register on every sensor on the planet." Major Tom replied flatly. "The Russians will have plenty of holes to investigate before they find the one your space ship inhabits," Major Tom assured the General.

Byrd pushed his lower lip up with his index finger and squinted his eyes as if he were pondering the meaning of life, which he was in a way. "Dial back the yield on each of them to between two and three kilotons. Mix it up so that the explosions are not all the exact same size. Make all of the distances from each other different. I don't want an obvious pattern."

"Yes Sir, impact in two minutes."

"When will the *Impegi* crash?"

"One minute and fifteen seconds."

"Close enough. the Russians will have a complete cluster fuck on their hands. This will buy us hours, if not days, before they figure it out," commented Byrd.

He glanced over at a startled Major Tom, "Well, today did not go as planned. I guess I better call the President and let him know I just nuked Russia."

"Better you than me," Major Tom said, shaking his head as he turned to go back to his lab.

"Where do you think you are going?" growled Byrd. "You just nuked Russia. Finish what you started. You run the command center while I go call the President."

"Yes Sir," said the Major.

Byrd turned and walked into his personal office at the back of the command center. Major Tom could see him picking up a red phone through the transparent glass walls.

Standing at the rear of the command center with his back to Byrd, he looked over the dozen or so officers in the room, some of them outranked him. All of them had more experience. "What the hell am I doing? I'm just an engineer," He thought to himself.

What was that phrase he had heard, when you wanted a status report? Oh, Yeah, "Sit Rep," he called out.

"Ten seconds to *Impegi's* impact," someone from the front of the room responded.

"It appears multiple shuttles or escape pods were launched. Fifty seconds to first missile's impact," was the reply from the officer sitting nearest to him.

Shuttles, that means survivors. That means the TEPNOS cannot detonate near the shuttles.

"Will any of the shuttle's trajectories place them near one of the TEPNOS blast zones?" Asked Major Tom.

"Five of the missiles are hundreds of miles from the shuttles' projected trajectory. However, one of TEPNOS may impact within 100 miles of the shuttles. . ."

"*Impegi* has crashed," interrupted another officer.

"Forty seconds till TEPNOS impact."

Forty seconds. That was not enough time to change the missiles trajectory, in any meaningful way.

"Terminate the TEPNOS nearest the shuttle craft," yelled Tom.

"Terminated," The special weapons targeting officer reported.

"Pull up all satellite coverage of Magadan," Tom spat out quickly.

The huge display monitors before the command center lit up with images of explosions and mushroom clouds forming over Far East Russia. The ever-expanding cloud of dust and debris slowly spread over the Magadan district, hiding the impact craters from view.

"All weapons detonated in uninhabited areas. Death toll will be due primarily to secondary causes, such as falls, heart attacks and the like," reported an officer.

Shortly after final impact, Byrd returned.

"How is the President?" Major Tom asked.

"Pissed off," as expected, "These idiot politicians think they are in charge. Don't worry Major. No president has challenged MJ-12. Well, at least not since Dealey Plaza."

Major Tom sucked in a deep breath as he realized that he still had a lot to learn.

CHAPTER NINE

Vosges Mountains, France
October 1944

Sergeant Dale Matthews sat in the deep fox hole that he had dug two days earlier, taking a final long drag on his last government-issued cigarette. He flicked the still smoldering, burnt stub into the puddle of freezing water pooling up around his boots. The other men and he had not eaten in nearly three days, and they were running low on ammunition. A few days earlier, the Germans had cut them off from the rest of their division and any opportunity to resupply. They had been ordered to "dig in" by Division, and were told that it would take several days for reinforcements to arrive due to the terrible weather and improvised road blocks set by the Germans. Up to this point, attempts to deliver food, ammunition, and medical supplies by air drop had failed.

Adam, one of Dale's foxhole mates, scrambled out of the muddy hole, keeping low, to gather a small tin bowl he had laid out to gather rain water. "I don't trust those damn Nazi's not to poison the creek, just to spite us," he grumbled.

"They use the same creek as us for drinking," Dale objected, "It would kill them, too."

"They could be getting water supplied to them from their rear. We are trapped with no other source. They poison the water and wait. We die, they win."

Dale could not argue with that logic. He pushed his tin coffee cup out of the fox hole. "I see your point."

"Does it ever stop raining here? I'm freezing, don't think I can feel my feet anymore," Tom Brown complained from another fox hole a few feet away. Tom, short with an olive complexion, was starting to go bald at a young age. Most of the squad was from Texas, but Tom was originally from New York.

"It's a wonder the rain even makes it all the way down to the ground. The trees are so thick; sunlight barely makes it through," Adam said. Overcast skies and dense tree cover had been hidden the sun for days.

"You got any . . ." Tom was interrupted by a loud explosion directly over their heads. Tom and the others instinctively dove deep into their fox holes. The German artillery was set to explode 100 feet above ground, upon contact with the tree tops. The exploding shell would rain down fiery shrapnel on their heads and shoulders.

They heard a scream from 20 meters away. They knew an American had been hit. Dale looked up from his fox hole to see if it was anyone in his squad. They had learned to cover up their fox holes with branches to shield from exploding shrapnel. The branches were not a perfect defense, but it was the best they could muster under these conditions.

Tom's foxhole buddy, Steve, stuck his head out from the branches covering his muddy hole and asked, "Whatever happened to the patrol they sent out last night?"

"Only five of the forty-eight men returned this morning. Krauts ambushed them," Dale hollered back over the pouring rain.

"Damn Nazi's," Steve spat.

"I heard the lieutenant saying we were completely surrounded by a full division of Kraut." Tom snarled.

"I don't think it's a full division, maybe a battalion or two." Dale replied.

"But, we don't really know. That's the problem," Adam complained.

Another loud explosion. Dale reached for his weapon, a Thompson machine gun, and peered out of his foxhole into the thick forest looking for signs of advancing German troops. On his hands and knees, Dale pulled himself to the edge of his foxhole and positioned himself, so that if he saw an approaching German, he could easily rise to a crouching position to fire his machine gun. Dale preferred the 20-round box magazine to the larger 100-round drum because the drum was heavier and more difficult to maneuver. Thompson had produced several models of the famous machinegun; earlier designs allowed for either a drum or straight magazine. The most recent design, made for the military, only allowed the straight magazine to attach.

Upon the order to "dig in," the battalion commander choose high ground and set up two heavy M1917A1 30 caliber, water-cooled machine guns; one on each end of the elliptical shaped fortification. Like cowboys circling the wagons, the battalion was positioned in an oval-shaped formation, with the water-cooled machine guns guarding both ends of the trail. Of course, they did not have chuck wagons to hide behind, nor were they facing natives with bows and arrows. They were surrounded by thousands of Nazis that were armed with machine guns, mortars, artillery, sniper rifles, and the occasional lite tank.

The thick, jungle-like tree canopy, combined with nasty storms, made air support for both sides nearly impossible. The fallen trees, mountainous terrain, and thick forest, that had allowed the Germans to fortify, now offered cover to the trapped American battalion. The 270 Americans had fortified the high ridge trail using downed trees and rock formations to create a strong defensible position.

Dale's twelve-man squad was near the center of the elliptical fortification, on the side facing away from the valley. The squad directly across the trail from him faced down the mountain toward the valley and town below them. The Germans knew exactly where the American battalion was and had been hitting them with mortars all day. The last attack from a company of Nazis was about an hour ago. The Germans had been easily repelled and broke off the attack after losing a dozen soldiers. Dale was afraid they were going to come back with two Battalions.

Squinting his eyes, he scanned the impenetrable forest for Germans lurking in the settling fog. The forest's shadowy canopy of trees, gloomy skies and the thick underbrush of fallen trees made it very easy for machinegun-toting Krauts to hide.

"Do you see anything?" hissed Tom from the foxhole next to him.

"Negative," he replied.

"Me neither," said Adam, leaning up against the inside of the foxhole with Dale. Adam was shouldering his weapon of choice, a Browning Automatic Rifle, or BAR for short. The BAR was considered a squad-based weapon, not a heavy machine gun, but not as light at the Thompson in Dale's right hand. Adam had his BAR set out of the foxhole, a tripod holding up the barrel that pointed up the mountain.

Treadwell, another member of the squad, slid into the foxhole like a baseball player coming into home plate. He was holding a new M2 carbine rifle, and his drab, olive uniform was covered in mud. The M2 carbine was an upgrade from the M1 carbine, in that it could be set to full auto and accepted a thirty-round magazine.

"The lieutenant just said Listening Outpost Two reported Germans approaching our position," he informed the others as he adjusted the helmet which had slid down his forehead. They had set up four listening posts total, each 1,000 meters out. The listening posts would report back to the fortified position but would not engage. Each listening post was heavily camouflaged and had a crank-powered, battlefield telephone to report back to the battalion. The main purpose of each listening post was to ensure that the Americans would get a warning before a German attack.

"They will be here any minute, everyone in position," called out Dale. All members of his squad were either dug into foxholes are behind fallen trees.

"I think I see movement, two hundred yards out," Tom whispered as he pointed up the mountain and to the right.

"Hold your fire until you have a clean shot. Conserve your ammunition, no automatic fire until they are inside 50 yards." Matthews said, as he lifted the Thompson up to his shoulder.

"I like to fire single shots at first, make them think they are up against a bolt action, then when they get close, open up, and switch to full auto." Adam smiled and rubbed his BAR like it was his favorite puppy. "Gets them every time," he said with a smile.

Boom. A single shot rang out. It was from ten feet away. Dale looked over and saw Evan give the universal thumbs up sign.

"I think I got me a Kraut," he said from behind a large fir tree. Evan was holding his M-1 Garand, a semi-automatic rifle. It was deadly accurate and considered to be an excellent defensive weapon. There were four soldiers carrying M-1 Garands in the squad. They would get the first kills because they were very accurate long range, but once the Nazis got close, the BARs would be more effective.

Bang. Bang. Bang. Three more shots, one right after another. This time from 20 meters to Dale's left. The squad directly next to Matthews was under attack. He could tell it was Garands firing, the Germans were still over 100 yards out. He squinted his eyes and saw the gray uniform of a German solider running between the trees 80 yards away. Then another and another. The next wave of Nazis had arrived.

He said to Adam, "See them?"

Adam nodded his head, and said, "Yes sir, barely through the fog." He squeezed the trigger on the powerful BAR. A deafening explosion followed, and then, "Damn, I missed."

Dale and his men were dug in and well-hidden, while the advancing Germans were running tree to tree. Now they were close enough to be seen, and the entire evening erupted in a deafening symphony of nearly 100 automatic rifles firing into the trees.

Dale spotted a Nazi 70 yards out crouching, behind a large tree. He was lining up a shot with a long rifle. He knew the Nazi was seconds from shooting an American. Dale took a deep breath, exhaled, and settled his iron sights on the Nazi rifleman. He gently squeezed the trigger of the Thompson machine gun. The Trench Broom, as his gun was also called, jumped to life and three bullets burrowed into the tree close to the Nazi's face. Bark and splinters broke free and sprayed into the Nazi's eyes. The Nazi jerked his trigger, and the rifle overshot its intended target. Dale instantly lined up his machine gun again and fired. This time the bullets slammed into the Nazi's face, and he jerked backwards and collapsed.

"Hell yeah!" shouted Matthews, "that's my thirty-seventh kill."

Adam grinned and said, "Still doesn't beat my 54 kills!" He peered down the barrel of his Browning and gave the trigger a good long pull, sending 10 bullets into a German soldier that had stuck his head up from behind a tree stump.

"Grenade!" yelled Adam.

Dale heard the thud of a grenade not six feet from him. He turned and saw the smooth, egg-shaped, German hand grenade land on the ground between his foxhole and the one to his left. He flung himself deep into the hole while grabbing Adam by his collar and dragging him down with him. The grenade exploded harmlessly, only feet away. Dale and Adam scrambled to stand, ears ringing from the explosion.

"Thanks. You saved my ass," Adam choked out, as he wiped mud and dirt from his face.

"Roger that," Dale responded, as he detached the magazine from his Thompson. He reached into the canvas ammo pouch attached to his web belt and pulled out a fresh magazine and slid it into place. He knew the magazine was in place when he heard and felt the metallic click. From down in the foxhole, he saw Evan firing from behind a tree at unseen Germans. He pulled back the charging handle, and the Thompson was ready to fire.

Dale and Adam cautiously rose from the foxhole, with their weapons held firmly at their shoulders. The Krauts had advanced to 25 yards. From a standing position in the foxhole, Adam fired the BAR at a German's head as it poked up from behind a large fallen tree. Splinters flew in every direction, as the bullets smashed into the tree just below the German's exposed head. Adam raised the barrel ever so slightly, and the German's head exploded in to a bloody mess.

Dale saw two Germans, 30 yards to his left, hiding behind a small outcropping of rock. He knew that his Thompson would likely be ineffective against their rocky defensive position. He could see they were setting up something behind the rock. Setting his Thompson on the ground, he took one of the pineapple grenades from his belt and wrapped his left index finger around the steel ring. He jerked the ring, activating the grenade. One, two, three. Dale knew it had a five second delay. Then, with one fluid motion he threw the grenade at the Germans behind the rock formation. The grenade never hit the ground. It exploded in the air only feet from the Germans heads, shrapnel ripping holes through their bodies as they were flung to the ground by the force of the explosion.

Dale, all but deaf from the gunfire and explosions all around him, looked right, then left, to see how his squad was doing. His entire team was holding their ground. No one had taken any hits.

The air was heavy with the noxious gasses of thousands of rounds being fired. A grayish white haze washed over the ridge.

"Mortar, incoming," shouted an unfamiliar voice from behind. Dale and Adam, instinctively, dove into their foxhole and hoped it would not explode directly overhead. Dale could hear the whistling sound of the mortar cutting through the air. It was a familiar sound; the Germans had been lobbing mortars at them for days. If it exploded to their right or left, the foxhole would shield them, but a direct hit would mean a shallow grave. Face down, covering his head with his arms, Dale heard the mortar explode behind him.

Leaping to his feet, he griped the wooden handle of his Thompson machine gun and raised it to eye level. Focusing on the iron sights at the end of the barrel, he saw a German soldier advancing 20 yards in front of him. Dale squeezed the trigger, and 10 rounds, half his magazine, slammed into the tree. One bullet finding its target. A gut shot. The German bent over and dropped to his knees, a fatal wound, the man would eventually bleed to death. Yet, Dale took aim again; this time sending three bullets into the mostly exposed soldier. The Nazi lurched backwards and toppled over onto the rocky ground.

There was the terrible roar of an incoming artillery barrage. Shells exploded in the tree tops, sending thousands of shards of hot metal down on the Americans. Everyone dove for their foxholes and scrambled to find whatever cover they could. Dale and Adam managed to pull their thatched, stick and branch shield over themselves as the hot iron buried into wood, dirt, and flesh. Once again, Dale and Adam took the opportunity to reload their magazines, and when the barrage of shrapnel had passed, they sprung out of their foxholes and ran, crouching the whole way, to a nearby fallen tree. Peering out from behind the broken tree, they could see Germans retreating.

They had been taught that soldiers in a fortified defensive position could repel an offensive force three times its size. The exposed advancing Germans took severe casualties, while the dug-in Americans were mostly protected by the earthen fortifications. The Americans had taken some casualties, but the lack of food, ammo, and medical supplies were going to be the death of them.

The squad began to advance from their hidden positions to the battlefield, where the Germans had just fallen. Slowly, tree-by-tree, they moved through the field of carnage searching for German weapons and ammunition. Mutilated German corpses littered the mountainside, strewed out in twisted and unnatural positions. Most had died from gunshot wounds, but arms and legs, dismembered from the exploding grenades were scattered about. The reality was, without reinforcements, the Americans would soon be out of bullets.

After searching the bloody corpses, the squad was back in their foxholes. Dale's squad had taken no casualties. He was sliding rounds into his empty magazines, preparing for the next wave, when the lieutenant approached in a semi-run hunching position. It was getting dark, darker than normal; the unseen sun was going down.

"How are your men doing, Sergeant?" the lieutenant asked. He was a lean man, with sandy blond hair. His slim frame was deceiving. Dale knew the Lieutenant was an excellent fighter, with hand-to-hand combat skills that surpassed any other officer he knew. Dale assumed he had obtained these fighting skills prior to entering the army, he figured maybe a boxer or something.

"No injuries, but we could sure use some K-rations," Dale reported. Generally, the men hated K-rations. They were dry, tasteless, and never enough food for a hungry man. The men preferred C-rations, which, while still not a gourmet meal, offered more flavor and calories.

"We have very little food left and even less ammunition, after this last German assault," replied the lieutenant. "Unless we get reinforcements, we can't last much longer."

Dale nodded his head in understanding. The Lieutenant, kneeling on one knee, went on, "That patrol we sent out last night took severe losses but came back with a German prisoner."

"Great, another mouth to feed," grumbled Dale.

"Yes, but we were able to get him to talk. While we are surrounded by heavily entrenched Germans, it seems there may be a pass, a couple thousand feet up the trail, that will bypass the German's main force. It may be a way off this mountain. I need you to recon that pass."

"Last night's recon team lost 43 men?"

"The team was too large; they were spotted. I want your squad to go recon up the trail a couple thousand feet and see if there is a way off the mountain where we can by-pass the German fortifications."

"We are running low on ammunition," Matthews objected.

"I can fully equip your squad. I want you and your men to leave once it is completely dark."

CHAPTER TEN

D ale Matthews and his squad huddled in the center of battalion's fortification. They were all cold, damp, and famished.

"I have a few cans of C-rations left," the lieutenant said, handing them to the men. They carefully divided the food the best they could so that everyone got some. The C-rations were designed to be enough calories for one soldier, hardly enough for twelve soldiers that had not properly eaten in three days.

"Can I get some of the meat and beans?" George Murphy asked. "That's my favorite," he said with a grin.

"I got a can of meat and spaghetti," Howard Meyers said. "Anybody want to share this with me?"

"I can help you out with that spaghetti." Raymond Treadwell said. There were not enough cans for everyone to have their own, so they shared what they had, eating directly out of the can.

"I also have extra ammunition and some new flashlights. These flashlights have red lens covers, so they are harder for the enemy to spot," the Lieutenant said, as he passed out the lights. The new flashlights were just like the old ones, an olive, drab, plastic frame with a ninety-degree angle on the lens and bulb assembly. The main difference was the red lens covers helped dim the light so that the enemy could not see them from a distance.

"This ridge is about seven kilometers from end to end, with no known roads," the lieutenant explained. "We are about two thirds of the way to the German fortifications. The mountain is only about two kilometers wide, and, to the best of our knowledge, we are surrounded. Last night, we sent four squads to see if they could get past the Krauts and back to the division, they failed. We must find a way off this mountain. I want you to go up the ridge toward the German fortifications with two objectives. First, I want you to see if there is another way off this ridge; and, second, try to spot any weaknesses in the German fortifications."

"Roger that, Lieutenant; and thanks for the C-rats," Dale added.

"Just find us a way off this mountain, Sergeant."

"If there's a way, I'll find it," Dale replied.

"All right men, finish up your chow, and we will be heading out," Dale ordered as he scraped the last spoonful of cold stew at the bottom of the tin can. Normally, the men complained about C-rats, but tonight they tasted unusually good.

"What's the plan?" asked Fred Perry, the youngest solider in the battalion, as he rubbed some newly grown peach fuzz on his chin. It had been said that he lied about his age to get into the Army.

"We continue up the trail, towards the German fortifications. We break into four-man groups, staying off the main trail. We'll keep an eye out for any passage that would be suitable to bring the battalion down into the valley," Dale said.

"Slow and easy," Adam said, "We are outnumbered and out gunned; soon we will be sitting ducks."

"If you see the enemy, do not engage. Only fire a weapon if you must. The goal is not to kill Krauts; it's to find a path off this ridge for the whole battalion," Dale reminded them.

"Is everyone ready? Anyone need to take a crap or piss? Now is the time to do it," Matthews said to the huddled squad.

"Safeties on and watch where you step. These Krauts like mines," Dale added, "last thing we need is one of us accidentally firing off a round."

"Adam, you are with me," he announced. "Tom and Steve, you are with me, as well. Everyone else, break into four-man teams."

Steve Dyer had the only M-9 bazooka in the squad. The M-9, sometimes referred to as a "stove pipe," was a rocket-propelled, anti-tank weapon that could also be used against an entrenched machine gun or armored vehicle. It had become less effective against German tanks since they upgraded their armor, but it was still somewhat effective at close range.

The men quietly advanced up the trail past the earthen fortifications. They passed the water-cooled, heavy machine gun that was set up behind logs and rocks. The machine gun fortification marked the end of their encampment; everything past that was German territory.

Dale stepped off the trail and into the woods. The goal was to find a path off the ridge. They were about 1000 feet off the valley floor, with steep cliffs and rugged terrain cascading to the village below them. If there was any hope of finding a passage down, they would have to travel as near as possible to the steep cliffs. It was one thing for a few men to travel in the woods at night, but moving almost 270 men in broad daylight was totally different. They needed a passable slope that offered cover from enemy fire. The only way they had held off the Germans superior numbers thus far was that they were entrenched.

The first thousand meters were easy, as expected, because the listening post had not reported any German activity in the last few hours. Dale did not know exactly where the listening post was, but he was sure they were about to pass it soon. He did not expect any communication from the post, as their job was to observe and report back to the battalion without exposing their position.

The air was cold, and the ground was soft from recent rains. The forest floor was thick with undergrowth. "This place needs a good fire to burn off some of this brush," Matthews thought to himself. Dale Matthews, Adam Bond, Tom Brown and Steve Dyer reached the steep cliff and stopped to survey the ridge and valley below them.

The four men crouched behind an outcropping of rocks that overlooked the valley and town below. Tom Brown had found a StG44 "storm rifle," on one of the dead German soldiers. The StG44 was an impressive assault rifle with select fire capabilities. It was accurate up to 300 meters in full auto and 600 meters in semi auto. However, that was not the most impressive feature of the weapon. It was outfitted with a rare ZG 1229 Vampire night vision scope. Most soldiers had never seen a night vision scope; some had heard of night vision, but none had used it. Earlier, Tom had spent several hours trying to figure out how to make it work.

Tom moved into position above the outcropped rocks and dropped to one knee. "I bet you're glad I found this rifle."

"Still, you went a little too far from the foxhole to get it; you could have been shot by a German sniper," Dale said.

"Had I not risked it, we would not have this night vision scope," Tom argued.

"Maybe they will give you the medal of honor," Matthews said sarcastically.

"If we get off this mountain, it will be because I found the pass," Tom remarked as he peered through the night vision scope on the top of the rifle. The fallen German had three magazines of 30 rounds to go with the rifle. They were a 7.92x33 round, a bit light for a sniper rifle, but highly effective at 200 meters.

"See anything?" Adam asked.

"No, just rocks and trees. It's all steep terrain. Maybe we should keep moving," Tom suggested.

The squad traveled slowly along the wooded ridge, carefully keeping an eye out for traps and land mines. Another 200 yards, and they stopped again. From behind a tree, Tom surveyed the steep cliffs ahead, looking for a good place for 270 men to descend a thousand feet to the valley. All he could see was steep cliffs and jagged rocks. That many men attempting to climb down at once would be easy targets for German snipers.

"Just going by what we have seen so far, I don't think we are going to find a passage to the valley," Tom complained.

"We're not giving up that easily," Dale whispered, "let's keep going." Dale had every intention of getting off this mountain alive; returning to the battalion without a solution was not an option.

"Wait," Tom hissed, grabbing Dale's shoulder and pulling him down. Tom handed the German StG44 to Dale. "Look there."

Dale and the others lay on their bellies, weapons pointed into the dark. Dale stared through the Vampire scope. The gun was heavy and awkward; the scope was large and made the rifle difficult to wield, especially from lying on the ground. He repositioned himself to lean against a tree so he could support the weapon by propping his elbow against his knee. At first, he couldn't see anything. It was out of focus. After giving it a minute to focus, trees, bushes, and rocks all came into view. He scanned the length of the steep cliff. He felt a gentle pushing on the barrel of the gun; it was Tom pointing the barrel in the direction of the Germans.

One, two, three, four Germans creeping along the ridge, mirroring their own actions. Except these Germans were heading toward them and the American battalion.

"I see four men. Two hundred yards out. They're heading in this direction," Dale whispered.

"If we had not stopped and used the night vision, we could have bumped into them in the dark," Adam said, as he lifted his BAR into position, as if he could see them.

"Easy does it." Dale waived at Adam to put the gun down. "We need to avoid these Krauts. They are not the mission."

"The mission is a failure. We can't go around them and we have not seen any evidence of a pass to the valley," Tom objected.

"We can't pass them, but they can pass us. Then we can continue," Steve whispered from behind. "Or we could light'em up with this bad boy," he said patting his M-9 bazooka.

Dale could almost see the gleam in Steve's eyes as he said 'light'em up.'

"No. Move off the ridge, twenty-five meters. Take cover; they won't see us as they pass," Dale ordered.

The squad slowly moved out of the Germans' projected path and took cover in the thick underbrush. The other two groups, 50 and 100 yards back, took cover as well.

Dale was settled in behind a fallen tree as the Germans were passing between him and the ridge. Three Germans materialized out of the darkness 20 meters to his left. They were traveling north to south along the ridge, heading toward the Battalion's encampment. Then, another five Germans materialized from the foggy darkness. The Germans were moving almost silently through the night, but there was not just eight of them, they kept coming, more and more.

Dale wondered if the listening post would even detect them. There were four listening posts reporting back to the battalion, but, at night and from this direction, Dale figured there may be no warning from the post.

Tom huddled up real close to Dale and whispered in a concerned voice, "Looks like every third one has a night scope. They could see us. More importantly, they can see the Battalion."

"Their night scopes cancel out the advantage our troops have by being dug in," Dale warned.

"Our troops will be firing blindly into the night while the Krauts pick 'em off," Adam said, shaking his head in concern.

"What can we do?" Tom asked.

"How many are there?" Dale asked Tom.

"Eighty, maybe 90. Looks like a couple dozen have night vision," Tom shrugged, as he assessed the enemy through the Vampire scope.

"Twelve against 90; we would just slow them down. It would alert the Battalion, and at least they would not get hit by a surprise attack," Dale said.

"Now look whose gunning for the medal of honor," Steve said.

"What if we circled in behind them and followed them back to camp? The last thing they would be expecting is an attack from behind," Dale proposed.

"While they are busy attacking the battalion, we will hit them from the rear. They will never expect it; hell, may not even realize from where they are being shot," Adam said with a smile creeping across his face.

"I may even get me one of those fancy German storm rifles, Vampire scope and all," Steve said.

As the last group of Germans were slowly creeping past, a loud explosion was heard about 50 yards back down the trail. A group of Germans, not 15 yards away, dropped to their knees and took cover behind some trees. They were not looking at the four men. They were staring down the trail to where the explosion was heard.

"What in the hell was that?" Muttered Adam, who was now lying on his stomach, beside Dale.

"Sounds like someone stepped on a land mine," Steve replied.

"I hope it's not one of ours," Adam said.

Just then, the sound of numerous machine guns firing broke the quiet night air. Dale could see sporadic muzzle flashes down the trail, near the place where he assumed the rest of his squad would be hiding.

"Shit. Must have been one of ours," Dale fretted. There was no sense in whispering now. The machine gun fire would prevent the Germans from hearing him.

"Look, there are six Krauts directly in front of us. We could take them out before they even knew what hit them," said Adam as he switched the safety off his BAR.

"Let's do it," said Tom as he lined up his newly acquired storm rifle on the German in the foremost position.

"Okay, our cover is blown. New mission is to support the battalion against this night raid, but hold your fire. Tom, you take those four Krauts," Dale said pointing to the ones furthest up the trail.

"Steve, you take the ones heading up the rear. Adam and I will deal with the ones in the middle, got it?"

"Got it," they all agreed.

Dale gave the hand signal and they stood from their crouching positions and opened fire on the unsuspecting Germans.

Five of the 10 Germans fell immediately. The remaining five took cover by diving behind trees, as their friends lie on the ground, bleeding to death. In a split second, the Germans realized where the Americans were and returned fire.

Tom, kneeling behind a large tree, took aim through the Vampire scope at the closest German, who apparently thought he was hidden behind a tree. The German was wrong. Tom's shot caught him just under the chin, and he fell back, grabbing at his neck, trying to stop the flow of blood.

At this point, the Germans must have realized the Americans had at least one-night scope, as they began to fall back. Dale surmised that his men had just saved the Battalion from a bloody night raid, as 20 more Germans materialized out of the night. The German reinforcements were still seventy-five yards up the trail, but they were moving fast. The Germans now severely outnumber the squad and were beginning to form a crescent shaped semi-circle around them.

"We got to get out of here fast before they completely surround us," Adam yelled at Dale, as he slid another boxy magazine into his BAR.

"We have to run, now," shouted Tom, over the roar of automatic gun fire.

"Retreat!" Dale shouted. The four turned and ran through the forest trying to escape the Germans. Dale could hear bullets whiz by his head and slam into the trees around him. They were running up the ridge, toward the trail with the steep cliffs at their backs, when Dale, in the lead, stepped into - nothing.

Dale was shocked, at first. Why had his foot not found land? Then, he was falling. He heard Adam behind him.

"Whoa," Adam called out, as he stumbled over the edge of the pit into the total darkness. Dale had no warning of the gaping hole and went in face first. Adam, a fraction of a second behind him, saw the hole but was unable to stop.

In the split-second Dale had while falling, he wondered if there were spikes at the bottom of the hole. Would he be impaled and left to bleed to death in this cold, dark place, or would a merciful German dispatch him quickly with a bullet to the brain? Dale Matthews did not have long to ponder his fate; he slammed into the ground face first with a dull thud.

A fraction of a second later, Adam came tumbling down and partially landed on him. Well, at least there were no spikes. But instead of the dirt, mud, and roots as he was expecting, his face was pressed against cold, hard concrete.

CHAPTER ELEVEN

Adam rolled off Dale, "Are you alright?"

"I think so," Dale coughed out, as he turned over and pulled himself up.

His eyes started to adjust to the darkness into which they had just fallen. Only, it wasn't a hole; it was a tunnel. A long concrete tunnel with no electric lighting.

"You two alright down there?" Tom's voice called down. Dale could see that Tom was about seven feet above him, peering through what appeared to be a small section of the tunnel that had sustained a direct artillery impact. Normally, a direct hit would not have collapsed a tunnel, but Dale figured it may have been due to a bad batch of concrete.

"Yeah, we're okay. Do the Germans know your position?" Dale asked.

"Negative. They are still 30 yards back in the brush, but approaching quickly."

"Get down here; we can hideout down here," Dale said.

Dale and Adam helped Tom and Steve descend into the tunnel. The hole Matthews had stepped through was only about four feet in diameter. In the dark, it would be hard to spot. If he had not fallen into the hole, they could have run past the opening without having seen it.

All four men were standing in the drafty tunnel, looking up into the dreary night. Surprisingly, the tunnel was slightly warm and dry. They positioned themselves away from the opening at the top of the tunnel and waited, hoping that the Germans would not see them. The German boots made crunching sounds in the snow above, as they canvassed the area, seemingly unaware of the tunnel below. The four men were safe, for the moment.

"Let's take five," Dale said. The men leaned up against the concrete walls that arched up toward the curved ceiling. All four men checked their magazines and did a bullet count.

"I bet the Krauts called off the night raid after that," Adam said.

"Assuming the other two groups engaged, I'm sure they were not expecting to be attacked on that ridge, that far away from the Battalion," Dale concluded.

"They lost the advantage of surprise. The Battalion was sure to have heard the shots. After that, the Krauts would assume we notified the battalion of their location," Tom added.

"So, what now?" asked Adam.

"Mission failed. We can't find a way off this ridge, now that the Nazis have spotted us. We focus on the second objective," Dale said, as he slid a magazine full of .45 caliber rounds into his Thompson machine gun until he heard a metallic click.

"What's the second objective?" asked Tom.

"You heard the lieutenant. We need to discover weaknesses in the German position. Something the battalion can exploit," Dale replied.

"How are we going to do that? While in this hole?"

"It's not a hole; it's a tunnel. And we are going to follow it," Dale said.

"What? Why? We know where it leads. It leads directly into an army full of pissed off Nazis!" Steve exclaimed.

"That's what we assume, but we won't know for sure until we check it out. This could be a way off the mountain" Dale explained.

Adam stood to his feet, brought the automatic rifle to his hip and said, "Let's do it."

The men turned on their newly issued military flashlights. The red lenses were a useful feature that, hopefully, would not alert the Nazis of their presence.

"Flashlights pointed to the ground," Dale whispered. They followed the winding, dark tunnel for about 300 yards until they could see a glimmer of light in the distance.

"Flashlights off," Dale hissed. The four men cautiously approached the light. The air grew colder as the light grew brighter. The tunnel was about four feet wide and seven feet high. As they approached the mouth of the tunnel they could hear voices.

The encroaching light was not like familiar electric bulbs, nor was it sun light. No, the flickering on the tunnel walls was dim, like flames dancing in the dark. Matthews slowly approached the end of the tunnel. He could see the tunnel open into a large space.

Six feet from the tunnel entrance, there were rows of large wooden boxes stacked three and four high, which obscured his view of the rest of the chamber. He waived his hand, indicating to Adam that he was advancing forward.

"What now?" Adam asked.

"I'm going to move up to those wooden crates and see if I can peek around them," Dale whispered.

Matthews signaled to the others to stay behind while he ran forward to the first row of stacked crates. Down on one knee, he peered around the box and further into cave-like chamber. There were crates and equipment placed all around the perimeter of the chamber, leaving the center open. On the other side of the chamber stood what appeared to be a large machine, not like one he had ever seen before. It was about 40 feet across and 20 feet tall. It was made of a gray metal, steel perhaps. It was disc shaped, taller and wider in the middle and tapered to the edges. At first, he thought it might be a new German tank, but then he realized it had no wheels or tracks. It wasn't a plane because it had no wings. It was sitting on two concrete pillars that held it up in the same way a dry dock would hold up a ship. The pillars were spaced twenty feet apart, and there appeared to be a hatch open at the bottom of the machine where a ladder extended down toward the chamber's cold stone floor.

Between the strange machine and the stacked crates Dale was hiding behind, were 50 chairs, all lined up in rows facing the machine. Standing between the chairs and the machine was an elevated wooden platform from where, presumably, a speaker would stand and address the audience. On either side of the rows of chairs, large Nazi flags were hanging from metal scaffolding.

Something about the scene was off, not just the unidentifiable machine and the make-shift pulpit. No, it was stranger than that. On the stage were six absurdly large chairs, suitable for giants. The six chairs were lined up along the back of the stage, facing the 50 chairs.

On the stage, in front of the six chairs was a six-foot-long, wooden table. Was it an alter? The table had a white marble top. Both alter and chairs were lavishly carved with symbols that Dale did not recognize. The entire concrete floor and wooden platform were covered with a red carpet that extended behind the platform and to the hatch on the bottom side of the disc-like machine. Atop the platform, were two shallow boxes of dirt.

Unlike the underground passage, the large chamber was lit by a combination of burning fire barrels, torches, and electric lights powered by the hum of local generators. "Why use fire-barrels if you have electricity?" Dale wondered. He knew that he had stumbled onto something important, but what was it?

Glancing around the room, he saw he was alone; then he looked up and noticed the chamber's ceiling. As expected, it was a concrete dome. Except, above the machine, there was an opening to the night sky. While the machine was about 40 feet in diameter, the circular hole in the chamber's ceiling was about 50 feet in diameter. Dale realized that the Nazis planned to fly the machine through the hole in the ceiling.

Knowing that he was well-concealed from view, he walked back to the tunnel and told the others what he had found.

"You said the room is not guarded; we can just steal the machine and fly away," Steve blurted out.

"None of us have been trained to fly our own planes. How are we going to fly that thing, whatever it is?" Adam asked.

"Adam is right, that's not an option," Dale insisted.

"We could destroy it with the stovepipe, we got six rockets," Steve said.

"Maybe, but we know the German's armor can stand up to the M-9," Dale objected.

"Their tanks can stand up to it. This is a flying machine. It can't be as heavy as a Panzer," Steve said, "I bet we can light her up from here."

"Then what?" Adam demanded.

"Adam is right, what then? Then the Krauts know where we are, and we may not even destroy the flying machine. I say we find good cover and see what happens," Dale said.

Suddenly, they heard a blood curdling scream. It was a woman's scream. Dale ran back to the box and peeked around the corner. Two hundred yards away, near the platform, he could see two guards carrying a woman towards the alter. Even from this distance Dale could tell it was a young woman. She could not be more than 25 years old. She was beautiful and wearing a flow-ing, ceremonial-looking, nearly see-through, white dress. She was struggling with the two Nazi soldiers, but they just kept drag-ging her towards the stage. Once on the stage, one of the soldiers held her still, while the other chained her to the platform as she screamed. The one that had been holding, released her, smacked her across the face and spat some German words at her. Dale did not understand what the German said, but he assumed it was a threat, because she stopped screaming. The two guards walked away laughing, then disappeared into a corridor behind the flying machine. The woman was alone on the stage, crying. Dale guessed she was French but could not be sure.

After discussing the situation with his men, they decided that rescuing the woman would most likely reveal their position. They needed to wait and see more.

It seemed like all the Nazi activities were centered on the other side of the large underground chamber, and it was unlikely that they would be discovered among the rows of wooden, swastika-emblazoned boxes. The men took positions where they could see the chamber, the stage, and the flying saucer.

A few minutes later, a German officer walked in and took a seat among the chairs lined up facing the saucer. Dale remembered people discussing 'foo fighters' and wondered if this flying saucer was what they were talking about. According to some, foo fighters were highly advanced enemy aircraft that could outmaneuver any American plane.

The room slowly filled with Nazi officers. They were wearing full dress uniforms with red armbands. Many were decorated with ribbons and medals. From their position behind the boxes, the squad could see what was going on. But everyone was speaking in German and none of them could understand it from 200 yards away. The last of the Nazi officers took his seat. Their backs facing Dale and the other three men.

Two more German soldiers appeared from the right side of the chamber, escorting another beautiful woman. Both women appeared to be healthy, and showed no physical signs of torture. The second woman's ankle was chained to the platform behind the alter, next to the first woman, each stood inside one of the shallow, boxes of dirt. Dale was getting a bad feeling about this. He knew something was happening, something bigger than these two women, something bigger than him and his men.

The two women looked at one another, each knowing that this was going to be a very bad day, if not their last. They trembled before the group of Nazi officers but kept glancing back toward the flying machine. Whatever was going to happen, it was going to happen soon.

A man began to walk down the ladder from the metallic saucer. He was wearing a full-dress Nazi uniform, complete with medals and ribbons. Dale guessed he was close to seven feet tall. Focusing on his face, he noted it was not like any other face he had ever seen before. The man had gray skin and large black eyes. Not black pupils, black eyes, like the eyes of an insect. Then Dale realized, this was no man at all. This was some kind of monster, perhaps not even from this planet.

The Nazi creature walked up the red carpet, onto the stage, and took his place in one of the large decorative chairs. Five more extremely tall, gray-faced beings emerged from the flying machine and took their places on stage. Each of the six creatures was wearing Nazi uniforms. Dale thought the insignias indicated they were generals. The audience sat completely still, and the large chamber was filled with a deafening silence.

Matthews glanced over at Adam, who was staring at the bizarre scene before them. The tallest of the six stood to his feet. He walked up to the altar and stood behind the woman on the right. Even from this distance Matthews could tell she was horrified. The hideous creature pulled out a jeweled blade and displayed it in front of the woman, she recoiled with disgust. He positioned the blade across her arm, then in one quick movement he sliced open her flesh. Her blood began to run down her arm and drip onto the soil. The creature chanted, "Blut und Boden," and the Nazi congregation repeated the phrase. Dale did not understand what was happening, but his bones rattled with disgust.

The second large creature stood, ceremoniously accepting the jeweled blade from the first creature as it returned to its place among the others. The second creature approached the woman, slowly penetrating the skin of her other arm. She screamed in pain, begged it to stop, but it did not relent. Matthews could see the backs of the Nazi officers' heads, they did not move, not one inch. The Nazis did not even whisper. They were not like the two German guards that brought the women into the chamber, laughing and carrying-on. Dale could not tell, but he was certain they were terrified.

The second creature finished his assault on the young woman, blood streaming down her arms, she was sobbing uncontrollably. A third creature lifted her head up by her long brown hair, and with lightning speed, lifted the ceremonial dagger and cut her throat all the way to the bone. Her blood sprayed all over the altar and onto the wooden platform. Splattered in blood, the woman chained beside her began to scream uncontrollably.

The creature returned to his chair momentarily and then walked back up to the altar. The young woman was still lying on the marble table, her blood flowing off the marble and onto the carpet. Seemingly, from nowhere, an ornate goblet appeared in the second creature's hand, and he began to collect the blood dripping off the table top. After what seemed like an eternity, the creature handed the bloody goblet to the tallest of his kin.

Taking the goblet from the creature with both hands. The tall one walked from around the altar and stood in the center of the platform before the Nazi officers and said nothing. He stood before them and lifted the bloody goblet to his lips and drank. Not a sound from the fifty Nazi officers, only the screams from the remaining terrified woman.

Dale was horrified, but what could he do in the face of such superior numbers? He knew that there was no way he could eliminate all fifty Nazi officers, the six creatures, and the guards that were surely lurking in the tunnels on the other side of the chamber.

Another of the creatures stood up and walked up behind the second woman who was tied to the bloody alter. The creature started to lift the jeweled blade into the air. There was no doubt as to this woman's fate. Matthews closed his eyes, trying to think of a way to save the young woman. What could be done?

A large explosion rocked the concrete chamber. Dale looked up and saw Nazi soldiers being flung 30 and 40 feet. The blast came from the center of the seating area, where a few seconds ago the chairs had been lined up in perfect order. Nazi soldiers were lying on the ground bleeding; some, dazed by the loss of limbs and blood. Dale saw one crawling away from the blast zone; others were running and limping away. Everyone was confused. It was complete bedlam.

Dale looked over at his crew, and to his surprise, Steve Dyer was standing up, in plain sight holding, the M-9 rocket launcher on his shoulder.

Dale knew the decision was made, and Steve would most like never see a court martial for what he had just done. There was no point in yelling at him for disobeying orders. He glanced over at Adam. Adam understood and nodded. They both stepped from cover and started firing their weapons into the crowd of fleeing Nazis.

The first few seconds were easy. The Nazis had been completely caught off guard by the explosion, which had immediately killed about 20 of them. The remaining 30 were in differing states of shock and confusion. The few that had their wits about them, enough to draw their pistols, were cut down quickly by Adam's BAR. At two hundred yards, a BAR will make quick work of a pistol-wielding Nazi. But that was just the first few seconds.

Through the haze of explosions and gunfire, emerged one of the creatures. The large creature was running directly toward the squad.

How fucked up is this? There is a seven-foot-tall creature, dressed as a Nazi general, charging directly at me. I can handle this. He has 200 yards to cross with no cover. I can fill him with lead long before he gets to me.

Dale took what seemed like forever to change his magazine and bring the loaded weapon to eye level. In those few seconds, the creature had closed the distance by half. The Thompson machine gun roared, and Dale emptied half the magazine in to the creature at 75 yards. The creature stopped, lurched forward, and dropped to one knee. Dale was certain he had taken out the seven-foot-tall monster when it leapt up, and began the charge again.

Dale jerked the trigger; this time making certain to aim for the creature's chest. He could see the impacts. He could see the creature stumble but not fall. Shit, it must be wearing body armor. Twenty-five yards, no time to reload. Dale pulled out his combat knife, but before he could get into a hand-to-hand combat position, the creature exploded into a ball of flame. Dale was thrown back from the blast.

Dammit. If we live through this I'm going to kill Steve Dyer.

The creature was dead, and if it wasn't, it wished it were because it was missing a leg and an arm. It was a short-lived victory. The next creature was charging, already half way across the space between them and the stage. A football field is all that separated them from the hideous beast. Steve was already reloading his M-9 bazooka. There was probably not enough time; this creature was fast.

Adam stepped out from cover and fired his BAR from the hip. Dale could see the bullets slamming into the creature. Holes were appearing all over his formerly neat, crisp uniform. The creature stopped 25 yards away, ripped open his Nazi uniform jacket to reveal a metallic looking undergarment. From a devise on the creature's chest, shot a beam of light, it resembled a lightning strike. The shard of light ripped through Adam's chest, throwing him backwards. Dale glanced at Adam's lifeless corpse. He knew Adam was dead, probably before he hit the ground. The wound in Adam's chest was the size of a grapefruit. The sickening, sweet smell of burning flesh filled Dale's nostrils.

His gun was empty, and the creature was moving toward him again. He dove for Adam's dropped Browning. Another loud explosion.

"Hell yeah," screamed Steve. I got two of those alien bastards."
We don't actually know they are aliens.
"Thanks!" His ears were ringing from the blast.

No sooner had Steve spoken he was hit by a shard of light. Half of his head disappeared into a mist of blood and brain matter.

Only two of us left. At least four creatures left. Not to mention dozens of Nazis. Not the best odds.

Standing to his feet after the blast that took out the second creature, he saw Nazi troops approaching from both sides and three creatures approaching down the middle.

"We got to go," Tom yelled. Tom had dropped his StG44 and was holding his standard issue M-2 carbine with a 30-round magazine.

Dale ducked down and grabbed the M-9 bazooka. It had one M6A3 rocket attached. *Damn. I wish I had time to look for the rest of the rockets.*

Dale and Tom raced back toward the tunnel.

Dale could hear the large creature closing the distance between them.

"That thing is right behind us," Tom yelled, as they ran through the dark tunnel.

Tom had a flashlight in one hand and his M-2 carbine in the other. The red beam was erratically bouncing around the on the concrete walls as they ran. Dale was clutching the pistol grip of the Thompson sub-machine gun, while his other hand held the M-9.

A large hand grabbed Dale's neck from behind. The hand and long fingers wrapped completely around his neck, like a baseball player would wrap his hand around the handle of bat. Dale was instantly flung backwards and crashed into the concrete wall. Both of his weapons disappeared into the darkness.

Dale's breath was knocked out of him by his impact with the wall. The monster had flung him 10 feet with all the ease of a teenager flinging a soda can. The monster grabbed him by his collar and lifted him off the ground. This large, gray, hairless beast was solid and strong. Dale stared into his large, black, bug-like eyes.

This thing is bullet proof and I don't even have a gun.

The creature's hands started to squeeze around his neck. Dale knew he only had seconds left. He reached down to his belt and wrapped his fingers around his US-M3 Utica combat knife. He gripped the leather and steel handle of the double-edged knife and flicked the snap button that held it in the scabbard.

He's bullet proof, and you won't get two swings with the knife.

With all his remaining strength, he rammed the combat knife straight up between the creature's arms and into its neck, just below the chin. He crashed back down to the floor as the creature released him. The seven-foot-tall Nazi general stumbled back, holding both hands over his neck. The creature stabled himself, and still holding his neck, started lifting his elbows upwards and shifting so that his chest plate was lined up on Dale.

Shit. He has that energy beam thing on his chest. He does not even need his hands to burn a hole through me.

Tom, standing ten feet from the creature, fired 15 rounds directly into the creature's head. It dropped to the floor. Dale was gasping for breath when he saw a shard of light zip through Tom's chest, leaving a gaping hole where his heart was located seconds before. Tom fell over, dead.

The creature that had drank the blood of the woman at the altar was standing 20 yards back in the tunnel. Tom's flashlight had fallen in such a way that it illuminated the M-9 bazooka. Dale knew the magazine in his Thompson machine gun was empty and that Tom had just about emptied his M-2 carbine. His only hope was the M-9 and the last M6A3 rocket. Dale lurched towards the M-9. Surprisingly, he was able to shoulder the weapon and spin around to face the creature before the creature could lay hands on him. Staring down the sights of the M-9, he saw the creature standing ten yards away. The creature was in the middle of the tunnel, arms to his sides like an old western gunslinger, the heat-beam weapon in the center of his chest faintly glowing, pulsing, and waiting to spit out a deadly shard of light.

"Sergeant Matthews," the creature said in a raspy deep voice.

How in the hell does it know my name? It speaks English?

"How do you know my name?" Dale asked.

"Does that matter at this moment? You have a rocket aimed at my chest, and I have a particle beam incinerator pointed at yours." The creature took a step forward.

"What are you," Dale challenged.

"Your language has no word that describes me. Suffice it to say, I am not from this world. Since we have been standing here, I have calculated the odds of your survival. If I fire my particle beam, there is a ninety-seven percent chance you will die."

"Yeah, is that so? Did you forget that I have an anti-tank rocket pointed at you?" Dale boasted with insincere confidence.

"I have calculated that I have a twenty-seven percent chance of surviving your next attack. The odds are in my favor. Even if your rocket is successful, my weapon is thought controlled, I need no hands to fire it."

"If you are so sure of your odds, then why all this talking? Why not just shoot?" Dale grasped his weapon tightly and shifted focus from the creature's chest to his feet.

"While my chances of surviving this duel are greater than yours, a twenty-seven percent chance of survival is not a gamble I wish to take today," the creature stated in a matter of fact way, as if he were considering going 'all-in' with a pair of queens.

"What do you propose? I'm not putting down my weapon," Dale said defiantly, somewhat relieved that there may be a way out of this situation. He knew he could not trust this otherworldly beast, but he figured the beast was pretty damn close on the odds.

"No need for you to disarm, simply start walking backwards until you no longer see me," the beast suggested.

Dale knew there were all kinds of problems with that solution. For starters, he could barely see walking forward, walking backward was likely to lead to some tragic slip-and-fall, and not one that could be remedied by some ambulance chasing personal injury lawyer. However, Dale was sure he was not going to get a better offer.

"What is your name?" Matthews shouted.

"I am Nox Bellator," the creature replied.

"How do I know you won't come after me when I leave?" Dale asked.

"I am not proposing a peace treaty between our nations, just a truce at this moment - in this tunnel. If we meet on the battle field again, I will surely kill you. As for today, I have more pressing matters to attend to," the self-proclaimed Nox Bellator announced in his raspy voice.

"Very well, I accept your temporary truce," Dale said, as he began to slowly back away.

CHAPTER TWELVE

Paris, France 1944

D ale Matthews sat in a wooden, low-back chair in the lobby of a formerly opulent hotel. He was wearing a clean uniform and had showered and shaved earlier that morning. After eating a decent breakfast in the makeshift mess hall, he was reporting to Allied Supreme Command Headquarters just outside Paris, France. Paris had been occupied by the Germans for the last four years, but a few months earlier, allied forces had pushed the Germans out and reclaimed Paris for the French. Now, Paris and its surrounding towns had become the headquarters for Allied operations. The city was bustling with thousands of troops moving millions of tons of supplies. Paris had become a critical part of the Allies' long supply line, as they prepared to cross the Rhine River and push further into German territory.

After his encounter with Nox Bellator, he had told his commanding officer of the incident, a decision he may live to regret. Apparently, his report was read by division command and then sent on to Allied Supreme Command because, a few days later, he was recalled from the front lines and ordered back to Paris. Dale enjoyed having a couple of days with decent food and sleep, but, he was very uncomfortable talking to colonels and generals. He thought he had finished yesterday, but then, here he was again today. How many times could he tell the same story?

It was obvious to Dale that a few years ago this hotel had been magnificent. The six-story, massive hotel was constructed with white stone blocks. He sat in a large hallway lined with decorative arches and white stone pillars. Everywhere he turned, there were recessed ceilings, crown molding, and fancy black and white checkered marble floors. There were still signs of the hotel's former glory: a deep, rich mahogany front desk; fancy crown molding and even a few delicate end tables were scattered about the lobby. The ornate rugs and so-fas had been removed and replaced with more practical desks and wooden chairs. Well-to-do Paris elites, with top hats and coat tails, had been replaced by dozens of soldiers wearing olive drab uniforms, running back and forth with orders and reinforcement requests.

A neat and trim officer approached Dale from around the corner. He was young but clearly professional and every bit of his uniform was pressed and perfect, not something Dale was accustomed to seeing among the officers to whom he reported. Dale stood at attention and saluted the dapper officer. By his insignia, he could see the officer was a Lieutenant Colonel in the Army Air Corp.

"At ease, Sergeant," the colonel said, in a gentle but professional tone. Dale relaxed his stance but was anything but 'at ease.'

"Come with me, Sergeant." the Colonel said.

"Yes, Sir," Matthews had given up on asking why, what and how; he simply followed the Colonel. They walked down several long, open, spacious corridors. Massive doors opened into vast ball rooms, that now served as makeshift offices for secretarial staff. They came to a conference room, that was insignificant compared to the others, and the Colonel opened the door and gesticulated for Dale to follow.

The small conference room was no less lavish than the rest of the hotel, with painted, wood panel walls and heavy crown molding. The ceiling had a circular recessed section that was painted a golden color. In the center of the room, stood a single table covered by a white tablecloth and surrounded by six high-back wooden chairs.

"May I get you something: coffee; tea; water?" the Colonel offered.

"Water, please," Dale replied. He was not thirsty, but based on how long previous meetings had taken, he figured after a few hours of repeating himself to some pretentious Colonel, his mouth would be dry.

"Have a seat. I will be right back," the Colonel politely, nodded toward the table and walked away.

"Thank you," Dale said, keeping up the charade of politeness, even though both men knew it was an order, and compliance was expected. Dale took the chair on the other side of the table, so he could face the door from which they had entered.

A few minutes after the Colonel brought back the glass of water another officer walked into the room. Dale could see from the three stars pinned on the collar of his khaki uniform that he was a General. Dale stood to attention and saluted.

"Good morning, Sergeant Matthews. At ease, take a seat," the General said, with a hand flourish toward the seat. The General appeared to be in his early fifties, with a touch gray creeping out, above his ears.

"I have already told the other officers everything I know," Dale insisted, in a respectful but defensive tone.

"I'm not here to interrogate you, Matthews. I have read the reports submitted by the previous interviewers, and I believe you. I'm General Ryan Bartlett with the Army Air Corps."

Dale nodded his head and decided to not speak, other than to answer direct questions.

General Bartlett pulled a folder from his brief case and placed it on the white tablecloth between the two men. Dale glanced at it, assuming it was transcripts of his previous interviews.

"The report says you killed three of these creatures." The General stated, leaning back in his chair.

"Not exactly. I assisted with killing two of the beasts. Quite frankly, I'm not sure I landed the death blow on either one them. I shot one with my Trench Broom. I mean Thompson machine gun, but it did not go down until it was hit with an M-9 bazooka. The other one I stabbed in the neck, but it did not die until it was shot in the head with an M-2 carbine."

General Bartlett nodded his head as if to agree with Matthews. "So, I read your description of the flying machine. Did you ever see it fly?"

"As I told the others, I never saw it fly. It was sitting on a concrete platform the entire time."

"What made you believe it was a flying machine, Matthews?" the General demanded as he was looking down his arrowhead-shaped nose at Matthews.

"I just assumed. It had no tires or tracks. It was made from a metallic substance and sat on the concrete pillars like a ship sits in dry dock." Dale thought for a moment. "There was also the opening at the top of the chamber directly above the flying machine. It looked to me like that opening was the only way for it to come into or go out of the underground chamber."

The General cradled his chin between his index finger and thumb, as if in deep thought, never taking his eyes off Matthews. Dale thought this seemed a lot like an interrogation. The General took his hand from his chin and pushed the folder on the table toward Dale, "Look at these."

Dale reached for the manila folder and opened it, to reveal dozens of photographs of disc-like flying objects. The pictures were all taken from different perspectives and positions.

"I see why you believe me now," Dale muttered. All the pictures were of metallic objects flying. None of the flying machines had wings, and they were all generally disc-like or cylindrical in shape.

"What you saw, did it look like any of the pictures," The General asked, pointing at the folder and pictures spread across the table.

Dale nodded his head and quietly responded, "Yes Sir."

"Matthews, what you saw, it is highly classified, and you cannot discuss it with anyone," the General warned, in a stern voice.

"Yes sir, I mean, no Sir, I won't tell anyone what I saw. I won't even discuss it with the men in my battalion." Dale knew by the three days of interrogations, that the three-star general was not going to tolerate the slightest breach of confidence.

"I know you will not discuss it with your friends in the battalion," the General replied, sitting up in his chair, he leaned forward on the white tablecloth and said, "I know, because you are not going back to your battalion. You are being reassigned."

O God what are they going to do to me?"

"Where to?" he stammered.

"You are being reassigned to the Army Air Corps. To the Alamogordo Army Air Base in New Mexico."

Dale took the first sip of his water. "I don't know anything about air planes," he said weakly.

"Upon arrival, your skills will be assessed. Then, we will decide what to do with you. By the way, you and your entire squad's history with the Army division will be permanently redacted from the records. You and your men were never on that ridge, never in that battalion, and never sent on that night mission. Do you understand?" It was clear from his facial expression that the General expected understanding.

"Yes sir. But what about my squad, they all died on that ridge."

"They all died heroes. They, and their families, will receive all the honors to which they are entitled, but they did not die on that ridge, on that night, do you understand?"

"Yes Sir."

CHAPTER THIRTEEN

April 25, 1945
Hamburg, Germany

Nox Bellator stood on top of the massive, concrete U-Boat base looking out upon the once great City of Hamburg. It was a dark and chilly night, but Bellator did not notice the wind or temperature because his interactive thermal body armor kept him comfortable in any climate. At seven feet tall, Nox Bellator towered over most humans. His size alone would strike fear into most seasoned warriors. Then you add his sophisticated armor and weaponry, he could terrify an entire battalion. His encounter with Sergeant Dale Matthews back in October had taught him a valuable lesson: never take off your armor. He had thought he was safe, well behind German lines, in a secret bunker filled with true believers. Yet, there was Matthews. Three of his most loyal soldiers were killed by Matthews. On that rueful night in the Vosges Mountains, he was wearing a dress uniform. Since then, he always wore his battle armor.

Nox was alone atop the massive edifice that stood in the waters of the Elbe River. The U-boat bunker was built to withstand numerous direct hits from the largest of the Allies' bombs. Even though the City of Hamburg was reduced to a burned-out rubble, the U-boat base had stood up to thousands of tons of British and American bombs.

The U-boat pen, Germans referred to it as "Fink II," was an enormous hardened structure and was designed to dock up to 15 submarines within the safety of its thick concrete walls. The structure, built right in the water, allowed submarines that had traveled up the Elbe River to the industrial City of Hamburg, to find refuge from Allied bombers.

Nox, a stranger to this planet, had first arrived in Hamburg 10 years earlier, and had overseen the expansion of the Nazi's U-boat program and the development of their experimental aircraft. Nox did not feel sadness or loss as he surveyed the hundreds of buildings that had been reduced to empty shells and crumbling walls. He was disappointed in himself. He was disappointed that he was not able to raise up the perfect army, and that his best efforts to organize these primitive humans had failed.

He estimated that the British and American's non-stop bombing of Hamburg had killed over 100,000 civilians. That did not matter to him. He knew the reports showed that one million civilians were left homeless after the endless bombing raids. Still, not his problem. Nox knew the City was about to fall to a British and American tank brigade. In a few days, the war would be over, and he would have almost nothing to show for the last 10 years -almost nothing.

Someday, fools would look back on history and question how Hitler could have lost a war if he had access to advanced alien technology. The answer was simple: a hand full of advanced antigravity fighters can't defeat over four million soldiers and hundreds of thousands of tanks and aircraft. Against Nox's advice, Hitler moved too fast. Bellator needed another ten years to get Hitler's factories to the point where they could mass produce advanced weaponry. Nox could no more mass produce antigravity fighters than an engineer could build an aircraft carrier out of coconuts and palm trees on a deserted island. Nox needed to build and repair his fighters with tools and equipment that the humans had not even discovered, much less, amassed in quantities large enough to supply a world war.

But, Hitler could not wait. Hitler saw Nox's antigravity fighter and particle beam incinerator, and he thought that alone could win a war against the rest of the world. If only he had tried harder to convince the madman to wait, just long enough to get a production line.

The City of Hamburg was surrounded by Allied troops and tanks. Sixty percent of the city was burned to the ground, and almost all the residents had evacuated. There were a few thousand German troops left, and they would be overrun in a few days. Nox was not worried for his safety; the antigravity fighter behind him could whisk him far away. He had a plan, not a plan to save Hamburg, but a plan to salvage some of his work.

Nox Bellator turned from the crumbling city and entered his antigravity fighter. His fighter craft was advanced far beyond anything the humans had engineered. It did not push through the wind with crude propellers and wings, but rather, it created a force field around the craft that allowed a planet's gravity to pass around it, like air passes around a wing. Without gravity pulling the craft towards the planet, the antimatter fusion reactors would power the flight system and move the craft at speeds over 5,000 miles per hour.

The flight systems were extraordinarily complex and completely controlled by either his thoughts or voice command. He could control the antigravity fighter from outside the ship, so long as he was wearing his body armor, which would transmit his thought commands to the craft.

Nox navigated the craft off the building and into one of several openings above the water by which the submarines would enter the

U-boat base. He landed his antigravity fighter on the dock behind a submarine mooring. This location within the submarine base had been specially designed to ensure Nox's privacy. Nox knew that his height, dark gray skin, and elongated facial features would draw unneeded attention. So, he intentionally limited his appearances among the rank-and-file German troops.

The antigravity fighter was sitting on the concrete pedestal, held up by three legs that had extended from the belly of the craft. Nox walked down the metal stairway to the submarine dock. A Nazi Admiral and two guards were waiting to greet him.

The admiral stepped forward and saluted as soon as Nox set foot on the base. "We have been expecting you Field Marshall Nox Bellator. Heil Hitler!"

Nox, who at this point, was no fan of Hitler, shrugged and gave a half-ass salute. "Admiral Armbruster, take me to your office."

"Yes Sir." The Admiral, who was acutely aware of the fact that Hamburg was about to be overrun by British forces and that Germany was destined to lose the war, was not terribly concerned with the formality of honoring Hitler.

The Admiral's office was very nice; the concrete bunker walls had been covered by rich wood paneling, and a dark red rug covered the floor. The Admiral had some personal effects displayed on a hand-carved curio cabinet that matched his ornate desk. Other than that, it was obvious that the Admiral worked at his desk. The large, executive desk was covered with papers, files, reports, memos, and plans. The messy paperwork extended past the fancy desk top and onto the surrounding floor as if the Admiral had them spread out for review.

Nox sat in a low back guest chair in the somewhat dimly lit office before being invited to do so. If the Admiral took offense to his guest sitting without invitation, he did not show it. The Admiral and Nox had been working together since prior to the inception of the war. Nox liked the Admiral, like a human would be fond of a favorite pet that could perform cool tricks. Nox thought the Admiral was intelligent - for a human.

Admiral Armbruster was one of the commanding officers of the U-boat base. He was average build, in his mid-fifties, with jet black hair, the wrinkles on his face, and bags under his eyes made it obvious that the war had taken a toll on him. Admiral Armbruster was proud of his family's seafaring history. Both his father and grandfather had honorably served as naval officers in the past. Armbruster did not blindly believe the Nazi rhetoric, but he was intelligent enough to play the political game to avoid a firing squad. Armbruster took great pride in his role in developing the cutting-edge underwater boats and in winning navel battles. There was honor in engaging an armed enemy at sea.

"Are the U-boats ready for their long journey?" Nox asked, in his raspy voice.

"Yes, the modifications were just completed this morning. Each of the Type IX U-boats can now carry 100 people, including the crew," the Admiral said with confidence.

"And the paperwork?" Nox had learned how important paperwork was on this planet.

"All four of the U-boats were reported missing in action, and there is no record that would indicate they are anywhere else but lying on the ocean floor. No one will come looking for these boats."

"Any weapons?" Nox knew the plan was to eliminate torpedo tubes and storage to make room for more passengers.

"Unfortunately, we had to eliminate all torpedo tubes to make enough room. We were able to leave both cannons on the forward and aft deck," replied the Admiral.

The Type IX U-Boats typically carried a crew of 53, were 251 feet long and displaced 1,034 long tons. With a maximum range of 15,000 miles and up to 24 torpedoes, they were perfect for attacking and sinking ships along the coast of North America and

Africa. The tradeoff for carrying 165 tons of fuel and torpedoes was that it was slow. With a maximum speed of 20 miles per hour, this would be a long trip.

"How many crew are necessary to man the submarine, now that we have no need to man the torpedoes?"

The Admiral paused, and put his hand to his face as if he were thinking. "I could probably operate each boat with as few as 25 men, seeing that the plan is to stay out of shipping channels, and to not engage the enemy. Basically, we are just moving people from here to Antarctica."

Nox nodded, his pitch-black eyes staring at the Admiral, not that the Admiral could tell as the creature had no eyeballs. "That means I can carry 300 men to Antarctica. One hundred and twenty-seven men are already chosen for the voyage. That means we can take 173 of your people."

The Admiral sat up in his chair. This was the first he was hearing about the other passengers; "I did not realize you were bringing other passengers?"

"Yes, I was unsure if I could get them here, but I was able to convince some of the V-2 rocket scientists to defect with us."

"I thought the V-2 scientists were relocated from Peenemunde Army Research Center after it was bombed by the British? How could you get them here from the Alpine Fortress?" asked the Admiral. If the Admiral was concerned with the word 'defect,' he made no mention of it.

Nox nodded. Nodding was a human gesture, but Nox had learned, not only the spoken language of humans, but also their body language. It seemed to put them at ease when he used familiar body language that they understood. He was also teaching himself to learn human facial expressions, not because he cared what they thought of him, but because sometimes he was forced to engage in diplomacy.

"After the scientists were moved from Peenemunde, they were taken to *Mittelwerk* in the Harz Mountains to work in an underground bunker. Some of my operatives were able to convince them to come with us. We helped them escape the Nazis when they were being transported from the underground base to the Alpine Fortress. Once in our custody, we could bring them here by boat, now on the Elbe River," Nox said.

Admiral Armbruster understood the importance of having V-2 rocket scientists. German scientists and aeronautical engineers were the most advanced in the world. They were good to have, if only to ensure the Americans did not have access to their knowledge.

"Very well, what shall we do now?" asked the Admiral.

"Is everyone on the list I gave you present?" asked Nox.

"I received your list of 224 names. A few of them had been killed and few transferred, but I was able to ensure that 217 of them were present at the yard today." Admiral Armbruster knew Nox did not appreciate failure, but, he was reasonably certain that he had come close enough to completing the assignment.

"How many of the persons missing from my list are dead?" Nox asked.

"Three."

"Four have been transferred?"

"Yes"

"Very well, that's close enough. Have them assembled in the briefing room in one hour," Nox grumbled.

"Yes Sir," The Admiral stood to attention and started to say Heil Hitler but caught himself.

"We can dispense with the 'Heil Hitler' at this point," Nox muttered, and he waived off the Admiral.

Nox sat in the empty Admiral's office for the next hour, contemplating what he would say to the 200 plus men. Nox was not only a warrior, but a cunning politician, as well. He understood that his alien forces were not strong enough to rule this world alone; he needed allies. He needed allies that were not so eager for war that they could wait for the perfect time. His plan was to rebuild, not the Third Reich, that brand was damaged beyond repair; no, he was going to rebuild in a new place, create a new world order.

The people on the list that Nox was assembling were not war hawks or greedy politicians; they were the best scientists and engineers he could manage to recruit. These were not just any scientists; they were scientists that he had either worked with or that knew of his existence. No one in that room would be shocked to see him.

Nox had 173 seats to fill on the recently reported missing U-boats. He hoped to convince 173 of the 217 men to join him. It would be unfortunate to launch the U-boats with empty seats. Nox did not need the scientists and engineers for their knowledge of human technology. Nox was more intelligent than any human that had ever lived, and understood the intricacies of technology centuries beyond what human scientists could even imagine. Earth's technology had not even developed enough to create basic tools to fix and repair the equipment Nox had brought with him from his home planet. Nox had to train humans on the basic concepts of his technology so that they could start planning to build factories that could produce advanced equipment. When you are stranded on a deserted island, you must invent an ax before you can chop down a tree. Then, you must make rope before you can tie the timbers together to build a raft. In this little parable, Nox felt like he was still swimming to the island.

Nox walked into the crowded conference room. The room was hot and stuffy from having over 200 people jammed into it. The group was a mixture of Nazi officers, yard workers, welders, planners, engineers, shipbuilders, and scientists. The walls were dark gray concrete. The men sat on metal chairs with no padding. Nox walked down the center aisle between the men, toward the front of the room. He had not made the same mistake he made in the Vosges Mountains; he was wearing full body armor and an interactive helmet with head up display vizor. At the front of the room was a wooden desk and on the wall before the men was a nautical chart of the Elbe River and coastal Germany.

Nox stood before the seated men. He was not nervous. He was hopeful, hopeful that he could convince 173 of these men to go to Antarctica to start over. The room was silent; you could hear a pen drop as he turned to face the group.

"Most of you have seen me around this base. Some of you have worked with me on developing new technologies for the war effort. If you have not seen or worked with me, you are here because I believe you are important to my mission.

For those of you that do not know me: I am Nox Bellator. I am not of this planet. The planet I come from circles a star that is over thirty thousand light years from Earth. We refer to ourselves as Ondagra, and our home world is called Botacoure. There are hundreds like me, right here on Earth, many of my fellow Ondagra are colonizing Antarctica.

"This war is almost over. The British and Americans have surrounded what remains of this city. They have us outnumbered and outgunned. The Soviets are advancing on Berlin, and it will fall in the next few days. The British, French, Soviets, and Americans will want revenge for the millions slaughtered by the Nazis. German soldiers and officers will be executed by the thousands; millions of your women will be violated and tortured. This is not a hypothetical; this is here, at our doorstep, right now.

I am offering to each one of you an opportunity to escape the penance of the fallen; but it comes with a price, a steep price. I have four U-boats sitting in the pen at this moment; each one has been retrofitted to carry 100 seamen and passengers to Antarctica, where we will start over, building a new world.

Many of you believe that Antarctica is nothing but millions of square miles of ice and sub-zero temperatures. You may even believe that humans could not survive the cold climate of Antarctica, but you would be wrong. Several years ago, we discovered a vast underground cavern, larger than the entire country of Germany. In the center of this massive underground cavern we discovered a warm water lake, as big as a sea. It was heated by an underground geothermal energy source. This huge lake radiates heat throughout the cavern and warms it to a comfortable temperature.

We have been exploring and mapping this cavern and the many underwater tunnel passages that lead to it. We have been building a city, a place we can seek refuge from our enemies, and where we can rebuild a new and stronger civilization.

I am extending the invitation to each one of you to join me on this journey. However, if you choose to go to Antarctica, you will never be able to return. Security demands that you live the remainder of your lives there. There is not enough space on the boats for you to bring your families, even if there were, we do not have accommodations for them.

If you choose this journey with me, you will not be allowed to say goodbye to your families or return home to collect your things. You will exit this room, walk directly to the U-boat pen and board. Everything you need is on the boat, including clothing, food and supplies.

If you choose to stay here, you will be taken hostage by the Allied invaders and suffer unspeakable humiliations at the hands of the enemy.

Who will come with me to Antarctica as free men?"

Nox knew it was a hard sell. Most of the men had families that they would not want to leave, "I will answer any questions, now."

A Nazi officer stood to his feet. He appeared to be in his early forties, with a strong jaw and closely cropped blonde hair. Like the other officers, he was in full dress uniform. "Will we be able to send for our families later?" he asked.

Nox had not anticipated that question. However, he knew the other men would be wondering the same thing. Nox immediately sensed that he would have more men volunteer for the mission if he gave them hope that they would one day be reunited with their families.

"Yes, of course. After things settle down we will make efforts to locate and transport your families to Antarctica. It may take years to locate them, depending on how the enemy handles the coming occupation," Nox said confidently. Nox did not really have a problem with families being at the Antarctica base; after all, he would need babies to help grow his would-be empire. The Nazi officer nodded and sat down.

A scientist raised his hand. Nox pointed at him, and the scientist rose to his feet. The scientist, well known by everyone on the U-boat base, was not a huge supporter of the Nazi party; he was more interested in scientific endeavors than politics. He was a man in his early forties, balding, and slight in stature.

"Mr. Nox, um, I have a question," the scientist shuffled his feet and looked at the floor.

Nox ignored the improper title, knowing the awkward scientist meant no disrespect.

The scientist continued, "If this huge cavern is underground, even if it is heated, how do plants and vegetables grow with no sunlight?"

Nox would have smiled if the muscles in his face would have allowed it; he knew he could convert many of them with this answer. "It is true that much of the cavern is underground and does not receive sunlight in the traditional manner. There are numerous natural openings at the top of the cavern, holes in the ground, that allow sunlight to directly fall on the floor of the cavern some 500 feet below, but that is not enough. When we found the cavern, there were numerous forests and plants growing in the spaces that had natural sunlight. We found thousands of acres of wooded areas with thick vegetation. But there were still hundreds of square miles of warm, but rocky, and barren land. Since then, our scientists have developed a system by which we collect sunlight on the surface and funnel it down to the caverns, with highly reflective tubing. When the sunlight reaches the cavern below it is 20 times brighter than it was on the surface because of our magnification equipment. We have already had great success in growing crops with the natural sunlight that is funneled through the ice in these magnification tunnels."

Nox saw several of the scientists nodding their heads in approval.

A commander stood to his feet. Nox looked at him and waived his hand, indicating for the Nazi commander to speak. Nox knew the commander was a natural leader and many men would follow him.

The Commander said, "What will be the command structure? Will we still be Nazis? Will Hitler be there? Will we keep our rank?"

Nox took a shallow breath; he knew this could be a critical point for many of the men. Nox never thought honesty was the best policy, but in this situation, it may be. He knew many of the higher-ranking officers were upset at Hitler because he had squandered their initial advantage. They knew that if Hitler had been less aggressive it may have kept the Soviets and Americans out of the war longer.

"Everyone will keep their current rank. There will be two command structures, a civilian command structure and a military command structure. The main difference, is that there will be a third command structure, one that supersedes both military and civilian command structures, and that will be the command structure of the Ondagra. All humans will fall under the authority of my people."

"Will we be slaves to the Ondagra?" asked the Commander.

"Are you a slave to me now? I am superior to you physically and mentally. Even now, you must obey my commands, but have I degraded any of you? Have I treated you unfairly or harmed you? No, of course not. I expect you to follow my orders because I know better than you, and you know that is true. It will be the same in Antarctica. You will be free to move about the cavern; there will be work for you. There will be food, shelter, and eventually entertainment. You just won't be allowed to leave or communicate with the outside world for security purposes."

After the men had asked their questions, Admiral Armbruster stood from the back of the room. The Admiral was admired and respected by the men as a fair and even-tempered leader. He said, "Germany is lost. The war is all but over. Many German officers will be killed or executed in the next several weeks. You know I would not ask of you anything I would not do myself. I am pledging my support to Nox Bellator. I will be on that U-boat, and I will work alongside Field Marshall Bellator, helping him build a new civilization. I will not order you to get on a U-boat. We only want those who willingly volunteer. I hope many of you will join me, today." The Admiral took a step forward and clinched his fist, "Right now. Stand if you are willing to get on these U-boats with me. Stand now!"

Five of the Admiral's executive officers stood. It had already been discussed, and the Admiral knew they were coming. Three engineers and 10 scientists stood. They too had already known what was happening and were expected to stand. Nineteen standing. Not enough. Silence.

Then, the Nazi commander that had asked the question about rank stood. His men took quick glances at each other, then stood, another 40 men. With almost 60 men standing, the momentum had almost turned in Nox's favor. He still needed over 100 more to stand. Nox knew he could say no more. The officers and ranking scientists had to convince their fellow soldiers and colleagues. This is where advanced planning pays off. Many of those standing had previously agreed to stand and help convince the others.

The Admiral walked forward from the back of the room. Nox loved his little pet.

Admiral Armbruster took the position next to Nox and said, "It has been an honor serving with each one of you. Over the last several years, we have seen many of our brothers-in-arms fall. But, you have kept the faith, and for that I am proud of you. This is not an easy decision, and I will respect you if you choose to stay. But, for what are you staying? This city will fall; there is no escape. Many of you will die at the hands of the Americans and Russians. Many of your families have already been killed in the fire bombings. Many of you imagine that you will be able to stop the British soldiers from violating your wives and daughters, but this is foolhardy. They will kill you first and then take your defenseless women. What future do you have here? Will you stay and be a slave to the Allied conquerors that hate us? Or will you come with me, where you can start over, not as a slave, but as an important part of a new world order? I can't promise you riches, fame, or even your families. But I promise that you will be a part of a movement that will make a permanent mark on the course of human history. The invaders will offer you chains and sorrow. Come with me and build a nation like this world has never seen!" Admiral Armbruster leaned back against the wooden table behind him. Seventy men stood up. Nox was so proud of his pet Admiral.

After a few more minutes of discussions, there were a total of 105 men standing, not quite what Nox wanted, but good enough.

Admiral Armbruster said, "All men that are standing, walk in a single file line to the submarine pen. Do not go back to your quarters. The rest of you wait here for further orders; I will be right back." The Admiral knew he would never go back.

Nox stayed at the front of the room, carefully studying the faces of the men that had chosen not to get on the submarines. After the volunteers had made their way toward the submarine pen, Nox said, "I too would like to thank you for your service to the Nazi party. The rest of you will be manning this base until the British arrive. Once they are about to take the base, I need you to scuttle all the U-boats. I'm going to the Admiral's office to gather your specific orders."

Nox walked down the center aisle to the rear of the room. As he reached the back of the room, he stood directly in front of the only door and turned to face the seated men. He withdrew, from a compartment in his armor, two canisters. They were of his own design, hydrogen-cyanide grenades. He thought it was ironic that these men would die from Zyklon-B, the same poison the Nazis used to kill the Jews. He flipped the rings on the grenades with his thumbs and tossed the pear-shaped, metallic devices into the center of the room. He quickly exited and secured the door behind him. The men screamed for a few minutes, and then there was silence. There could be no witnesses; he did not need captured German soldiers telling the Americans about a seven-foot-tall, gray alien. This mission always had two goals: the first was to recruit talent for Antarctica; the second, to tie up loose ends.

Nox Bellator walked to the submarine pen where Admiral Armbruster was waiting.

"All the volunteers are aboard. The U-boats are ready to launch," Armbruster said, "should we leave the Nazi insignias on the Boats?"

"We should keep the insignia on the boats. We still have a lot of Nazi controlled water to travel through, no need in having *everyone* target us. When you get to Antarctica, we can decide on a new uniform and emblem, for now, maintain the Nazi command structure," Nox said.

"Will you be joining us?" asked the Admiral.

"I do not plan to go to Antarctica. The Ondagra will get you set up in there. I have a few humans to call on," answered Nox.

The Admiral boarded the U-boat. Nox noticed the number on the side, it was U-196. Nox knew it was the Type IXD2 that had gone missing five months earlier. He watched as the last of the U-boats disappeared into the dark Elbe River, pleased with his success.

CHAPTER FOURTEEN

Berlin, Germany
April 30, 1945

Nox gently landed his antigravity fighter in the garden of the Old Reich Chancellery in Berlin. Even though his craft was equipped with optical stealth technology, and neither the Germans nor the Soviets could see the craft, he still radioed ahead to Hitler's Bunker. No point in having them mistakenly shoot at him.

Hitler had taken to his bunker weeks earlier, when the Soviets began their non-stop bombing campaign. Prior to that Hitler had spent most of his time in the government buildings above the bunker. As Nox approached the square entrance of the concrete bunker, several Nazi guards came out of the small opening. Their weapons were ready, but not pointed at Nox; they were expecting him.

Nox was not concerned about the guards, he had been to the Old Reich Chancellery on several occasions to discuss matters with Hitler. Nox and the guards descended the concrete stairs to the bunker, 28 feet below the gardens. The bunker was protected by almost 10 feet of reinforced concrete that could withstand a direct hit from almost any conventional bomb.

At the bottom of the stairs, he was led into a conference room. There were several doors on either side of the room, leading to bed chambers, kitchens, communication rooms, and Hitler's private study. For such a small space, the bunker was surprisingly decorated with rare oil paintings and gilded furniture.

Hitler, Goebbels, and Krebs stood at the other end of the cramped conference room. Their faces were easy to read: they knew the end was near. The German troops defending Berlin would run out of ammunition soon. Generals in the field were already engaging in unauthorized discussions regarding how to surrender to the Soviets.

The plan had been discussed. One of Hitler's many body doubles would be shot and burned. The scene would be staged to make it appear that Eva Braun, Hitler's new wife, committed suicide. The Soviets would find their bodies and, hopefully, assume the couple had committed suicide. The goal was to allow Hitler and Eva to disappear to Argentina and live the rest of their lives in anonymity. That was Hitler's plan. Nox had other ideas.

"Are the look-a-likes in the bunker?" Nox asked. Introductions were not necessary.

Goebbels responded, "Yes, they are in the Fuehrer's private chambers."

Nox walked up to Hitler and held out his large hand. "Give me your Luger."

Hitler was under no illusion as to who was in power at this moment and dutifully handed the weapon to Nox, "Yes Sir."

The pistol was almost difficult to hold; it was tiny compared to the size of Nox's oversized fingers. Nox walked past the three of them and into Hitler's chambers. A single shot was heard. A few minutes later, Nox walked back into the room. "I forced Eva's look-a-like to ingest cyanide."

Nox pointed at Goebbels. "Take pictures, burn the bodies in the garden."

Nox then turned to General Krebs, "Wait two hours and notify the Generals in the field that the Fuehrer is dead."

Nox then reached into a hidden compartment within his body armor and pulled out a small container. Handing it to Krebs, he said, "A gift for you. This contains enough cyanide to kill both of you. I suggest you use it before the Soviets take this bunker."

Nox then turned to Hitler, "Your U-boats were launched for Argentina a few days ago. All your belongings will arrive as planned. I personally saw to it that your instructions were followed. You and Eva will live out your days in a villa in the Andes Mountains. Go get Eva now; we need to leave."

Lying was easy for Nox. The trick was to shroud your lie in a believable truth.

Nox turned to Goebbels and Krebs. "You both need to ingest the poison before the Soviets get here. I expect absolute secrecy about Hitler's whereabouts."

"I will take this secret to my grave," Krebs assured Nox.

Hitler and Eva emerged from one of the back rooms, each carrying a small travel bag.

"Follow me," Nox said.

As they exited the bunker, Nox shot each one of the German guards with his thought-controlled particle beam incinerator. Less witnesses.

CHAPTER FIFTEEN

May 1, 1945
The Kremlin, Moscow

A s Nox entered Soviet airspace, he disengaged his optical stealth so that his flying saucer could be seen by the Russian military. He intentionally slowed his craft so that the Russians would be able to fully take in what they were seeing; he needed to demonstrate his superiority to Stalin long before they met.

As expected, Soviet air defenses began firing into the sky. Nox was not concerned; there was no possibility of them striking his craft.

Nox wanted to make certain that Stalin and the Soviet commanders were watching. He did not take a direct route to Moscow, but rather, intentionally flew his craft over known military installations to draw as much fire as possible.

After two hours of spectacularly evading Soviet air defenses, he had attracted three Russian military planes. They seemed to be following him at a distance. Nox could have easily shot down the

Soviet planes, but his goal was not to kill Russians, only to clearly demonstrate his military superiority.

As Nox approached Moscow, the anti-aircraft weapons stopped. Nox assumed they gave up and decided to stop wasting ammunition. He had not shot a single Russian plane or engaged a single Russian anti-aircraft position, he had simply allowed them to shoot at him.

As Nox approached the spot where he believed the Kremlin to be, he was shocked. The Kremlin, which had been built hundreds of years earlier as a walled city, sat on a 68-acre parcel that was completely enclosed by ten-foot-thick brick walls. Along the 7,332 feet of red brick walls stood 20 towers. Inside the huge governmental complex were numerous structures that housed ornate governmental and administrative offices, lavish churches with golden onion-shaped domes, and extensive ammo depots.

A couple of years earlier, in the Moscow campaign, Hitler had expended considerable resources bombing Moscow and the Kremlin. Nox knew what the Kremlin was supposed to look like because of the numerous pictures he had seen. Nox made it a point to study the great cities of all the major countries on Earth, especially those of his enemies. Nox was expecting to see shiny golden domes atop buildings that had miraculously been spared by the many bombing runs Either that, or burned out ruins.

To Nox's surprise, where the Kremlin was supposed to be, stood a row of tenement apartment buildings. It looked like government or army housing, certainly not the elaborate Neo-Classical architecture that was supposed to be the Kremlin.

Were his instruments off? Was he in the wrong place?

As he sat in the cockpit of his antigravity fighter, trying to reconcile what he knew to be true against what he saw before him, his focus shifted, and the Kremlin he knew to exist appeared before his eyes.

*Had the Russians invented active optical stealth? How could his esti-
mates of their technology be that far off?*

Then he realized the truth. The Russians had not developed optical stealth; they had used a 1,000-year-old ploy. They had painted the
Kremlin to look like a series of unimportant apartment buildings.
The once elegant gold domes were painted brown to deceive German
pilots looking down to drop their payload of destruction. The impressive brick walls of the Kremlin were painted to look like the sides of
buildings with rows of nondescript windows. False shells of buildings
were built up around the Kremlin, like a Hollywood movie set. Nox
realized immediately why the Nazi pilots could not accurately target
the Kremlin, they could not see it from the sky.

Those clever bastards.

Nox looked for the perfect place to set down the AG Fighter. Red
Square was directly outside the walled Kremlin. Running along another side of the walled compound was a river. The walls came together
into a triangular shape. If he landed in Red Square, then the people
that mattered most would have to leave the walls of the Kremlin to
meet him. That would be okay, but would make for an anticlimactic
moment. Nox knew this was a time for diplomacy. He chose to set his
craft down in Cathedral Square in front of the *Assumption Cathedral.*
Cathedral Square is an open space that is centrally located within the
complex and visible from many important buildings.

Nox sat in his cockpit for a few minutes, simply for effect. He
knew exactly what he was going to say. Waiting to exit the fighter
was for the human's benefit, just like the blood sacrifices. Nox did
not really like the taste of blood, nor did he derive any energy from
killing certain people. He just knew that it solidified his control
over them. Nox was certain Stalin and his top advisors would have
already been gathered and discussing the situation. There was not
a battalion of Russian soldiers in front of his craft. Instead, Joseph
Stalin walked out from the Soviet Senate building with five soldiers and began to make his way towards Nox's craft.

Both Nox and Stalin had played their roles perfectly. Nox had telegraphed his position of power. Stalin knew he was powerless against Nox's superior technology; so, he chose not to embarrass himself by surrounding the ship with impotent guards.

This guy is a true leader, a vicious, murderous leader, but someone I can work with.

Stalin stopped about 30 feet from the disc-shaped craft that was resting on its landing gear. He was wearing his iconic long, gray trench coat, shiny black boots, and military cap. The five soldiers were standing a few feet behind him, with submachine guns ready at the hip position, but not aimed at the craft.

Nox walked down the ramp that had extended from the bottom of the craft. He was surprised at how little damage the Kremlin had sustained during the war, unlike Berlin, the Kremlin was in good shape. One could no longer see the sumptuous elegance of the Neo-Classical design through the façade of scaffolding and paint, but Nox was sure it would shine again soon.

"Welcome to the Soviet Union," Stalin said. "My apologies for the barrage of anti-aircraft fire earlier."

Stalin was a talented politician. One does not rise to that level of power without knowing when and how to use diplomacy. The fact that he was personally in the square, demonstrated to Nox that the leader of the Soviet Union was giving proper deference to the situation.

"I have come in peace. I do not wish to harm you or your people." Nox made his first communication to the Soviet leader very simple and clear. He was aware that the demonstration of superior air power would cause the Soviets to be concerned.

"I am Joseph Stalin. I am the supreme leader of the Soviet Union. May I ask to whom I am speaking?"

"I am Nox Bellator. I am from the planet Botacoure, far from here. I have a proposal to make; one, I think will be mutually beneficial."

"Would you like to come into the Senate Conference center to discuss your proposal?" The Soviet leader raised his hands, palms up, to signal peaceful intent.

"If you have your men lower their weapons, I would be happy to sit and discuss my concerns," Nox said. He was not concerned that the soldiers could harm him. Five men armed with machine guns would be no match for his armor and particle beam incinerator.

With a hand motion from Stalin, the men lowered their weapons. "Please come this way," he said.

It was a short walk to the Senate building. The magnificent structure was a mustard-colored, 18th century neo-classical building, with engaged columns partially built into the walls. Stalin led Nox into a large conference room. Unlike the outside of the building, which had been disguised to look unimportant, the conference room was a display of gaudy opulence. The walls were covered with thick, hand-carved wood, paneling arching up towards a vaulted ceiling. Gilded lamps sat upon marble-top furniture stationed against the walls. A large mahogany conference table sat in the middle of the room, surrounded by an army of high-back well-upholstered chairs. On the far side of the large room was a massive stone fireplace that reached up to the decorative ceiling. The floors were white marble, and the ceiling was hand painted with whimsical geometric shapes and colors.

Stalin walked to a chair near the door and pulled it out, "Please have a seat."

"Thank you for your hospitality," Nox said. Maybe this would be easier than he thought. Nox sat in a chair, it was a large with a high back and luxurious embroidery. The chair had to be strong, if his seven-foot frame clad in battle armor weighing nearly 500 pounds did not crush it.

Stalin sat in the chair directly across the conference table from Nox. Two guards with machine guns stood in the doorway, but the rest of Stalin's entourage left the room.

Stalin, unaware of exactly how powerful Nox may be, was trying to be as polite and diplomatic as possible. "May I get you something to drink?"

"No, thank you," said Nox, unsure as to whether Stalin would attempt to poison him. Nox's battle armor could detect all known poisons, but there was no need to put that system to the test.

Nox continued, "I would like to form a treaty between your people and mine, a trade agreement of sorts."

"I'm interested." Stalin was sitting straight up, hands folded on the table, looking directly into Nox's black eyes.

"I come from a planet far from here. I have technology that allows me to fly through space at incredible speeds. I possess weapons far beyond your wildest imagination. I can help your people build communication devices that will make your best radios and radars obsolete. I can assist you in rebuilding and advancing your infrastructure in a fraction of the time it would take you with your current equipment."

Stalin nodded, "And what do you want in return?"

"I want to be appointed as General of the Russian Armed Forces, with access to all systems. I want to be the commanding officer over all the military installations in Moscow and I want all research and development under my command. I will operate in full secrecy; only a few of your highest-ranking officers will know of my existence. I will need to triple your research and development budget, and I will have sole discretion as to how to use it. My orders will be carried out by staff generals, so the rank-and-file are not aware of my existence. I will answer only to you, the supreme leader of the Soviet Union."

Stalin took a deep breath. "You are asking me to turn over all control. You want to install yourself as supreme commander and make me a puppet. How can I trust you? How can I know that you will not overthrow me once I give you so much power?"

"A very good question, but there is a simple answer. I cannot rule your people. They would never trust or accept me as a leader.

If they knew of my existence, they would revolt. That is why I must be kept in the shadows. I have no need for a regime change. I have no desire to enter into a world war. Hitler went against my wishes by pushing the world into a destructive war that destroyed much needed infrastructure. I want to build your planet into something new, something better, not decimate it with bombs."

"How do I know you can deliver all of this?"

"For two hours, your air defenses were unable to stop me as I flew through your skies. What more demonstration do you need?"

"Your plane is impressive. I have no doubt that your craft is advanced far beyond anything in my air force. I can see your body armor is made of a substance unknown to me. I assume you did not walk into my Senate chamber unarmed, and yet, I see no weapon. Clearly, you are who you say you are, and I assume you have the means to inflict massive damage to my military. Yet, you are promising to deliver this technological advantage to me. Why?"

"It is true that I can assist you in rapid technological advances. But, I offer technology to you, not as a gift, but rather in trade. Botacoure is very far away, which makes resupply difficult. I have many craft, like the one sitting in your Square, but finding fuel and replacement parts is burdensome. I need to advance human technology and industry so that I can have the resources I need to maintain my equipment."

Nox continued, "I am not asking for control of your military to take over your country. I am asking for control so that I can direct the research and development to create the technology I need. Your scientists and engineers are not advanced enough to handle this on their own. As I develop the technology I need, I will share it with you and your scientists. You will get better armor, better rockets, better warheads, better communication devices, better infrastructure, and equipment that will make it easier to spy on your enemies. I will give this to you because I need your cooperation in this partnership."

"I would like a demonstration of what you can do for me."

Nox stood and turned toward the door where they had entered the opulent room.

With his back to Stalin, and his hand on the chair that he was just sitting in, two shards of bright light flashed from the square box on the breast plate of his armor. Both guards at the door fell to their knees, and toppled to the floor; both were dead before their faces smashed into the fine marble tiles.

Stalin leapt to his feet, trembling with rage. Nox turned to him and said flatly. "You asked for a demonstration."

Nox held his hands up to Stalin, "I mean you no harm. I thought his would be an excellent way to prove what I have to offer."

"Those were two of my best men," Stalin stammered.

"I'm certain you saw that I did not raise either of my hands to your men. The weapon attached to my chest is controlled by my thoughts alone. I have demonstrated my ability to produce results. Now I will demonstrate my willingness."

With an ever-so-slight whirring sound, a pistol appeared at Nox's hip. Nox rarely used a particle beam pistol; it was overkill when paired with his thought-control weapon. Nox withdrew the pistol from its hidden compartment and placed it on the table before Stalin.

"A gift for you," Nox said.

Stalin lifted the weapon; it was slightly heavier and larger than the U.S. 1911 pistol.

"Fire it," insisted Nox.

Stalin took aim at an innocent vase filled with lovely lavender flowers sitting on a marble-top table. He squeezed the trigger. A flash of light left the barrel of the handgun; the vase exploded, leaving a burnt smoking hole in the wall behind the where the vase once stood. Stalin smiled.

"Thank you for the gift. What shall I call you?"

"Nox Bellator, Marshal of the Soviet Union," Nox replied.

Stalin stood for a moment, pondering the proposed arrangement.

"I almost forgot. I have another gift for you," Nox said. "It is still in my fighter. Shall we walk back to the craft?"

"Of course, I would love to see the inside of it."

"Would you like for me to take you for a ride in it?" Nox's highest priority was ensuring that Stalin would appoint him as the General responsible for Soviet research and development.

"I would like that very much," the dictator replied.

A handful of soldiers accompanied them back to the square where Nox's craft was waiting. Nox disappeared back into the craft, "I'll be right back."

A few minutes later, Nox reappeared beneath the craft with two prisoners, one male and one female, hands tied behind their backs, with black hoods over their heads.

Stalin chuckled, "What makes you think I need two more prisoners?"

Nox pushed the two, bound prisoners toward the dictator. When they were five feet from the dictator, Nox ripped the black hoods off their heads. Stalin roared with laughter. It was Hitler and Eva Braun.

"This is the best gift I have ever received, Marshal Bellator." Stalin nodded at Nox to emphasize the word 'Marshal'.

"I'm glad you like it, Sir. I think it would be best if we keep this gift a secret, just between you and me," Nox warned. Nox emphasized the word 'Sir.'

"Of course. The Fuehrer and his bride will receive my undivided attention for the remainder of their lives," Stalin said with a wicked grin.

CHAPTER SIXTEEN

Moscow, Russia
Present Day

It had been over 70 years since Marshall Bellator and Stalin had struck a deal. Nox sat at the head of a long conference room table in an underground facility, 29 levels below the surface. Underground facilities had come a long way since WWII. The conference room looked more like what you would find in a corporate headquarters in New York City than the old concrete walls of yesteryear. The table, surrounded by high ranking Russian officers, was closer akin to a board room table than the hand-carved gilded tables of the past.

Even though they were deep underground, there were *faux* windows that glowed with artificial sunlight. Instead of nautical charts and maps on the wall, behind him was a huge display monitor. Built into the conference room table before each of the chairs was a display that could control the big screen at the head of the room.

Nox was uncomfortable in his hand-tailored suit and silk shirt. The suit was more than fine, it was superb. Nox still preferred his armor. The lesson that Dale Matthews' squad taught to him in the Vosges Mountains still stuck with him. But today was an exception. Today's events had been in the planning stages for almost 10 years. Today he was going to meet, in person, for the first time, the *Council of Three Hundred*.

Until now, the number of living humans that had seen Nox were fewer than one hundred. In a few hours, Nox would be transported from his deep underground bunker to the classified Russian Air Force base, where he would speak to 300 of the world's most powerful people.

Many members of the *Council of Three Hundred* had heard of Nox Bellator, but less than a dozen had ever met him. The *Circle of Ten* were the ten sitting members on the Council of Three Hundred that Nox had personally chosen to be in his inner circle. The *Circle of Ten* was a secret group within the Council, chosen by Nox because he felt they would do his bidding. Ten members in his pocket was not enough to sway a Council vote, but it was enough to have trusted eyes and ears in the Council. The *Circle of Ten* came in very handy when he needed points made, favors requested or a whisper campaign started. All 10 of his inner circle sat on the best committees, though only two were chairmen.

After the fall of the Soviet Union, Nox bestowed upon himself the title: *Marshal of the Russian Federation*. He outranked every flag officer in Russia. He answered only to the President of the Russian Federation. Only one person had held this rank in the past. Most of the Russian people did not even know the position existed. There were over 1,000 flag officers in the Russian military. Of those, only a handful knew of Nox. He gave his orders to the generals under his command and they directed the rest of the military. The rank-and-file officers and enlisted just assumed the orders originated from a three or four-star general.

"Have all of our guests arrived?" Nox asked.

"The last guest's plane touched down 20 minutes ago. They are gathering in the Grand Hall as we speak. It will take 15 minutes to transport you to the conference center," General Ivanov said.

The three-day conference was taking place on Nox's secret air base, just outside Moscow. Nox had a conference center and hotel built specially for this occasion. After all, when you are hosting 300 billionaires, security and luxury are absolute requirements. The conference hall was a negotiated compromise. Nox insisted on no weapons, but the billionaires insisted on bringing their private security details. The hotel and conference halls were divided into two sections: one for the world leaders and another for their security details. The leaders would all pass through several layers of security, but their bodyguards would have to stay behind. In all total, there were over 2,000 people staying in the hotel during the conference.

Nox stood to address his generals. What he was about to do had never been done. "The time of sovereign nations is coming to an end. We must lead the way into a new world order, where there is one flag, one currency, and one military. We need to stop wasting resources fighting one another and come together to fight the enemies of the planet."

"I understand it is hard for you to comprehend a world without borders, but you must. Otherwise, humans will fade into history, a mere footnote in the annals of more advanced civilizations."

"Marshal Bellator, we all have faith in you, but if the Americans refuse to join us in this new world order, how can it succeed?" General Popov asked.

"Leave the Americans to me. They will come peacefully, or I will bring them to their knees. But, we are not even close to that stage, yet. First, we must unite the people behind one currency. We are close. The Euro is an example of how a one-world currency can work. More than that, there are international credit card companies already in place, with built in currency exchanges. Soon, converting to a one-world currency will be as simple as pressing a button on a computer."

"The Americans will never give up their precious freedom and democracy. They will never submit to a one-world government," Popov objected.

Nox knew if he could not convince his own men, he could never convince hundreds of the world's richest and most intelligent men.

"The Americans have already surrendered their freedom. They are just too brainwashed to see it. We have been indoctrinating their children through public education for decades. The average American has no idea what the word 'freedom' means. The Americans spend all their time and energy fighting over marriage regulations, bathroom policies and ancient battle flags, they are weak and stupid. Americans will lay down their liberty as soon as they believe they can trade freedom for safety and security. I will ensure they get that opportunity. If you need an example, look at the NSA spying programs. Hitler would have been impressed. Americans gleefully turning over their private communications to the government; the Fuehrer would have been swollen with pride, had he lived to see the NSA!" Nox took a moment to assess the faces of the men before him and continued. "This is a long road; once we get the elite onboard, the rest will fall into place. Once they are sold on a New World Order, every media outlet on the planet will be talking it." Nox's voice rose. "It will be on the lips of every grade-school teacher. The Saturday morning cartoons, and church pulpits will be singing the praises of a single government. You just wait and see. People are sheep, and I am their unseen Shepard."

General Popov pressed further, "but do really think the American people will surrender their sovereignty after seeing a few slick television commercials?"

"In just eight years the American people went from being opposed to gay marriage to favoring it. What Changed? Did they all turn gay? No! They were bombarded by favorable images of LGBTQ people in the media. The homosexual went from being some stranger, to that likable guy on my favorite TV show. The same can be done for a New World Order; only we will not just have the television outlets, but the public schools, as well. Don't forget, the biggest publisher of school books sits right here on the Council of Three Hundred."

The Generals all nod in agreement, whether out of adoration or fear, it did not matter to Nox.

CHAPTER SEVENTEEN

Moscow, Russia
Present Day

Ten black SUVs raced across the tarmac from the underground bunker to the brand-new Grand Hall and hotel. Hundreds of expensive private jets were sitting just outside the hotel entrance. There were not enough hangars to house all the planes, so they were lined up in rows along the runway.

General Popov, sitting across from Nox in the luxury SUV, said, "There must be 200 million dollars' worth of private jets sitting on the runway."

General Ivanov added, "It's disgusting, the wealth these greedy bastards have while others starve."

General Papov laughed. "That's the pot calling the kettle black. You have two mansions and a fleet of cars, General."

"That's different. Those things belong to the people. I merely care for them while I'm serving the military."

"Ha," Papov laughed. "I would like to see what would happen to one of the 'people' if they tried to borrow the 'people's' car from you. It would be off to Siberia for them, would it not?"

"You always side with the Corporations, Papov."

Papov responded, "If you are merely a caretaker for the 'peoples' mansions and luxury cars; then why can't a person that delivers valuable products or services to the people also be a caretaker for their possessions? What makes you so special? It seems to me that we take the people's money by force through taxation; while the people voluntarily give their money to the business owner in exchange for goods and services."

"You are impossible, Papov. Sometimes I can't believe you are Russian."

Nox interrupted the two bickering Generals, "Hey, you both have valid points, let's focus on the situation at hand."

Papov crossed his arms and Ivanov smirked. The debate was over, for now. Nox was in the first SUV, with Papov, Ivanov and the driver. The entourage of generals and staff following behind him.

The convoy of SUVs pulled up to the Grand Hall. Within minutes, Nox was whisked to the stage. Most of the guests had taken their seats. Nox was the first speaker. Nox stood behind the oversized steel podium, which had been specifically designed for him. He had insisted on the larger podium because he felt it would somewhat disguise his height. It was steel, to add an extra layer of protection, in case of an assassination attempt. While he was not wearing his body armor, he was wearing conventional bullet-resistant clothing. Nox held either side of the steel podium with both hands as he began his speech.

"I would like to welcome all of you to Moscow. Over the next several days I hope to meet each of you personally. Gathered in this room are the richest most powerful humans on the planet. The people in this room have

a combined personal net worth of over 5 trillion dollars. More importantly, the people in this room control nearly 90 trillion in global assets. Almost every major world event occurs as the direct result of the actions of someone sitting in this room.

Since WW2, the very rich and powerful have worked together to ensure that we do not have another world war. As we learned in the 1940s, world wars destroy infrastructure, resources, and wealth, changing the balance of power and the course of history. After the Great War, the remaining elite classes gathered together to form organizations to ensure that it would never happen again. For the most part, you have been successful in avoiding world war and nuclear war. Preserving your immense wealth and passing it to future generations. Each one of you in this room could lose everything if there were another world war; that is why you come to these conferences every 10 years.

Together, we have helped form some of the most influential organizations on this planet. Working with global organizations, one-world Commissions, and Councils on foreign affairs, the Council of Three Hundred and its members have had a hand in developing international policy. These groups, and others like them work tirelessly to bring about the much-needed New World Order.

If the first world nations refuse to share the wealth and power with the developing nations, there will not be peace. While Europe, Asia and North America seem to be working together and reaping the benefits of globalization, the Middle East is suffering in absolute chaos. Until we give them a seat at the table, they will continue to revolt against western culture.

While you are safely tucked away behind the large stone walls of your luxurious mansions, you are still vulnerable. While many of you have inherited your money, all of you have your money invested in the global market. Whether you are a king, a monarch, a drug cartel, or the owner of some international enterprise; you need taxpayers and customers to support your lifestyle. If your customers or taxpayers stopped paying, eventually you or your heirs would become paupers. As much as you despise the common people, you need them as much as they need you.

There are a few things that could disrupt your plan of continued domination of this planet. A nuclear war or asteroid could kill enough taxpayers and consumers to disrupt your cash flow. A conventional world war could eliminate hundreds of millions of taxpayers. I do not believe we are on the verge of a nuclear war or even a serious conventional war. Years ago, back in the 1960s, we all but eliminated the possibility of the superpowers engaging in all out nuclear war though MAD. Mutually-Assured-Destruction is not the physical destruction of bombs exploding; no, mutually assured destruction is the financial destruction of the country that starts the nuclear war. Globalization of commerce tied all our economies together so tightly that no one would dare start a nuclear war for fear of destroying their own economy.

This policy was successful for several decades. Unfortunately, it only works against developed nations that have too much to lose. A rouge nation that has no assets or quality-of-life is not afraid of mutually assured destruction.

But that is not the threat I have come to discuss with you today. There is another, greater threat facing this planet. As I stand here today, a seven-foot-tall, gray faced, black-eyed alien, from a world 35,000 light years from here, I promise you, an invasion from another planet is imminent.

I have no intentions of invading your planet. However, numerous species from other planets have been visiting Earth for thousands of years. I happen to know that many of them are beyond the scouting stage. Some of them are seriously evaluating colonization of the planet. No nation on Earth has the resources to defend the planet from a full-scale invasion, but if you pooled your resources, you may have a chance.

Think of all the resources wasted in duplicate administrative branches, not to mention all the resources wasted competing with one another. Imagine if all nations came together as one, with a one-world Parliament. We could have a Constitution for all of mankind, put aside our differences and work together to advance our civilization beyond the stars.

I may not look like you, or even think like you, but I call this planet home. I cannot return to my home world; this is my home now. I do not want to see it ruined by some powerful, invading force.

In this room are the most powerful leaders around the world. In this room, we have kings and presidents. In this room, we have the titans of industry, computer science, banking and insurance. In this room, we have the underground entrepreneurs, hackers, leaders of drug cartels and the like. We may fight with each other in the public eye. We may be conservatives or liberals in front of the cameras, but we are all here, today, with one goal in mind. We must preserve our way of life. The commoners cannot do it; they lack the resources and knowledge to make it happen.

The reason we are here today is to discuss how and when we will bring about the New World Order. Over the next few days we will break up into small planning groups. Hopefully by the end of the conference we will have a workable timetable."

Nox stepped back from the podium and microphone. Not one of the elite billionaires said a word, silence. A few of the well-dressed men were nodding in approval, others sat there stone faced. Then one stood to his feet and started clapping, then another and another. Within seconds there was a standing ovation. Nox had nailed it.

Nox walked off stage into an entourage of Russian Generals, all frantically talking at once.

"General, I'm sorry, I mean Marshal Bellator, we have a huge problem," one of the Generals said.

"All of you, stop talking, General Ivanov, what is going on?" Nox pointed his finger at Ivanov.

General Ivanov said, "The reports indicate that there have been six large explosions in Far East Russia, the north-east section of the Magadan Oblast, to be precise, near the arctic circle. The explosions seem to be in the two to twenty kiloton range. They could be nuclear detonations."

"Why are we not sure what they are?"

"We were tracking an object coming from low earth orbit. It started to lose altitude and crashed into the Earth. We don't know what it is, but it slowed down before it crashed," the General explained.

"If it slowed down, it can't be an asteroid or space junk. It must be a vessel of some kind. Do we have any idea how large it was?"

"No. We were tracking its decent. Several smaller objects seemed to break off, or fly off, we can't tell for sure. But at the time of impact, there were six large explosions in the district, not just one. Best we can tell, at this point, there were six different explosions. Each struck with the force of a small nuclear bomb," the General said.

"How does one ship create six impact craters? Do we know what caused the six impacts?" Nox asked.

"No. There was nothing on our radar to indicate what caused the other five impacts. But, because they are so close to each other and happened at the same time, we don't know which one was the object we were tracking," reported the General.

CHAPTER EIGHTEEN

Dam Neck Naval Base
Virginia Beach, VA
Last July

Mike Evans peered out of the window of the C-40A Clipper troop transport as it landed at Dam Neck Naval Base in Virginia Beach, Virginia. The C-40A Clipper is the Navy's version of the Boeing 737-700. Even though he appeared to be in his mid-thirties, Mike had been working at Hill Air Force Base in Utah for over 50 years. He had come to Virginia Beach for some long-deserved rest and relaxation. He traveled to Virginia Beach on the C-40 troop transport, but soon a driver and security detail would be pulling up to the tarmac to whisk him to an ocean front hotel.

For over 50 years he had been helping the humans build faster, stronger, and more fuel-efficient aircraft. His real name could not be pronounced by the human tongue, but a close approximation would be: *Sicarius*. The human leadership had insisted that he and his fellow Vitahicians use regular names to draw less attention to themselves. He was originally from a planet in the Cygnus constellation, over 620 light years away. He had been on Earth for decades and had no hope of ever returning home.

There were dozens of Vitahicians living on Hill Air Force base as permanent residents. They were called "guests," but it seemed more like a prison. He and the other Vitahicians were given military ranks and paychecks. They could move around the base and utilize its facilities. They blended in with the human population very well, as they looked very much like humans. They aged more slowly than humans, but on a highly transient military installation, people did not stick around long enough to notice certain residents did not appear to age.

Mike's day-to-day life was not like that of a prisoner. He lived underground in private quarters, the size of a large apartment. He went to work every day, performing duties that matched his skill set. He could go to the commissary, bowling alley, grocery store, movie theater and any other of the base's many amenities. However, he was not allowed to leave the base or interact with the public without an escort. He was able to leave the base several times per year, with an escort, to go on what humans referred to as a vacation.

Many years ago, Mike had lost all hope of ever being satisfied with his station in life. He grew to resent his American "hosts," thinking of them more like prison guards than co-workers. Most of the Vitahicians liked the Americans and enjoyed helping them develop new technology. They believed that by helping the Americans develop better technology the Earth would become a good ally and trading partner for the Vitahicians.

Mike was tired of playing the long game. Waiting decade after decade for the humans to get their act together was more than he could stand. Mike was certain that his long life would be over before the humans ever reached the point where they were able to become a meaningful ally to his people. Mike wanted, needed, something more, something to fill the mundane routine of working and sleeping.

Mike, like the other Vitahicians, was well paid for his services. He had no wife or children, rarely left the base and lived in underground quarters provided to him at no cost. His frugal lifestyle and lack of bills had allowed him to save most of his money over the years. Mike planned on having a lot of fun on this vacation with the money he never had time to spend. Except for drinking alcohol, which did not agree with their digestive systems, Vitahicians enjoyed many of the same activities as humans.

Mike's security detail consisted of two ex-military types wearing dark suits and driving a single SUV. The luggage was placed in the SUV; Mike climbed into the back seat and they started off toward the beach. After struggling through heavy traffic down General Booth Boulevard and Atlantic Avenue, Mike found himself in a large hotel room on the twelfth floor of an expensive ocean front resort. After handing the valet a ten-dollar tip for bringing up his luggage he turned to his security detail, "Do you really have to stand here in the room with me?"

"No Sir, we can stand outside the door, if you would like," said the bulky man. Both men on the protective detail were wearing black suits, black aviator style sun glasses and appeared to know how to handle a situation.

Where do they find these goons?

"Do you guys always wear black suits? It's 105 degrees out there," Mike asked with a slight chuckle.

"We will have to accompany you whenever you leave the room," said the larger man, ignoring Mike's question. The men turned to walk out the door.

"If I go lay on the beach, will you two stand in the sand behind me wearing those black suits?"

"I think the boardwalk will be close enough," said the smaller of the two stone-faced agents. On the drive in, Mike had noticed that the Virginia Beach boardwalk was about five miles long, and made of poured concrete, not actual wooden boards.

After a day of relaxing on the beach, Mike decided to walk down Atlantic Ave to a steak restaurant that had received many good reviews, it appeared to be a small family owned restaurant with a silhouette of a bull on the outside of the building. Mike was thankful that Vitahician scientists had developed a pill that, if taken prior to eating, would allow for easy digestion of human food. He did not make a habit of eating human food, but from time to time he liked to splurge. The food was excellent. The two agents sat at a nearby table and did not appear to eat anything other than a few rolls. Mike planned to charter a boat and go deep sea fishing the next day, but tonight he was going to head across the street to a bar where a local band was playing. Mike paid the bill and left an extra twenty for the cute waitress. As he walked out the door, the two agents followed.

"I'm heading across the street to listen to the band; do you have to follow me?" Mike asked the two agents. Mike was wearing khaki shorts, a brightly colored collared shirt and tan loafers. He knew the two men in black suits would stand out like vampires in the Vatican.

"Look, I want to relax, have a few drinks, listen to some music, and maybe pick up a woman. You two goons are going to draw all kinds of unwanted attention to me."

"We have our orders." If the man was upset about being called a 'goon' he did not show it.

"Hey, can you at least wait out in the parking lot? How much trouble can I get into at a bar?" Mike asked, as they crossed over Atlantic Avenue.

The two men glanced at each other. They knew Mike was not a normal person. They knew he was a V.I.P. of some sort, but they did not know of his extraterrestrial origins.

Mike pressed, "Listen, what if I get some cute little piece-of-ass to come home with me tonight? Are you two clowns going to have to stand over the bed while I bang her?"

Mike looked like a human, and the average person would never suspect he was not of this world. He wanted to get the maximum enjoyment out of his vacation before heading back to the confinement of his underground bunker.

Goon number one hesitated for a painfully long moment, but then his stature relaxed. Mike knew he had won. "Okay, I don't know why we were instructed to keep such a close eye on you, but you seem to be a decent guy. We will stay in the parking lot, but if you cause problems, you won't be able to take a shit without us watching."

"Thank you, thank you," Mike said enthusiastically, putting his hands together and taking a slight bow. Mike really had no intentions of doing anything illegal. He just wanted to have a few minutes without big brother watching him.

"If anything goes down, if you feel unsafe for any reason, take this," the agent handed him a small plastic device, the size of a key fob. "Press the red button in the middle of the key fob, and we will be there in seconds. Its range is two miles, but, here in the parking lot, we should not be more than 100 yards away. Keep it in your pocket."

Mike took it. He assumed the key fob also contained a GPS tracking system and listening device, but it was still better than having those guys bumping into him in the bar.

Mike walked up the wooden stairs onto a large deck. He pushed through the crowded room full of drunken sailors, college kids, and vacationers. The bar was decorated in a muddled nautical theme with crab pots, anchors, surfboards and other items relating to beach life.

Mike navigated his way up to the crowded bar, sliding in between two scantily clad co-eds that had been drinking copious amounts of alcohol. After a few minutes, the bar tender approached him, "What can I get for you, sweetie?" The bar tender was wearing a tiny black spaghetti string top that barely covered her breasts and short tight cutoff jeans that allowed her butt cheeks to peek through when she bent over.

"I'll take a water," Mike said.

The waitress frowned, "Would you like anything in the water?"

"Just ice, ma'am. I have to drive home. Could you put it in the high ball glass? I don't want to look like a cop," Mike said with a grin.

"No problem," the waitress slid the glass of water to him across the bar, smiled, and winked. Mike was accustomed to getting attention from the ladies. It did not take him long to figure out that human women found him attractive.

Mike glanced at two drunk co-eds on either side of him; they were way too young. He made his way to the back open-air deck. Beyond the deck was the boardwalk, sandy beach, rolling ocean, and starry night. He found a chair near the band and sat down. He was there for one purpose: to find a woman.

There's a woman in this bar that has already decided that she is going to have sex with a stranger tonight. My job is to figure out which one that is – don't waste time with the rest of them.

He scanned the bar, checking out each woman.

Too drunk. Too married. Too many girlfriends.

He took another sip of water. Across the bar he saw a woman, appearing to be in her mid-thirties, leaning up against the wall. She was making love to an icy red drink with a gaudy umbrella in it. Mike waited a few minutes; no boyfriend appeared. Mike walked over to her.

"Hi there, I'm Mike. Do you like this band?"

She smiled and raised her finger to display a large wedding ring.

"My bad. Your husband is a lucky guy," Mike said. Mike was tall, fit, and had deep blue eyes. His blonde hair, which normally was combed back for work, was fashionably unkempt. He was 220 years old, but did not look a day over thirty-nine. Mike was confident he would find the right woman.

After striking out a few more times, Mike went back to the bar to refill his glass.

"Same thing?" the bartender asked with a smile.

Mike nodded his head. When she spun around his eyes dropped to the super tight cut off shorts.

"Like what you see?" the bar tender had turned around so fast Mike could not divert his eyes. She was still smiling.

"What's not to like?" he replied. The water was free; he handed her a ten-dollar bill, and said, "keep the change."

He headed back outside, took up a seat near the band. They were playing eighties chart toppers – something about Egyptians.

The night is still young. I will find my girl.

A Russian woman walked up to him and asked, "Is this seat taken?" She had short blond hair and an athletic figure. Her hazel eyes confidently held contact with his.

Mike halfway stood up, waived at the empty chair, and said, "Be my guest."

After a few drinks and small talk, she asked if he would like to go for a walk. On the beach, the wind was blowing, and the temperature had dropped to a comfortable 82 degrees. The wind blowing from the Atlantic Ocean was thick with the smell of salt.

"Let's take our shoes off," Mike said.

"I love walking barefoot in the sand." She smiled up at him.

After kicking off their shoes and leaving them on the board-walk, they strolled to the shoreline where the waves were washing up on the sandy beach. The salty water felt good on Mike's feet. Hand-in-hand, they walked along the beach, feet sinking into the sand as the foamy surf hurried up to meet them. Her name was Nikita Smirnoff, and she was from Moscow, here on a work visa.

"Oh, where do you work?" Mike asked.

"I work for a Russian cargo shipping company. We do a lot of business with the Portsmouth International Terminals," she replied.

"Sounds exciting."

"Not really. It's kind of boring."

They continued talking as they walked down the beach, focusing only on each other. Mike had all but forgotten about the two goons that were supposed to be escorting him.

Shit. If I wonder off too far off they will be up my ass for the next 10 days.

"I think we need to head back to the bar," Mike said, hoping not to give Nikita the wrong impression.

"Oh, that's too bad, I was really enjoying our walk," she sounded genuinely disappointed.

Damn. I really want to close the deal on this one. If those clowns-in-black cock-block my night, I'm going to be pissed.

"I'm having a great time, too. I was hoping we could go back to my hotel room. I have a nice suite overlooking the ocean. Twelfth floor."

Damn. Was that too forward?

"You must think I'm easy," she teased, trying her hardest to sound offended.

"No, not at all. We were just having such a good time. I just thought. . ." Mike's voice trailed off.

"I'm just kidding. I would love to go up to your room. Do you have one of those little mini-bars?"

"Hell, yeah. You want to get trashed?" Mike asked enthusiastically. Mike never 'got trashed,' but he knew many humans got excited about drinking alcohol. He had also discovered that the best way to throw a bucket of cold water all over a situation was to explain why he did not drink alcohol.

"You can't get too trashed, cowboy; you got some work to do." She smiled and laughed while gently pushing him.

"You don't have to worry about me. I'll definitely get the job done," Mike said with a wink.

"Oh, I'm looking forward to it."

"Do you have a car parked at the bar?" Mike asked.

"What, you can't wait till we get to the hotel room?" Nikita said with exaggerated indignation and a laugh.

"Nothing like that. I just walked here. My hotel is 30 blocks away."

"Yep, I'm in the parking garage across from the bar. I can drive us to your hotel."

Good! Now I can get those goons off my back.

"Can we stop by the bar first, I need to use the head."

"No problem," she said.

Once in the bar, Mike took a lingering look at her and grinned. "I'll be right back," he drawled.

Instead of using the head, Mike made his way back to the front of the bar. He checked to see if she was watching and then slipped out the front door. One of the agents had gone and retrieved the SUV while Mike was inside. The passenger window slid down with a slight electric purr.

"Having fun, Mr. Evans?" the no-neck agent asked from the passenger seat.

"Yes, I got a girl that wants to come up to the room, can you guys stay out of sight?"

"Way to go Mr. Evans. Is she hot?" The smaller of the two goons asked, while raising his hands to his chest as if to mimic having large boobs.

"That's really professional," Mike said with insincere offense.

"Hey, we got to have some fun too."

"Really, you still have sun glasses on?" Mike said sarcastically. "Listen, she's going to drive me back in her car. It's over there in the garage; you can be cool, right?" Mike pointed at the two-story parking garage.

"Yeah, yeah. We'll stay out of sight."

"Thanks. I didn't tell her I had the men-in-black following me. Thought it may put a damper on things," Mike doubled tapped the roof of the SUV with the universal 'okay to go' signal and ran back in to the bar. He spotted Nikita in the back, near the band, and made his way over to her.

"Damn, I thought you might have fallen in or something, cause I knew damn well you were not going to ditch me," she said jokingly.

Mike laughed, "Everything is all good. Let's go put a hurting on that mini-bar."

They had to go out to Pacific Avenue, the next street over, to make their way back to the hotel because the police had blocked off Atlantic Avenue for foot traffic only. Back in the hotel, Mike opened the mini-bar.

This mini-bar will cost me more than a damn hooker. Oh, Well, you only live once.

"What's your poison?" Mike asked, while leaning over and peering into the mini-fridge.

"Vodka, of course." She laughed as she flicked her high heels off.

Mike filled a glass with ice and slowly poured the vodka. He sauntered over to Nikita with the glass, but when she reached for it, he pulled it away. She smiled at the game, and when she made a grab for the glass, he pushed her up against the wall. Wrapping his free arm around her waist, he slipped his tongue into her mouth. She was a good kisser, and she already tasted like vodka. He disposed of the drink, and his hand dropped from her waist to her firm buttocks, he squeezed. He could feel her heart pulsing as his right hand slid up her the inside of her blouse and cupped her left breast. Next thing he knew she was on the bed, and he was on top of her. Two hours later, they collapsed on the twisted sheets, naked and exhausted.

The next morning, Mike woke to the scent of a strong ocean breeze. The curtains were billowing inwards from the wind, as it pushed through the open glass door. Sunlight was pouring into the room from the balcony that overlooked the ocean. That's where he found her. Her naked body silhouetted in the dancing curtains, with a cup of coffee pressed to her lips. He stood up, aware of his own exposed body, and walked toward her. She turned to him and smiled.

"Aren't you worried about someone seeing you naked?" he asked with a cocky glint in his eye.

"I think we are well past that, don't you?" she retorted, as she pushed her blonde locks out of her face, to gaze at him.

"I didn't mean me," he told her, his voice growing heavier as he filled the space between them.

"We're twelve stories up, it would not be much of a show," she challenged.

"It was one hell of a show last night," Mike chuckled.

"It was wonderful. I hope we can do it again."

Mike answered the plea in her voice, as he pressed his lips against hers.

CHAPTER NINETEEN

Virginia Beach, VA
Last July

Nikita Smirnov felt the cool beach air blow around her naked body, after round two this morning. She was standing on the balcony caressing a fresh new cup of steaming hot black coffee that she had made in the complimentary hotel coffee maker. It did not even cross her mind that early morning joggers may look up and see her exposed and lost in thought on the balcony. Last night did not go as expected.

The previous evening, she had gone to the bar with some of her girlfriends from work. The plan was to get drunk and crash at a friend's house near the beach. Then she saw him. She knew what he was the second she laid eyes on him. She had been looking for him, it, for three years. As soon as she saw him, she had excused herself and called her contact in New York. When she asked for instructions, her contact said, "Honeypot. Don't let him out of your sight until I arrive."

Last night's sex was amazing. She would have slept with him regardless of the mission. Now she had to keep him in sight until the Master arrived. The Nordic visitor seemed to be alone on vacation; it should not be hard to convince him to hang out with her. She knew how to keep him occupied until reinforcements arrived. She heard footsteps behind her.

"Are you trying to make history repeat itself?" Mike teased.

"I should probably try to finish one cup of coffee?" She giggled, twisting her index finger in her short hair.

"Well, don't let me stop you. You will be needing your energy for later tonight."

"Tonight?" she probed.

"It was one hell of a show last night," Mike chuckled.

Mike picked up on the nervous tremor in her voice and mistook it for insecurity. "I had a fishing trip planned for afternoon, but I'll be back on land tonight."

Nikita could not risk losing this asset, and she was kind of hurt at the seeming lack of desire to stay with her. Pushing up on her toes, she crushed her lips to his. She pushed him toward the bed, "I don't want you to miss your fishing trip," she teased as he melted into the bed beneath her.

"This is kind of like fishing, only the payoff is much better," Mike hinted.

A few hours later, they found themselves in a small hole-in-the-wall restaurant that advertised an all-day breakfast. A walk down Atlantic Ave led them to many different local shops and venders. The place was crawling with cops, like the city was preparing for a riot or something. They ended up in a beachfront bar listening to a local musician playing Caribbean music. They found a seat on a second story deck overlooking the boardwalk and the ocean.

"What would you like to drink?" Mike asked, "coffee, Vodka?"

"I'll take a sex on the beach," she replied with a seductive grin.

Mike laughed, "I think I can arrange for that."

"No silly, that's the name of the drink," she touched his arm as she giggled.

I think I really like this guy. I hope the Master is not going to kill him, or worse.

The waitress came out wearing a light blue polo shirt with an embroidered emblem of a palm tree over her left breast. She had khaki shorts, tennis shoes and her light brown hair was pulled back in a ponytail, "What can I get you two?"

"Why do they have so many cops all over the place?" Mike asked the waitress.

"Pst," the waitress blew air through her lips and rolled her eyes. "The city is a bunch of totalitarian assholes. They just want to arrest locals, and even tourists sometimes, to raise revenues for the city."

Mike frowned and said, "Well, that doesn't sound very nice of them. I thought maybe they had received information that a riot was about to happen, or something."

"Nothing like that. I promise you. I have worked on the beach for five years. It's this way every summer. You don't have anything to worry about as long as you don't piss off a cop."

"Wow, okay. I'll make sure I don't piss off any cops. Thanks for the advice. I'll take a soda and she will have a . . ." Mike's voice trailed off.

Mike glanced over at Nikita, looking for help. She smirked at him.

"Sex on the beach," Mike finished the sentence.

The waitress looked offended. "Oh my!" she exclaimed, covering her mouth with her hand. She started laughing, "I'm just kidding. Of course, we have that."

Mike and Nikita laughed at the waitress's good humor. She then took their orders and disappeared back into the bar.

"I have had so much fun with you today," Nikita said, shielding her eyes from the bright sun light.

"I'm here for the rest of the week," Mike said.

"I know. I hope to spend most of it with you." Nikita adjusted her chair to avoid the direct sunlight to her eyes.

"Don't you have to work?" Mike asked.

"Maybe a little, but I have some time-off saved up."

A strange sound blared from Nikita's purse. She pulled out her cell phone and checked the screen, "I have to take this."

"Of course," Mike replied.

Nikita rushed off, down the stairwell and out onto the crowded boardwalk.

"This is Nikita. We are on an encrypted line," she said into her seemingly normal cell phone. She glanced back at the two-story bar and grill to make sure Mike had not followed her.

"Do you still have the package?" asked the raspy voice that she knew to be Calidus Delusor.

"Yes, the package is under my control. What would you have me do with it?"

"How long do we have?"

"To do what? I have not been told what my objective is, only to keep the package in sight."

"How long until the package is returned home?" asked Calidus.

"He will be here for another eight days. What is my mission?"

"You need to turn him," Calidus Delusor said flatly.

"Turn him? Are you kidding me? I have not been trained on how to turn an asset. He may kill me, or have his men kill me," she protested.

"He has men? How many? Are they professionals?"

"Yes, he doesn't know, but I spotted them following us back to his hotel. They are keeping a distance, but they are constantly following us. I think there are two on his security detail. From what I can tell, they seem to be well trained."

"You need to determine if he would be willing to defect. I need to know what he wants, so I can offer it to him."

"If I fail?"

"Failure is not an option. If you fail as a spy, you will have to learn to how to be an assassin quickly," Calidus warned.

The line went dead.

Shit. I'm not a spy. I've never flipped an asset. I take pictures of things and forward them to the bosses.

She had never met the Master, but she assumed he was some sort of alien, nothing like the handsome Mike Evans. She walked back to the bar and up the stairs. Mike was still sitting in the same seat where she had left him, staring into a tall glass filled with ice and cola.

"Everything okay?" Mike asked.

"Oh yeah, it was just work. They had misplaced a file," she lied.

I hope the Master does not ask me to kill Mike. I don't think I could do it.

"Do you have to go in?"

"No, they gave me the rest of the week off," she lied again.

She pushed the cheap, plastic, outdoor chair over toward Mike, put her hand in his lap, and said, "Have you ever just wanted to escape? You know, get away from it all."

Mike leaned forward, gazed into her hazel eyes and said with a big grin on his face, "With you, I would go anywhere."

She smirked and punched his arm, "I'm being for real. Haven't you ever just wanted to run away from it all?"

Mike sat back, inhaled a deep breath of fresh ocean air, thought for a moment, and said, "Yes, all the time. I hate my job. I want to quit every day."

"Why don't you?"

"It's not that simple."

I bet. You're an alien from another planet locked away in an underground military base.

Nikita had been trained to look for Nordic aliens. She was working near Virginia Beach because it was a military town with thousands of soldiers, sailors, and top-secret DOD contractors. She was a soft-spy. Her job was to collect intel and report back, not to engage the target, just observe and report. She had a real job, in a strategic location where she may see useful information or people. She could go years without reporting anything of importance to her bosses. But then, in one night, she could send in one report that would justify all the money they had ever paid her over the years. Last night was that night. Until now, she had never felt bad about the information she had passed on to them. It seemed like little bits of unimportant data.

"It couldn't be that boring?" she asked as she adjusted her plastic chair to a position where she could look directly into Mike's eyes.

Mike shifted in his seat; he was obviously uncomfortable.

"I told you, I'm an analyst for the government."

Nikita knew to stop pushing. She still had eight days to crack him.

That evening was dinner and dancing at an ocean front grill and pub. Late that night they returned to the hotel room, and Nikita opened a bottle of wine. She had bought a little black dress for the evening and matching black high heels.

"I know you don't drink, but would you have just one glass with me?" Nikita did not expect the ruse to work, but she thought she had to make another attempt.

"You know I don't drink," Mike said with a weak smile.

"I know. Do you ever drink? I mean why did you stop?"

"It does not sit with me well. It makes me feel ill," Mike answered truthfully.

"Well, I'll have a glass and snuggle up with you on the bed. How does that sound?"

"That sounds like a good idea."

Nikita kicked off her high heels and flopped down on the king-sized bed next to him. "I've had such a good time with you. I wish this would never end." Nikita pushed to get him to open up.

Too much? I hope I don't scare him away, but I have to get him to trust me.

"I've had a great time too. I would love to see you again, but my schedule at work doesn't allow it."

"If you could go anywhere in the world, where would it be?" Nikita asked, switching the subject.

"Well, I came here for vacation, and so far, I'm having a great time," Mike said.

Nakita tried again, "My job is so frustrating. I have this boss that hits on me every day. All the women are bitches, and the work is so boring I want to claw my eyes out. I wish I could just get away for a while."

"I know the feeling, I feel like a prisoner at my job," Mike said with a sigh.

Prisoner. Interesting word choice. Maybe he wants freedom?

"If you could have any job on the planet, what would it be?" Nikita pressed on, hoping for a break through.

Mike took a deep breath and paused for a long moment.

Should I say something? No, give him a chance. He may be close to giving me something I can use.

"I would want to be a politician. But not just any politician, a politician that would change the world."

Nikita was shocked.

CHAPTER TWENTY

Nikita and Mike returned to the hotel room after another fun day at the beach. They had been inseparable for the last seven days. Nikita was worried that she would not find an opportunity to breach the subject of Mike coming to work for her bosses. It was after midnight; they had gone dancing at a club on the rooftop of a nearby resort hotel. Nikita had put down a few too many white Russians. Mike had been drinking water with a lemon all night. Nikita could not help thinking her job would be a lot easier if she could get Mike drunk.

"I've had a wonderful time this past week. I wish we could spend more time together," she told him. She had been dropping hints like this all week, hoping to get him to open up about his job.

"It's been great; I'm really glad we met," Mike said, as he pulled off his pants. They had been having sex almost every night since they met.

Damn. The sex has been great. I'm sure it would have been even better if I wasn't trying to get him to become a spy. I wish I had met this guy under different circumstances.

Nikita's smart phone buzzed in her purse. She knew by the tone it was an incoming text message. She looked at the number, at first not recognizing it; a second later, she realized it was Calidus from New York. It read: 'Call you in five minutes.'

Shit. I can't take the call in here, or on the balcony. Mike can't hear this. What about the hallway? No, other guests could overhear.

"Honey, I got a special treat for you tonight," she whispered in Mike's ear, while running her hand up his thigh.

"Oh my, I can't wait," he said with a big grin.

"But first I must take a long shower," she said, kissing him on the lips. Her hand settled on his package, and she gave a light squeeze before hurrying into the shower.

That should keep him preoccupied while I take this call. Maybe I would be a good spy.

The bathroom was nicely apportioned with an earth tone tile floor, granite countertops, and a tub-shower combo. On the granite counter top was an assortment of complimentary soaps and shampoos with the hotel's logo on them. Nikita turned on the shower full blast, not bothering to adjust the temperature. She stripped down naked and sat on a towel draped over the closed toilet lid, waiting for her encrypted smart phone to vibrate.

I have nothing to tell Calidus. I have made no progress towards flipping this guy. I hope I don't have to kill him. Shit. I've never killed anybody before, let alone someone I like.

The phone lit up in her hand.

"Hello," she said in a rushed voice, holding the phone up to her ear. Mike had turned on the television. Between the loud infomercials and the shower going full blast, there was no way Mike could overhear her.

"Do you have any news to report?" Calidus asked, in his throaty voice.

"He has not been willing to admit where he works or what he does. I don't know how to breach the subject with him," Nikita complained.

"What does he say about his job?"

"He never says anything good about it. Says he would like to get away. He claims he is a low-level government analyst, but, he won't go beyond that."

"How does he feel about you?" Calidus asked.

"I think he really likes me. He told me he would miss me when he goes back to work. Every time I discuss us keeping in touch, he just blows me off by saying it's impossible."

"Can you use the affection he has for you to turn him?"

"The only think I can think to do is to admit to him who I am and that I know who he is, too."

"If you admit who you are and he does not turn, you have to kill him. That is an all or nothing position. You can't let him return to work once he knows about you. It's risky. Can you handle killing him if you fail?"

"I think so," she barely whispered.

"'I think so' is not good enough. If you try and fail, he must die. I want to be present when this happens. When will you do it?" Calidus asked in an agitated voice.

"How can you be present?"

"My craft is invisible. I will be close enough to help, but far enough away he won't suspect my presence."

"I will do it tomorrow night, near Williamsburg, Virginia."

"I will be in the vicinity. I will be monitoring the whole thing through your cell phone."

"How will you know my exact location if I need help?" Nikita asked.

"Through the GPS on your phone. Leave your phone on. I will be there if you need me."

Nikita showered, dried off, and hopped in the bed next to Mike. After making love, Mike collapsed between her legs resting his head on her lower abdomen.

"That was amazing," Nikita said, laying spread eagle on the bed.

"You weren't so bad yourself," Mike answered, in between deep breaths.

"You're out of breath?" Nikita said jokingly.

"Just a little," Mike said as he rolled off her onto his side of the bed.

"Let's go to Williamsburg tomorrow," Nikita said. "It's only about two hours away from here, and I can drive."

"Why would we want to go there?" Mike asked.

"There's lots of stuff to do in Williamsburg; a ton of history occurred there. Plus, there's an amusement park and wineries up that way."

"Okay, whatever you want to do. I'm ready for a change of pace anyway."

The next day flew by. Mike and Nikita spent much of the day riding roller coasters at the amusement park, then they headed to downtown Williamsburg for some window shopping. After dinner, they headed into the countryside toward a local winery that had live music in the evenings.

The winery sat atop a hill overlooking a river. To get to the winery and tasting room, they had to drive down a gravel road twisting and turning through rows of grape vines lined up along the hilly countryside. At the top of the hill, stood the large two-story structure that housed the winery. The large building had been designed to resemble a rustic mountain lodge. The pair walked up the heavy wooden timber steps to the wrap-around deck on the first floor. They crossed the country style wooden porch into the main wine tasting room. The wine tasting room had a stone floor and a huge stone fireplace. The fireplace's chimney reached up two stories past the heavy wooden ceiling trusses. Off to the left, was a wooden bar that sold wines by the glass or bottle. Behind the large bar and tasting area was a glass wall that allowed visitors to look past the tasting room into the work area, which contained several large stainless-steel vats where wine was produced.

"What a lovely place," Nikita said. She was starting to worry that she would not be able to close the deal with Mike.

"Oh, it is really nice. I really like those leather couches and end tables carved from cross sections of large trees."

"Let's get a bottle of wine and sit on the deck," Nikita said.

"I don't drink, remember?"

"I'll drink for both of us," she giggled.

"I can drive home if you need me to," Mike said as he reached around and drew her in with his right arm.

God. I hope so.

All the seats on the deck were taken; so they walked past the band, down the steps and onto the well-manicured lawn. There was a circular fire pit made from medium sized boulders surrounded by a dozen Adirondack chairs. Mike and Nikita sat in two chairs by the fire where they could still hear the music. Nikita poured herself a healthy glass of red wine.

"Are you going to miss me when this vacation is over?" Nikita prompted.

"You have no idea how much I'm going to miss you."

"Maybe we can stay in contact?" she asked.

"I can give you my email address, and if you are ever in New Mexico, I would love to see you." Mike frowned and slumped down in his chair.

"What about the weekends?"

"I really can't get away for weekends very often," he replied.

"Are you just using me for sex? I'm just a booty call for you when you are here in Virginia?" Nikita laughed and raised her glass up at him.

"No, no, I really like you, but my job is demanding."

"What if you could leave your job, would you want to be with me?"

"Of course, I would love to be with you; I just can't."

Did he just drop the L word? He did not say he loved me just that he loved to be with me. Is that the same thing?

"Are you secretly married?" she whispered, leaning forward, as if someone were listening.

"I already told you, I have no family, and that includes no wife."

"Good. I would hate to think you are cheating on your wife," Nikita laughed.

I have to stop drinking. I have to be on my A game. One, or both of our lives depend on it.

When Mike was not looking, she poured out the glass of wine to make it look like she had drunk it.

"Hey Mike, let's go for a walk in the vineyard."

"I don't think it's allowed," Mike protested.

"I promise you will not regret it." She tilted her head down and puckered up her lips as if to pout.

She grabbed Mike by the hand, and they slipped into the darkness. Their eyes quickly adjusted to the night, and they walked by moonlight toward the cliffs that overlooked the river. The large rustic lodge of a winery faded away into the distance. The sound of music was replaced with the soft sound of the river lapping at the small sandy beach at the bottom of the steep cliff.

Nikita dropped to her knees in front of Mike and unbuttoned his jeans. She pulled down his zipper and took him into her mouth. Mike closed his eyes and took a deep breath. A few minutes later Mike patted her on the head indicating that she should be prepared for the big finale. She didn't stop until it was over. She rose to her feet and hugged him. He hugged her back and whispered, "That was incredible."

"I wish I could do that for you more often. There is a way out for you."

He stood back with a puzzled look on his face.

"I know who you are. I know you are from another planet. I know you work for a top-secret government agency, building weapons. I can help you escape."

"What? How do you know? How can you help me escape? You are a spy?" Mike was clearly horrified. "Oh, my god. They could kill me just for talking to you. Do you know I have body guards? They will probably be here any minute. Shit." Mike shouted.

"I disabled their tracking device; we lost your security hours ago," Nikita said. "I made them the first day we met."

"You were sent here to spy on me? All this time we have spent, it has just been to what? Get me to leave my job and come work for you? I feel like such a fool. I was falling for you, but you played me. You played me for a fool."

"That's not true. I really like you. I would have spent this past week with you regardless of my job. I had a great time and would do it again! Yes, I met you because of my job, but that's how a lot of people meet. Yes, I was doing my job, but the sex, the sex I did for myself, for us." She was desperate for him to understand her.

Should I drop the L word? Things are really coming unglued here. Shit, if I have to kill him, can I even do it? Where is the Master?

"So, what now? If I say no? What if I just walk back to the winery?"

"Don't, please don't! I love you. I want you to be with me. I know that means you have to quit your job, but we can offer you so much more. We can make you free! You want to live out in the open; it can happen. You want to be a politician; it can happen. You want to be with me, it can happen. Just don't turn around."

He stood there, looking into the tears pouring out of her eyes. He knew she believed what she was saying. Whether it was true or not, was another story. She could believe every word she said, but she could still be wrong, dead wrong.

"I believe you. How could your people promise so much? The U.S. Government will chase me down if I leave. You know that."

"I don't work for a government. I work for an alien nation. A nation that controls all governments, including the U.S. Government."

Mike looked confused, "But how?"

"Trust me. Are you willing to come with me? Are you willing to trust me?"

Mike looked directly into her earnest eyes. "Yes," he answered. "I will go with you."

No sooner had the word passed through his lips, did the Master's antigravity fighter materialize. It was hovering at eye level, just over the cliff, 40 feet below the slow-moving river. Mike jumped, startled by the sudden appearance of the strange craft. It silently moved towards them so that it was above the vineyard, between the cliff and them.

"What is that?" Mike asked.

"It's a space ship. You should know that, Mike." Nikita rolled her eyes.

"Damn it. I know it's a space ship. I meant, what is it doing here?"

"That's my boss, our boss now."

A hatch opened near the bottom of the craft, and stairs descended to the soft earth below. Calidus walked down the steps and directly up to Mike.

"My name is Calidus Delusor." The alien stood seven and half feet tall and had a dark gray complexion with large black eyes. He appeared to be thick and muscular, but his body was mostly covered by a dark metallic armor.

Mike looked up at the beast towering over him. "Nikita tells me you can offer me a better deal than the Americans?"

"I can offer you freedom from your captors. I have a secret base, as large as a small country, where you could move about freely and work in the field of your choice. But coming to work for me is a reward."

"A reward for what?"

"You must bring me something, something of value from your current employer."

"What do you need?" Mike asked.

"In time." The beast paused, "You must first prove to me your loyalty."

CHAPTER TWENTY-ONE

Mike stood before the powerful creature. He had never seen a Large Gray alien in the wild. He had seen them in captivity; most of them had been killed in battle. Seeing one in person, standing almost eight feet tall in full battle armor, was frightening, to say the least.

This thing could kill me at any moment. Every word I speak could be my last.

"What would you have me do?" Mike asked, fearing the answer.

"You must prove that you are loyal to me," the creature hissed in its throaty voice.

"But how?" Mike asked again. The creature stood between Mike and the disc shaped craft near the cliffs. Mike noticed that all the clouds had disappeared and that thousands of stars were sparkling in the sky behind a bright, full moon.

The self-proclaimed Calidus Delusor pulled a Glock 22 from a concealed compartment within the armor on his right leg. In the blink of an eye, Calidus was holding the pistol by the barrel with the handle facing toward Mike.

"Take the gun," Calidus ordered.

Why does he want me to take the gun? Is it a trick, so he can kill me? But why do that? He has the upper hand he can kill me anyway.

Mike reached out and took the pistol. Calidus released his grip on the barrel. Mike dropped the hand with the pistol to his side, telegraphing to the creature that he was no threat.

With an evil twinkle in his pitch-black eye, Calidus said, "Now, shoot Nikita."

Mike saw the terror and surprise in Nikita's eyes, she took a step backwards.

"No, why?" Nikita took another step back. It was clear she was surprised by Calidus' command.

"I have done nothing but serve you. I did everything you asked. Why would you have him kill me?" she demanded in a trembling voice.

"Shoot her." Calidus' voice was louder and more terrifying.

Mike looked back at Calidus. "Why do you need me to kill her? She has done nothing wrong. There has got to be another way for me to prove my loyalty."

"Shoot her, or I will shoot you both," Calidus demanded, his voice raising.

What if I turn the gun on Calidus instead? I could shoot him, and then Nikita and I could run.

"Please, Calidus Delusor, I want to prove my worth. I will do anything else you wish. I will kill someone else for you. I love her."

Nikita looked at him.

"The only way to prove your loyalty is to kill her now," Calidus hissed.

If I don't kill her, he will kill us both. Maybe this is just a test. Maybe she is in on it. Maybe if I pull the trigger, I will prove my worth and she will be okay.

Mike turned to Nikita and slowly raised the Glock. Nikita was less than five feet from him. The moonlight reflected off her face, showing the fear in her eyes.

156

She is a spy. She probably practices looking scared in the mirror.

"No. Don't. Please don't shoot me," She screamed.

Mike pointed the Glock directly at her face. He peered down the short barrel, the fixed barrel sights lined up on her tearful eyes.

"Please don't shoot me. I love you," she sobbed.

I have no choice. The beast would not hand me a weapon that could kill an Ondagra. This pistol probably only has one shot anyway. I bet the bullet would bounce off his armor.

With that justification, Mike closed his eyes and jerked the trigger. The gunshot was deafening, as the Glock recoiled in his hand. He dropped the weapon and opened his eyes. He saw Nikita reach for her face and fall back in the dirt between two rows of grape vines.

"Why did I have to do that?" Mike cried, as he began to hyperventilate.

"I have to be able to trust you. If you would kill the woman you love, then maybe I can use you," Calidus said.

"What next? Do I come with you?" Mike asked, between short, and shallow breaths.

"No. You go back to work and pretend this never happened. I will be in contact with you," the large creature explained.

"But how? I stay on a top-secret military base where all communications are monitored." Mike glanced over at Nikita's body.

The large creature stepped toward him and withdrew an ornate dagger from his armor. With his other hand, the creature grabbed Mike's wrist, and with lightning speed, sliced open his forearm. Blood flowed down Mike's wrist and fell into the soft soil.

"Hey, what the hell. Why did you cut my arm?" Mike demanded, as he glanced over at Nikita's motionless body.

The creature, still firmly gripping Mike's hand, said, "We will have a psychic connection. One that your human security forces will not be able to detect."

"You need to implant a devise in me for a psychic connection?" Mike asked skeptically.

"No, the psychic connection is completely biological, but it only works when we are within 50 miles of one another."

"Well, I'm going to be in Utah," Mike responded flatly.

Calidus pulled a small, hairy device from a compartment on his chest armor.

"Hey, what's that? Is it alive? Is that hair? They will be able to detect a device in me."

"You ask too many questions. This implant is biological and contains no metal. The human scanners will never be able to sense that it is inside you. This device will amplify your thoughts, so that I can communicate with you from thousands of miles away. Just say my name, and it will activate; then we can speak."

"What do want me to take from the humans?" Mike said, as his breathing became more relaxed. But, even in this tense situation, the guilt from killing Nikita was starting to weigh heavily on his mind.

"You will know when you see it. Until then, go about your day as if nothing has changed. I will be waiting to hear from you."

Nikita's body twitched. Mike spun around to see her struggling to pull herself up off the ground. She made a coughed and gasped for air. Mike rushed to her side and dropped to one knee to help lift her head.

"Are you okay?" he asked, as he helped her turn over.

How can this be? How could she be alive? I shot her in the face.

Calidus stepped toward them, his hulking body blocking out the moon light. "She should be fine. You shot her with a cotton ball. The cartridge had gun powder, but I replaced the lead bullet with a wad of cotton. She had no idea."

"You. Fucking. Asshole. You shot me in the face!" Nikita screamed. She jumped to her feet. Mike stood up with her, holding her steady.

"I'm so glad you are okay," Mike sputtered in shock.

Nikita thrust her knee into Mike's groin as hard as she could. Mike doubled over in pain and dropped to his knees.

"You love me? You're an asshole!" Nikita screamed.

Nikita punched Mike in the face. Mike could not block the powerful blow to his left cheek and eye because he was still clutching his aching balls with both hands.

"You tried to kill me. How can you fuck me and then try to kill me?"

Calidus stepped back. "Well, I see you two have a lot to talk about. Nikita, you can get your revenge, but make sure he gets back to his hotel in one piece. He works for me now, just like you. Is that understood?"

CHAPTER TWENTY-TWO

Last Week

Major Morgan "Snap" Slade stepped from behind the low, stone wall and fired the laser rifle at the AK-47 wielding man wearing a black hood. The 100-kilowatt laser beam instantly burned a hole through the chest of the hooded gunman. The gunman dropped to his knees and fell face-forward into the dirt, still clutching the archaic Soviet assault rifle. Snap ducked and ran forward, toward the blackened hulk of a late model pickup truck, keeping his eyes on the compound the whole time.

Snap and his twelve-man squad were attempting to neutralize a terrorist compound that was holding an ambassador's daughter hostage. Intelligence reports indicated that the compound contained 25 insurgents and three hostages. Peering around the front bumper of the wrecked truck, Snap could see three terrorists on the compound's wall. Snap's *Head Up Display*, or HUD for short, built into the visor of his helmet, indicated that the hostile nearest to him on the wall was armed with a rocket propelled grenade launcher, or RPG for short. "That's the one to target first," Snap thought.

Snap stood from his concealed position and easily lifted the forty-pound laser rifle, also known as a DE Rifle, up toward the RPG wielding terrorist. The HUD in his visor glowed red when the laser locked on the target, Snap squeezed the trigger. A flash of light burned a hole through the center of the hostile's chest. The target fell off the wall, dropping his RPG. Snap immediately shifted his weapon toward the other two terrorists, the HUD glowing red in his visor when the laser had locked on both targets at once. Both terrorists fell from their positions on the wall, their AK-47s having never fired a shot.

The HUD indicated enemies in red and team mates as green dots on the visor screen. Most of his team was still behind him, and the remaining terrorists were inside the walled compound. "I'm going to breach the door!"

"Roger that, Major," Josh Miller said through the communications device that was built into his helmet.

Snap ran toward the steel door. The 200-pound armor suit he was wearing, commonly referred to as FALOS armor, also known as *Fusion-powered Armor Light Operator System*, allowed him to run at 25 miles per hour because it was powered by a *micro modular fusion reactor*, or MMFR for short. Snap reached the door and kicked it with his right foot. The titanium exoskeleton that supported the weight of the heavy armor easily smashed down the steel door.

Snap immediately backed away from the gaping hole that had once been a heavy security door. His squad ran through the opening, weapons ready. INTEL suggested that they would have to secure the building in less than four minutes if they hoped to save the hostages. Once in the compound, the team ran toward the two-story building, taking out two more rooftop terrorists as they ran. Breaching the building was even easier than breaking down the compound door. Half the team entered the building; the other half branched off to secure the rest of area.

Inside, the building was dark, as all the windows were boarded shut. Snap's visor automatically switched to night vison.

"Target eliminated," Snap heard in his COM system.

"Target eliminated." This time it was Moore.

"Target eliminated," Martin said.

Snap ran up the stairs to his left. As he turned on the balcony, he saw a man holding an AK-47. He was too late. The man opened fire at point blank range. A barrage of 7.62x39 rounds slammed into Snap's chest.

Shit. Am I going to die? This can't be how it ends, in some shitty town in the middle of nowhere.

The kinetic force of the rounds pushed Snap down the stairs, but they did not penetrate his FALOS armor. Snap regained his balance and aimed the DE rifle at the masked man. The man knew it was over; he tried to back up and run, but it was too late. Snap pulled the trigger before his targeting system locked on to the man. It did not matter. At this range, Snap could not miss. The masked man was nearly cut in two by the laser.

"Target eliminated," Snap said into his COM so that the rest of his team would know.

"Courtyard clear," Jackson reported.

Snap turned right at the top of the stairs to see a long, dark hallway with several closed doors. The helmet's built-in night vision allowed Snap to see in the dark. He kicked the first door on the right, and it swung open with the sound of splintering wood to reveal an empty room.

The next two rooms were empty, also. Williams and Johnson were at his back.

"Rear of compound, clear," crackled over the COM system.

"First floor clear," Neal West said.

"Rear entrance clear," Ryan Taylor said.

Where are the hostages? There are more doors upstairs. They must be here.

Williams and Johnson were wearing the same exoskeleton armored suits that Snap was wearing. Williams pointed at the next door, indicating that he would kick it down and that Snap and Johnson should rush in. On his cue, Snap rushed into the dark room, Johnson directly behind him. Snap felt a crushing pain, as the terrorist's huge fist slammed into his face. He tumbled back, and Johnson shot the terrorist with his laser gun. Snap, sitting on the floor, looked up and realized that the terrorist was nine feet tall and wearing advanced battle armor. Snap jumped to his feet, the FALOS suit easily lifting the hundreds of pounds of armor and laser gun.

Snap tried to raise his DE rifle up to the huge hostile, but he was once again knocked to his knees. Three more flashes of light. Three more direct hits. It seemed his laser was completely ineffective against this insurgent's armor. Snap's eyes focused on the giant's face; it is not human. The tall creature had taunt grey skin. The rest of his features were shielded by his helmet.

The creature threw its hands up, as if to surrender, and three shards of light burst from a device on its chest. Williams, Johnson, and Taylor were violently thrown against the wall and slumped to the floor. Snap knew they were dead. The creature stood over him. He tried to raise his DE rifle, to no avail. The shard of light cut through Snap's armor and flesh like a hot knife through butter. Everything faded to black as Snap lost consciousness.

Snap's eyes popped open and he jolted out of bed. He was in a large hospital room with multiple beds. His chest was on fire, and his throat was dry and itchy. He looked around the large room to see the rest of his team lying in medical beds. None of them are wearing armor; rather they were wearing traditional hospital gowns, and hooked up to medical monitoring devices.

"Soldier, you got your ass whipped," barked General Benjamin Paxton. The General was standing in a doorway, a few feet from

Snap. "You are going to have to do a hell of a lot better than that if we are going to win the next war."

"Yes Sir, what was that thing, Sir?" Snap asked.

"That was an Ondagra. He and his kind are from a planet called Botacoure. His name is Ater, and he is working with us to help get you boys ready for the next war."

"What?" Snap asked, with a dumbfounded look on his face.

"We have a lot to discuss, Major Slade. I want you and your squad in my office in one hour." The General surveyed the hospital bay. "Make that two hours."

CHAPTER TWENTY-THREE

Hill Air Force Base, Utah

General Benjamin Paxton's office was seven levels below the surface of Hill Air Force base. The structure was referred to as a Deep Underground Military Base, or DUMB for short. The General's office had a large desk, conference table, and a dozen chairs. The only people present were, the General, his chief of staff, and Snap's squad.

"Men, you just encountered your first extraterrestrial, or alien, if you will. His name is Ater Velens, and if you had met him anywhere but in a training exercise, all of you would be dead," General Paxton said from behind his desk at the front of the room.

"When your team came here from Delta Force on a special duty assignment, you thought you were here to perform field tests on new equipment. While that was part of the reason you were here, we were testing you, to determine if your squad had what it takes to be a part of our command. You passed the test, and now, you are one of the few people on this planet to have knowingly seen an extraterritorial. You are about to be read into a program that is so far above Top Secret that the last five Presidents didn't even know of its existence." General Paxton reached into his desk and retrieved a laser pointer.

"Your team has been training for several months with the next generation FALOS suit. You are now aware of many of its advanced functions. What you don't know, is that, in addition to all the functions you have been training with, the suit is outfitted with electro-chromic plates and light emitting diodes that create a chameleon effect, giving you a cloak of invisibility." The General strode out from behind his desk to the table where the men were sitting.

"The problem is this," the General cleared his throat. "You are not even close to being the most advanced combatant on this planet. Even with these advantages, you are still the underdog when facing Ondagra battle armor."

Snap and his squad were dumbfounded. You could hear a pin drop.

"Another thing you need to know, the FALOS suit that you have been training on, was not designed by human scientists. The FALOS suit was developed by Nordic aliens that work with us on this and other secret facilities. The MMFR, fusion technology, that powers the armor is only made available by our alien benefactors. Without special light elements, that are not available here on Earth, we would not be able to generate enough power to operate the FALOS armor."

"You have got to be shitting me," muttered Justin Thomas from the second row.

"What was that soldier?" General Paxton barked.

"Nothing Sir"

"You will all have the opportunity to ask questions at the end," General Paxton assured them.

Paxton continued, "These Nordics, as we call them, are from our own Milky Way galaxy, about 620 light years from here. They refer to themselves as Vitahicians and call their home world Vitahic.

There are a few thousand of them here on Earth. Most of them live on U.S. military bases. They have been visiting our planet for hundreds of years, but they contacted the government about 70 years ago. The Nordics and the Government have a good working relationship, unlike the Ondagra. The Ondagra you met in the training exercise has defected and now helps us. Part of his job is training new recruits, like yourselves. From this point forward, your squad will be working closely with Ater Velens and the Nordic aliens. Any questions?"

Senior Master Sergeant Justin Thomas stood up, while partially raising his hand. "I have a question, General."

"Yes, Sergeant Thomas."

"So, all the UFO stuff we see on the internet is real? Roswell, New Mexico is real?" Justin sat back down.

The General cleared his throat. "Yes, for the most part, all the stories you see on the internet are real. Of course, some of them are faked or exaggerated; but, generally speaking, they are true. The government has spent billions of dollars trying to discredit the UFO crowd, you know, make them look like crack-pots. The reason we do that, is to keep the public in the dark. Yes. The Roswell incident happened. We recovered an alien space craft and made contact with an alien species. Any other questions?"

Snap stood.

"Major Slade." The general pointed at Snap.

"Presumably, we are in some kind of war with the Large Gray species, or Ondagra as you call them, and we are being recruited to engage them. Given that their technology is advanced far beyond our own, how do we fight them?" Snap asked.

"Excellent question, Major Slade. Tomorrow you begin combat training with Ater Velens. He will teach you how to exploit their weaknesses - their very few weaknesses."

Senior Master Sergeant James Martin raised his hand. "How many of these Ondagra are operating on Earth?'

General Paxton shook his head. "Truthfully we don't know. We believe the number to less than 1800, but we can't be sure. On the top end, 2400. But, if they learned to reproduce? Who knows."

After a few more questions, the General said, "Okay, we have several days of orientation to go through; we don't need to solve all the world's problems this afternoon. Keep in mind, everything you learned today is Top Secret SCI. More details will follow in the next few days. Tomorrow, you are to report to Dugway Proving Ground for training with Ater Velens."

CHAPTER TWENTY-FOUR

Dugway Proving Ground, Utah

*D*ugway Proving Ground, or DPG, sits about 85 South West of Salt Lake City. DPG is adjacent to *Utah Training and Testing Range*, also known as UTTR. DPG is almost 800,000 acres; together, DPG and UTTR cover almost 3,900 square miles of land.

The next morning, the squad piled into a fifteen-passenger van and were driven to Dugway. DPG consists of hundreds of miles of flat, treeless desert. The military complex is surrounded by mountain ranges on three sides.

From Hill AFB, it took over an hour to travel to the DPG main gate, where they were waived in with a salute. Once through the main gate, they drove several miles through barren salt flats, until they came to the main installation. The main installation was a cluster of buildings, hangers, and housing surrounded by miles of empty desert. It only took a few minutes to pass through the small town-like area. Then, they were heading toward a huge mountain in the distance.

Snap, sitting in the first row of seats behind the driver, leaned forward and asked, "I thought we were stopping at Dugway?"

"Yes Sir, heading to Granite Peak Installation," the young Sergeant said, as he turned off the pavement onto a gravel road.

"Granite Peak Installation? I thought they closed that after WWII," Snap questioned.

"I've been here for six years. It's been open the whole time. It's a top secret underground bunker. Not many people, even here on Dugway, know what goes on in there." The Sergeant continued to drive along the gravel road, through the flat desert, toward the looming mountain.

"What's up, Major?" Neal West asked from the second-row window seat.

"Seems we are heading to Granite Peak Installation."

"Thought that was closed decades ago?" Neal pulled himself up to the bench in front of him.

"Supposedly, they closed GPI after WWII. It was a huge self-contained facility right here on Dugway. GPI had its own barracks, mess hall, administration, laboratories, utilities and runway."

"Why did they close it?" Neal asked.

"War was over; they cut a lot of bases and programs. During the war, it was used for biological weapons testing."

As they traveled, the mountain blotted out their view of the sky, so that all they could see was a solid rock face through the windshield of the van. They stopped at the foot of the mountain, before a large half circle opening in the rock. The entrance to the underground bunker was cut directly into a sheer rock wall. A heavy metal gate was affixed to a concrete frame that defined the outside entrance to the passage.

"No guards?" Neal asked.

"No need for guards. They have been watching us approach for the last 45 minutes. If we were a threat, several attack drones would have been dispatched before we were even close. The gate will open in a minute; they know this van. We are expected." The Sergeant stretched his arms and legs from a seated position, "Long drive."

"Look, the gate is opening," Neal said. The gate slowly rose off the ground and disappeared into the stone ceiling.

"Here we go, Gentlemen. Welcome to Wonderland," the Sergeant said with a chuckle, as he drove the van into the dark tunnel. Inside the underground passage, was a paved road leading down to a large open space. The walls of the tunnel were rough granite rock and arched up toward a dome-shaped ceiling. Once in the large open cavern, they could see numerous vehicles and self-contained, modular metal buildings. The space reminded Snap of an airport parking garage that was under construction.

"Here we are, end of the line. Hope you gentlemen enjoyed the ride, no tipping allowed," the driver said jokingly. "Lieutenant Black will be here in a few minutes to take you to your next stop."

"Thanks for the lift, Sergeant," Snap said, as he jumped out the side door of the van. The rest of his men followed suit.

A few minutes later, a medium built man walked through the door of the mobile, shipping container-like admin office and right up to Snap. "Good morning, Major, I'm Max Black. I'm here to escort you to level fifteen."

"Morning, Lieutenant Black," replied Snap.

"Please follow me," said the young lieutenant, obviously more of an administrative type than a warrior.

Snap and the men followed Lieutenant Black through a man-sized tunnel, bore through solid granite, to another large chamber. The man-sized tunnel was next to a larger tractor trailer sized tunnel that led to the same cavern. This chamber was more militarized than the first parking-garage type chamber.

Immediately upon walking through the short tunnel, they found themselves at a security check point. There were waist high concrete barriers set up to corral visitors toward a guard post. On the other side of the long concrete barriers were military personnel armed with TAR-21 bull-pup rifles. On either side of the check point were 50 caliber machine guns mounted on armored turrets.

Snap could see over the concrete barriers, past the check point, to the rest of the cavernous space. In the middle of the granite cavern was a ramp, that was large enough for a tractor trailer to drive down, into an underground facility. The ramp was surrounded by thick concrete walls and there appeared to be a large steel door that could come down to secure the tunnel. The ramp leading to the tunnel was guarded by a squad of soldiers and one M3 Bradley fighting vehicle.

Lightning Squad easily passed through the security checkpoint. Once on the other side, Lieutenant Black pointed them toward another 15-passenger van and indicated that they should climb aboard. Once settled into the van, Lieutenant Black drove the van toward the ramp that descended even deeper into the mountain. He was stopped at the mouth of the tunnel by a security team that checked over the passenger van, presumably for bombs. They passed through the second check point and onto the ramp, making wide left turns as they descended. The large ramp reminded Snap of driving round and round in a multi-level parking garage. Each level was clearly marked with large numbers painted on the wall near the heavy gate giving entrance to that level. Even this far down, the ramp was wide enough for a tractor trailer to pass. Each level they passed had small parking lots, with a few empty vehicles.

They reached Level 15, and Lieutenant Black pulled the van to the curb, near the large metallic blast doors.

"Your stop. Your ID card will open the blast doors," Lieutenant Black said from the driver's seat.

"You're not coming in with us?" Snap asked.

"No Sir, what's behind those doors is not within my need-to-know. Good luck, Major."

"Alright, everyone out," Snap said.

The unguarded, steel blast doors were large enough to allow a single tractor trailer to drive through. Snap walked up to a display monitor and raised his ID. A few seconds later the heavy doors slowly raised from the concrete surface to reveal a wide-open area resembling a loading bay. Two guards armed with holstered semi-automatic pistols walked toward them.

"Good morning, Major Slade. We are here to take you to the training center."

"Roger that."

Level 15 was much larger than Snap had expected. As they walked through the open bay area they could see all types of equipment, some familiar, some not. There were saucer-shaped craft, tanks, and other armored vehicles in various states of disrepair. Skilled technicians were upgrading existing equipment and working on developing new types of armored fighting vehicles with exotic weapons systems. On either side of the large work zone were numerous doors that led to areas unknown.

"Part of orientation will be a tour of Level 15. You will be staying here for a while. Look over there," the security guard pointed toward a set of non-descript double doors with no markings, "over there is Level 15 temporary housing. You'll have sleeping quarters and a small dining facility."

They continued walking. "Here we are, the training room. Someone will be with you shortly."

"You're not coming in?" Snap asked.

"Nope. My job was to see that you got to this point. Just walk through those doors, and someone will be with you shortly," the guard said, as he turned to walk away.

"Very well." Snap pushed open the plain metal door and walked into a large open room. The auditorium-sized room was very plain, with no decorations on the walls, and only three doors on the back wall. It reminded Snap of a high school gymnasium. To the right, were twelve chairs set up in three rows, all facing toward a blank wall. To the left there were mats on the floor like you would see in a karate studio.

"What the hell are we supposed to do here?" Sergeant Williams asked.

"I guess we just stand around and wait for someone to show up," Justin Thomas replied.

"I wonder what that big ass dome is for," Senior Master Sergeant Smith asked as he pointed toward the center of the ceiling.

"Damn, that thing looks like it is 10 feet across. I bet it's some sort of surveillance device," Sergeant Williams said.

By this time, most of the team was looking up at the large black dome. "It has some sort of reflective quality, I don't think it's is a video monitor," Snap mumbled.

A great white flash of light instantly blinded Snap. A deafening crash of thunder forced them to cover their ears, as they felt a brief weightlessness sensation. Snap and the others were thrown to the floor by a violent force. Snap's eyes were wide open, but he could not see. He struggled to focus and refocus, but his eyes could see nothing but white.

I can't see. I'm blind.

Snap pulled himself to his hands and knees. The temperature was different; it was much hotter and very humid.

I can't feel the concrete floor anymore. It feels like dirt or mud. Where the hell am I?

"I can't see. Williams, Robins, are you here?" Snap called out to his squad.

"I can't see either; I was blinded by that flash of light," Williams said, in a frantic voice.

"Can anyone see? What the hell is going on?" Snap yelled out.

"Major, my vision is starting to come back, but all I see is green," Moore said, from what seemed like far away.

"Where are you, Moore?"

"About 20 feet to your left, Major. I think we are in some kind of jungle."

"Is that rain? I think the temperature just went up 40 degrees!" Senior Master Sergeant Davis proclaimed.

The bright white light was fading into a mellow green. Snap could start to make out leaves and vegetation. The ground was soft, and his face was being sprinkled by a light rain.

"Is everyone okay?" Snap yelled out.

"I'm good, ears are ringing a bit," Ryan Taylor called out.

"My head is pounding," Miller said.

"I think I twisted my ankle when I fell," James Martin hollered. "But, I'll be okay."

Snap looked around, his vision better. He could not see his entire squad, due to the thick underbrush. The squad suffered no serious injuries. It seemed the physical effects of the event were quickly wearing off.

"What the hell was that? Where are we?" Jones asked.

"Maybe we're in a hologram?" Moore guessed.

"What the fuck? You can't feel a hologram!" Brown exclaimed. "We must have been transported to another location."

"Transport? How? They don't have that kind of technology," Josh Miller said.

"Really? What makes you think that?" Ryan Taylor said sarcastically. "Have you not been paying attention? We are wearing alien armor and carrying laser cannons – seems like they could teleport us to wherever they wanted?"

"Bullshit. If this were a hologram, my hand would pass right through this tree," Miller said, as he slammed his hand into a tree trunk. "Damn that hurt." Miller quickly pulled back his fist wincing in pain.

Snap looked around; several members of his team were outside his field of vision, due to the thick underbrush and dense jungle.

"Hey, I found something" Jones yelled.

Snap and the others pushed through the thick leaves, being careful not to step on a booby trap, toward the sound of Jones' voice.

"Where are you," Snap asked, in a slightly elevated voice.

"Over here."

Snap and the others followed the sound of Jones' voice. Pushing through the green foliage, their boots sunk into the soft, wet soil. Snap pushed back a large, leafy branch that revealed Sergeant Jones standing over a wooden crate. Jones easily pushed off the lid, to display a cache of weapons.

"Where the hell are we? Why the fuck is there stash of weapons here?" Jones muttered.

"We were supposed to find these, it's no accident." Snap concluded as he reached for the first weapon, an AK-47. Snap examined the gun, and pulled back the charging handle. "Seems to be in good working order."

"These were left here for us to find. Check the firing pins. Make sure they haven't been tampered with," Moore said.

Snap looked through the crate to find there was a wide variety of weapons, including assault rifles, sub-machine guns, large caliber pistols, and even a rocket launcher. The rest of the squad had arrived and were going through the crate.

"What the . . . a double-edged battle ax?" Miller asked, holding up the weapon.

"Look here. Why would we need a sword?" Johnson said as he lifted the sword from the crate. Johnson twirled the blade in his right hand, to check the balance. "It's sharp," he said, pulling his left index finger away quickly.

"Hey, watch that thing. You almost cut my arm off. Who the hell do you think you are, fucking Zorro?" Ryan Taylor shouted.

"I'm a little concerned," Snap said, "why would they – whoever they are- give us such an odd assortment of weapons? They are not only from different manufactures and countries, they are from different time periods."

"Maybe it's an experiment of some kind?" Williams said, shrugging his shoulders.

"You are God Damn right it's an experiment, and we are the fucking lab rats," Davis shouted. "We need to get the fuck out of here before the inevitable shit hits the proverbial fan."

"Hold on," Snap ordered, "everyone grab a weapon first, then we can figure this out." Snap lifted a GM6M Bull-pup anti-material sniper rifle from the crate. The GM6 shot a 50 caliber BMG round, the same round that was used in anti-aircraft machine guns. It was known for its ability to stop trucks, airplanes, and light armor. Snap detached the magazine to reveal five very large 50 BMG rounds.

Very odd weapon to have in the jungle. This may come in handy if we run into one of those Ondagra.

"Hey, Snap, is that new *Exacto* round? You know, the one that can self-course correct in mid-flight?" Neal West asked.

"Holy shit! I think you are right. I have never seen one of those before. Supposedly, it locks onto the target and follows it like a guided missile," Snap said.

"It's a sniper rifle round, great for distances, but here in close quarters, it's pretty much useless," Neal pointed out.

"I don't know Neal; I got a feeling we are going to need this, even in the jungle. It may come in handy if we run into alien armor."

Snap leaned into the crate and picked up a WW2 era combat knife. He flipped it around a couple of times to ensure that the weight was right and tucked it into his belt.

"Everybody got a weapon? Check them out; make sure they all work. Any ideas on where we are?" Snap asked, in a rhetorical way, since he was pretty sure none of his men had any idea.

Senior Master Sergeant Thomas stepped forward, holding a Russian AK-12 assault rifle, "We're not going to figure out how we got here or where here is by standing around in the woods. The way I see it, either we were transported here somehow, or we are in some hypnotic trance or something. Either way, we need to move until we see something we recognize."

"Agreed. Since we can't see the sun through the canopy and rain clouds, and we have no idea where we are, I say we just start walking in this direction," Snap pointed into the jungle.

"What was that?" Miller asked.

"I didn't hear anything," Jackson said.

"Over there, behind that tree." Miller dropped to one knee and raised the WW2 era M-2 Carbine to his shoulder. The rest of the men took cover behind trees.

"There, see it!" Brown hollered, while pointing at some moving brush.

Snap turned to where Brown was pointing and saw a figure darting between trees about 20 feet out. The figure was hard to make out; it was almost translucent, as if light were passing through it making it difficult to see. Then, it disappeared into the green jungle.

Shit. We are up against something with invisible armor. I have no armor, and a sniper rifle. I should have grabbed a machinegun.

Davis, Miller, and Moore clutched their chests at the same instant, and silently fell over, like dominos, faces first into the dirt. Snap could see a light trail of smoke reaching up to the sky from a grapefruit-sized hole in Davis' back.

Shit. That fucking alien.

"Where did that come from?" Snap yelled, while crouching behind a tree.

"I don't know," Ryan Taylor replied.

"It happened too fast," barked Jackson.

Snap saw the translucent figure running toward Anderson, who was facing the wrong direction, staring into the woods. Snap switched off the safety, dropped to one knee and aimed the 25-pound anti-material gun toward the blurry creature.

I can't get him in my sights. He will be on Anderson in a second. Too Late.

The nearly invisible, creature jammed a sword through Anderson's back and lifted him into the air like a rag doll. Anderson slid down the sword like a human shish kabob. The creature slung him off the sword, and Anderson's lifeless body hurdled through the air, slamming into a tree.

Snap pulled the trigger as the bones in Anderson's corpse broke against the tree trunk. The sound of the BMG round exploding caused his ear to start ringing instantly.

Miss. Shit. Four rounds left.

The eight-foot-tall beast was gone, blending perfectly with the thick, green leaves. Seconds later, it reappeared directly in front of Brown. Brown dropped, clutching his neck as blood sprayed through his fingers. Snap squeezed the trigger again. Miss.

Three rounds left.

Through the noxious haze of gun smoke, the creature looked directly at Snap and charged. The heavy sniper rifle was difficult to lock onto a target in such close quarters. Snap felt the creature's clawed hand close on his neck. The creature arched forward in pain as thirty rounds from an M4A1 carbine slammed into his back. It was not enough to kill the beast, but enough to make him release Snap. The creature's attention was diverted for a second; a shard of light shot from its breastplate and cut down the carbine-wielding Smith.

While the creature was still focused on Snap, who was scrambling behind a tree, Jackson fired the Magnum Research single action revolver into the beast at point-blank range. It screamed. Jackson fired the hand cannon a second time; a copper-colored fluid burst from the beast's armor. The creature leapt toward Jackson, knocking him down. Snap came from behind the tree and fired the 50-caliber rifle at the beast on top of Jackson.

Dammit. How'd I missed again? Just too close for this rifle.

Thomas stepped up and swung the battle ax down on the beast while it was still on top of Jackson. The beast leapt up, revealing a mangled Jackson, and the incinerator weapon on his chest glowed blue. Another flash of light, and Thomas' battle ax dropped. Snap charged, raising the GM6M, at 11 feet away, he pulled the trigger. The beast dropped. Then, there was a blinding flash of light and Snap was violently thrown to the ground.

CHAPTER TWENTY-FIVE

Granite Peak Installation

Once again, Snap was back in the training room on Level 15. Slowly, the room stopped spinning, and Snap forced himself to stand up. All his men were alive and shaking off minor aches and pains. Anderson, who a few minutes earlier had been impaled by a sword, was checking out his stomach and chest with both hands. In a couple of minutes, they were all standing in the training room.

"Told you it was a hologram," said Tim Moore.

"Bullshit. No way it was a hologram," Brown argued. "You can't feel a hologram. I felt that shit. I felt it for real."

"Quiet," Snap ordered. The men stopped talking and looked toward Snap and then at the eight-foot-tall beast they had just been fighting.

"I am Ater Velens. This is my base. You will follow my orders while you are here. Do you understand?" Ater towered over them. He was no longer wearing his battle armor, but he appeared to be wearing form-fitting, translucent suit.

"How should we address you?" Snap asked.

"I do not stand on ceremony or titles. You may call me Ater." As Ater moved, the colorless suit reacted to the movement by changing to different hues of a translucent blur.

"Ater, could you explain what just happened to us?"

"Half of your squad was killed by one Ondagra," he hissed with a hint of disgust.

"Ondagra?" Jackson asked.

"Ondagra is the name for my people; like you refer to yourselves as humans, we refer to ourselves as Ondagra. My kind, the Ondagra, come from Botacoure, a planet that is located thousands of light years from Earth."

"How did you transport us to a jungle?" asked Snap.

"Major Slade, I did not transport you anywhere. You never left this room. This room is one big holographic projector. The tiles on the walls, floor, and ceiling are each able to project millions of holographic images at once. Combined with that black dome above us, they create an alternate reality that will trick the eye and mind." Ater pointed at the hexagon-shaped tiles on the walls and floor.

"Not possible," Snap said. "We felt the rain on our faces, the trees, the ground and the impacts of your weapons. You can't feel a hologram."

"Almost true, Major. You don't feel the holographic projection. In this room, you are surrounded by billions of flying nanobots. These nanobots interact with the hologram, and when they detect that you are about to come in contact with an object in the holographic world, millions of them contact your skin in the appropriate location with the appropriate pressure so that you think you are touching an object, a tree, rain, or a weapon."

"I picked up a weapon and fired it. I felt the pistol grip in my hand; I felt the recoil."

"You saw a holographic image of a weapon. When you went to grab the handle, you really grabbed a hand full of nanobots that applied the correct amount of pressure to the palm of your hand to make you believe you were lifting a weapon. The nanobots are too small for the human eye to see; each one is controlled by microchip that is 1,000 times smaller than a white blood cell. This is a training room. Everything that happens here is recorded for later review," Ater said, as he waived his hand toward the wall.

Instantly, an image appeared on the plain white wall. "Replay last twenty minutes," Ater commanded, speaking to the projection on the wall.

"That's us in the jungle," Ryan Taylor said in surprise. The wall-sized video display showed a perfect image of the squad sorting through the crate, examining the weapons in the jungle.

"This is a video replay of the simulated attack on your squad. We use the replay as a training exercise, to help you learn what you did wrong. I like running this simulation on new recruits before they are aware of the holographic technology. It gives me a true understanding of each of your strengths and weaknesses. I find soldiers become braver after they realize they are in a simulated hologram," Ater said, as he crossed his huge arms over his muscular chest.

"When you attacked us, you were wearing advanced body armor, but now you are wearing some type of invisibility suit. How did you change so quickly?" Snap asked.

"I did not change. When you killed me with the 50 BMG, the training exercise immediately ended, and seconds later you were able to see me in this suit. I was wearing this reflective suit during the entire training exercise, it projects the appearance that I am wearing armor. All of you will receive suits like this for training, and when you put them on, they will look and feel exactly like you are wearing the FALOS armor that you wear into combat."

"You were able to kill half of our squad before being neutralized, and we are one of America's most elite fighting forces. Those don't seem like very good odds for the battlefield," Sergeant Martin said.

"Fighting the Ondagra will not be easy, but you will perform better than this training exercise suggests. You were not wearing armor during the training exercise. Some of you had weapons that were capable of killing an Ondagra, but you were not trained in how to use those weapons. Once training is complete, your chances against a Large Gray, as you call us, will be much improved."

"Not that I don't appreciate it, but why are you helping us to fight your own kind?" Snap asked.

"I had a falling out with our leader here on Earth, Nox Bellator. He is secretly trying to rule the Earth through proxy corporations and shadow governments. I have grown to appreciate the freedom and creativity that some humans enjoy. Nox would slowly destroy all of that," Ater explained.

"Are you the only Ondagra working with the U.S. Government?" Snap asked.

"I am now. I originally came here with a delegation of Ondagra in 1954. There were 40 of us sent here to work with the Americans. Nox was trying to play both sides of the cold war. After a long series of unfortunate events, all of them returned home in the early eighties."

"Except you."

"I could have returned home. Nox wanted me to leave this place. But I grew to dislike Nox's way of doing things. It's not that I love Americans, it's that I really dislike Nox Bellator."

Snap knew he could not begin to understand the Ondagra's facial expressions, but he sensed he could trust this Ondagra. "So, how did we do for our first training exercise?"

"Compared to previous groups, you did remarkably well. Many squads take far higher casualties before the simulation ends. Over half of the time, I kill the entire squad before they can neutralize me."

"During the first training exercise, back in the desert compound, after taking out the terrorists, why were our laser cannons not effective against you?" Snap questioned.

"The Ondagra developed their armor among a group of solar systems where there are several warring planets. The primary enemies of the Ondagra use directed energy weapons, not ballistic weapons. For a thousand years the Ondagra have been developing armor to defend against lasers and beam weapons, but we have not focused on projectiles, like bullets. Don't misunderstand, the Ondagra's armor will stop small caliber bullets, but it will break down under a barrage of sub-machine gun fire or high caliber weapons. That is why the 50 BMG works so well."

"Easy, we all get outfitted with 50 caliber rifles and go hunting," Ryan Taylor said with a laugh.

"Not so simple," Ater replied. "The GM6M Lynx sniper rifle has a five-round magazine, and compared to a particle beam accelerator, it has an incredibly slow rate of fire. The Large Gray will be able to fire 100 lethal particle beams at you for each high caliber projectile fired at him. It's like charging a machine gun nest with a musket," Ater cautioned.

"That's right," Snap said. "Targeting Ater with that heavy rifle was not easy."

"Pistol rounds like 9 mm, or 45 are pretty much ineffective against Ondagra armor. Larger rounds, like .308 or 7.62x39 may be effective with multiple strikes from a fully automatic weapon. There are very few conventional, man-portable weapons that deliver a lethal blow to the Ondagra's armor. As you saw, the 50 BMG Lynx is one of the few that will deliver a kill strike with one hit."

"So, will we each be issued one of those?" James Martin asked.

"No. Four of these will be issued to your squad. Remember, I said man-portable. There are several squad based weapons that will effectively take out Ondagra armor. The mini-gun will easily slice through his armor and deliver multiple kill shots per second."

"Now that's what I'm talking about," said Justin Thomas.

"Normally, squad weapons require multiple soldiers to operate, but, in your FALOS suit, you will easily be able to carry a mini-gun and thousands of rounds of ammunition."

"How many of those will we get?" Snap asked.

"Four squad members will have mini-guns. A FALOS suit and mini-gun is almost an even match against Ondagra armor. Remember, even with a mini-gun, the Ondagra has an advantage," Ater cautioned the squad.

"What's that?" asked Miller.

"The FALOS suit can only carry a few thousand rounds of armor piercing ammunition. The Ondagra's particle accelerator weapon has unlimited shots and is much lighter than a mini-gun," Ater replied.

"So, what's next in our training, Ater?" Snap asked.

"The rest of the day will be spent debriefing you on the Ondagra threat to global and national security; on their technology, types of crafts, weapons and weaknesses. Tomorrow you will begin training on a new piece of equipment; I think you will enjoy it."

The team sat through several hours of presentations from various speakers, including combat veterans, DOD contractors, National Security Agency representatives, and scientists. After the training and briefings, the squad was dismissed to their temporary quarters for the evening.

CHAPTER TWENTY-SIX

Granite Peak Installation

The steward took the squad to the guest housing area. Lightning Squad had their own suite of rooms; there were enough suites to house up to six squads at a time. Each suite had a small central living space with several couches, chairs, and tables. On either side of the living space, there were two doors, leading to sleeping quarters. Three of the bedrooms had four bunks each, and the fourth had only two bunks.

The steward, a bald, middle aged man, stood in the middle of the room wearing black cargo pants and button-down shirt like the security forces they had seen earlier. He had introduced himself as Jim Connor and mentioned that he was former Special Forces.

"Gentlemen, you will find a fully stocked bathroom in each of the bedrooms. We have already placed three days' worth of clothes in the closets for you. If any of the sizes are wrong, just let us know. The DFAC is staffed with a chef during normal meal times, but if you get hungry, feel free to go there any time. You are the only squad here this week, so the place will be pretty quiet."

"I think that covers it," Snap said. "Thank you. So, where can we get something to eat?"

"Out the door, turn right, and it's down the hall on the left, across from the gym." Jim pointed down the hall.

"Thanks," Snap said as Jim turned to leave.

"Let's head down to the mess hall and check it out," Lieutenant Neal West said to Snap. Neal was the only other officer in the squad.

"Sound good to me," Snap replied.

The two men walked down the hotel-like hallway, passing several doors that led to unoccupied sleeping quarters. Unlike the large cavernous areas, the crew's quarters were not carved from rough granite. Rather, the corridors had nice finished walls and were decorated with modern wallpaper and prints of landscapes. If it were not for the fact that there were no windows, you could forget you were underground. The hallway opened into a small lobby. Off to the left was a small but functional mess hall; to the right was the steward's quarters and gym.

"I wonder if the chef is still on duty?" Neal asked.

"Let's see," Snap responded, as they walked into the dining room area that had twelve rectangular tables, surrounded by armless metal chairs. The stainless-steel kitchen was partially open to the dining room, with a pass through and an extra-wide doorway.

"Hello." Snap announced their presence as they entered the commercial kitchen. In the middle of the kitchen stood a stainless-steel island with an impressive array of pots and pans hanging from a rack attached to the ceiling.

"Good evening, Sir." Another middle-aged man emerged from around the corner, wiping his hands on a dish towel. The chef was of average height and build, and was wearing black beneath his white apron and hair net.

"Evening, Chef, I'm Lieutenant West, and this is Major Slade. We are going to be staying here for a few nights."

"I know. I'm Chef Parker. You can just call me Chef if you like." Chef extended his hand to Snap. Chef had a firm handshake, and made solid eye contact.

"Good to meet you Chef. So, what's for dinner tonight?" Snap asked, returning the firm handshake. It was obvious to Snap that Chef was more than a simple fry cook.

"Well, Major, since there's only twelve of you here tonight, I thought I would just cook something to order. I have a menu here, but if you would like something special, just let me know, and I will see if I can whip it up for you."

"Excellent," Snap said, as he picked up the laminated one-page menu. All your basic pub food was available, plus a couple of main entrees.

"What do you recommend?" Snap asked as he glanced over the menu.

"I make a mean seared filet mignon with a caramelized onion curry sauce. Alongside it, I place a healthy serving of asparagus in a smooth hollandaise sauce. Then, we finish the evening off with bananas foster a la mode," the chef said, almost gleefully.

"That sounds delicious. I will have that." Snap handed Chef the menu. "You got a beer around here?"

Chef pointed at refrigerator in the dining hall that was stocked full of a variety of beer. Snap and Neal each grabbed one and headed back into the kitchen to talk to Chef.

"So how long you been working here on Level 15?" Snap asked, as he took a swig from the brown bottle.

A slight look of concern crossed Chef's narrow face. He paused for a moment, as if to reflect, and said, "Over 20 years."

"Wow, you have been a Chef for 20 years?" Snap asked, obviously surprised.

"No. I started out like you, an operator. The work took a toll on my body; so, they moved me to the kitchen."

"You didn't want to leave Level 15 and try something different, you know, in the private sector?" Neal asked.

Chef looked puzzled for a minute, as if that thought had never crossed his mind, then said, "Nah. I wanted to stick around here."

"Place looks empty, where does everyone else eat?" Neal asked.

Chef shuffled his feet and fumbled with a bloody steak, "I don't serve them. They have their own quarters and DFAC. I only work in the temporary guest quarters."

"Compartmentalization?" Snap asked.

"Yes Sir. They don't want the guests in the permanent resident section. Afraid they might overhear something they shouldn't." Chef started tossing some ingredients together in a mixing bowl.

A few more members of Lightning Squad stumbled in and placed orders. Chef was getting busy flipping burgers, grilling steaks and operating the deep fryer. Snap and Neal went to the linen clad table in the back of the dining room to wait for their steaks.

"Wow, two days ago we were just a regular squad, training to fight radicalized terrorists in the Middle East, and now, we find out the world is crawling with aliens," Neal said, shaking his head in disbelief. "I mean Holy Fucking Shit. This is like some freaking science fiction horror movie," Neal said in a whisper.

"I know, it's pretty unbelievable. Ever since the forties, the government has been covering up all this shit. I'm sure you have noticed that ever since we saw the Large Gray, what did they call him? An Ondagra? We have not been allowed out of their sight? Much less been permitted to call anyone," Snap said.

"Did you know about any of this prior to yesterday, Major?" West asked.

"Nope, I was in the dark, just like the rest of you." Snap took another sip of his beer.

"How do you think they have been keeping this a secret for the last 70 years? I get that they keep the circle small, but still. No one spills the beans? After 70 years?" West shook his head in disbelief.

"But there have been leaks and plenty of them. Look at all the stuff on the internet about astronauts and pilots claiming to have seen saucer shaped discs and aliens from other worlds. Those pilots are immediately discredited and made to look like clowns. Look at all the whistle blowers that died in mysterious accidents after giving an interview about Area 51 or some other above top-secret project." Snap made fist a with one hand and leaned his chin onto it.

"Yeah, I always thought those guys were just crazy."

Snap shook his head in disagreement. "They can't all be crazy. There are too many of them. Generals, admirals, astronauts, scientists, and presidents have all confirmed the existence of, not only aliens, but also the cover up. They can't all be wrong, especially when they risked their own careers to disclose the truth. It all makes sense now."

The last of the squad arrived and were seated at the other tables. None of the enlisted men sat with Snap or West. Snap stood up, "You want another beer?"

"Yes Sir."

Snap returned with two more cold ones. "Do you think they are telling us everything? I mean, about the Large Grays."

Neal took a sip of his beer, rocked back on the rear legs of his chair, and took a deep breath, "No, definitely not."

"According to the scientist that spoke this afternoon, we don't know how many there are, where they are located, or why they are here. Hell, Ater is one of them, and he could not give us a straight answer as to what their goals are, or why they are here."

"Yeah, he knows a hell of a lot more than he is telling us. How could he not know exactly how many there are, why they're here, and where their bases are?" Snap asked.

"I liked it when you asked if there were any other aliens visiting the planet. Did you see the look on his long, gray face?" West laughed.

"Yeah, like, how could he not have seen that question coming?" Snap smirked.

"Did you believe his answer? That there are no other aliens on the planet but the Large Grays?"

"Well, if you believe the internet, and I'm starting to, then you have to assume they are all full of shit."

West said, "So, we now know that aliens exist, our government has been in contact with them for years; they have been actively covering up their existence for decades, and even now, after telling us about them, they are still lying."

"Yep that about sums it up." Snap raised his beer bottle. West tipped his bottle toward Snap's brew as if to giver a toast. They chuckled.

"I think we are FUBARed."

"Yes Sir."

Dinner was served by Chef. The steaks, smothered in caramelized onions, came out on piping hot white china plates.

"If you need anything else, just let me know," Chef said.

"This looks great; I think we will be fine," Snap replied.

"I'll be out later to prepare your bananas foster."

"I can't wait." West said.

Chef walked toward one of the other tables surrounded by four soldiers that had mistakenly ordered the mushroom smothered hamburger.

"Those guys should have ordered the filet mignon," Snap said with a laugh.

"Yeah, they don't know what they are missing." Neal sat up in his chair, "On a serious note, though, during orientation, they warned us that disclosing anything we learn about extraterrestrials is punishable by death. We don't even get a trial. Does that bother you?" Neal pondered.

"Yes, of course. But that's not what worries me the most. I'm pretty sure I can keep my mouth shut. What worries me the most is the fact that I know they are keeping a lot of secrets from us. There is no way that they don't have any idea how many they are, or where they are when they got at least one of them right here on this base," Snap said.

"We are the only squad here right now? We have been here all day; this place is designed for at least six squads. Have you seen any other soldiers? Plenty of scientists, spooks, techs, but not one combat solider, except us. Where are they?"

"You think they are all in combat, right now?" Snap asked, while chewing a stalk of tender asparagus.

"Could be, for all we know, there could be a full-blown against the Ondagra, and we don't even know it." Neal took another bite of his smothered steak.

"So, to what do you attribute all the rapid advancement of technology? Roswell? Or, do you think that aliens have been working with the government to develop the tech?" Snap asked.

"I definitely think alien technology was involved, whether it be crashed saucers or alien intervention, I don't know. At the very minimum, you have Ater here for a couple of decades helping develop tech."

"I just get this feeling that there is more to the story, a lot more," Snap said, as he slowly cut his filet.

CHAPTER TWENTY-SEVEN

Lightning Squad reported to the training room the next morning. Ater was already there when they walked in.

"Good Morning, Ater," Snap called out from the door, as he entered the large room.

"Gentlemen, we have an exciting day planned for you. Today we will be training on the *Fixed-wing Individual Glider Assault System,* or FIGAS for short. We will not be in a hologram room or simulation. Today, we will be going up in a plane and jumping without a parachute. Literally," Ater said eustatically.

The men looked at each other, unsure of what to think.

Before any of them could object, Ater waived his hand, and a three-dimensional holographic image of a FIGAS appeared before the men. The image was an eight-foot-long wing with two small jets attached to the bottom of the wing. There was no fuselage, just a harness system that allowed a man to put it on, like a camper would wear a backpack.

Ater continued, "This fixed wing jet pack will allow you controlled flight to your destination from the plane. Unlike a parachute, which merely allows you to float to the ground, this will allow you to fly, up to 10 miles to your chosen destination. This is far superior to a parachute because the pilot does not have to be as exact in dropping you and you, can fly to better landing zones in a combat situation."

"The FIGAS offers a one-way trip. It will not take off from the ground. It must be launched from a high point and glide, under power, to its landing zone. The FIGAS does not have its own power source, it attaches to the Modular Micro Fusion Reactor built into your FALOS armor. The guidance systems of the FIGAS are all integrated into the HUD built into the helmet of your FALOS armor."

"Since we are using the fusion reactor in our FALOS suit to power the jet wing, will we still be able to fire our laser while in flight?" Snap asked.

"Good question. It is true that constant use of the laser places a strain on the fusion reactor. However, our scientists have been able to adjust the laser's power requirements while in flight. Essentially, the laser will be reduced to 50 kilowatts while in flight, or roughly half power. Still powerful enough to dispatch soft ground forces."

Snap nodded his head, "That will work."

"How hard is it to fly?" Williams asked.

"It's as easy as falling out of an airplane. The jet wing is fully voice-command controlled. Flight data will appear in the HUD. You can use your laser targeting system and flight control systems at the same time. The wing has a built in 3-axis gyro that automatically engages the thrusters to ensure you are upright and stable; all you have to do is adjust for speed and direction."

After a few hours of training in the hologram room, the men headed to the lockers to put on their FALOS suits. Each man had his own suit that was uniquely fitted to not only his body, but his voice commands. While not being worn, the FALOS armor was able to stand on its own with the weight of the suit being held up by the exoskeleton. The micro modular fusion reactor could go months without being refueled, as the alien technology made it extremely efficient.

Snap stepped up to his FALOS suit, which looked almost like a robot, standing all on its own. It was a completely self-contained unit, the heavy armor resting on the titanium exoskeleton. The suit was designed to anticipate the operator's movements and assist with lifting heavy loads or executing preprogrammed maneuvers. If the operator wanted to override any preprogrammed functions, there was a voice command feature.

The suit's natural color was white, but it would automatically change colors to blend in with the environment. If the operator was in the desert, it would change to a sandy color, if in the jungle, to green. The suit had thousands of miniature light-emitting diodes built into the armor that would project an image on the suit. In an urban setting, the suit could project one of hundreds of pre-programmed images, or it could project an image from the local setting. It did not make the operator completely invisible, but it made the operator difficult to see in any environment.

The suit came with a laser rifle that could be attached to the modular micro fusion reactor for non-stop fire power. When the laser was not in use, it would be charging. The laser was capable of firing 200 shots when fully powered. If the power in the laser were depleted in combat, it could be reattached to the fusion reactor and fired without being powered up.

The head up display built into his helmet allowed for communications with his men, headquarters, and other devices. The HUD could track the enemy's movements, friendlies' movements, his vital signs, targeting, and power supply, and it could interface with other equipment, like the jet wing.

Equipping the armor took time. First, there was a carbon boride fiber under suit, similar to a diver's wet suit. This was bullet resistant and would act to control the temperature of his body.

Then, the largest part of the suit, a single piece of armor that covered his chest, back, and torso, was called the main unit. The arms and legs attached next, locking into the main unit. The weight of the main unit and helmet were supported by the leg units through a mechanical spine in the back of the suit that held it all together.

While the suit took several minutes to put on and run a complete system check, it did have a manual quick release lever if the operator had to exit the suit in a hurry. Once in the suit, the operator was 80 percent covered in advanced, nearly impenetrable armor. The suit had two weaknesses. First, it was not equipped for swimming or being in deep water. Second, and the more troubling weakness, was that it was susceptible to failure upon a direct hit from an Electromagnetic Pulse weapon, or EMP for short.

After locking his helmet into place and powering up the suit, Snap ran a diagnostic on all systems. The head up display showed each critical system in red until it was checked; then it turned green to indicate it was in working order. Even though the suit weighed several hundred pounds, its design made it seem weightless.

Snap turned to West, "Neal, you all good?"

"Yes Sir. All systems go."

Snap looked around and saw that all his men were finishing up their initial checks. Their helmets covered their heads completely; so, all talking was done through the communications device. When Snap spoke, the default setting was for the sound of his voice to be heard in all of his men's helmets. If Snap wished to speak to only one of his men, he would start by saying that man's name. The communications system had an artificial intelligence component that determined to whom one was speaking based on word content, voice inflection, geographic proximity and retinal monitoring."

"Alright men, let's go learn how to fly."

Lightning Squad climbed into a large troop transport vehicle designed to carry a squad of men wearing FALOS armor. Behind them was Ater's personal SUV. He too, was wearing full battle armor. The two vehicles exited Level 15 and drove up the circular ramp to the mouth of the Granite Peak Installation bunker. It was the first time the men had seen sunlight in a couple of days. They drove the short distance from the mouth of the tunnel to a runway used exclusively for GPI operations.

Thanks to their powerful exoskeletons, they effortlessly jumped out of the transport vehicle. Ater's SUV pulled up beside them, and he stepped out, displaying the matte black finish of his impressive armor.

"I want his armor," Williams said.

"He can hear you," Davis replied.

"Why are all the Airmen lying face down on the tarmac?" Snap asked Ater.

"They are not allowed to see me or the FALOS armor. They are required to lay face down and cover their heads with their hands when we pass," Ater said. "Security protocols. If one of them sees us, then they are threatened and forced to sign additional nondisclosure agreements."

Lightning Squad entered the C-17 Globe Master III cargo plane from the rear ramp. The rear cargo ramp had been extended down so that trucks or tanks could be easily driven up into the cargo compartment. The squad sat in the integral sidewall seats; the center seats had been removed to make room for cargo, in this case, the fixed wing jets. The FIGAS units were suspended from the ceiling waiting for the squad to step into the harnesses immediately prior to jumping.

After several minutes had passed, Snap peered out onto the tarmac and noticed that the Airmen were still lying face down. "Ater, why are the men still lying on the ground?" Snap asked.

"They are not allowed to stand up or look around until all top-secret equipment and personnel are onboard."

"But we are all here."

"No, we are still waiting for the last member of your team."

"My whole team is here," Snap replied.

"Just wait." No sooner had Ater spoke, then a troop transport raced past the face-down men and up to the rear cargo ramp. A nine-foot-tall man emerged from the rear of the transport and ran up the ramp toward the squad.

"Holy shit!" Snap exclaimed, as he leapt to his feet. The rest of his squad jumped up.

"What the hell is that thing?" Neal West asked, as he reached for his laser rifle.

"At ease men, do not touch your weapons," Ater commanded. The men stared at the nine-foot-tall man who was built like a football linebacker.

"Is he human?" Neal West asked. The question did not sound absurd to Snap.

In seconds, the huge man closed the distance between the ramp and the squad and was towering over them.

"Meet 028," Ater said.

"028, are you fucking kidding me? His name is 028?" Williams said into his HUD, before realizing everyone could hear it.

"028 does not speak much, other than to give and receive commands."

"How do you know if he likes you?" Neal asked.

"If you see him and live to discuss it, he liked you," Ater said.

"I'm not calling him 028," Ryan Taylor said. "That's not a name."

"What do you intend to call him?" Snap asked, glancing over at Ater.

"Well, anything is better than 028, how about we call him Bob?" Ryan asked.

"Bob would be a lot easier than 028. What do you think, Ater?" Snap asked.

Ater paused for a moment, as if the thought of naming the giant had never crossed his mind. "That's fine. You can call him Bob. You hear that, 028, for this mission, your call name will be Bob."

"Bob is not wearing armor," Snap pointed out. Bob was wearing kaki canvas cargo pants, a black t-shirt, combat boots, and a black watch with a large combat knife strapped to his belt.

"Bob does not need armor. He is an even match against a FALOS armor." Ater said.

The men took their seats. Bob took two seats.

"Snap, I bet he weighs over 500 pounds," Neal whispered.

"Neal, Ater never answered the question about whether Bob was human," Snap said into the HUD com system.

"Snap, he looks mean, shell shocked, or something."

"Neal, he has a thousand-yard stare, kind of like he is a robot. He only takes orders, but from who?"

"Snap, I hope to God he takes orders from you," Neal said into the HUD.

The pilot announced that they were above the drop zone, not that drop zone was the right term since they were going to be flying out the rear of the plane on jet packs.

"Is Bob coming with us?'

"Yes." Ater replied. Bob leapt up from his seats, grabbed the only yellow, fixed wing jet pack, tossed it on like a school boy slings a knap sack over his shoulder when heading off to the bus, and jumped from the open ramp.

"He did that in 10 seconds, flat" one Williams said in astonishment.

"He has no FALOS suit. What powers his jet wing?" Snap asked.

"The MMFR on your FALOS suit powers your wing. His is powered by four micro turbo diesel engines," Ater said, as he stepped into the harness of his own fixed wing jet. "The landing zone coordinates will appear in your HUD."

CHAPTER TWENTY-EIGHT

Far East Russia
Magadan Oblast
Present Day

Commander Forte stepped from the rear of the ten-man shuttle onto the rocky terrain. All seven shuttles were sitting in a row beneath an overhang that would hide them from any Russian planes flying overhead; and shield them from the cold winds. The crew were pouring out of the shuttles and exploring the shallow cave-like shelter.

Commander Furier exited the shuttle, shivering. "Damn, it's cold out here. I thought our uniforms were supposed to protect us from all weather."

Commander Forte looked at her, smirked, and said, "They are helping. It's minus forty-seven degrees outside. We would be dead if they were not working." Forte glanced down at her shapely figure, she crossed her arms over her ample chest. Forte was pissed at her for not fully disclosing the nature of the cargo. "You know we are going to have to talk about the Element 115."

She stared at him through her curly mane that was hanging down in her face. Her ice blue eyes fixed on Forte. "You know, you don't outrank me here."

Forte could see she was still shivering, the platinum streaks in her hair stood out even more in the natural light. He didn't want to fight over this point right now; he had more important problems to solve. "You are a supply officer; I am a commanding officer. I may not have a ship, but you don't have a cargo. As this is a tactical situation, I am the ranking officer. That aside, we should work together to get the remaining cargo to the Americans safely."

Commander Furier nodded her head in agreement.

The seventy survivors of the crash gathered behind the shuttles under the shelter of the overhang. Commander Forte stood on a small rock so he could see the remaining members of his crew.

"Crew of the *Impegi*, I want you to know that we are going to survive this tragedy. I know many of you are grieving the loss of some of your friends. There will be time to mourn them soon enough. Now, we must focus on survival. Our mission is not complete." Forte surveyed the group, they were all cold, shivering, and scared.

"I have been in contact with the Americans. They are working on a rescue mission. We have crashed in hostile territory. The enemy has advanced weaponry; so, we need to stay hidden until the Americans come to retrieve us."

"We are going to break up into small groups to set up camp. Captain Pilosus, take 10 crew and start to devise a camouflage for the front of the cave entrance."

"Yes Sir." Pilosus replied.

"Captain Cordatus, start formulating a plan for food, water, and heat."

"Commander Furier."

"Yes, Commander Forte."

"Figure out what we have in the way of armor and weapons. Take a team to the crash site and monitor it. Report back all activity."

"I thought we were told to stand down?"

"We were, and we are. I just want INTEL. We need to know what we are facing. Just report back activity, do not engage."

"Yes Sir."

CHAPTER TWENTY-NINE

Granite Peak Installation
Present Day

Snap and Neal West sat a table waiting for Chef to bring them their dinner after the FIGAS training exercise. Most of the squad was relaxing in the mess hall or finishing up with their showers. Snap had ordered a bacon cheeseburger, rare with a side of something Chef called wilted lettuce. Neal had ordered a Santa Fe chicken sandwich. Both were wearing civilian gym clothes.

"So, what about Bob?" Neal asked with a snicker.

"He looked human, sort of. Aside from being nine feet tall, not talking, and having an expressionless face that only a mother could love, I suppose he was okay," Snap replied. "I thought you were going to draw down on him there for a second."

"He startled me. Good thing I didn't. Ater said he is competitive against FALOS armor. Can you believe that? How can flesh compete against a titanium exoskeleton?"

"Nothing surprises me anymore," Snap said, shaking his head. "I guess we will find out soon enough."

Chef walked up to the table holding two steaming platters. "Evening gentlemen. Here are your entrees. Is there anything else I can get for you?"

"Thank you, Chef," Snap said. "I think we have everything we need here." Snap examined his burger, "It looks great."

The wilted lettuce, as Chef called it, was a leafy, lite, green lettuce, tossed with chopped up radishes and scallions, with hot bacon grease poured over the mixture. "Now, this is my kind of salad," Snap said.

"Bacon grease poured over lettuce, that's a salad I can get into. Mine is pretty good, too," Neal said, as he took a big bite of the sliced chicken breast smothered in cheese, and grilled onions and peppers.

After a few minutes of silent enjoyment of Chef's culinary masterpieces, Neal asked, "So, what made you want to join the Air Force?"

Snap took a gulp of his unsweet tea, leaned back, and said, "My grandfather. He was in WWII. He really inspired me to join."

"Were you close to your grandfather?" Neal asked.

"Not really, I wish we were closer. After he retired from the Air Force, he had a second career in the civil service. He was gone a lot. My dad spent some time in Nam, but never talked about it much."

"My dad was in Vietnam, too. He retired from the Marine Corp," Neal said.

"That's the way it works now, with a volunteer military. Many military families serve for generations, while the civilian population has no idea what we do. It was better, back before WWII; when everybody served. It was not military-life versus civilian-life; it was just American-life, everyone had skin in the game." Snap took another bite of his juicy cheeseburger.

As Snap was chewing a mouthful of well-seasoned hamburger, the lights turned from white to red, and a siren went off.

"What the hell is that?" Williams shouted from a across the small room.

"Everyone report to their assigned positions. This is not a drill," a hidden loud speaker announced from somewhere in the ceiling.

"What do we do? Where do we report?" Neal asked. The pulsing red light was casting strange shadows across room. The men were starting to stand up, but not sure of where to go.

"I don't know. We were never told where to report in case of an actual emergency." Snap rose to his feet, unsure of his next step.

Ater slammed open the door and barraged into the room. The men were shocked to see the menacing figure outside of the training room. "Everyone to the training room. You need to change into your FALOS suits immediately. We have a real-world situation to deal with; and time is of the essence."

"What's going on?" Snap asked.

"No time. You will be fully briefed in the air. Get your men suited up. This is not a training exercise."

Thirty minutes later, the men were standing on what appeared to be a deserted runway just outside Granite Peak Installation. The troop transport that had brought them to the desolate location was heading back to GPI.

"Snap, what the hell are we doing here, standing in the middle of the desert all alone." Neal said into the head up display of his FALOS suit.

"I don't know," Snap replied. "But it doesn't feel like an exercise."

"Snap, you don't think this is just another one of those trick training exercises to evaluate us under pressure?"

Ater's voice interrupted the conversation, "This is not a training exercise. I assure you of that. Your ride will be there shortly."

"Ater, I thought only Snap could hear me if I said his name first," West protested.

"Control can hear everything you say, even directed conversation," Ater replied.

"Great. I will have to keep that in mind," Neal muttered.

"Neal, look." Snap smacked Neal on the arm and pointed at the ground. Ten yards from where they stood, the ground was opening, sliding along a mechanical track.

The false desert floor opened to reveal a deep, dark, perfectly square hole. The squad heard a mechanical humming sound. The bottom of the hole began to ascend, and, as it got closer to the top the team could make out a triangular shaped craft. The platform reached the surface and locked into place; the hole disappeared. The black triangular shaped craft was much larger than a fighter jet, but still smaller than a cargo plane. It had no wings or nose, but the men could tell by its design it was meant to fly.

"What the. . .?"

"Is that what I think it is?" Williams asked.

"Well, it's sure as shit ain't no UFO, since it just came out of our base," Johnson replied.

"It's a UFO to your mom," Davis said.

"Alright men, cut it out." Snap ordered.

A ramp descended from one of the equal sides of the triangle, revealing a well-lit metallic interior that resembled the inside cargo compartment of a transport plane.

"This must be the rear of the craft," Snap said.

"Not precisely," Ater said from the command center.

"Board the plane," Snap ordered his men. On board, they could see their fixed-wing jets suspended from the ceiling. The sidewall seats were designed for soldiers wearing bulky FALOS suits.

"Where's the pilot?" Williams asked.

"If he were up your ass you would know," Johnson replied, with a chuckle.

"Fuck you man. I was serious," Williams retorted.

"Get strapped in. You will be briefed as soon as you are in the air," Ater said. A couple of minutes later, they were cutting through the atmosphere at nearly 8,000 miles per hour.

CHAPTER THIRTY

Magadan Oblast
Present Day

Commander Caliana Furier sat in the pilot's seat of the jump shuttle, perched directly on the ridge overlooking the crash site. Not only was she the highest-ranking officer in the jump shuttle, she was the same rank as Commander Forte. His mission was to safely get them to Earth; her mission was to ensure the safe passage of the valuable cargo. Both had failed. Furier and the other nine crewmen in the shuttle were dressed in full battle armor.

The other jump shuttles and Forte were back in the cave. Commander Furier and her team were wearing 10 combat suits that they found in the jump shuttles. The other four combat suits were being worn by officers back at the cave. Furier and the team exited the rear of the jump shuttle, leaving it in stealth mode.

"Everyone stay in chameleon mode," Furier said, as they exited. The battle armor not only added an extra layer of protection and warmth, it was also capable of rendering the operator nearly invisible. The Americans FALOS suit was based on the same technology, only the Americans' suit was even more advanced. Each of the suits had helmets with communications systems that allowed the crew to speak with each other. Unlike the more advanced FALOS suits, their communications could not be monitored by a command center. Additionally, they could not receive a data-link from the Americans command center, meaning they were not receiving real time updates regarding enemy troop movements. Their armor had built in radars, which would give them limited INTEL regarding movements within a 25-mile radius.

"What are we doing here?" Catrix asked. Catrix was one of the ship's engineering crew. Much like many of the survivors, he had no combat experience.

"We are here to observe and gather intelligence on the ship and cargo. Ultimately, we would like to recover as much of the Element 115 as possible. Also, many of our fellow crew are back in a cave freezing. If we could recover some equipment to help them; that would be nice."

Genu, one of the crew's navigation team, was staring through the only pair of binoculars found in the shuttle's emergency supply locker. The ridge they were standing on was not a natural formation; it was created as the ship crashed, driving through the otherwise flat, rocky terrain. The ship was situated, in three large segments, at the bottom of the very long trench that was dug into the ground as it crashed.

"Look, there's the command tower. Looks like it broke off the super structure in the crash," Genu said, pointing over toward the tower, whose top level was barely above the ridge line.

"It's remarkably intact for such a violent impact," Commander Furier said.

"I guess Commander Forte really knew what he was doing by activating the plasma shields the way he did," Genu said, completely unaware of the ongoing rift between Forte and Furier.

"Yeah, I guess we have to give him credit for that," Furier mumbled.

"Commander, the tower looks pretty much intact. Why don't we go down there and access the crew's quarters? We could salvage some blankets, clothes and food for the crew back in the cave."

"I don't know. It could be very unstable in there; decks could collapse any minute," Furier said.

"We will be careful. Also, we are woefully outgunned if the locals show up before the Americans. We should recover some weapons from the armory, just in case," Sergeant Fabris said. Fabris was one of the few military personnel standing on the ridge with Furier.

"Most of our people are not trained to use weapons," Furier objected.

"An armed group of civilians is better than an unarmed group of civilians, in my opinion, Commander."

"Okay, it's better than sitting here doing nothing. But our first priority is food and clothing, our people could die from exposure before a single shot is fired."

"Understood, Commander," Sergeant Fabris responded.

"How do we get in and up to the crew's quarter's level? We can't just take the elevator," Furier said.

"No, it would have no power. We could take the stairs," Fabris offered.

"The stairs would be a long walk through a lot of potentially unstable space. If a level were to collapse we may not be able to exit," Commander Furier pointed out.

"We could fly the shuttle directly up to the level we want to access and break in from the shuttle as it hovers. Maybe, if we are lucky, we find a damaged area where there is already a hole in the superstructure for us to enter," Situlas said. Situlas was the only other female on the mission with Furier. She was the loadmaster for the *Impegi*, her job had been to make sure weight was distributed evenly throughout the ship. She had worked with Furier, as she was Quartermaster, and they knew each other well.

Furier nodded her head in agreement, "But how do we break in? We have no cutting tools and the shuttle has no offensive weapons."

"True, but we have two laser rifles. We could use them to burn a hole in a weak spot on the hull, maybe near a portal."

"How long would it take to burn a hole through the hull of the ship?"

"Under normal circumstances, probably an hour. However, we may be able to find a weakened spot, maybe one that is already breached. We won't know until we take a closer look."

"Everybody, back in the shuttle. We are going to breach the hull and recover supplies for the survivors," Commander Furier said.

The short shuttle ride to the tower was surreal. No one said a word, as they flew over the debris field that was once a magnificent spaceship. Most of the crew just stared out the portals taking in the destruction.

"Here we are. Looks like we are near what was level 10 of the tower," the Commander said. The shuttle was hovering about five feet from the wall of the tower.

"Let's fly around the whole tower, see if there is an opening or weak spot. We may not have an hour to burn an entrance with the laser rifles."

The Commander maneuvered the shuttle away from the wall and around to the other side of the tower. There, they could see the command center blast doors were closed, as they should have been. However, several decks below that had sustained severe damage and the hull walls had been ripped away from the superstructure.

"Look, there's an opening," yelled Genu, as he pointed to the gash in the tower that was about the size of a residential home.

"Commander, if you can level off the shuttle, we can lower the rear ramp and step off into the tower," Situlas said excitedly.

"Roger that," Furier said as she brought the shuttle around and backed it up to the gaping hole in the side of the ship.

"Little bit closer," Fabris said, as he pulled the manual lever to lower the rear ramp. The ramp slid down, leaving the back of the shuttle open to the elements. The cold wind rushed into the shuttle, not that they could feel it through their armor.

Fabris, standing on the edge of the ramp, looked down to the barren tundra below. "Must be at least a 150-foot drop, be careful."

"I wish we had some safety harnesses," Genu said as he gripped a handle bar by the ramp. "Look there, we can see straight into the galley."

"Commander, we need to get a little bit closer. We are about seven feet from the tower wall. It's not safe to jump yet," Fabris said into his COM.

Commander Furier slowly edged the shuttle closer to the wall. "I can't get any closer, and we got too much wind. It could blow us into the wall."

"This should do it, four feet and we can jump," Genu said.

"Jumping from a small shuttle onto a large stationary deck is one thing. Jumping back onto this moving shuttle from that deck will be something else entirely," Fabris said, as he eyed the jump with suspicion.

"Commander, I'm jumping now. Hold her steady!" Genu yelled as he ran through the empty cargo bay to gain momentum for his jump.

Genu leapt from the shuttle and landed squarely in the galley, dropped to one knee, then rolled. The roll was not just from the momentum of the jump; the deck was no longer level, but had settled into an angle. Walking on the decks of the *Impegi* would be like walking up or down a steep hill.

Genu stood to his feet and held up both of his hands in the universal victory sign. The galley looked like a cyclone had run through it. All the furniture, plates, equipment and chairs had slid down to the lower side. The downward slope at which the ship had settled was not so steep that Genu could not stand on it; it just made walking more difficult.

Fabris jumped next and landed with equal grace, "Made it!" Catrix and Situlas both jumped from the shuttle.

From the ramp, Lignos said, "I'm next."

"No, Lignos; no one else is going."

"They may need my help."

"They will definitely need your help when they are jumping back onto this shuttle, as it is bobbing up and down in the wind. The rest of you stand by the ramp and receive the supplies they bring to us."

"Boarding party, we need food, clothing, blankets, medicine, and weapons. Retrieve them if you can, and bring them back to the shuttle."

"Roger that, Commander."

Over the next 20 minutes, the team recovered boxes of food, clothing, blankets and medicine. The team on the ship tossed the boxes and containers to the crew on the shuttle.

"I don't see any weapons," Commander Furier said over the COM.

"There is a collapsed bulkhead three decks down that is blocking the armory," Fabris said.

"That reminds me, in the cargo hold we had some light armor and short-range attack craft. I wonder if any of that survived?" Commander Furier remarked.

"Hell, given that we are thousands of miles from friendlies, and I'm sure the locals are on their way, I'd love to find out," Fabris said.

"And so, we will," Commander Furier said. "So, we will."

CHAPTER THIRTY-ONE

Over the Pacific Ocean

Lightning Squad was seated in chairs along the interior walls of the craft, facing each other. The compartment where they sat did not appear to be triangular like the exterior of the craft.

Williams timidly sat in the sidewall seat next to the mountain of a man, known only as Bob. Bob was not wearing the hardened armor of a FALOS suit, but unlike the fixed-wing jet exercise, he was wearing a light-weight fabric armor and cold weather gear. Bob's helmet that shielded his eyes displayed the same HUD and COM system as the rest of the squad. Next to Williams, Bob still looked like a giant.

"Hello," Williams said to Bob. Bob turned to face Williams to acknowledge the greeting, but only grunted. Bob had what appeared to be a permanent scowl on his hard, weathered face.

Williams pressed further, "So, you are going to be working with us on this mission?"

Bob grunted again in recognition of the question and then tilted his head forward, his attempt at a nod.

Williams, determined to figure out the huge man, asked, "I see you are not wearing armor, why is that?"

"No need armor." Bob's deep voice and enunciation made each word sound like a sentence unto itself.

"Good evening, men," a voice filled each of their HUD units. Then a live video feed flickered on the HUD in each of their helmets. It was a man they had never seen before.

"My name is General Byrd; I serve in the Air Force's Space Command division. Your squad has been selected to execute a critical mission. Mission failure could upset the balance of global power for centuries. A few minutes ago, an interstellar space craft crashed in Far East Russia. This ship contained a rare and valuable element, known as Element 115. Element 115 is used in making ultra-lite, super strong anti-gravity fighter craft. The country that possesses this shipment will control the skies for the next 100 years."

"This is Major Morgan Slade. Why was my squad picked for such a critical mission? We have not completed training. How do you know what was on a crashed interstellar space ship?"

"Excellent questions, Major Slade. You were not our first choice. Honestly, you were not our second choice, either. Unfortunately, due the extremely short window of opportunity to recover the cargo, your team was the one that could be scrambled the fastest. To answer your second question, we were expecting the shipment; it was coming from one of our off-world trading partners."

"Off world trading partners, what the fuck?" Davis whispered. Of course, everyone could hear him. "Sorry," he mumbled.

"You are in a TR3C anti-gravity plane. It was designed as part of the Aurora program. It will have you over the target area of Far East Russia in about 30 minutes. The nuclear-powered plane is incredibly fast and virtually undetectable by enemy radar. You will be on the ground before the Russians know you are there, hopefully, before their troops arrive on the scene. The mission, while it may be difficult to execute, is simple in plan: recover the Element 115 before the Russians realize it exists," General Byrd explained.

"Secrecy is important on this mission. We cannot offer you support without starting World War Three. Your priority is to make certain the Russians do not discover your location. If you are discovered, then it will only be hours before you are overrun by their military. There is over 100,000 pounds of Element 115 on the crashed ship. You must locate and recover it before the Russians arrive. Engaging the Russians would be an act of last resort. If you are captured, we will deny affiliation."

"What about the FALOS armor? If caught, won't they be able to identify us by those?" Snap asked.

"We are not the only ones on the planet with that technology. It would be a stretch, but we would sell it."

"Roger that, but how do we transport 100,000 pounds of Element 115 out of Russia undetected?" Snap asked.

"Another good question, Major," the General said. "In a few minutes, a massive anti-gravity cargo plane, the NATT, will take off and head toward Far East Russia. That plane, while considerably slower than the one you are in, can carry thousands of tons of cargo. It has the most advanced stealth capabilities in the world and is nearly invisible to both electronic surveillance and the naked eye."

"While that craft is traveling to your position, you will locate and remove the cargo from the wreckage. The NATT is capable of hovering and vertical takeoff; it will land near the crash site and you will load it up," Byrd said.

"It seems like a simple plan, but what about the Russians? A large space ship crashed in their territory, won't they be looking for it?"

"We anticipate that you will arrive minutes before they dispatch their jets for recon. We were expecting this space ship, they were not. They don't know it is a space ship, much less that it holds valuable cargo. They will be sending high altitude jets to scan the area, not knowing for what to look. Eventually, they will send helicopters and paratroopers, but hopefully you will have removed the cargo by then," Byrd said.

"General, why paratroopers?" Snap asked.

"You are being dropped in Far East Russia, in January. It is minus 47 degrees outside. All roads to the Magadan district are virtually unpassable. The only way in or out is by plane or helicopter," Byrd said.

"Roger that, General. If we land minutes before the Russian jets do a flyover, how will they not see a crashed spaceship?" Snap asked, knowing that his FALOS armor would shield his heat signature from the enemy aircraft.

"That brings me to my next point, Major. We have a new piece of technology that is critical to this mission. We have a *Projected Invisibility Dome*, or PID. This device, about the size of a small truck, is capable of projecting a holographic image over a space the size of three football fields. It combines phased array optics with computational holography to project a three-dimensional image that will camouflage the ship from any direction, including the sky. It can project an image of anything we like, a building, forest, car lot, mall, bowling alley, anything. In this case, the PID will project an image of the surrounding terrain over the crashed ship. The device also acts to hide heat and radiation signatures. You will have to get that PID up within minutes of hitting the ground."

"None of my men have been trained to use a PID. It is unlikely we can calibrate it with only minutes before the Russian jets arrive," Snap complained.

"We have the scientist that developed it on site, he will walk you through each step via your HUD. If Russian ground troops arrive before you remove the cargo, you will need to take them out using the squad's EMP rifle. You can't risk them letting Russian Command know your location."

Snap was puzzled by this. "Why would the Russians not know the location of the crash site?"

Radio silence.

"Um. They have several sites to check out. They will not know which site you are at until a recon unit reports back that they spotted the crashed ship."

"Why are there multiple sites?"

Radio silence.

"That's classified," General Byrd answered.

Schematics of the *Impegi* and information about the Nordic survivors were downloaded into the squad's HUD units. The briefing was completed and Admiral Byrd closed the communication link.

"Holy shit. We are invading Russia!" Williams said.

"I'm not worried about it; I can fuck up any Russian with my 100-kilowatt DE rifle," Johnson said.

"These DE rifles can take out a tank or chopper, no problem," Williams said. "Only good commie is a dead commie. Ha," Smith said.

"Guys, remember what Ater and the General said. We're not the only ones with these weapons and tech. Not to mention how the Large Grays have beat us in simulations. And, don't forget about Bob. He's an even match against one of us. It is very likely that we will not be up against simple Russian soldiers. We need to keep our eyes open and be prepared for the worst," Neal said.

"You really think they would put us up against an army of Grays or a battalion of Bobs on our first mission?" Davis asked.

"This mission was not meant for us. Don't forget that," Snap said. "We are here because first string was not available."

"Sounds like second and third strings were unavailable too," Neal mumbled.

"Major Slade, I did not know there were any five-star General's in the Air Force?" Williams asked. All of Lightning Squad had noticed the five stars on the General's lapel.

"Neither did I, neither did I," Snap replied, shaking his head. "Normally, five-star generals are only seen during war time."

"Ten minutes to drop zone." The unseen pilot's voice was heard in the HUD units.

Snap stood to rally his unit. "Men, a few minutes ago we were in the DFAC. Now, we are about to leap from a plane over enemy territory to recover a priceless cargo from another world. You all heard the General; the stakes could not be higher. Failure could shift the balance of power for a century. The only thing standing against Russia achieving the resources to rule the world is this squad. Everyone, put on your FIGAS units; it's time to earn those paychecks."

Lightning Squad stood in the center of the compartment in front of their FIGAS jet wings that were hanging from the ceiling. The FIGAS jet wing easily snapped into place over the fusion reactor built into the back of their suits. Once snapped into place, the FIGAS system was powered by the fusion reactor. The FIGAS strapped on with a harness, like a back pack, and had a quick release lever that would allow the operator to quickly disconnect, if necessary. It also had a built in manual parachute for emergencies.

"Why do we have to fly down in this winged contraption?" Williams asked. "Couldn't the pilot just land and let us off? This is an antigravity craft, right?"

"The craft has the ability to land vertically, but the longer an American plane stays in Russian airspace, the more likely it will be discovered. After the TR3C drops us off, it will immediately leave Russian airspace to avoid detection, probably through the *Russian Air Defense Gap* over the Artic," Snap said.

The craft slowed. The ramp opened, revealing a semi-dark, sunless sky. The lights in the craft dimmed to red as a countdown clock started in each of their HUD units.

Snap placed each arm through a metallic harness that fit snugly into his battle armor. He heard the clicking sound, like a seat

belt, as the FIGAS wing became one with the FALOS suit. The
HUD is his helmet lit up and began displaying automatic diagnostic checks. He noticed the countdown clock in the right hand of
the display.

"Davis, Williams, push the equipment rover off the ramp,"
Snap ordered. The two men pushed the truck-sized mobile unit
off the ramp and into the purplish sky. The mobile rover unit had
a self-guiding parachute with coordinates pre-programmed. Upon
making landfall, it would automatically begin traveling toward the
squad, guided by a tracking system that locked onto their location.

As the rover plummeted toward the ground, the squad made
their final systems checks. Bob, the quiet giant, leapt from the craft
with his special fabric armor and uniquely designed jet-wing. Neal
jumped next. Half the men had jumped before it was Snap's turn.
Snap walked to the edge of the ramp; he could feel the wind whipping around him despite his heavy armor. All systems showed green
in his HUD, he bent his knees and pushed himself away from the
craft. For a moment, he was weightless, falling through space.

The jets on the tips of his eight-foot wingspan automatically engaged, keeping him level, face down toward the Earth. Snap had
full mobility of his arms, his laser rifle held in his right hand. The
location of the landing zone was programmed into the FALOS
suit. Unless an enemy presented himself, Snap would only take
control of the flight system moments before landing.

"Engage optical stealth mode," Snap said into the COM system.
The hardened surfaces of Snap's FALOS suit and jet wing were covered in light emitting tiles that would reflect his surroundings, in
this case, an overcast sky. The rest of the squad followed suit.

Snap was at such a great altitude that he could easily make
out the curvature of the earth and the mountains in the distance.
Snap's HUD showed the outside temperature was negative 47 degrees, but it was a comfortable 72 degrees in his FALOS suit. At
this height, there was not enough oxygen. Snap's battle armor

had a breathing apparatus that not only allowed for high altitude breathing, but also protected against most biological and chemical weapons.

The Russians had recently deployed numerous advanced SA-400 missile launchers to Siberia. Initial reports suggested that they were capable of tracking and destroying hypersonic craft, such as the TR3C, but so far there was no indication that they had been detected. On his HUD, he noticed that the TR3C that they had just jumped from had veered off toward the *Russian Air Defense Gap*. Snap believed that the FIGAS wings were too small to be detected by most Russian radar systems.

As Snap's FIGAS unit brought him closer to the surface, he could see the barren landscape of Russia's Siberian region. The ground was covered in an untouched snow. Even though Snap could see for miles in every direction, there were no signs of human habitation: no houses, factories, towns, or automobiles. Nothing but snow, rocks, and lonely land filled his view. To his left, away from the mountain range, he saw the crater with a thin line of smoke drifting up into the semi-luminous sky.

"What are those mushroom cloud looking things on the horizon?" Williams asked.

"Which direction?" Davis asked.

"All directions," Neal said. "There are large pillars of dark clouds rising from the ground in the distance – in every direction."

"West, they appear to be a couple of hundred miles away from our landing zone," Snap said.

"There is more going on here than they told us about," Neal said, with concern in his voice.

"No shit, Neal. I think we are seeing compartmentalization at its finest," Snap replied sarcastically.

"Does anyone see the equipment rover?" Snap asked.

"It's tracking about a half mile East of the target zone," Williams said.

General Byrd's voice came across the COM, "Russia just dispatched six Mig-31s from Kamchatka, about 1,100 miles away. They are over an hour out, but you need to get that portable invisibility dome up in a hurry."

"Won't they need to refuel?" Snap asked.

"Affirmative, the target location is on the outside of their range, they will be able to refuel at the Magadan airport. They will fly over your location with full tanks."

CHAPTER THIRTY-TWO

Moscow, Russia

Nox and his trusted officers had rushed out of the lobby of the brand-new conference center and back to their black SUVs. The trip back to Nox's bunker was quick as the SUVs sped across the base at over 90 miles an hour. Standing in the command center at Nox's underground base, the men stood around a large monitor that displayed a tactical map of Far East Russia and the Arctic Circle. Nox was happy that the humans had developed to the point where they had flat screen display technology; he hated the old paper maps of WWII.

"What is our situation?" Nox asked.

"Up on the screen we have a map of Far East Russia, which includes the Kamchatka Peninsula. There are six red dots in the north-east section of the Magadan Oblast, where we believe the explosions occurred."

"We don't know where the explosions were?" Nox asked, placing an emphasis on 'know.'

"No sir, we have no visual confirmation, other than our satellite images."

"No reports from local inhabitants?" Nox asked.

"No, it is a very remote part of Russia; there is less than one person for every 10 square miles of land in this region."

"Have we deployed jets to do a fly over?"

"They are being readied as we speak."

"How long until they are over the site?"

"Could be two hours."

"Two hours! Why so long?"

"The impacts occurred near the arctic circle. We have very few military assets in that region. The closest military airfield is in Kamchatka. Our fighters will have to refuel in Magadan before continuing to the crash sites."

"I don't think this is an asteroid. I want reports immediately as we get them. I want Special Forces on Mil-35s heading to the sites immediately. Don't wait until the jets report back," Nox said.

"Dispatch one helicopter to each site. Divert as necessary depending on the reports from the fighters. How long will it take for the helicopters to arrive?" Nox asked.

"Several hours. Again, we have very few assets in the region."

"Can we dispatch ground forces?"

"No. The roads are impassable this time of year." The General shook his head and looked at the floor.

"So, we can build a supersonic plane capable of Mach 3 speed, but we can't build a road?" Nox asked sarcastically.

"This district is very poor with a very small population. The weather conditions make it a very undesirable place to live. The population has been shrinking for two decades now. It's hard to justify road construction expenses for so few people."

"How many dead?" Nox asked.

"Almost none." The General was happy to finally have a good answer to one of Nox's questions.

"Really? Six mega impacts, spread over hundreds of miles and no deaths? How is that possible? Pull up the map again, and overlay it with the latest population map."

"Well, very few deaths, compared to the explosions." General Popov said as he pulled up the population map. The population map placed little red dots where people were known to have lived.

"Overlay the suspected blast radius based on current information."

The Russians stared at the map in disbelief.

"It could not have been better. There is no better way to place five nuclear explosions that would have killed less people. What are the odds that a naturally occurring phenomenon would impact six times, each time, killing the least possible amount of people?" Nox asked.

"Not only that, General Bellator, look at the distances between the explosions. Each impact is two to three hundred miles apart, almost in a cluster. If it were natural, some of the impacts would be close to one another," General Popov said.

Nox stood back and stared at the map. "This is intentional. Its purpose was not to cripple our military or harm our people. It was not for shock and awe because almost no one saw it."

Nox sat down in his custom-made, over-sized, black, executive roller chair. "No, the person who did this was trying to hide something."

"What do you suppose that is, General Bellator?"

"I don't know. The question is: was their intent to divert our attention, or destroy the object?"

"Seems to me, they wanted to divert out attention," Popov said.

"Why is that?" Nox asked.

"You don't need six nuclear explosions to destroy something."

Nox stood up, slammed his fist on the table. "I want all of our assets in the region moved to the Port of Magadan. Send the Pacific carrier group to Magadan. Dispatch a squadron of Mig-31s to Magadan airport. Start moving ground forces toward the impact sites. I don't care if they have to hike in; make it happen. Whatever is going on in Magadan, we are going to be ready for it."

"Yes Sir." Popov quickly left the room to start preparing the operation.

"I want my antigravity fighter prepared for take-off, I'm going to lead this operation from Magadan. I feel that I need to be close to this one. Something important is happening, and I need to know what it is."

CHAPTER THIRTY-THREE

Hill Air Force Base, UTAH

It had been over six months since Mike Evans had last seen Calidus Delusor in Virginia. Mike had returned to his monotonous life at Hill Air Force Base in Utah. He had not seen Nikita since she survived him shooting her in the face on Calidus' orders. After Calidus flew off in his space craft, Nikita and Mike had suffered through the awkward two-hour drive back to the Virginia Beach ocean front.

The drive back was awkward, but not silent. Nikita was furious at both Mike and Calidus. She was mad at Calidus for not giving her a heads up on the fact he was going to have Mike shoot her as a loyalty test. She was furious and disappointed that Mike had shot her. The shot would have been fatal had Calidus not exchanged the lead bullet for a cotton ball. She explained to Mike that the compact cotton ball, while not as hard a bullet, was still very painful.

Mike listened to her all the way back to Virginia Beach, holding his aching balls most of the way. It was clear that she really liked him, maybe even loved him, prior to the shooting. He tried to explain that he did not believe the gun was loaded with real bullets and that he believed it was just to test his loyalty. He further explained that he felt he had no choice, that Calidus would have killed them both, had he failed to comply. Mike explained that they had a chance of survival if he shot her, but no chance of survival in a fight against an armed, Large Gray alien. Mike could not convince her.

The night ended with a civil exchange of pleasantries in the hotel parking lot, more like colleagues leaving work than lovers parting ways. That was the last time he saw her. He had her phone number memorized, but he never attempted to call her for fear of being caught by his American 'hosts.'

Now, months later, he still dreamed about her at night. On the base, he had no female companionship. Several weeks after getting back to Hill AFB, he tried to contact Calidus using the hairy, biological implant in his arm. Calidus had explained that the Large Gray's telepathic abilities were limited to a 50-mile radius, but that the implant would allow communication over great distances. It worked, but it took several attempts over a three-hour period before Calidus responded. Mike was not sure if that was a problem with the transmitter, receiver, or just bad reception.

On the two-hour drive from Williamsburg to the Virginia Beach oceanfront, between Nikita's emotional outbreaks, Mike learned a few valuable things. The most important thing he learned was that there was a huge underground base in Antarctica. This base was the size of a small country, with thousands of humans and Large Grays working side-by-side to build a new civilization. Nikita said it was technologically advanced beyond anything he could imagine, which was saying something, because he could imagine a lot.

Mike Evans, as the humans called him, lay in his bed staring at the ceiling, dreading the next few minutes, when he would have to get up, shower and pretend to love his job. The last time he used the hairy transmitter, Calidus had informed him that there was a decent sized group of Nordics that, like him, were tired of waiting on the Americans. Calidus made it sound like they were planning something big. Mike had been contacted by the leader of the Vitahician underground movement, via coded messages, but he had never met any of them.

Mike was painfully self-aware of his situation. He knew he should not feel this way about Nikita, she should not be plaguing his mind. He wondered if he really loved her, something most Vitahicians back home did not often experience; or, was the dissatisfaction with his life in general, causing him to cling to her. Back on his home world, he believed he would have had a much more fulfilling life, with familiar social structures in place. Here, on Earth, he rarely saw the sun, or engaged I personally fulfilling activities, leaving him open to reckless, and destructive fantasy.

As Mike lay in his bed, only minutes before he would have to face the day, fantasizing that Nikita was snuggled up next him, he was jolted by a loud knocking on the door to his underground apartment. Mike leapt from his bed; a cold dread sunk to his stomach. No one ever came to his door, especially at this hour.

Shit. Have they found out about me? How could they? I've been careful.

"Just a minute. I'm coming," Mike yelled so that it could be heard through the metal door.

Mike grabbed the first pair of shorts he could find in the darkness and stumbled to the door. Opening the door revealed two young airmen, not the armed escort he had feared. "What can I do for you?" Mike asked, more than a little relieved by the fact they were not carrying machine guns.

"We have been sent to bring you to air command headquarters," the young Sergeant said.

"Can I get dressed?"

"We have orders to bring you in ASAP. Make it quick, no shower."

A few minutes later, they were in a Humvee, racing across the base towards air command headquarters.

"Do you know why they want me so early? I'm a scientist; they never need me at headquarters?" Mike asked.

"Couldn't tell you, Sir. Way above my pay-grade," the young Sergeant said, as he navigated a turn onto another street. "What I can say, is the whole base is on high alert, everyone is running around like World War Three just started."

Mike was rushed into a non-descript building and down a couple of hallways, until he was standing in a crowded room full of officers and scientists. The lead scientist in Mike's team came up to him.

"Mike, I'm glad you could make it," the human scientist said to him. Sabine Weber, had been working at Hill with Mike for over fifteen years.

"I didn't know I had a choice." Mike responded flatly. Mike did not dislike Weber; he was just bored with Weber's non-stop, pro-military political slogans. Mike was surprised at how many seemingly intelligent people could be brainwashed so easily. He assumed they just accepted the party line because their paychecks depended on it.

"Ha, you're funny. This is serious. They want us to make seven C-17 Globe masters invisible."

"Shouldn't be a problem. We make planes invisible all the time. Normally, they are much smaller fighter craft. Why send a ground pounder to my apartment at 6 AM?" Mike asked, still not getting what all the fuss was about.

"You just got up? You want some coffee? How about a donut? They have coffee and donuts over there." The helpful scientist pointed to the other side of the crowded room.

"Thanks. I will get some coffee in a minute. What's going on?"

"Oh, they need the full Houdini on seven C-17s within two hours," the scientist said, stuffing a glazed donut into his mouth.

"What? That's impossible. Why such a rush?"

"Classified. Need to know. All we need to know, is that they want a full Houdini package on all seven, pronto. Best I can tell, they are to be used as support for a mission that has already started. I think this is the backup plan."

"How do you figure?" Mike asked.

"I overheard some of the top brass talking about the NATT taking off this morning. Sounded like they were heading off to Russia to pick up a package." The scientist used his sticky fingers to make quotation signs when he said 'package.'

"They want the full Houdini?" Mike asked. Everyone understood that the full Houdini meant invisible to radar and the naked eye.

"Yep, everything, right now. This is big, Evans, real big." The scientist patted Evans on the back with the glaze covered hand that had held the donut.

General Durant walked up to Mike Evans, as the donut eating scientist went to select his next doughy victim. Mike wished he had made a break for the coffee and donut table.

"Good morning, Mike," The General bellowed, as he grabbed Mike's hand and began to vigorously shake it.

"Morning, General."

This guy must be on his fifth cup of coffee already.

"Have they told you what we are doing this morning?"

"Something about giving seven C-17s the full Houdini."

"That's right. I've always liked you, you know that. How long have we known each other, Mike?" The General, who had spider veins across his cheeks, was a real blow hard to his men, but he was very polite to the scientists.

"About 20 years, Sir."

"Seems like just yesterday they were debriefing me about your people being here on Earth."

"Nope, it was twenty years, three months, and sixteen days ago when we first met. May I ask why we have to get the job done in two hours?" Mike was hoping for something of value to report to Calidus. Maybe he could trade the information for his ticket out of America; maybe he could be with Nakita in Antarctica.

"All I can say, is that this is the biggest thing to happen on Earth in 70 years. We must recover some very valuable cargo from a very sensitive locations. Secrecy is of upmost concern, and our window of opportunity is very small." The General was as gleeful as a kid on Christmas morning.

Mike knew he was not going to get anymore, so he did not bother to ask. "We will need 500 men to get the job done in two hours."

"You will have 200 hundred," the General said, as he walked away.

I've got to contact Calidus. This may be my ticket out of here.

A few minutes later, they were being whisked away to a remote section of the base, where seven C-17s sat on the airport apron. Several busloads of airmen were being transported to the site where the planes were to be upgraded. The men piled out of the busses and waited for orders. Mike and the other scientists gathered at the front of the staging area; materials were being driven from the hangers to the site on flatbed trucks. Military police were setting up a perimeter so that unauthorized personnel would not come near the project.

"What are they going to do with these airmen that are not read into this program?" Mike asked a General standing next him.

"Probably just shoot them." The General laughed. "Just kidding. They have no idea what they are doing, or what the result will be. They won't even know the plane is invisible. They will sign NDAs and be told if they ever speak of what they saw here today, they will be criminally prosecuted."

Mike nodded his head in agreement.

This is how they keep the public from knowing of our existence. A mixture of lies, half-truths, and threats. I should do something about that one day.

The airmen started placing the electrochromic tiles on the huge cargo plane. Each tile was one-foot square, and the plane was 174 feet long and had a 170-foot wing span. The Air Force's second largest conventional cargo plane weighed in at 282,400 pounds. Once all the squares were placed on this plane, an electric charge would run through the tiles, connecting them all. Each tile had an embedded microprocessor that allowed it to work with all the other tiles, forming a super computer on the new skin of the plane. Each tile was only a few centimeters thick and attached to the plane with a super adhesive. Once attached to the plane, the tile was not going to come off.

The electrochromic tiles, working together as one *Exoskin*, would project a three-dimensional image around the craft. The image could be of anything, another plane, the moon, a UFO, a cloud or simply blue sky. Either way, the observer sees what the *Exoskin* is displaying, not the plane itself. In the past, while invading foreign territory, pilots had displayed the image of an enemy fighter. A TR3B may appear to be a MiG-31 while flying over Russia.

Still, it was a huge job; fifty percent of each tile had to be touching the other adjacent tiles for it to receive the charge and connect to the network. If even half of a tile's edges did not touch other tiles, then the device would not activate, and there would be a hole in the invisibility cloak. A few holes, did not matter due to the altitudes and speeds at which a plane travels. But when it landed, a few holes could be all that is needed for the enemy to spot the plane. The airmen worked tirelessly to attach each square tile to the plane in such a manner that all the squares would connect to the other tiles.

As the airmen were getting close to finishing their part of the job, Mike knew his role was about to begin. Mike was part of the team that set up the pilot's controls to operate the *Exoskin* and to make sure all the tiles had come online and were functioning properly. If he did his job right, the plane would disappear right before the eyes of all those on the tarmac.

"Excuse me, I have to go to the bathroom," Mike said to the officers and scientists standing around watching.

"No problem, Mike."

"I'll be back in a minute," Mike said as he started to walk toward one of the hangers.

Mike had walked about 50 yards when he looked around to make sure no one was near him. "Calidus Delusor, are you there?"

"Calidus Delusor?" Mike put his finger to his ear as if Calidus' response would be audible. Of course, the response, if any, would not be heard through Mike's ear. Mike waited a few seconds for a reply.

"Calidus Delusor, can you hear me?" Mike said again, as he hurried to the bathroom in the hangar.

No response.

What should I do? Should I sabotage the mission? Make it so the Globe masters will become visible over Russia?

Mike pushed open the door to the grimy old restroom. The small bathroom had tiny square blue tiles on the walls and a dim, flickering fluorescent light. The restroom was empty; he was alone. Mike knew it could be hours before Calidus responded. He did not have hours; he only had minutes.

Whatever they are doing, I will be out of the loop as soon as those planes take off. For me to remain useful in this situation, I must be on that plane.

Mike formulated his plan and hurried back to the worksite. Mike sprinted up the rear ramp of the C-17, and into the cargo hold area, which was large enough to carry an M-1 Abrams tank or a Chinook helicopter. The floor of the massive cargo hold, capable of carrying 169,000 pounds of military might, could be converted from a smooth surface to a roller system for loading boxes or palettes.

In the cockpit, there were four chairs for pilots and crew; three were occupied by technicians, men and Vitahicians he knew well.

"Hey, where are we at on the project?" Mike asked.

"Five of the planes have all the tiles on them; the other two do not. This is the first plane we have been able to start working on, as far as bringing the tiles online. We have 30 minutes to finish the job, if we are going to stay on schedule."

"Not good. Once this puppy is in the air, with a cruising speed of 515 miles per hour, it will take nearly 9 hours for the C-17s to reach their destination. That's not even accounting for the fact that they will have to refuel midway across the Pacific," Mike said, as he plopped down into the co-pilot's seat and linked his laptop to the C-17's flight controls.

After a few minutes, Bill Wall, the technician sitting in the pilot's seat said, "I think we have it done."

"Good. I'll radio the General and let him know we are ready to activate Houdini," Mike said, as he raised the hand-held walkie-talkie.

"General, this is Mike Evans onboard the first C-17. We are ready to activate Houdini."

"Roger that, Mike. Whenever you are ready."

"Go for it, Bill," Mike said. Bill flipped the newly wired accessory switch on the flight controls.

"Houdini activated," Mike announced on the radio.

"Good job guys, the plane just disappeared. Right here on the tarmac."

"Any holes in the Exoskin?" Mike asked from inside the plane.

"A few small ones on the wings. No big deal. Let's move on to the next plane. We are way behind schedule."

"Roger that," Mike said as he stood from the co-pilot's seat.

A few minutes later, Mike stood with the General, as his team hurried to the next plane.

"Impressive, isn't it?" the General said rhetorically. "Two Hundred and eighty-two thousand pounds of plane can just disappear."

"Technically, Sir, it did not disappear. It is still there; you just can't see it."

"I'm aware of how the technology works, Mike. Can we get the job done on the other six?"

"No way can we finish six in twenty minutes, Sir. But I have a suggestion. My team and I can travel with the planes and finish the programming mid-flight."

"Can that be done?"

"Of course. The tiles will have to be placed on the outside fuselage before takeoff, but the internal setup can be completed in flight. May I ask the nature of the mission and why it so imperative that we leave in, what, eighteen minutes?" Mike asked while looking at his watch.

"Strictly speaking, this is above your clearance, but given the circumstances, I will let you in on the plan. We have already deployed our only NATT, the *Flying City*. If Flying City is successful, then there will be no need for the C-17s. However, if the Flying City fails, then the C-17s must be in the region for backup. To be an effective back up, they need to be on their way now."

"Will they be escorted?"

"They will be flying into enemy territory as it is. We have a Pacific carrier group moving into position now. They will offer limited support, but their main defense is the Houdini. If they are detected over Russian air space, no number of escorts will be able to save them."

"Let me go with them. If they get into a jam, my scientific expertise could be the difference between mission success or failure."

The General stood on the airport apron, his breath visible in the air, contemplating the proposal. "You are too valuable to lose, Mike."

This is my one shot at getting on that plane. This is the mission; this is my opportunity to give something of value to Calidus Delusor. This is my ticket out of here, freedom, and another chance with Nikita.

"Am I more valuable than the cargo you are attempting to acquire in Russia?"

The General pondered that for a moment. "At the risk of sounding unkind, I would have to say no. The cargo to be recovered in Russia is more valuable than any man on the planet, probably more valuable than any 10,000 men."

What could possibly be that valuable?

"Then, there's your answer. You need my team on the planes, not only to keep the mission on schedule, but in case something goes wrong." Mike pulled the hood of his large coat over his head to shield him from the wind.

The General nodded his head. "How many men on your team?"

"Fifteen, Sir."

"You can take three. The rest stay here."

Great. I'm on the plane going to an unknown Russian location, to pick up an unknown cargo. I have no idea how I'm to take possession of the cargo, or how I am going to deliver it to Calidus. If I am caught, I will be executed, and Calidus is not answering his little hairy bug phone. How could anything go wrong?

"How are we going to get the cargo on to the C-17 once in Russia? I'm pretty sure the Russians are not going to let us use one of their airports?"

"No. That's the beautiful part. If plan A does not work, plan B is to fill the shuttle crafts with cargo and fly it up to the C-17s. We are going to load the C-17s mid-flight," the General explained, and then hurried off.

Shuttle craft? What shuttle craft?

CHAPTER THIRTY-FOUR

Richmond, VA

Governor Robert Fisher was standing in his plush office, staring down at the head of a 22-year-old would-be intern as it bobbed back and forth. Her hair was bleach blonde, but not in a slutty way; she had it pulled back in a bun. He grabbed and twisted the hair on the back of her head and pulled her in even closer. He could hear her choking a little, but not too much. Her horn-rimmed glasses smashed up against her face, and he erupted down her throat. Reflexively, she pulled back; he released his grip on the back of her head. She coughed a little and wiped off her mouth, as she awkwardly stood to her feet.

"Nice, Jessica, very nice," the Governor said, as he drew in a deep breath.

"My name is Cathy," she protested, as she straightened the stylish glasses on her nose.

"Sure, it is honey." The Governor pulled up his zipper.

"You're an asshole. Did I get the job?" she asked as she tucked in her blouse.

"Yeah, yeah. You got the internship. Next time, no teeth."

He stared at her firm ass as she hurried out of his office. His cell phone rang. Not many people had his personal cell phone, and they knew not to call unless it was important. The list of people that have his number is short: his wife, kids, chief-of-staff, his poker buddies, a few select Senators, and the President.

"Hello?" Fisher said into his smart phone, as he gazed into the ornate mirror hanging on the wall to straighten his $225.00 solid red power tie.

"This is General Stone Byrd, Space Command. We have a problem. A big problem."

"What is it?" Governor Fisher asked. He had forgotten about MJ-1 of Majestic Twelve. Of course, he had the private number. It had been a long time since MJ-1 had called him. After all, the Governor was MJ-12, the lowest ranking member of the elite group.

"I need you to gather the entire Majestic-12 group in DC within the hour. I will address everyone at once," General Byrd said.

"May I ask the nature of the problem?" Fisher asked.

"Let's just say it's of the apocalyptic variety."

"Shit. I will be right on it. Does the President know? He knows a little, but not everything. I wanted to bring it to the full Majestic Twelve before I read him in," Byrd said.

"Okay, I'm on it."

"Say, you sounded a little out of breath when I called," Byrd asked with a chuckle. "So, you're interviewing interns?"

"How did you know?"

"I will call back in one hour. Have everyone there." The phone went dead.

Robert Fisher was serving the first year of his term as Virginia's Governor. He knew that there were six other MJ-12 members in the Washington, DC area. Four others were spread around the country, and General Byrd was on the Moon Base. He could not have his secretary make the phone calls; he had to call them himself.

He knew they would all attend the meeting, regardless of what they were doing.

Robert Fisher stepped out into the hallway, where is secretary gave him a knowing look. "What can I do for you, Governor?"

"I need you to get the helicopter ready. I need to be in DC ASAP. Also, call Congressman Charles Foster and have him arrange for a secure conference room."

"Yes Sir. I'm right on it."

"Oh, and then take the rest of the day off," Fisher said.

"Sir, you have a little something on your pants." She pointed to her inside thigh, glanced down at his leg, and smiled.

"Thank you, Jessica; you're a life saver," he said as he wiped his pleated pants with a monogrammed handkerchief given to him by his wife.

Jessica moved in close to the Governor and whispered in his ear, "I don't make messes like that." She then hurried off to arrange for the helicopter.

It was a quick helicopter ride from Richmond to the Russel Senate Building in Washington, DC. Charles Foster, a congressman from South Carolina, was waiting in the designated conference room.

"Good afternoon, Congressman. Glad you could make it on such short notice," Fisher said, as he entered the room. Charles Foster, Chairman of the powerful Ways and Means Committee, held the rank of MJ-10, and thus was the Governor's superior.

"I didn't think I had a choice. What is going on? We have never been ordered to a meeting on an hour's notice. Normally our meetings are set months in advance," Charles complained as he took off his dark blue suit jacket. Charles slung the jacket over the back of the leather conference room chair and plopped down.

"I don't know exactly what this is about. MJ-1 said it was apocalyptic."

"That sounds ominous," Congressman Foster replied.

General Donald Barnes entered the room. "What in the Sam hell is this about? I got a war over in Afghanistan to fight; I don't have time to be pussyfooting around with you space cadets." Barnes was wearing the standard Army Combat Uniform with the digital camo pattern.

"Stone Byrd said it was apocalyptic, Sir," Governor Fisher replied. Donald Barnes, a four-star general, was MJ-3, which meant he was senior to both the Governor and Representative.

The next to walk through the door was Fleet Admiral Kevin Butler. The five-star Admiral had the designation MJ-2, the second highest ranking member of Majestic Twelve, second only to General Stone Byrd, who was currently on the Moon Base.

"Gentlemen, to what do I owe the dubious honor of this meeting?" Admiral Butler said as he took a seat next to the boisterous General Barnes.

"General Byrd called us here so that he could break some important news to us at the same time. He will be calling on an encrypted line shortly," Governor Fisher said.

Nolan Sanders, Inspector General for the Department of Treasury walked in next. Sanders was a slight man with wavy salt-and-pepper hair. He had the mannerisms of a bookish accountant, but the temperament of a rattle snake. Sanders was MJ-11, the second lowest ranking member of the Majestic Twelve. He did not say a word, just looked around the room, and took a seat.

Anthony Diaz and Byron Long walked in together. Diaz was the Assistant Deputy Director of Intelligence for the National Security Council. Byron Long was the Deputy Director of the Central Intelligence Agency.

"Gentlemen." Byron sat in the seat closest to the door.

"Afternoon." Diaz sat in the seat next to Byron and crossed his arms.

A few minutes later, the six large video monitors flickered to life. The four other MJ-12 members were displayed on the screens, all four sitting behind their desks.

"Good afternoon, glad to have you with us," Fisher said from the middle of the table, because the General had taken his seat as some sort of power play, or just to be an asshole.

Lisa Russell, an Astronomer at the National Advanced Optics Astronomy Observatories at Kitt Peak said, "Good afternoon. Sorry I could not be there in person."

Brent Ross, Quantum Physicist at the Jefferson National Accelerator Facility in Newport News, Virginia, said, "Hello everyone. This is really short notice; anyone have any idea what this is about?"

They all shook their heads and replied in the negative. The fifth screen came to life, and General Stone Byrd appeared before the group, everyone stared at the monitor.

"Can everyone hear me?" Byrd asked.

"Yes Sir," Governor Fisher said. The scientists on the other monitors all replied in the affirmative.

"I'm sorry about the short notice, but I have grave news to report. Less than two hours ago, the *Impegi* crashed into a remote region of Far East Russia, near the Arctic Circle. As you know, the *Impegi* was the ship bringing us over 100,000 pounds of Element 115. This shipment was of incredible value, not only because Element 115 is so difficult for us to create here on Earth, but because we were going to use it to greatly increase our 7th generation antigravity, stealth fighter fleet." Byrd took a moment to drink from a bottle of water.

"Why is it so important that we build more 7th generation fighters?" Lisa Russell asked quietly. Lisa, thirty-five years old, was the newest member of Majestic Twelve. Even though she was the youngest, her scientific background afforded her a higher MJ ranking than some of the older members.

Byrd responded, "For Ms. Russell's benefit, since she is the newest member, we will briefly, discuss the underlying problem. Ten years ago, intelligence reports seemed to indicate that an advanced race was planning a full-scale invasion of Earth. Our information, though not independently confirmed, suggests that the invading force will consist of around 300 mother ships, each capable of transporting 400 fighter craft. We estimate, that based on their technology, they will have a thirty-to-one kill ratio, against our conventional fifth generation fighters. Our anti-gravity fighters will fare better, but will be wiped out in the face of overwhelming numbers. We need to build 100,000 7th generation fighters, or AG Fighters, to even be competitive."

"How many do we have now?" Lisa asked.

"Seventy-four."

"What? How many can we build per year?" Lisa asked, clearly shocked by this revelation.

"At this time, we can produce about 30 per year. However, this shipment of Element 115 would allow us to increase production to at least 1,500 per year."

"That's still not close to enough. How much time do we have until they arrive?" Lisa asked.

"We don't know exactly. We have not been able to independently confirm the invasion force even exists. However, the intelligence we have been able to gather suggests that they will arrive in about nine years."

"Okay, I'm just processing this out loud. We can produce 1,500 advanced fighters per year, and we may have nine years to prepare. That's 13,500 fighters against their 120,000 fighters, not to mention their mother ships."

"We can only produce the 1,500 fighters if we recover the cargo from Russia. If not, we can only produce 30 fighters per year. Our scientists are working around the clock to discover ways to advance production. Hopefully we will have a break through before it is too late," Byrd said.

"This is a global problem, is it not? I mean, we all get wiped out if the alien force wins? Why not take this information to the Russians and ask to work together?" Lisa asked.

Everyone grew silent and glanced back and forth at each other.

Byrd said, "You are too young to remember this, and have not been around long enough to have heard about it. But, the last time a person suggested we divulge information to the Russians regarding aliens, a U.S. President was assassinated."

"You mean Kennedy? That was over aliens?" Lisa sounded shocked.

"Well, disclosing the information that we have about aliens to the Russians, to be precise," said General Donald Barnes, as he dug a pen into a yellow pad.

"Don't you think things have changed over the last 50 years? Especially since we are now facing global extinction?"

Byrd interrupted, "That brings me to my next point. As the *Impegi* was crashing, I launched six nuclear missiles at Russia in an effort to distract them from the crashed ship."

"Holy shit, you did what?" That outburst was by Fleet Admiral Kevin Butler, MJ-2, the only person that would dare challenge MJ-1 in such a manner. "You could have moved up our extinction event by nine years!"

"I used our new TEPNOS missiles. They are invisible until impact, and they came from space. They were not launched from one of our silos," Byrd said calmly. "I had to make a quick decision, and it is done."

"God dammit; I always wanted to nuke Russia. When it comes time for the job, the space cadets get the honors! It just does not pay to be in the Army." General Barnes slammed his fist on the table. "Next time Russia gets nuked, I got dibs on the trigger."

"No one is nuking Russia anymore," the Fleet Admiral said. "What next?"

"I sent an elite team into Russia to recover the Element 115. They should be on the ground any minute," Byrd said.

"Dammit, once again, I'm out of the loop. My special forces can run circles around your space cadets," General Barnes said.

"So, let me get this straight. You nuked, and then invaded Russia, without consulting us or the President?" Lisa said in disbelief.

"In a word, yes. But, we are an hour into the mission, and Russia has not blamed anyone. I used low-yield nukes and hit low population areas. Russia is moving assets into the area to investigate, but our men should be able to get in and out before the Russians are fully aware of the true situation."

Lisa said, "How many assets are the Russians moving to the crash site?"

"It looks like all of them."

"How many is that?"

"Best we can tell, couple hundred fighters, two carrier groups, three armored divisions, artillery and ground troops. But they are moving very slowly. The roads are impassable due to the weather," Byrd said.

"They will have air superiority soon," the Fleet Admiral said. "We have a very short window of time."

"I agree," Byrd said. "But, that is not why you are here. Part of the reason I brought you here is to inform you of what happened. The main reason you are here today is to help decide what to do next."

"What's that?" Barnes asked.

"Well, there's trillions of dollars' worth of cargo sitting in Russia. That cargo, aside from its immense value, is the only way we will be able to defend ourselves in the suspected alien invasion. What are we willing to do to protect it?" Byrd paused for effect. "WWII was fought over far less."

Barnes said, "You are asking us for a full-scale invasion into Russia? The consequences would be nothing less than World War Three, maybe a nuclear holocaust. The dead would be measured in the billions. It would make WWII look like a walk in the park. But, if you are asking me if we would win? Then, yes, we would. Even if China stepped up, it would be tough; we would take millions of casualties at home, but we would win." Barnes had a certain glee in his eye, like a kid on Christmas Eve.

Lisa, the newest member, clinching her fists, said, "I can't believe I am hearing this. You guys are seriously discussing going to war with a nuclear super power over an element used to build air planes. Who cares if we get the element, if half the world is uninhabitable for a thousand years because we started a nuclear war?"

"The mission must be clandestine. We need a backup plan to our backup plan. We need all our assets in the area operational and prepared for action. How do we air lift the cargo out of there?"

"Our latest Aurora project, call name *Flying City*, is a massive cargo craft capable of transporting 750,000 pounds of cargo. Officially, the plane is designated a *Nuclear Powered Antigravity Tactical Transport*, or NATT for short. It was designed for delivering heavy cargo directly to the battlefield undetected. Think of the TR-3B, only much larger. It is enrooted to the target destination to retrieve the men and cargo." Byrd explained.

"Ha. That's not impressive. The Russians had a cargo plane that could carry almost 600,000 pounds of cargo over 20 years ago," Donald Barnes said.

"It is impressive. Trust me, this is no An-225 Mriya. While that was impressive for its day, the Flying City carries 200,000 pounds more cargo and has stealth features, including invisibility. But that's not the special part, this plane uses our latest antigravity technology and flies at Mach Two."

"Wow. Now that is impressive. You have a plane that can carry over a half million pounds of cargo at 1,500 miles per hour? All while being invisible?"

"That's right. The antigravity technology means we don't have to fight gravity for takeoff or while in flight. All power is directed toward directional thrust. If you think that is impressive, we are damn near having an electromagnetic pulse drive that when combined with the antigravity technology, will more than double our speed capabilities."

Donald Barnes stood up and straightened out his ACU, adjusted his belt, and said, "Gentlemen, this is a good plan, but those Russians are sneaky bastards. This plane may be the answer, but we need a backup plan. We need to have other planes and assets available in the region in case something goes wrong and our boys need back up."

The group stayed for a few minutes later discussing the plan, then dispersed.

The Governor's personal cell phone rang again as he walked out of the conference room. He looked down at the number; it was one he recognized.

He swiped the glowing screen and put it to his ear. "Hello Mr. President; this is Governor Robert Fisher."

"Robert, I have something really important to discuss with you. Do you have a minute?"

"Yes, Sir. I was just sitting here going over some paperwork; I could use the distraction," Robert lied.

"So, you know, Virginia will have an open Senate seat coming up in a couple of years."

"Yes, looks like Chuck is looking to retire soon. I heard the party chairman was considering a run?" the Governor replied.

"Yes, but some of us think there is just too much controversy surrounding the chairman. We need a good, middle of the road, populist. Somebody like you, Robert. We have to watch out for our friends in the progressive wing of the party; they seem to be gaining momentum."

"Thank you, Mr. President. It seems a bit early to start a campaign, but, I would be happy to serve in whatever capacity I can."

"It's never too early to start laying the ground work. So, it would be okay for me to float your name as a possible candidate?"

"It would be my honor, Mr. President."

"Excellent. Let me make a few phone calls. I'll get back to you in a week or so." The call ended.

CHAPTER THIRTY-FIVE

Magadan Oblast

Gliding over the crash site at 125 miles per hour, Snap was in awe at the sight of the massive debris field. The sunless sky reflected enough light to clearly make out large sections of the once great interstellar ship. The ship had broken into three large sections, and all were lying in a long, deep trench that had been dug out as the ship crashed into the ground.

"West, I'm surprised that the ship is this much intact," Snap said into his COM system.

"Yeah, it's like a fifty-story building toppled over. If it' superstructure had collapsed anymore, I'm not sure we would able to locate the cargo."

"Looks like the bottom five to ten levels have been completely collapsed under the weight of the ship."

"Major, let's hope the cargo is not in one of those levels. It will would take weeks with heavy equipment to access those decks."

"What's wrong? Don't think the Russians will let us bring in a couple dozen heavy cranes?" Snap asked, with a chuckle.

"Lightning Squad, commence with landing procedures. Let's put down fifty yards north of the largest segment of the ship, near the middle of the crash zone."

"Roger Wilco," Senior Master Sergeant Williams replied.

"Johnson, do you have control of the landing rover?" Neal asked.

"Yes Sir."

"How far away is it?"

"Still descending, about 500 yards to the southwest."

"Can you get it any closer? Time is of the essence, here."

"Roger that," Johnson replied.

Snap guided his FIGAS over the crash site again, this time looking for easy access points to the large ship. Snap was also looking for defensible positions in case the Russians arrived. The barren land was covered in icy snow. There were plenty of boulders and rock formations to hide behind, but that would offer no protection against a missile launched from a MiG-31.

"Bob, this is Snap. Could you take the EMP cannon and set up on the south west ridge? Taylor, you go with Bob. If it appears a Russian aircraft spots us through the optical stealth, try and take it out with the EMP cannon. Don't shoot down a plane unless you suspect they have seen through our invisibility dome."

"Roger that," Taylor responded, as he steered his FIGAS unit toward the ridgeline.

Bob followed Taylor to the ridge overlooking the crash site, while the rest of the team landed near the center of the site. No one was injured in the landing and the men easily dismounted from the FIGAS units. As soon as Snap landed and freed himself from the fixed wing, he looked up at the sky to locate the rover that was slowly descending by parachute.

"Johnson, can you get that rover to land inside the trench? We don't have time to carry it down here if it lands on the ridge."

"Roger that," Johnson said. Johnson was operating the flight controls to the parachute from the display on his left forearm. "There, that should do it, we cleared the ridge."

The rover, the size of a small truck, could travel along a flat surface at 35 miles per hour. Rather than having tires, it had tank treads. The primary purpose of the rover was to transport the 2,150-pound *Projected Invisibility Dome*, but it was also carrying other equipment to assist in the recovery.

Snap, standing next to Johnson, said, "There it is," as he pointed to the rover as it slammed into the earth. "Moore, Martin, go recover the rover."

"I think I can guide it in from the controls on my display," Johnson said, as he tapped the screen on his forearm.

"Johnson, no, let them go help recover it. It may be caught on a rock or something. They can help guide it in. We may not have time for any mistakes."

"Major Slade, I just received the data download with instructions on how to set up the PID, I'm pretty sure I can handle this," Jackson said.

"I just received an update; Russian fighters are 30 minutes out. We have to get this set up, now."

Senior Master Sergeant Josh Miller ran up to Snap, holding a compact, laser range finder in his left hand. "We have a problem."

"What's that?"

"Well, the ship was originally 1,700 feet long and several hundred feet tall."

"So, what's the problem?"

"The debris field is over 3,000 feet long and 400 feet wide."

"And, the punch line?" Snap asked.

"The PID only projects a holographic dome over 900 feet of space."

"What the fuck, how did somebody miss that? General Byrd, are you still listening to this? This is going to be one short mission!" Snap yelled into his HUD.

"I'm still here. Calm down. We will think of something," General Byrd reassured them from the comfort of the Moon Base.

"It better be quick. The Mig is 20 minutes out. They might just see us hanging out in their backyard and drop a bomb on us."

"I have a tech here, and he is advising me that the dome can be reconfigured to be shaped more like a rectangle. This will cover more of the craft. You said the debris filed was 3,000 feet long and 400 feet wide?"

"Basically. There are some outliers, but most of the wreckage fits in those dimensions."

"Okay, our models here are saying that we can recalibrate from a 900-foot dome to a 2,000-foot-long rectangle. That narrows the width to the 400 feet you need."

"But it still leaves 1,000 feet of the wreckage exposed to the sky." Snap said.

"I understand. We are going to have to make some tough decisions here in the next couple of minutes. You flew down from the sky, yes?"

"Of course."

"Which means you saw exactly what the Russian pilot is going to see, correct?"

"Yes"

"Wrong, Major Slade. You knew what you were looking for, and you knew exactly where it was located. The Russian pilot has thousands of miles of land to search over for an unknown object."

"I see your point, General. But still, this is a space ship, it kinda sticks out."

"Okay, but what was the first thing you saw as you descended on the site?"

"The control tower, it sticks up higher than everything else," Snap replied.

"Good, then what?"

"The largest intact section of the super structure, set in the middle of the wreckage."

"Good, what was the last part you noticed?" the General asked.

"The smaller debris fields surrounding the three main pieces," Snap said.

"There you go, set up the PID so that it covers the control tower, the large section of the super structure and anything else you can cover."

"What then?"

"Sit tight and hope the Russian pilot, which is flying at over 900 miles per hour, misses it. Their analysts will see it eventually, but hopefully, it buys you a couple of hours without Russian paratroopers. Good Luck."

"Damn it," Snap whispered.

Snap focused his attention on the men retrieving the rover. "We need to move the rover over there," Snap said, pointing at the largest section of the super structure.

"Position it closer to the tower, and line it up near the center of the trench."

"Jackson, we need to calibrate this thing to cover a 2,000-foot-long rectangular shape."

"That's not going to be enough."

"It's the best we can do," Snap responded.

"Oh shit," Jackson said, shaking his head.

"Lightning Squad, Johnson is going to configure the PID to conceal most of the crash site. We are not going to be able to ghost the whole thing. All we can hope for is that the Russians will miss it on their first pass. The rest of you, grab your equipment from the rover and start looking for the Element 115. Schematics of the ship have been down loaded to your HUD."

"Where are you going to be?" Neal asked.

"I'm going to be out here with Jackson. Bob and Taylor will be monitoring the Russian radio transmissions as they fly over. We may be having some fireworks soon; so, keep your eye out in the debris for anything that might prove helpful."

"Roger that, Major."

The men of Lightning Squad grabbed their equipment and started off to the dangerous mission of sifting through debris, looking for the unstable Element 115. Johnson stood at the rear of the rover, in front of the control panel, tapping on a weather resistant keyboard.

"Bob, any movement up on the ridge?"

"Negative, Major."

"Stay down. We have our first fly over in five minutes."

"Roger that," Bob said.

"Jackson, how are we doing on the PID?"

"Just about done. There we go. Ready to light up the Christmas tree?"

"Hell yeah, let's do a Houdini before this Russian bird flies by," Snap said.

Mark Jackson dramatically smashed down the button on the keyboard, and nothing happened.

"What the fuck was that?" Snap asked.

"I don't know. It should have worked."

"Do I have to remind you that a Russian MiG-31 carries dozens of missiles?" Snap asked, sarcastically.

Jackson was frantically pounding at the key board, but nothing seemed to work. Snap looked over his shoulder to make sure the rest of the men were already inside the downed space ship. Snap took a deep breath and walked around the rover, examining it closely.

The PID was built into the rover, so that it was really one device. The equipment had been stored in saddle bag type compartments on the outside of the rover. The rover itself was constructed mainly of steel and had been painted white. Sitting above the tank-like treads was a large armored container-like structure affixed to the rover platform that stood about seven feet high. On the side of the rover was a hand lever; above it was written 'pull to activate.'

Snap pulled the lever, and the top of the container opened. A crystal sphere rose out of the rover and began to spin. As the man-sized crystal sphere spun it began to glow, and then shards of light shot from the sphere, reaching farther and farther away from the rover.

"Bob, what are you seeing up there?" Snap asked.

"I got a Mig-31 three minutes from visual."

"Jesus Bob, that's the most I have ever heard you say."

"I can still see you, the ship and the fucking fireworks display that you and Johnson are putting on," Bob said from the ridge above.

Just then, the shards of light smoothed out and disappeared. The crystal sphere glowed with a dull, whitish gray color, radiating evenly from its surface.

"Bob, what do you see up there?"

"A MiG-31 in the distance"

"And?" Snap asked.

"And you have disappeared."

"Hell yes. What else?"

"The tower and super structure have completely disappeared, looks like freshly fallen snow banks," Bob replied.

"And the bow of the ship?"

"It can be seen, but it is buried up against the trench wall. So unless you are looking for it, you could miss it."

"Stay tuned into the pilot's radio frequency. If he says anything that makes you believe he sees us, shoot him down with the EMP cannon," Snap ordered.

"Roger that."

Snap and Jackson stood next to the rover monitoring the diagnostic reports for the three-dimensional projected holographic image.

"Everything looks fine. We have enough power to last several hours. Just under 75 percent of the ship is hidden from view," Jackson said.

The MiG-31 flew overhead, and Bob did not take a shot at it with the EMP cannon.

"Major Slade, no radio communication from pilot. If he spotted us, he didn't mention it."

"Jackson, stay here with the rover. Leave on the PID until the MiG is safely out of the area, then shut it down to conserve power. I've got cargo to move," Snap ordered, as he stomped off toward the ship's smoldering hulk.

"Bob, good work. You and Taylor stay up on that ridge and keep an eye out for any Russian movement."

"Roger that."

CHAPTER THIRTY-SIX

Moscow Russia

Nox Bellator stood on the flight deck next to his anti-gravity fighter, five levels below the tarmac, just outside of Moscow. There were five antigravity fighters sitting in a circular formation on the flight deck, directly below a large shaft that led to the surface.

"Open the blast doors; I will be leaving soon," Nox commanded the Russian officer.

"Yes Sir," he replied, as he quickly moved to the control panel.

"General Bellator, we have received reports back from Magadan," Popov said.

"And?"

"So far, the pilot's reports are less than helpful. All six sites were located. All six show signs of massive explosions. Well, actually, one shows a smaller blast radius."

"Anything else stand out about the smaller site?"

"Not really, just that its impact zone was strange in appearance, not as symmetrical as the others."

"Anything else?"

"Based on the pilot's reports there were no signs of manmade debris or people at any of the locations," Popov replied.

"When will we have the analyst's reports on the pictures taken from the fly over?"

"That is our top priority; they should be complete before you land in Magadan," Popov said.

"I'm not going to Magadan first," Nox said.

"Where will you be heading first, Sir?"

"I'm going straight to the anomalous site," Nox answered.

"By yourself? Do you want back up?"

"I commanded an interstellar warship for hundreds of years. I think I can handle a crater in Siberia."

"Very well. I will make sure the folks at the Magadan airport expect your delayed arrival."

Nox was wearing his full armor and helmet. He stood head and shoulders over the Russian General. "Where are we on troop deployment?"

"Sir, I have deployed the Pacific Fleet to the Port of Magadan. They should be there in 10 hours, along with air support. We keep the Sea of Okhotsk free of ice and open for shipping traffic year around. Magadan Airport however is another story. It is under a winter storm advisory and is facing near whiteout conditions. Your antigravity fighter can make it, but the fighters are having trouble landing. Also, it is a small airport, not really prepared for large scale military functions. Moving planes through there will take time."

"How long until I get boots on the ground at these locations?"

"The fighters detected low levels of radiation from the impacts."

"I didn't ask about radiation levels, General."

"No Sir. We will have paratroopers at each location in a few hours."

"How many?"

"We can drop 90 paratroopers from a Mi-26 T2 helicopter. They are being readied now, as we speak."

"Very well, I want boots on the ground at each location, ASAP. I will be at the anomalous site in a little under one hour."

Nox turned and entered his anti-gravity fighter. In a few minutes, he was flying through the gray, winter Russian sky at over 7,000 miles per hour. The anti-gravity technology allowed for the smoothest of rides, even through the harshest weather conditions. Nox verbally commanded the ship to the known coordinates and leaned back in the pilot's seat to ponder what he might find in Magadan.

Nox, a leader of leaders, did not give into fantasy easily. But lately his plans to unite the Earth under one rule had stalled out. The *Council of Three Hundred* were bickering over the same old crap and unable to see the big picture. He needed a break, something to force the world leaders back to the table. This may be just the thing, or it may just be a strange meteor shower.

Then, his thoughts wondered to the past, a time when things were simpler. When politics were black-and-white, good was good, and evil was evil. He thought of his old adversary: Dale Matthews. Often, he wondered how Dale was doing. At this point, Dale was a very old man, weak and frail. But that's not how Nox remembered him. Nox remembered Dale as the fearless warrior that stared him down in an underground tunnel. The only man that ever bested him. He would pay Dale a visit someday, someday soon, because Dale did not have much time left.

As Nox was mentally visualizing what Dale would look like after roaming the Earth for 90 years, the emergency siren rang, and the cabin lights faded to red. Nox was jolted back to reality. Apparently, his technologically advanced anti-gravity fighter was not completely impervious to harsh Russian winters.

CHAPTER THIRTY-SEVEN

Magadan Oblast

Snap checked the schematics of the ship, which had been downloaded to the display on his forearm. Snap glanced at the massive ship; even crashed, it rose over a hundred feet into the air. Inside, the ship was dark, making it difficult to walk through the scattered debris, boxes and smashed up cargo. The Element 115 was supposed to be on Deck 12 of the superstructure. The tower was of no interest to Snap and his team; it was several hundred feet away in a separate debris field.

Snap climbed through charred rubble to reach the first level that was not destroyed in the crash. He estimated that the first seven levels have been completely obliterated under the weight of the ship. His FALOS armor made the climb easy, if not relatively safe. Inside, the broken ship was dark; he oriented himself with the schematic on his forearm display. Cargo and passenger elevators were destroyed. Snap found the nearest stairwell. He carefully moved up the stairs, scanning for signs that it may have weakened to the point of near collapse.

Once on Deck 12, He realized just how massive the ship had once been. This section of Deck 12 was over 600 feet long. It appeared to be structurally sound, except for the fact that both ends were exposed to the elements where the rest of the ship had been sheared off. At the top of the stairs, Snap looked to his left, where he saw where the ship had been ripped apart, and snow was just starting to blow onto the exposed metal decking. When he turned to his right, he saw six of his men, in FALOS suits, searching through debris. The high-powered LED beams, coming from the sides of their helmets, pierced the darkness, making of them easy to spot.

"Lightning Squad, find anything yet?" Snap asked into the COM.

"Not yet, Major." The men did not turn around and look at him approaching; they just continued moving containers from where they had piled up along one side of the ship during the crash.

"Damn. There must be 3,000 containers on this section alone," Snap said.

Neal West responded, "Yeah, and they are all piled up on top of one another. Even with our FALOS suits, it takes two of us to move one container. Moving three containers at a time, it will take a long time to find what we are looking for. If it is even in this section of the ship."

"Our data link gave us a description of the containers, but without an actual picture, we don't really know what we are looking for," Jackson said.

"Are these containers you are moving powered?" Snap asked.

"Don't appear to be, Major. They look like regular storage containers, dry goods, equipment, and electronics," Williams replied.

"The description says the units we are looking for have independent power sources to maintain the integrity of the Element 115. Do you suppose those power sources are still functional?" Snap asked.

Neal said, "I don't see why not. If they are independent of the ship, unless they were damaged in the crash they should still work."

"Major, most of these boxes appear to be undamaged. I see no reason why the Element 115 containers would be damaged, if they are in this section of the ship," Miller added.

"I'm thinking if they are powered, they may be emitting some type of light source, even if it is just an indicator light," Snap said.

"We have not seen anything like that, Sir," Williams said.

West said, "Maybe we should turn off our LED spot lights and look in the dark for a light source."

"Everyone, turn off your helmet lights," Snap ordered through the COM. The 600-foot section of Deck 12 went dark. It took a few minutes for their eyes to adjust to the darkness. The only thing they could see was a faint light of falling white snow through the large openings at either end of the superstructure.

"I don't see anything," Neal complained.

"We can't see well enough to move containers in this darkness," Williams said.

"We are not going to move containers. Just walk around and look for a container emitting light of any kind," Snap said.

Twenty minutes later, they returned to the middle of the deck. None of them had seen a light being emitted from a container.

"We have to find a way to locate the Element 115 without moving 3,000 containers," West declared.

Snap remarked, "We did not see anything with the spotlights off, but our vision is still impaired by the low-level light in our HUD."

"Sure, but that's a very dim, green light. It should not affect our vision that much."

"But the glow would affect our vision a little. We should turn off our HUD and lift our visors, so we have no light competing for our eyes' attention. In total darkness, our eyes should be able to adjust to find any light source," Snap said.

"Yeah, but it's not really total darkness. We do have some light coming from outside the ship," West insisted.

"True, but that is still less than the HUD in our helmets."

"We can't be without helmets for long, it is minus 47 degrees outside," Moore said.

"Suck it up, buttercup," said West.

"Men, this is going to be a bit chilly, but I need you to turn off your HUD and lift your visors. We are going to look for any light source being emitted from the piles of containers," directed Snap.

"Hot damn, it's colder than a Tajuana whore's heart!" Miller exclaimed.

"You would know, Miller," Justin Thomas said, with a laugh.

"Holy shit, my face has never been this cold before," Moore cried.

"Five minutes, seven minutes tops, and then you can put your visors back on," Snap countered. "Everyone look for any container that is emitting light of some kind."

A few minutes later, Justin Thomas yelled from 50 yards away, "Hey, I think I got something." Everyone ran toward him.

"See, look there," Thomas said, pointing at a container stacked up behind several other large containers, so that only a small corner of it was visible.

"Damn, you are right. I see it. Let's move these boxes and see what we got back there," Senior Master Sergeant Anderson said.

Visors went back down so that faces would not get frost bite and the men went to work digging out the container that was emitting a tiny light. A few minutes later, it was pulled free of the other boxes and sitting in the middle of the deck. The squad stood around it as Snap examined the container. It was roughly the size of a large coffin, with handles along the sides. The container was made of a metallic substance, and the top had what appeared to be a touch screen display, emitting a soft blue light.

"It looks like the display is showing us monitoring data from the contents," Snap said.

"Can you read it?" Moore asked.

"No. But, if they set up their display data like we do, it appears all systems are operating within acceptable ranges," Snap said. "Of course, it could also be a self-destruct countdown, and we have five seconds to live. How the fuck should I know? I don't read alien."

"Okay, let's start digging through this section here," West said.

An hour later the men had stacked up two dozen containers of Element 115.

"That's 80,000 pounds of the Element. I thought there was supposed to be 100,000 pounds here," Snap said, as he leaned up against a large pile of discarded containers.

"We have searched most of the area around here, and have not found any other containers with Element 115."

"There has got to be more. Keep looking," Snap ordered.

Bob's voice came over the COM, "We have a large helo landing 200 yards behind my position, looks like a Mi-26 T2."

"Can you take it out with the EMP rifle?" Snap asked.

"Negative, Major. The weather is pretty bad out here, got less than 50 yards of visibility."

"Move into a position where you can take out the helo with the EMP rifle. Don't give away your position until you have a clear shot. We don't want them communicating to their command that we are here, or that this is the site where they should be looking."

"Roger that Major; I will hit the chopper with the EMP before they figure out we are here and have an opportunity to radio for backup."

Bob, the newest member of Lightning Squad, if that is in fact what he was, slung the EMP rifle over his shoulder, while toting the six-barreled machine gun in his right hand. Bob, at nine feet tall, made carrying the modified M134D-H minigun and 4,000 rounds of 7.51 ammo look easy.

Bob said into his COM, "Taylor, you stay here and watch over the squad. I'm going to deal with the helo that just landed behind our position."

"Roger that Bob"

The snow was blinding. Bob switched his HUD to thermal imaging as he hunched over and sprinted towards the helo. Through the blinding snow, Bob could not see the helo, but his HUD showed the red heat signature of the helo in the distance. The red splotch on his HUD, indicating a heat source, began to spread and widen until it was not one, but dozens, of red spots on his HUD.

"Major Slade, the helo has deployed dozens of men. They are approaching my position. It is unlikely I could eliminate all of them."

"Have they seen you?"

"No."

"Then continue with your mission. Take out the helo. We will deal with the Russians," Snap said.

Snap turned to Lightning Squad, "Alright, we have Russians approaching. One hundred and fifty yards out. Unknown strength. Williams and Johnson, you take positions up here on Deck 12 and cover us. The rest of you, follow me." Snap and the men headed toward the stairwell.

West hurried along next to Snap, "There are only ten of us, two on Deck 12, two on the ridge and six on the ground, and one of those is operating the PID. How many Russians did Bob say there were?"

"He didn't. But we know a Russian helo can carry nearly 100 troops; so, I'm guessing."

"Looks like the Russians are at company strength," Bob said into the COM, from one hundred yards behind the ridge. "They are fanning out into squads and will be on the ridge in about five minutes. Squads are about 50 yards apart from each other. I don't see how we could take them out quickly."

Snap said, "Take out the helo. We can handle the Russians, just don't let them radio back."

"The Russian command will know we are here when the helo fails to report," West observed.

"Yep. Better the Russians suspect we are here, then have it confirmed. Once they receive visual confirmation that we are here, they will hit us with everything they can muster. If they just think a helo went down in a snow storm, they may hesitate," Snap said, as he and the other men reached ground level.

"Williams, Johnson, make sure you got that ridge covered where Bob and Taylor were. That's where the Russians are going to appear first. Don't shoot until we have confirmation that Bob has shut down the helo."

"Roger that."

"Lightning Squad, take up defensive positions every 20 yards or so along the trench. Hopefully we can hit them as they attempt to repel down the rock wall. Don't fire until my mark," Snap ordered. The five men ran along the bottom of the trench and took up positions amongst the debris with the ship at their backs. Each man was hidden behind rocks or pieces of the ship's hull, with their DE rifles trained on the ridgeline above them.

"Ten to one odds, Major," Davis said from behind a jagged piece of debris, 20 yards to Snap's left.

"I like those odds, Davis. Our FALOS suits and laser rifles should give us a decisive advantage – not to mention the element of surprise," Snap said from behind a collapsed bulkhead. From his vantage point, Snap could clearly see the crater's ridge.

"Bob, we are in position. Once you take out that helo, we will ambush the Russians as they descend the ridge. You need to make your way back to the ridge and attack them from the rear. You and Taylor should be able to force any stragglers over the ridge with your miniguns. We will catch these Russians in a cross fire, they won't even know what hit them," Snap said.

"I see three men on top of the ridge. Looks like they are pre-paring to repel down," Davis said over the COM.

"Where?" Snap asked.

"Your ten o'clock."

Snap switched to thermal and looked to his left. There they were, and then four more appeared.

"Bob, have you neutralized that helo? We have visual. Russians on the ridge," Snap said into the COM.

The first Russian began the decent. From the position the Russians chose, the drop was only about seventy feet to the base of the newly carved out trench. It would not take them long to be on the ground. Once on the ground level, they would have more places to hide, and would be more difficult to target. If they made it to the ship, they would have countless places to hide – it would be like searching through a corn maze.

"I'm lining up the shot now," Bob said over the COM. "Direct hit. Target immobilized. Do want me to finish off the flight crew?" Bob asked.

Snap thought about it for a minute. He needed Bob to set up the crossfire, so the Russians could not simply run away from the ridge. On the other hand, if he left the flight crew alive, they may find some way get in contact with Russian command.

"Eliminate the flight crew, then get back to the ridge ASAP."

"Helo down. Everyone else, wait until the first Russian hits the ground, then light'em up. Start with the targets on top of the ridge - the ones that have not started down the cliff."

The first Russian touched the snow-covered ground at the bottom of the trench. All five men on the ground began to fire at the Russians as they repelled down the rocky cliff. Lightning Squad's DE rifles made very little noise and only emitted a tiny trace of light. At first, the Russians had no idea what was happening. Fifteen Russians fell from the ridge before any of them realized they were under attack.

Twenty-five Russians, wearing cold weather gear, were shot as they clung to the slippery rockface they were attempting to descend.

"Holy shit. This is like shooting fish in a barrel," Davis yelled.

"Forty down, and they still have not fired a shot," Williams said from Deck 12 where he was sniping Russians that were hiding just over the ridgeline.

"That means there are about 60 left, and they are digging in behind the ridge – where we can't see them from down here."

"I can see them clearly from my vantage point," Williams said. "I moved up several decks, I'm looking down on these Reds."

Williams had used his select fire switch to change his DE rifle from assault to sniper mode. In addition to single fire, three-shot burst, and full auto, the laser rifle offered two other firing options. These other options included sniper mode and anti-armor mode. Anti-armor mode used more power and caused a serious delay between shots. Theoretically, anti-armor mode, if used often enough, could diminish the fusion fuel cell, even though no one had ever seen that happen.

"I don't think they are called 'Reds' anymore," West said.

"Another one down," Williams called out. "I don't care what they're called, as long as they drop."

Snap and the others had slowed down their rate of fire because the Russians had retreated to behind the ridgeline.

"I got no targets, Major," Davis said.

"Yeah, we got the easy ones dangling on the side of the cliff. The rest have taken up defensive positions along the ridge," Snap replied.

"Bob, where are you and Taylor? The Russians have retreated behind the ridgeline where we can't see them."

"We are making our way into position behind the Russian line."

Taylor, on the ridgeline with Bob and the remaining Russians, switched his FALOS suit to invisibility mode. The thousands of light-emitting diodes and electrochromic panels displayed images of a snow storm across his heavy plate armor. His titanium, exoskeleton frame made wielding the minigun and thousands of rounds as easy as picking up a bowling ball.

He walked the ridgeline, boulder to boulder, shooting unsuspecting Russians. Bob, who did not have the advantage of invisible armor, stayed behind Taylor, taking out any survivors. A few Russians were able to fire off a couple of shots before being pulverized by the rotating multi-barrel machinegun, but they missed by dozens of yards. At no time did Taylor feel like the enemy could even see him, much less effectively target him.

A quick squeeze of the modified trigger on the M134D-H sent dozens of rounds into the soft Russian targets, leaving nothing but a bloody mess where an enemy solider once stood. A few Russians decided to take their chances with the ridge, but Snap and the men on the ground made short work of them. A few minutes later, the last Russian was dispatched to meet his maker. The minigun in Taylor's hand was not even warm.

"That's the last one," Taylor said into the COM.

"Roger that, what's your status up there?" Snap asked.

"Bob and I are fine. Between the two of us, we just spent about 1,800 rounds of ammunition."

"Shit. You only had 60 targets," West said as he headed back over towards Snap.

"Yeah, well, they wouldn't hold still," Taylor said, as he surveyed the bloody carnage along the ridgeline. Taylor walked the cliff's edge with a Desert Eagle pistol in his hand, making sure there were no survivors.

"What did these Russians do to deserve this? I mean, they came out here to check on a crashed ship or asteroid, and this is what they get for their efforts? Hell, we are in their country," Taylor said, as he lined up a head shot on a Russian that was struggling to breathe with a bubbling hole in his chest.

"It's not fair, or right. It is what it is. We all know the risks when we put on the uniform and pick up a weapon. Today, we had the better weapons, tomorrow – who knows?" Snap said.

"The helo is destroyed. Flight crew is dead. It looks like they were unable to get a message to Russian command," Bob reported in his abrupt manner.

"Bob, Taylor, stay on the ridge. The rest of you get back to Deck 12, we need to get that cargo to ground level for pick up," Snap ordered.

"We don't have long before the Russians come looking for their missing helo," West said.

"Bring them on, with these FALOS suits and laser rifles, fighting Russians is as easy as stepping on cockroaches," Chris Johnson said into the COM.

"Those Russians thought they were looking for an asteroid or something. We caught them completely off guard. I'm sure the next ones that are sent will be more prepared," Snap warned. "Let's not get too cocky."

"Hopefully, we can get the hell out of here before the next wave of Russians comes around."

"*Flying City* is sixty minutes out," General Stone Byrd reported.

"Anything can happen in an hour," West muttered.

CHAPTER THIRTY-EIGHT

Magadan Airport

Nox Bellator hurried down the ramp of his antigravity fighter. Once on the ground, he spun around to examine his favorite craft. Nox had diverted from his course to the crash site when the warning alarms sounded. The last few minutes of his trip had been like flying a toaster through a tornado; now he could see why. Nox stood in a private hangar, which appeared to have been rapidly cleared for his arrival. The forty-foot-wide disc shaped craft was covered with ice and snow; it would need to be deiced before he could take off again.

"General Bellator, I am General Kotov, it is a pleasure to meet you, Sir," said the older man in a trembling voice.

Nox turned around to the sound of an unfamiliar voice. He could see the fear in the General's eyes. This is why Nox preferred to only deal with Generals he knew, or at least officers that had been properly informed of his features.

"Do not be afraid, General. I too am Russian. I was first commissioned by Stalin himself after WWII. I assume General Popov has given you instructions."

"Yes, Sir. As you can see, we have cleared out this hangar for you. There are guards posted at the door, with instructions not to allow anyone to enter."

"General Kotov, you understand that you and your men were not supposed to see me or my ship."

"Yes Sir. These are my best men. They know not to tell a soul."

"General Kotov, do you believe in souls?" Nox asked.

"No Sir, not particularly so, Sir. It's just a saying."

"General, if I ever hear of you, or your men, mentioning this encounter, I will see to it that, not only you, but your families' souls are immediately relieved of their mortal coil. Do you understand me?"

"Yes Sir. No one will ever mention your presence."

"How long until my team gets here?"

"Couple hours, Sir."

"Two hours? I don't have two hours. I need to get to the site. General, when was the last time you and your officers actually did some manual labor?"

"Excuse me, Sir?"

"I need you and your officers to deice my craft. No one else. Deice my craft now. I want reports every fifteen minutes from the units deployed to the crash sites."

Nox turned to enter his craft, when General Kotov spoke, "Would you like your action report now, Sir."

Nox slowly turned, reminding himself that there were good officers in the Russian Air Force that were not aware of his existence, "Yes, General. Now would be fine."

"We have landed troops at each of the impact zones. Five helos have reported back, all with the same findings; big craters, minor radiation and little else. Multiple attempts to contact the sixth helo have failed."

Nox sensed this was the break for which he had been waiting. "Which helo failed to report back? Which site was it?"

"The Mi-26 that did not report was sent to Site Four, Sir."

"Is that the site where the MiG pilot reported an anomalous impact crater?" Nox asked, with masked glee.

"Yes Sir, that's the one."

Damn. If it were not for my craft icing over, I would have already been there.

"How long until my craft is deiced?"

"Sir, it will take about 40 minutes to deice and apply anti-icing chemicals."

"Make it happen. No one other than you and your staff officers are allowed in this hangar," Nox said, as he hurried up the ramp into his craft.

Nox plopped down into the chair in his cockpit. It was set up similarly to the cockpit of a modern jet. It never shocked Nox that humanoids of all different planets had equipment that looked the same. After all, humanoids had similar features: arms, legs, heads and hands. It made perfect sense that they would arrive at the same solution to a scientific problem. Nox's craft had been upgraded several times to be able to interface with human technologies. In addition to the otherworldly features, Nox's craft had command and control functions for most Russian military assets, including communications.

"Get me General Popov," Nox spoke into the craft's communication system. Nox preferred the voice command feature, even though he could control certain aspects of the craft thru thought commands.

"This is General Popov. What can I do for you, Sir?" General Popov asked.

"Where are you, right now?" Nox asked.

"I'm in Moscow, at the bunker."

"Excellent. How many next generation BAS units do we have operational?"

"Other than yours, and the other resident Ondagra, we have ten Battle Armor Systems with trained Russian operators," General Popov said. "What do you have in mind?"

"How many Ondagra are there at the base?"

"Three that I know of."

"I want the three Ondagra and the 10 trained operators deployed in an antigravity fighter to Site Four. I believe there are enemy forces on the ground there, and they shot down our Mi-26. Make sure that you take extra care when applying the anti-freeze to the exterior of the craft; that's what forced me to divert. I should be at Site Four within an hour."

"Consider it done, Sir."

CHAPTER THIRTY-NINE

Magadan Oblast

"We need to carry these containers to the ground level and outside for pickup. When the NATT arrives, we need to be able to load up quickly and get the hell out," Snap to Lightning Squad from Deck 12 of the crashed *Impegi*.

"We have several containers to carry off this deck to ground level. Each of you grab an end, and we will walk them down the stairwell," Neal added.

"There's seven of us. You six, grab three containers, and I will stay up here and look for the missing units," Snap said pointing the men to the large containers.

Carrying the heavy containers down multiple flights of broken and uneven steps was challenging, even with the aid of their titanium exoskeletons. Forty-five minutes later the containers were lined up, like coffins on the frozen tundra, ready for transport. Snap found no more of the missing containers.

"So here we are, in the open, sitting ducks for any Russian fighter pilot to light us up," Williams said, as the squad stood by the line of containers on the ground.

"Our sensors would tell us if there were any Russian planes on approach," Snap said. "All we have to do is wait for the NATT to come pick us up, and we are home free."

"What if they have stealth planes? Our sensors would not alert us to those," Williams pointed out.

"It's unlikely that they have stealth planes this close to the Arctic Circle. Those assets would be stationed near Europe and Moscow," Snap replied.

"How far out is the NATT?" West asked.

Snap checked the display on his forearm, "Fifteen minutes out."

"Should we bring Bob and Taylor down off the ridge?" West asked.

"Not yet. We may need them, still. Leave them up there until we are ready to leave," Snap said.

"Snap, since we have a minute here before the Transport arrives, I got a question for you," West said into the COM so that only Snap could hear him.

"West, what's that?"

"So, how did you get the nickname 'Snap'?"

"Ha," Snap chuckled, "That's a funny story. We got a minute. Back in junior high school, I was about 14 years old. I had this super-hot science teacher, long blonde hair and big tits."

"Nice."

"Yeah, well, one hot summer day, it was pouring rain outside, and she ran into the classroom holding her briefcase over her head with both hands. She was wearing a very thin, almost see-through silk blouse. Her blouse was soaked and pulled tight around her breasts because her arms were up over her head."

"Sounds like quite a sight for a fourteen-year-old."

"Shit. I'd like to see that again, now! Just as she was coming through the door in her drenched silk blouse, the AC cuts on, and it was full on headlights – her nipples poked through that silk shirt. Let's just say it didn't leave much to the imagination."

"Nice."

"West, as soon as she came through that door, my eyes went straight to those hard nipples, and I yelled at the top of my voice, 'Snap Dog, tits!'"

West and Snap chuckled.

"Every boy in that class started laughing. The teacher dropped her brief case and cupped her own breasts – that's when the girls started laughing. Needless to say, I got sent to detention. When I got back from detention, everyone started calling me Snap Dog. Funny thing is, we never saw that teacher's pointy nipples again - she must have gone out and bought padded bras."

"That's hilarious."

"Yeah. That story followed me around for a long time. In college, they shortened my nickname to 'Snap.' Even my mom still calls me Snap."

"Your mom found out?"

"Yeah, she thought it was funny too," Snap said with a chuckle.

The entire squad's HUD units sounded at once, indicating an approaching aircraft. It was their built-in *Identification Friend or Foe* system, or IFF for short, informing them that the NATT was on approach.

"Hell yeah, mission accomplished," Williams said.

"Not so fast, we can celebrate once we are out of Russian airspace with the cargo," West cautioned.

"This is Flying City, we need a visual confirmation of the LZ," an unfamiliar voice boomed through the squad's COM.

"Roger that, Flying City. This is Major Morgan Slade. Turn off the PID, Jackson," Snap ordered. The *Projected Invisibility Dome* flickered off.

"Flying City, can you see us?" Snap asked.

"Clear as day," the voice responded.

"We are standing with the cargo; it's only 80,000 pounds. Can you land close to us?'

"No problem. We will be vertically landing and will hover 10 feet off the ground. You can load the cargo via a drop ramp; we will be heading home in 10 minutes."

"Roger that," Snap said with a bit of excitement.

All the men looked up into the sky, expecting to see a large transport plane hovering over them, but there was nothing but dreary winter flurries.

"Look, there, about 75 yards out," Johnson said as he pointed to the snow swirling in the sky.

"I see it, just barely," Davis said. Slowly, as it approached, the NATT came into focus, the images of blowing snow being projected on its fuselage, just a hair off from the real snow surrounding it.

"It's perfectly invisible at 300 yards, but as it gets closer, the invisibility is less effective. Within 25 yards, it's hard to miss," West said.

"Yeah, still impressive. Flying Mach 2 at 30,000 feet and it's impossible to detect. You can only see it after it's already up your ass," Snap said, as the plane stopped its vertical decent and hovered just above the surface.

The Flying City, appropriately named, had no real wings and sported an aerodynamic fuselage that was 165 feet wide and 174 feet long. The NATT, or Nuclear-powered Tactical Transport, stood 40 feet tall and was triangularly shaped, like the TR-3B, but was white, rather than black. Unlike the TR-3B, the Flying City had a clearly designated front and rear. One smooth, aerodynamic point of the triangular shaped fuselage was a cockpit area with windows for the pilots. The back of the plane had powerful jet thrusters. The other side, which was facing the containers, had a ramp that was extending downward toward Lightning Squad.

"Holy shit, it's like a triangle shaped building, how does it take off with no wings?" Williams asked.

"The antigravity technology reduces its weight by nearly 90 percent. When you combine the fact that it is incredibly light, with the powerful thrusters, it does not need that much lift to take off. One day, antigravity technology will develop to the point where they will be able to float a 200-ton building like an air balloon," Snap said.

The ramp touched the ground, revealing the massive interior cargo space. Lined up along one side of the cavernous space were 20 sidewall jump seats.

"Go, go, go. Get these containers on the ship," Snap yelled.

Davis and Johnson grabbed the first container and began running toward the ramp, when several explosions rocked the large craft. It shuttered and dropped several feet closer to the ground. Fire burst from the open hangar, and the ramp crumpled as it was jammed into the rocky surface.

"What the hell was that?" West yelled.

"Major Slade, we're under attack. We took several hits from an energy weapon of some sort. The cockpit is filling with smoke."

"Fuck me," Snap said. "Bob, can you see what hit the transport?"

"No. I can't see anything. I'm switching to thermal imaging." Bob scanned the skies with thermal and still saw nothing. Then, three streaks of light from a cloud slammed into the transport, again.

"I see the craft. It has optical stealth, hard as hell to see in the snow," Bob said. "I have marked it with my HUD. Hopefully, it will keep up."

"Damn, they have Next Gen fighters. How did they get those here so fast?" West asked.

"They know we are here; this isn't going to be easy," Snap said.

"Three more direct hits," the pilot said over the COM. The transport was on fire, but it was still struggling to hover in place.

"Flying City, this is General Stone Byrd, you need to retreat, now. Get out of there. Major Slade, dig in. Defend the cargo." Byrd's voice boomed through all their COMs.

"Yes Sir," Snap said.

Fuck. How long can I defend against the Russian military?

"What the fuck? They are leaving us here?" Johnson asked, as the transport wobbled away, partially on fire.

"Bob, you still got that Russian craft in sights?"

"Yes Sir, it's hard to see, but I got it marked."

"Hit it with the EMP. Taylor, you hit it with the mini gun. Let's see how it stands up to 2,000 rounds." Snap ordered.

Bob and Taylor began firing at the barely visible craft, unable to tell if their rounds were connecting with their target.

CHAPTER FORTY

Commander Furier stood beside the jump shuttle atop a rocky ledge overlooking the entire crash site. Her team and the jump shuttle were all in chameleon mode, unseen by the men at the crash site. They had left Catrix and Fabris back at the crash site to try and recover an armored vehicle or anything else of use. So far, there was no indication that the squad of Americans had discovered Catrix and Fabris. They had taken the clothes and food back to the survivors hiding in the shallow cave. She and her team were over two miles from the location where the transport had just been attacked by an unseen craft. The transport had taken off and disappeared behind a mountain. It was unclear if the attacker pursued.

"What is going on?" Genu asked Furier. "Can I see?"

"Just a minute," Furier said, as she squinted into the binoculars. "Their transport was just attacked, there were a few small explosions."

"Who attacked them?"

"Impossible to tell. But whoever it was, they had chameleon technology and energy weapons," Furier said, shaking her head.

"Do you think that transport was part of our exit plan?" Genu asked.

"If it was, it's not anymore. The transport is gone. Looks to me like it was seriously outgunned." Furier handed the binoculars to Genu and said, "I'm going to tell Forte."

Furier sat in the jump shuttle's cockpit and pulled up the COM. Her armor, while the inspiration for the modern FALOS suit, was technologically inferior when it came to data transmission. The humans, who had little technological development in the arena of space travel, were somewhat advanced when it came to mass data collection, management, and dissemination. Not to mention, her battle armor had been sitting in a storage locker for 30 years while the humans continued to develop theirs.

"Commander Forte, can you hear me?" Furier spoke into the shuttle's COM system.

"Loud and clear. What's your status, Commander?" Forte asked.

"As you know, the Americans landed a few hours ago and have been pulling out the Element 115. It looks like their transport plane came to pick it up and was attacked."

"Say again Commander."

"It was attacked by what appeared to be a craft with chameleon capabilities," Furier said.

"And?"

"The transport was outgunned; it flew away. I cannot confirm whether it was destroyed by the attacker."

"Not good. I think that was going to be our ride out of here," Forte said.

"From the size of the plane, it looks like it could easily have carried us, all the Element 115, and half our shuttles," Furier complained.

"I'm certain that was our extraction plan. We need to be prepared for a longer stay. I'm glad you were able to recover those supplies."

"Supplies are going to be the least of our worries when the locals come looking for us. How long can the 70 of us hold out against an organized military?" Furier asked, almost frantic.

"Commander, calm down. We don't have to beat their army. All we have to do is hide until the Americans devise another rescue plan."

"I want to help the Americans on the ground at the crash site," Furier said.

"How? It sounds like the Americans already outgun you. What can you do to help them against an AG Fighter?"

"I don't know. But I could add 10 guns to their side."

"Ten guns for what? To shoot at an invisible craft. I think not. Stand down. We have been ordered to protect the cargo in our possession, not defend the crash site. Let the Americans on the ground do their job; we will wait for orders from Moon Base," Forte commanded.

Furier said nothing.

"Do you hear me, Commander? That is a direct order. Stand down, and stay put, do not make contact with the Americans until we are told to do so," Forte said firmly.

"Understood," Furier replied.

Furier took a deep breath and adjusted the COM to contact Catrix, who was still in one of the lower cargo holds of the *Impegi*. "Furier to Catrix, can you hear me?"

"This is Catrix. We can hear you. Can you see what's going on out there? It sounded like an explosion or something."

"It looks like the American's transport was attacked by an unknown aggressor."

"And, do we have a ride out of here?"

"Looks like it was shot down, total loss. How are your efforts going?"

"Surprisingly well. Fabris and I may be able to salvage some of this equipment. I'll keep you posted. Should we contact the Americans?"

Furier sighed, "You and Fabris stay out of sight for now, but if the situation changes, and they need help, use your own judgment."

Furier stood on the ridge, staring through her binoculars at the column of smoke reaching for the sky just beyond the skyline.

CHAPTER FORTY-ONE

N ox had departed the Magadan airport 20 minutes earlier, leaving the timid General and his staff officers with instructions to stay on the base until General Popov arrived and had an opportunity to debrief them. Even though his craft could comfortably seat 10 passengers, Nox enjoyed flying solo. His craft had now been properly prepared for the weather and he had reduced speed to 700 miles per hour so that he would have a better chance of not missing something important on the ground. As he approached the location of where the Russian helo had made last contact he started paying closer attention to the surface. However, the crash site was clearly visible, along with the huge nuclear-powered transport plane sitting next to it.

Of course, the Americans were already here. How did the MiG-31 *fighter pilot miss this huge debris field on the first pass?*

Nox saw a squad of men preparing to load large containers into the large white cargo transport. Nox did not know what cargo they were loading. The only thing he knew for certain was they were not Russians, and they were not supposed to be here. He assumed they were Americans, maybe Chinese; only a few nations could produce the battle armor these soldiers appeared to be wearing. If they were going through all the trouble to load these containers, the contents must be valuable.

Nox gave it no further thought. Statistically speaking, he knew it was unlikely he would face a technologically superior craft in Siberia. Nox pushed the flight controls into a dramatic dive and opened fire on the large, unsuspecting transport plane. All three shots from his particle beam weapon made contact, slicing through the thin fuselage of the plane. Nox pulled back on the flight controls, and his craft veered to the left. Nox was impressed that the enemy transport plane was not destroyed upon taking a direct hit from his particle beam weapon. He decided to bring his craft around for another attack.

This time, the armored men were scurrying about like little ants whose hill had been kicked over by some thoughtless bully. He fired again, three more direct hits. This time he could see flames flickering through the craft.

Silly Americans. They think they can waltz into my country and do anything they want. I'll teach them a lesson.

Before Nox could finish his thought, his warning siren went off, and his cabin lights dimmed to red.

Not again. What now?

Nox glanced at his control panel and then out the window, just in time to see a mountain of a man firing a mini gun from the hip position.

What the fuck?

Nox was not prone to expressing himself by using human slang, but the situation seemed appropriate. Ten more bullets slammed into his fuselage. More warning sirens. Three penetrated the craft's armor, venting atmosphere. His craft was almost impervious to lasers and EMP weapons. Only the most powerful particle beams could penetrate his shields, of which the humans had none.

Even the human's best rapid-fire heavy machine guns where not effectual when shot from an armored platform because his craft was faster than most bullets. Under normal circumstances, he would be a couple thousand feet up, traveling at such a high rate of speed, that he could easily outmaneuver even a Phalanx Close-In Weapons System. But here, he was flying low and slow, the shooter was not miles away, but only a few hundred yards away. Nox had no time to correct course or speed up. More bullets ripped through his cockpit.

Damn these Americans.

As he decided to sweep around and take a shot at the gunman on the ridge, he noticed the transport plane had decided to take off.

That thing can still fly? Six direct hits and it's on fire. What's that pilot thinking?

Rather than lining up a shot on the ridgeline-mini-gun-toting giant, Nox broke off to chase the transport; figuring that cutting off their means of escape would be better than taking out a sentry.

The transport attempted to engage it's Exoskin, rendering it invisible, but the trail of smoke gave away its position. It tried to punch up the speed, but Nox easily kept up with the damaged NATT.

Nox initiated the auto fire feature of his particle beam weapon, which essentially just shot a constant spread of directed pulsed particle bursts in a spiral formation at the target. Hundreds of individual particle beams ripped through the NATT, shredding it like a log tossed into a wood chipper. The nine-billion-dollar plane slammed into the ground, just beyond the sightline of the Americans.

Nox was ecstatic. It had been decades since he had personally shot down an enemy craft. He jerked the flight controls to swing back around and take another pass at the Americans, but he quickly thought better of it and continued in a westward direction.

Why fight the Americans alone when I have reinforcements on the way? They aren't going anywhere, I saw to that.

He would have chuckled at that thought, had his vocal chords evolved in a manner that would have allowed for laughter. Instead, he flew 10 miles west and set down his craft on an isolated snowy plain, far from the prying eyes.

Nox activated his COM system, "General Manpugna, where are you and your crew?"

"General Bellator, we are about 15 minutes west of Site Four," General Manpugna said. General Manpugna had been a loyal officer since the beginning, even before crash landing on Earth so many decades ago. General Manpugna had been in charge of securing the perimeter of the Antarctica base, but he had transferred to Moscow to assist Nox with the Council of Three hundred.

"I'm sitting on the ground, 10 miles west of the site. Land here so we can plan the next move. How many soldiers do you have?"

General Manpugna said, "Myself, two other Ondagra and 10 Russian operators."

"Thirteen. That should do it. We also have several hundred paratroopers in route. They may already be there by now."

"Do you think they could take out the Americans before we arrive?"

"Not a chance. These are not regular Americans; they are all equipped with Next Gen FALOS suits, and they took out a company of paratroopers in minutes. Best we can hope for is that they slow down the Americans until we get there."

"I've locked onto your COMs signal. We will be on your position in three minutes," General Manpugna said.

Nox trotted down the ramp to the icy ground below. A quick survey of the exterior of his fuselage revealed a dozen bullet holes.

Could have been worse. After all, that giant clone was firing a mini gun at point blank range.

Nox lifted his helmet visor for a minute to take in the frigid air. Normally, cold temperatures did not bother him, but the ice pellets seemed like little bullets being fired at his exposed face. A saucer shaped craft, identical to his, landed 10 yards from his position. He knew the fighter well, it had been on his interstellar ship when it crashed, rendering them permanent residents of Earth.

The ramp slid down and General Manpugna crunched through the icy snow toward Nox.

"Welcome to the battle, General," Nox said.

"I'm glad to be here, old friend. It has been a long time since we battled a worthy adversary. I hope you have not grown weak from fighting the politicians with words and paper."

"Never," Nox replied. "I have already destroyed their transport plane. They are sitting ducks waiting to be led to their destruction. I almost felt bad, it was an impressive nuclear-powered plane, with optical stealth. Had I not arrived just as I did, they would have likely escaped."

The other two Ondagra were standing next to General Manpugna. All were wearing the same battle armor as Nox, impervious to any directed energy weapons, vulnerable to only the most powerful, high-velocity rounds.

"What's the situation?" General Manpugna asked.

"There is a squad of soldiers guarding the crash site. They are heavily armed and wearing advanced battle armor – like ours."

"Reinforcements?" Manpugna questioned.

"None that I can tell. I don't think they have a means of escape either."

"So, we have them outnumbered and out gunned. We just walk in and take them out," Manpugna asserted.

"Not quite, General. They are heavily armed, have comparable armor, and have the advantage of a defensive position. We should let the Russian paratroopers go in first and soften them up."

"They will destroy the paratroopers. You're sending them to their death," Manpugna objected.

"Maybe, but the paratroopers may deplete their ammunition supply, giving us another advantage when we attack," Nox responded.

"Very well. When do the paratroopers attack?"

"In about seven minutes," Nox said.

"How many paratroopers are you sending in?"

"Three hundred. I diverted helos from other sites. They took out the last group of paratroopers in under 15 minutes. They took out the last company of Russian paratroopers as they descended into the trench. It looks like they hit the Mi-26 with an EMP burst so it could not radio for help. I say we give these paratroopers 30 minutes to fight the Americans, and then, we go in."

"Smart plan, give the Americans no time to regroup," Manpugna added.

CHAPTER FORTY-TWO

The NATT had disappeared behind the mountain range, along with the nearly invisible attacker. The squad stood beside the containers, wondering what to do next.

"Lightning Squad, get these containers back into the ship's hull. We are going to dig in and prepare for a fight," Snap ordered.

"How long till backup arrives, Major?" Davis asked.

"Unknown."

"Bob scared it off with the mini gun," Davis yelled.

"I don't think Bob scared it off. It took off to chase the NATT," West said. "It will be back."

The team could hear an explosion and a plume of smoke rose from behind a snow-covered hill, just beyond their line of sight.

"I bet that was our plane, being grounded," West said, in a somber tone.

"Get these containers back to the ship, they need to be hidden and protected. Unless I miss my guess, that was just the first wave," Snap said. The squad grabbed the heavy containers and hurried them back to the *Impegi* wreckage.

"Bob and Taylor, get off that ridge. When that craft returns with his friends, you won't have any cover," Snap ordered.

"Roger that, Major," Taylor said, as he began to use one of the dead paratrooper's repelling lines to descend.

The attack craft that took out the NATT did not return as expected. The men gathered on Level 7, the first level of the disgraced *Impegi* that was not obliterated upon impact. The crew had not spent much time on Level 7, as their instructions were to locate the Element 115 on Deck 12. Level 7 had sustained tremendous damage; the floors had buckled, bulkheads collapsed, and some areas were completely unpassable.

Lightning Squad and Bob gathered in a circle inside the hull; the large containers stacked up behind them. Across all their HUD units, a voice boomed, "This is General Stone Byrd. It appears we have had a little set back. The NATT that was sent to recover you and the containers was shot down. It's going to be awhile before we can get you an alternate extraction route."

"How long?" Snap asked.

"Several hours. We have seven C-17s en route to your position."

"No way is that going to work. The Russians have a stealth fighter with an energy weapon over our position. As good, or better, than our TR-3B. It will wipe out those C-17s in 10 seconds flat," Snap said into his COM.

"We have been monitoring the action on the ground. I know they are operating an Antigravity Fighter in the area. I'm not saying it won't be a challenge, but these are not ordinary C-17s. They too have optical stealth."

"Damn. You put optical stealth on a C-17?" Williams muttered.

"Not just one, seven," Byrd replied.

"Okay. You have seven stealth cargo planes heading this way. I'm pretty sure the Russians aren't going to lend you an airport to land them; and we can't load them up in the sky," Snap said.

"We are working on a plan, Major. In the meantime, you need to dig in and survive until the C-17s arrive."

"How long do we have to hold off the Russians?"

"Best case scenario – four hours. Looks like you got three Mi-26 helicopters heading your way. Three hundred and six Russians onboard. Stone out."

Snap looked at his men, "We need to set up defensive positions."

West said, "We could take the top of the ship, high ground."

"Negative. They have air superiority. That AG fighter could come back and chew us up. They could have several of them, we just don't know," Snap said.

"Agreed," Williams said. "The rooftop and ridgeline are too exposed. We could get trapped with our backs to that ridge and along comes that AG fighter with his laser cannon, and we are done," Neal said.

Then it's settled. We make our stand here, inside the ship, where we have some cover between us and that fighter," Snap said.

"Anyone see any good spots to set up a defensive perimeter. This level, or should we go up to a higher level?" West asked.

"I think we make our stand right here on Level 7. It's the first level that is not destroyed; ground troops will have to come through here. We place two snipers on Level 8 for back up," Snap said.

"What about the rooftop? The helos may drop some of those Russians on the top and then they could move down the stairwells and get in behind us," Johnson said.

"Not going to happen. You and Williams are going to booby trap those stairs with explosives, all the way down," Snap said. "How many laser tripwires do we have?"

"Thirty," Taylor said.

"Alright. Johnson, Taylor, go set directional explosives in both stairwells. Make them pay dearly for each flight they come down."

"Roger that."

"Also, set up several video cameras. Position them on three of the upper levels, just so we can see their progress as they are coming down those stairs."

"You got it, Major."

"And this time, don't set the fucking cameras so close to the explosives. Like you did in Kabul."

"Roger that, Major. Learned my lesson that time. Video cameras and high explosives don't mix."

"Robins and Taylor, start moving some of this heavy steel debris toward the middle of the deck, set up some good cover for when the Russians breach," Snap ordered.

"Moore and Jackson, go up one level and dig in. I want you both picking the Russians off from a distance. Remember, you must have both sides of the ship covered. Coordinate with Taylor and Johnson. Make sure they don't booby the level you are on."

"The rest of you, fortify this level. West and I are going to work our way through wreckage on this level and see if there is anything we can use to our advantage," Snap said.

Snap and West turned away from the gaping hole in the hull and walked toward the crumpled floor and crushed bulkheads. Unlike Deck 12 that was in fairly good shape, the cargo on this level had been mostly demolished. The two men could only see about 200 feet into this section of the ship due to collapsed bulkheads and piled debris.

"Snap, what are we looking to find?" West asked.

"Two things. First, I want to see if there is another way into this section that the Russians could use to flank us. Second, we have never seen this section of the ship. It could have weapons that we could use; you just never know."

They both flipped on their powerful LED spotlights which cut through the darkness. Unlike Deck 12, with thousands of manageable containers, Deck 7 was full of broken space craft and vehicles.

"Shit, look at all these destroyed fighters. I bet we are looking at 100 billion dollars' worth of junk," West said.

"More than that," Snap mumbled.

There was no clear path through the jumbled heap of fighter planes. Snap and West climbed over a pile and found a clearing near the overhead where they could push through to the other side of the pile of destroyed planes. Just past the wrecked planes were three tanks. The tanks had fared better than the planes, probably because they were locked down and had stronger armor.

"I wonder if those tanks work?" West asked.

"We will have to find out," Snap said as he climbed down off the mountain of twisted metal and reached the deck below.

"Look, we can see all the way to the other side of the ship," West said.

"Yeah, that's a route the Russians could take to flank the squad."

"If we could get these tanks operational, we could use them to defend this side of the ship."

"Remember, this is alien technology. We may not even be able to operate them. They could have a bio identification ignition system for all we know. Hell, they may be thought controlled and only compatible with an alien brain," Snap said as he approached the first tank.

All three tanks appeared to be in good shape, but the floor had buckled up around one of them; so, moving them would have been impossible. Snap went to place his gloved hand on the first tank when a figure stepped out of the darkness behind him.

"Drop your weapons, or we will shoot," the stranger commanded.

Snap froze, then glanced at West to his right. They both knew they had been had. There was no way they could spin around, spot the targets in the dark and fire their weapons before the strangers unloaded a whole magazine of God knows what into them. It was possible their advanced armor would stop most of the bullets, but that would be taking one hell of a chance. For all Snap knew, the stranger could be toting an RPG.

Snap nodded at West, detached his laser rifle from the Micro Modular Fusion Reactor on his back, and lowered the weapon to the deck. West followed suit, and they slowly turned to meet their captors.

Raising his hands, Snap said, "My name is Major Morgan Slade. This is Captain Neal West. We have come here to recover the Element 115 onboard this ship. May I ask who you are?"

Snap vaguely recognized the battle armor of the two men standing atop a demolished shuttle. Both had energy rifles pointed toward him and West. Their armor was clearly not Russian; it seemed like an older version of their own armor. Snap deduced that these were survivors of the *Impegi*.

The men ignored Snap's question and said, "Who are you with?"

Snap, understanding the man's meaning, and believing them to be on the same side, replied, "We are Americans. We have come to remove the cargo and rescue you. But the enemy is here too, and they shot down our plane."

The man that had been speaking looked over at his partner to see a nod. They both lowered their rifles. The one on the right said, "I'm Catrix and this this Fabris. We were crew aboard this ship. The others have relocated a few miles from here."

"There are other survivors? How many?" Snap asked, in a surprised tone.

Fabris told him that the rest of the crew had taken supplies and valuable cargo offsite to hide it from the enemy. Snap explained that they had been attacked by local military and were expecting another assault soon.

"So, any of these tanks work?" Snap asked.

Catrix grinned. While technically he was not in their chain of command, it was obvious to both him and Fabris that Snap was the leader in this situation. Catrix answered, "Yes, Sir. We just found a fully functional tank with, what seems like, a clear path through the debris. I even took the liberty of arming it with 20 photon shells, all ready to go."

Catrix proudly pointed at the newly armed tank.

CHAPTER FORTY-THREE

The tank was relatively small, only slightly larger than a Humvee. It had been unstrapped from the deck and appeared to be ready to roll. Fabris, using his exoskeleton armor, easily leapt onto the turret and disappeared inside. The other three men joined him.

Fabris slid into the driver's seat, which closely resembled that of a jet plane and said, "This machine is incredible. It can reach speeds of 125 miles per hour, track dozens of targets at once, and fire 25,000 rounds a minute."

"That sounds great, but can it target an invisible AG Fighter?" Snap asked.

"Well, not exactly. But, if the fighter slows down enough to target ground forces, we may be able to hit him."

"What kind of range does this thing have?" Neal asked.

"The laser canon has a range of about 1,200 meters, but the mini photon gun has range of two miles."

"Photon gun? Holy crap, we are going to vaporize some Ruskies today!" Neal said, slapping his armor-clad hands together.

"Unfortunately, I think this is all going to be close quarters combat. We probably will not be able to capitalize on the two-mile range," Snap said with a sigh.

"I'll take the photon gun, anyway," Neal said as he climbed into the main turret.

"I got the laser cannon," Snap said, as he climbed to the top of the tank into the semi-protected turret. The laser cannon was similar in size to a large machine gun and was mounted on a turret that allowed for nearly 180-degree maneuverability.

After a few minutes of Catrix explaining the controls, Snap and West felt they were ready for combat. Catrix and Fabris settled into the bowels of the tank from where they would navigate, and the four began to make their way through the wreckage of the once great interstellar craft.

While Snap and West had been familiarizing themselves with the new tank, the rest of Lightning Squad had been setting up perimeters, booby traps, and digging into fortified positions. As the tank was slowly climbing over the last mound of rubble before it reached the frozen tundra three loud explosions were heard.

"What was that?" Fabris asked over the tank's communication system.

Snap, who had been listening to his team the whole time, said, "That was the first wave of Russian paratroopers making their way down from the top decks."

Catrix asked, "Any idea of how many?"

"They started out with about 300, minus however many just triggered that explosion," Snap said with a brief chuckle.

Three more explosions were heard, this time closer.

"Another dozen gone," West surmised.

For the last several minutes, there had been radio silence from the team. Snap knew this was because they were bracing for the paratroopers to make their way into the kill box.

Johnson and Taylor who were two levels up from the rest of the group, would be the first to see the paratroopers descending the stairwell. In a perfect world, the booby traps would have thinned out the Russian ranks before engaging the two men.

Two more explosions.

"They are one deck above us. Cam three is showing their approach," Ryan Taylor calmly stated into his COMM so the entire team could hear him.

"Good job on not setting the cameras too close to the explosives this time," Williams added.

"Looks like about 30 of them have made it this far," Johnson said.

"Anybody got eyes on the rest of them?" Snap asked.

"Not yet, Sir," Josh Miller responded from the main deck with the rest of the team.

The last of the stairwell booby traps exploded, only one deck above Johnson and Taylor.

"Three more down," Johnson reported.

"Twenty-Seven Ruskies, I like my odds," Ryan Taylor said, as he fired his DE rifle at the first soldier appearing from the stairwell.

The first couple of Russians fell in the stairwell, but the rest of them were able to fan out into the open hangar bay and find cover behind broken equipment and bulkheads. Johnson and Taylor had chosen their positions well and enjoyed the high-ground advantage, but now they did not have clear shots at the Russians. Most of Lightning Squad were two decks down and counting on Johnson and Taylor to cover this entry point so they could focus on the rest of the paratroopers that presumably would attack from ground level.

The tank climbed over the last pile of rubble and broke free of the *Impegi's* broken outer bulkhead. A twinge of fear washed over Snap as the tank fell to the hard tundra below, but the tank was undamaged.

"Hell, yes, free at last!" West exclaimed, with a little too much excitement.

"Maybe so, but now we are a sitting duck for that Russian AG Fighter," Snap reminded him.

Catrix interjected, "Did I forget to mention we have limited stealth?"

"What does that mean?" Snap asked.

"The tank is invisible beyond 100 yards when we are not engaging the enemy."

"So, we can sneak up on the bastards?" Neal asked, as he rotated the turret toward the unseen enemy.

"Yes Sir," Catrix replied.

"Visual contact," Williams exclaimed through the COMM, as shots were heard.

"Enemy combatants advancing on our position," Josh Miller said from the makeshift fortification. "Looks like about a one hundred."

"Should be more than that; where are the rest of them?" Snap muttered mostly to himself.

The tank was several hundred yards away from the fighting, on the other side of the *Impegi's* debris field. A rocket whizzed by and exploded several yards to Snap's left.

"Shit. Well, there they are," Snap answered his own question; again, mostly to himself. "Ruskies, about hundred strong, advancing from the south," Snap said into his COMM.

"Everyone hold your positions. West and I can handle these guys," Snap ordered, as he sighted in on the Russian that had fired the RPG from nearly 100 yards out.

"Major, they are spread wide and are not advancing directly on our position. I'm not sure they know where we are," Fabris said.

"But the rocket, they had to be aiming at us," West pointed out.

"Yes, but that guy is just barely inside the 100-yard range; we are still invisible to the rest, until we fire."

"He will tell his comrades," West said.

"Maybe, but having them suspect we are here is better than confirming it," Catrix objected.

"Hold your fire," Snap ordered. "Can we stay just outside their line of sight?"

"Yes, for a few more minutes," Catrix replied.

"How well will this thing hold up to an RPG, Catrix?" Snap asked.

"RPG, Sir?"

Snap realized the alien was not familiar with Earthly weapon terminology and corrected himself, "Rocket propelled grenade, shoulder launched explosive."

"Ahhh, I see. We could probably take four or five direct hits from an explosive matching the weapon that just missed us," Catrix said, as he maneuvered the tank just outside the 100-yard mark, thus maintaining their invisibility.

Snap had been studying the display on his forearm of his FALOS armor, which was marking the enemy as red dots approaching the *Impegi.* Very soon, all the red dots would be within 100 yards of the *Impegi* and there would be no place where the tank would remain invisible.

Snap said, "The Russians are spread out over 200 yards and advancing toward the rest of the unit at the front of the ship. If they trap us against this bulkhead, we could easily be flanked, and surrounded, and tank or not, I don't like those odds."

"Agreed, Major. Your orders?" Fabris asked.

"Turn around, go back. Hopefully we can get behind them and have them trapped up against this bulkhead."

Fabris expertly turned the tank and quickly moved along the bulkhead, trying to evade the advancing Russians. Snap and West watched the red dots on their displays closing in, hoping they could get behind the wall of advancing Russians before they were spotted.

Johnson and Taylor were holding off the Russians two decks above the rest of the unit, but they were not reducing the Russians' numbers as quickly as they had hoped. The remaining paratroopers had all found positions and were exchanging fire. Ten paratroopers had started to flank Johnson and Taylor by hiding behind several large metal storage containers to their right. The other 15 or so had made it to a crumpled bulkhead to their left. Johnson and Taylor, holding the higher ground about 30 yards away, had stopped the Russian advance, but could not get a clear shot.

The two men who were perched atop a large pile of containers that had slid down to one side of the deck across from the stairwell and they could not clearly see the Russians hiding behind the smaller pile of containers.

"If I could just get a little higher, I could see those Ruskies," Taylor said, pointing upward at a partially collapsed metal walkway above them.

"That's almost 20 feet up, you'll have no cover," Johnson objected.

"I've jumped twenty feet before in this FALOS armor. Besides, you can cover me."

"Don't do it. They got us flanked on two sides. I doubt I can cover both at the same time," Johnson argued.

Catrix expertly wielded the light tank behind the advancing Russians while maintaining their invisibility. Now, the Russian paratroopers between them and the large bulkheads of the crashed ship were still advancing toward the front of the ship, where the rest of Snap's team was dug in and waiting. The wind picked up, fiercely swirling snow to near whiteout blindness.

Snap checked his forearm display, it was still showing red dots directly ahead of him. "West, we should engage the enemy now.

Between the snow and our invisibility, we should be able to evade and overpower them."

"Roger that."

"Fabris, maneuver the tank toward the enemy, try to keep most of their forces in front of us."

"How are you going to target the enemy in this blinding snow?"

"We've got that covered. The built-in radar should give us an advantage over the paratroopers," Snap said, as he gripped the duel handles of the large gun and rotated his wrist to see the screen on his forearm.

"Major, this is all on you. I can't fire this gun based solely on the radar. If I hit an unseen rock directly in front of us, it could destroy the tank," West said.

"Agreed," Snap said, as he fired the laser cannon in the direction of three red dots.

The laser cannon made no sound as it sent a barrage intense light beams racing into the snowy whiteness. Three red dots slowly faded away from the display screen on Snap's forearm.

"Good shot, Major," West said, as he watched the dots disappear.

Fabris added, "Major, don't forget the snowy conditions are going to greatly reduce the range of the laser cannon."

"What's my range in this shit?"

"Four hundred yards, tops," Catrix said.

"Damn."

"We are in a complete standoff," Ryan Taylor said to Johnson. "I will have a clear shot from that walkway."

"Okay, I got your back," Johnson barked.

Taylor stood and bent his armor-clad legs to prepare for the jump. Twenty feet is close to the maximum distance the exoskeleton can leap. Still behind the stack of containers, as soon as he jumped, Taylor would be exposed to enemy fire.

"READY. SET. GO," Taylor yelled.

Johnson stood from his covered position and began firing his laser rifle at the Russians who were peeking from behind the broken containers.

One Russian's head disappeared in a spray of red mist. Another stepped back to avoid being splashed with his comrade's blood.

Taylor's left hand missed the metal railing, but his right hand made contact and clamped down on the cold steel. Taylor hung suspended in the air, struggling to pull himself to the higher walkway.

As if in slow motion, Johnson, from the corner of his eye, saw a Russian step from behind the bulkhead with an RPG already shouldered and pointed upward. In a split second, the rocket was launched in a cloud of flame and smoke. Johnson, who was not an overly religious man, said a quick prayer, as he glanced toward Ryan Taylor. Direct hit on the center mass of Taylor's FALOS armor. Ryan disappeared in a fiery explosion. Johnson did not need to look for Taylor as the smoke cleared; he knew there was no chance of survival.

"Taylor down," Johnson called out, as he lined up a shot and squeezed the trigger.

"Damn," Snap muttered, as he fired another volley into the dwindling snow storm. "West, we are regaining some visibility, it looks like you may have a clear shot with the cannon."

"Roger that, Major."

"Catrix, it looks like there is a cluster of targets about 900 meters to the right; if you can get us up to that embankment, I may have a clean shot," West said.

"Roger that, but we have to conserve the photon shells, we only have twenty," Catrix said, as he sharply turned the tank toward the mound of earth.

"How does this small tank generate enough energy to power a photon gun?" West asked, as he prepared to line up the shot.

"It doesn't, off course. The shells we use don't contain explosives and projectiles, but rather concentrated energy that, when released, projects a ray of intense heat. They are best used against armor."

As the tank crested the mound of earth, the wind died and the Russians could barely be seen in the distance. The white clad paratroopers were near the end of the ship where Snap's team was waiting.

"Looks like about 40 of them," Snap observed.

"They are kind of spread out; I don't know if we can get them all," West complained.

"Target the center of the group," Catrix said.

West pointed the cannon at the center of the group and squeezed the trigger. A bright flash shot from the cannon with a sizzling whoosh. The air around the tank was instantly hot and sparked with flame. The flash of light struck near the center of the soldiers advancing toward the gaping hole in the ship. When Snap's eyes adjusted from the blinding light, he zoomed in on the spot where the soldiers had been. The ones nearest the center had been vaporized or turned to charred ash. All the snow had melted and the paratroopers on the perimeter of the group were all lying on the ground, seemingly dead.

"The photon cannon releases a ray of light that is twice as hot as your sun. The targets that are not instantly burnt from the release of heat, suffocate as the oxygen around the initial impact is burned off," Catrix explained. "Terrible way to die, not that I can think of a good one."

After another 20 minutes of fighting, all the paratroopers that had landed on the ground were either dead, or fleeing across the frozen tundra, where they would surely die from exposure. Snap and West joined the rest of the team on the main level where they heard gunfire above them. The team raced up the stairwell to find Johnson defending against 14 remaining paratroopers. The paratroopers fought and died well, as the armor-clad team easily flanked their position. Once the paratroopers were eliminated the team gathered at the spot where Taylor had been killed.

"Poor Ryan," Johnson said, shaking his head.

"Rest in peace, old buddy," Josh Miller choked out, as he looked down at the bloody mess of armor and flesh that had once been his friend.

"Should we bury him?" Catrix asked.

"Major, who are these guys?" Davis asked, halfway lifting his gun in Catrix and Fabris' direction.

CHAPTER FORTY-FOUR

Nox piloted his AG fighter alone. The other Ondagra and the BAS operators were in General Manpugna's AG Fighter. The plan was for Nox to give cover fire, while Manpugna deployed the soldiers. As Nox approached the crash site, he could see no movement, no para-troopers, only blackened tundra and corpses.

Both fighters slowed to deploy the BAS operators and Ondagra, when a flash of light raced past his fighter, causing him to lose flight controls. In seconds Nox regained control of his craft in time to see a cleverly disguised tank slowly fade into the wintery whiteness.

Once again, Nox's control panel lit up with warning alarms, his weapons systems were completely offline. An unfamiliar tension rose in Nox's chest and throat, anxiety, or anger. He had not felt this way since his interstellar ship crashed in Antarctica decades earlier.

"I've been hit. All weapons lost. I can't cover your landing. I'm going after the tank. You and your men secure the target," Nox barked into his COMM.

Nox fought the urge to fly his craft directly at the enemy tank, knowing he must preserve the fighter. He veered to the right, making several evasive maneuvers as he picked up speed and gained altitude. The tank fired no more shots and was now completely undetectable on the ground below, blending in with the swirling snow.

Damn. That tank makes these AG Fighters far less useful.

Nox felt he was out of the tank's range, and he circled back toward the site in time to see 10 Russian operators and two Ondagra run from Manpugna's AG fighter toward the crashed ship. Even from the sky, Nox could see flashes of light and explosions, as the operators met the Americans at the perimeter of the debris field. The Americans had positioned themselves inside the wrecked ship's bulkheads and were shielded from air attacks. Nox's craft would be ineffective at this stage.

Nox spoke into his COMM, "Manpugna, I'm going to land and look for that tank. You stay in the sky and provide air support when the need arises. With weapons down, I'm no good in the air anyway."

"Yes Sir. Want me to draw fire from the tank? So, you can find it?"

"Maybe. I'll let you know. Don't get shot down, they have a photon gun."

Nox landed his fighter several hundred yards away and engaged the invisibility. A few minutes of searching for the tank turned up nothing, and Nox decided to join the Russians battling at the ship.

Nox joined Manpugna at the inner rim of the debris field just outside the hulk of the ship that remained somewhat intact. The Americans were just inside the hulk exchanging fire with the Russian BAS operators.

"No tank?" Manpugna asked.

"Could not find it. I'm sure it will show up at the most inopportune time," Nox snarled in disgust. "What's the situation here?"

"Appears to be seven American operators set up on the first three decks, all wearing advanced armor with directed energy weapons, except the one with the heavy machine gun. He's not wearing armor, or winter gear. Not sure what the hell he is?"

"Probably a genetically engineered warrior, super strong and fast. I've seen reports that they can trade blows with a BAS unit with their bare hands. He's the one who shot my fighter before you got here."

"Great," Manpugna muttered. "Nearly a fair fight against our fourteen."

"Don't forget the tank; there could be two or three Americans operating it," Nox reminded.

"Yeah, what if there are survivors? From the initial crash?" Manpugna pondered.

"Anything's possible. We could be out numbered."

"True. But time is one our side. We can reinforce, not sure they can," Manpugna said, as he shouldered his rifle and stepped out from the debris.

Nox leapt over the twisted metal wreckage and sprinted toward the opening. He drew the American's fire like nails to a magnet, bright flashes of light smashed into the ground all around him. The first three direct hits caused seconds of white blindness but did little damage to his advanced armor.

Good. My armor is still superior. The Americans and their Vitahician benefactors still don't have what it takes to beat me.

Nox ran along a path that provided the most cover from the American weapons, knowing that they had rockets and heavy machineguns that could cause him substantial damage. Two overly confident Russian BAS operators followed Nox and were cut down in flashes of light.

Nox yelled into his COMM, "Operators, do not follow me, your armor is not strong enough to withstand a direct hit. The Ondagra armor cannot yet be duplicated on this planet."

Inside the hulk, and shielded by a large collapsed bulkhead, Nox was drawing intense fire from the Americans. He stepped from the broken bulkhead and fired at one of the Americans who had revealed himself three times in the same position. Perfect timing. The bold American stepped into his line of fire and a large smoldering hole appeared in the center of his chest.

Josh Miller was dead.

Nox had little time to enjoy the small victory as he was nearly struck by a hail of heavy machine gunfire. Rolling back to cover unharmed, Nox thought to himself, 'that giant has got to go.' Two more Ondagra joined him inside the hulk, while the other Russian operators were being effectively held to the debris field by the Americans holding the high ground.

Nox gave the order to charge the Americans, and chaos ensued. In the swirling, white mayhem of madness, Nox came face to face with an American in FALOS armor. Reflexively, Nox struck the American in the helmet with his metal clad fist. The American stepped back, apparently momentarily stunned, and Nox raised his rifle and fired.

The American expertly dove to the right, and the flash of light singed the metal deck. In a split second, the American had tackled Nox, and they were both on the ground. The alien easily overpowered the invader, and, using brute strength ripped the American's helmet off.

Nox raised his right hand, intending to smash the American's head like a cantaloupe.

What. The. Fuck? It was Dale Matthews? His old adversary from the Great War? How was this possible? Dale would be nearly 100 years old, yet, here he was?

Nox froze in confusion. Nothing made any sense.

Am I going crazy? That was not normal for Ondagra. Could this planet be driving me insane?

Nox lowered his fist, he could not kill Dale Matthews. *Why?*

Nox was suddenly struck by a barrage of machine gun fire in the back, throwing him to the ground. Nox raced for cover before the giant clone could get another shot.

Shaken and wounded, Nox retreated from the battlefield and returned to his fighter. The wounds were not fatal, but his armor had sustained significant damage from the machine gun. Nox monitored the progress of the Russians from his fighter craft as he tended to his wounds.

How was Dale Matthews here in Siberia? Why had he not aged?

CHAPTER FORTY-FIVE

S nap grabbed his broken helmet and stumbled to cover. Neal West and Bob were the only two of his team that had seen the incident.

"Thanks, Bob. You saved my life," Snap gasped between cold breaths. Bob could not hear him because the COMM system was in the detached helmet.

Neal pulled Snap to cover behind a twisted bulkhead. The Russian operators were now all inside the ship's hulk, and advancing.

Snap's face was freezing as he gulped down frigid air. "Did you see that?" Snap asked Neal, who was directly in front of him. Snap was fumbling with his broken helmet, trying to reattach it to his FALOS armor.

Neal helped Snap somewhat reattach the helmet and COMM. "It's damaged beyond battlefield repair," Neal said. "But this should work for now."

"Thanks. Did you see that alien? Why did he freeze? He had me dead to rights. I knew I was a dead man."

"I saw it. Thank God for Bob."

"It wasn't Bob. The alien recognized me and lowered his fist. He had time to kill me before Bob shot him."

"I don't know, that's pretty messed up. Maybe we will never know."

The Russian operators had settled back into positions, with their backs to the frozen tundra, and were trading fire with Lightning Squad. Davis and Moore had made their way to Snap and West's position to give cover, while Snap got his helmet back on.

"Looks like one of the big ones is trying to flank us on the right," Timothy Moore said, while pointing to movement behind some wreckage.

"I can't get a clear shoot at him," West said, as he inched his way into a better position.

"Doesn't matter. The big ones can't be harmed by our DE rifles," Snap said, as he switched to his 50 BMG Lynx. "Maybe this will help."

"Damn. I was hoping we would never need that thing again," West whispered.

"Semi-automatic 50 caliber *Exacto* rounds. But only five shots per magazine," Snap said.

The Ondagra sprang from the rubble and landed in the middle of the group, swiping the Lynx sniper rifle from Snap's hands. The powerful rifle clattered to the deck, which was slowly turning white from the wind-blown snow.

"Fuck," Timothy Moore said, as he was flung against a pile of jagged metal debris that had seconds earlier been affording him cover.

Davis and West, knowing their rifles were useless, grabbed the seven-foot-tall armor-clad alien and attempted to wrestle him to the ground. Snap scrambled for the rifle, as Moore slowly picked himself up.

The Ondagra flung West off with ease and rolled over, pinning Davis to the ground beneath him. The device on the alien's chest began to glow bright blue, and Snap knew Davis was about to be incinerated. Snap, lying on the ground, raised the powerful sniper rifle at the alien and fired three times. Snap could feel the recoil of the 50 caliber rounds through his armor. The alien lurched to the left, and the flash of light from his chest missed Davis.

"You hit him," West yelled, as the alien leapt from the ground and scurried away before Snap could line up another shot.

Davis and Moore lie on the ground, not moving. Moore sat against the pile of jagged debris, with a grapefruit-sized hole burned through his armored stomach, a thin trail of steamy smoke was climbing upward.

Snap, knowing Moore was dead, crawled over to Davis, lying where the alien had left him. "Davis, Davis, can you hear me?"

West grabbed Snap's sniper rifle and took up a defensive position behind the twisted metal. "Snap, is he alive?"

Davis had two perfectly round holes punctured through his armor. Snap recognized them immediately, the BMG round had passed through the alien's armor, through the alien, and through Davis' armor. Snap rolled Davis over to see if the bullets had passed through him, there were no exit wounds. Two BMG rounds were lodged in Davis.

"West, Davis has been shot. He needs medical attention." Snap began to detach the helmet for a better look at the wounds.

"Is he going to make it?" West asked, as he peered into the scope of the sniper rifle towards the elusive enemy.

Davis' eyes fluttered open.

"He's alive, but I can't tell how serious the injuries are. Got to get his FALOS armor off." Snap began taking off the chest armor that was now adorned with two round holes.

Davis screamed and pushed Snap away. Snap tumbled backwards and Davis, half clad in armor, jumped on top.

"What the fuck," Snap was cut short by Davis' fist slamming into his already damaged helmet. Snap punched Davis in the chest hoping to connect with the wounds. Davis rolled off Snap howling in pain.

Snap grabbed Davis to control and comfort him. "It's okay man, we got you. You're safe."

Davis' eyes were open, but Snap could see that they were glazed over, like he was somewhere else.

"Davis, wake up. Wake up." Snap yelled, as he slapped Davis on the face.

Davis continued to scream, "Stay away from me you monster. Get away from me."

West turned from the battle to see what was going on with Snap and Davis. "Snap, what's wrong with Davis?"

"I don't know. He's in some sort of trance. Thinks I am one of them." Snap continued to cradle Davis in his arms, while he struggled to get free, screaming about demons and monsters.

"It might not matter. With Moore and Davis down, the Russians are advancing. Looks like we are outnumbered now," West said, as he peered out from behind cover.

Davis stopped struggling, Snap could see recognition in Davis' eyes – he was back. Snap released his grip on Davis.

"Major, Major," Davis managed to spit out between gulps of cold air.

"Davis, take it easy. You've been shot. I need to see the wound. Let's get the rest of this armor off."

"We don't have time, Major." West yelled. "The Russians are charging our position. I need you here now." West fired two more rounds from the sniper rifle, dropped it, and switched to this DE rifle.

Snap scrambled to the top of the pile of scrap metal and began firing at the advancing Russians.

"There's too many of them. We're not going to make it," West said, as the several Russians encroached on their position and began to flank them.

Snap and West were on top of the heap of metal, and Davis lay below, where he could not move because of his injuries. Davis could not see the battle from his vantage point. Snap was focused on the Russians in front of him, firing his DE rifle when he heard a shrill scream.

Davis screamed from his lowly position. "Snap, drop the DE and pick up the Lynx."

Snap dropped the DE rifle and dove for the 50 BMG.

"RELOAD." Davis screamed.

How the fuck can Davis be giving orders from behind the pile of rubble? He can't see shit.

Snap's instincts told him to do what Davis said, despite it making no sense. In seconds, the boxy magazine clicked into place, and the charging handle locked one 50 BMG into the chamber.

"YOUR THREE O'CLOCK."

Snap spun to his right to see nothing. *How can he see anything?*

"DOWN."

Snap lowered the rifle down just in time to see an Ondagra emerge from the twisted metal. He squeezed the trigger. The Ondagra lurched backwards and tumbled back down the pile of debris.

"Shit, Davis. You just saved my life. But how could you have known that?"

Before Davis could answer, ten more soldiers emerged from the blinding snow behind the Russians.

Shit. Just when I thought it couldn't get any worse.

"We have ten more operators joining the party at our twelve o'clock." Snap said into the COMM.

"Roger that, Major," Williams confirmed.

Then, the newcomers opened fire on the Russians. The Russians seemed to be just as surprised as Lightning Squad. Between the newcomers and Snap's men, the Russians were surrounded and started falling quickly.

"Who the hell are they?" Johnson asked.

"I think they are the remaining crew, *Impegi* survivors," Snap said, as he picked off a fleeing Russian.

A few minutes later, the remaining Russians were dead or running off into the snowy oblivion. Snap leapt down the pile of rubble to Davis lying below. Now that Davis had gotten his armor off, Snap could see the two bullet wounds.

"Shit, Davis. You look terrible."

"Thanks to your terrible aim, Major."

"Hey, I hit what I was aiming at. If not, you would be a cinder right now."

They traded awkward glances and then looked toward Moore, who had caught the sizzling beam that was meant for Davis.

Davis shook his head, "That was meant for me."

Snap applied pressure to the wounds with sterile bandages from a concealed first aid kit hidden within each of their armor suits.

"You're lucky. The bullets lost most of their velocity when traveling through the alien armor," Snap said, as he tossed a bloody bandage on to the deck.

"I don't feel lucky, Major."

"How did you know about that Ondagra sneaking up on me?" Snap asked, as he chemically cauterized Davis' wounds.

"I saw him," Davis answered.

"You could not possibly have seen him. He was nowhere near you, and he was on the other side of the rubble."

Davis sighed, "Since you shot me, I have been having visions – hallucinations. I can see the alien that you shot."

"Is he still alive?"

"Very much so. You hit him. Not fatal. He is back at his ship being patched up now."

"How could you know that?" Snap asked, bewildered.

"I just know. I know that I know."

Snap finished dressing the wounds and helped Davis put the armor back on.

"We're not done yet," Snap said, as he helped Davis over the mound of metal and crushed containers to meet the *Impegi* crew.

CHAPTER FORTY-SIX

Snap, with Davis by his side, approached Lightning Squad, who were gathering just inside the bulkheads of the *Impegi*. The wind was whipping through the fractured hull, carrying with it freezing snow. The newcomers were joined by Fabris and Catrix. The *Impegi* crew were wearing the same battle armor, which closely resembled the FALOS armor of Lightning Squad.

As he joined the group of soldiers introducing themselves to each other, he noticed that the *Impegi* crew had raised the visors on their helmets, so that their faces could be seen.

"Hello, I'm Commander Caliana Furier," the woman with stunning ice-blue eyes said, in perfect unaccented English, as she extended her hand in the customary way.

Shocked by the sight of such an attractive woman in this desolate place, Snap stuttered, "Hello, I'm Major Morgan Slade."

"This is Commander Forte," Furier said, as she gestured toward the man standing to her right. "He was the, as you would say, CO of the *Impegi*."

"Pleasure to meet you Sir. Major Morgan Slade," Snap said, as he raised the visor on his damaged helmet.

"The pleasure is all mine, Major Slade. I understand your team is here to rescue us," Forte said with a sarcastic grin.

"Yes, well, so far, the rescue mission isn't going as planned," Snap replied, with an emphasis on 'rescue.' "We have three down and one wounded," Snap said, nodding his head toward Davis.

"Major, what is the extraction plan?" Forte asked.

"Commander, we have seven C-17 cargo planes en route. They can't land, but supposedly, we can fly your jump shuttles up to them."

"Huh, that sounds like a dangerous training exercise; more like a suicide mission in hostile territory, with at least two enemy AG fighters in the area," Forte said with concern.

Snap took a deep breath, glanced at Furier's ice-blue eyes, and said, "It's not quite that bad. The Cargo planes are running optical stealth and have a battery of defensive weapons."

"Our jump shuttles have chameleon mode," Furier said with a smile. "That's something working for us."

"Speaking of the jump shuttles, where are they?" Snap asked.

"Couple miles away, hiding. They can be here in a minute when we are ready to finish loading them up. When will the C-17s arrive?"

Snap looked at the display on his forearm. "About 20 minutes. Let's finish loading the jump shuttles and get out of here."

"Major, let me introduce you to the rest of my crew. Then we will load the jump shuttles."

The two men walked up to the *Impegi* crew, who were mingling with Snap's team, recounting events from the battle. As Snap shook hands with Genu, he saw out of the corner of his eye a Russian through a gaping hole in the structure three decks up. The Russian was pointing an RPG directly at Snap's team.

Fuck. My visors up. No way to drop the visor and acquire targeting data before that asshole pulls the trigger. Hundred fifty yards away. Chances of bringing rifle to shoulder, manually targeting and firing before he can pull trigger- zero.

"RPG," Williams screamed, and pointed up.

A flash of light from behind Snap and the RPG exploded in the Russian's hands, killing him instantly. Snap whirled around to see Commander Forte lowering a laser rifle from his shoulder.

"That was one hell of a shot, Commander. Did you do that free-hand?" Snap asked, in amazement, noticing that the Commander's visor was still up.

"Yes Sir."

"You saved all of our lives, Commander," Lignos said.

"Thank you, Commander," Catrix said, sighing in relief.

"Wow. I had no idea you had skills like that, Commander," Genu said with admiration.

"Good thing he does, or we would all be crispy right now," Stella said, as she squeezed the Commander's hand and smiled.

"West, Williams, Johnson, secure a perimeter. The rest of you, move these containers out into the open, where we can load up the jump shuttles. We're out in ten."

The jump shuttles materialized a few dozen feet from the wreckage. The men, aided by their exoskeleton armor, easily carried the remaining containers to the jump shuttles.

Commander Forte warned Snap, "We can't get all the Element 115 on the jump shuttles. They are near max capacity."

"We don't need to get far. We just need to get up a couple thousand feet to meet the C-17s," Snap said.

"I don't know. If we overload the jump ships and are attacked, we have no maneuverability," Forte said, shaking his head.

"We only get one shot at this. Once the jump shuttles are in the air, we are not coming back to reload. We leave the rest of the cargo for the Russians."

In a matter of minutes, Snap and the other operators loaded up the shuttles, to standing room only for the soldiers and survivors.

"Okay, we are full. Everyone find a shuttle and pile in. Let's go," Snap commanded the crew, and waived his arm toward the shuttles.

"What about the remaining containers, Major?" Johnson asked. "Should we rig them with explosives?"

"There's too many of them, and they are still spread through-out the ship. Set time delayed explosives on the ones we have out, forget the rest," Snap ordered.

After seeing that all the operators and survivors had climbed aboard a jump shuttle, Snap entered the one that Furier was pilot-ing. There were three *Impegi* crew squeezed in-between the con-tainers that were stacked to the ceiling. Snap made his way to the front of the shuttle and sat beside Furier in the cockpit.

"Is this really going to work? I mean, we really are going to fly this shuttle right into the belly of a C-17 cargo plane mid-flight?" Furier asked.

"We're going to do it. Will it work? Not my department. The eggheads Stateside say it can be done. And it's our only option now," Snap said flippantly. "I hope you're a good pilot."

"So do I," Furier said with a grin.

The shuttle hummed to life and gently rose out of the snow. Snap could see the other shuttles rising, almost floating. One by one, they faded from view, as they activated their chameleon mode.

"Where do you suppose the Ondagra fighters are?" Furrier asked.

"I have no idea. Hopefully, they are damaged or have left the area with wounded," Snap replied, as he snapped his safety har-ness into place.

A few minutes later, the C-17 cargo planes could be seen in the low-level clouds before them. They were flying low and slow, with their rear bay doors open. Snap could see the first shuttle move into position and attempt to enter the cargo bay.

"Holy shit. Those eggheads got something right," Snap exclaimed, as the first shuttle nudged its way into the cargo plane.

The C-17 activated its optical stealth and faded from view. Two more shuttles successfully docked in their cargo planes and disappeared into the clouds. Snap could see two men standing ready to help them enter at the cargo bay door. Furrier was about to make the final push into the open bay when there was a loud explosion, and the shuttle spun out of control.

"What the fuck was that," Snap yelled, as the shuttle raced toward the ground, the C-17 no longer in their field of vision.

"We were shot by a particle beam. Brace yourself; we are going down," Furrier said coolly, as she attempted to regain flight controls.

Snap braced himself. Seconds before impact, Furrier engaged the craft's shields.

CHAPTER FORTY-SEVEN

B ob stood nine feet tall and had skin like Kevlar. He could lift a small automobile over his head and toss it like a brick. But the most remarkable thing about Bob was that he had absolute total memory recall. Every second of Bob's lonely existence could be instantly remembered in the clearest of detail.

Bob wasn't born in a test tube, but he was conceived in one. He remembered the dark warmth of his mother's womb, the bright light, and the scientist's cold hands. He could not remember his mother's face because he never saw it. Upon his birth, he was rushed to a scientific research lab, where he grew up with other children like him.

Bob received the best education. Beginning at three years old, he was taught languages, history, geography, computers, politics, but mostly he was taught war. There was no art or music in the curriculum for his fellow child soldiers. He wasn't given a name, just a number: 028. Bob knew he would die in combat; he was told that repeatedly during his lessons. He sometimes wondered if he had a soul. Would he burn in hell for all the people he had killed?

His teammates in this mission had given him the name Bob. He liked it. It was the first time anyone had given him a name, and for that, he would always be grateful. He hoped that when he got back to base, that they would let him keep his new name.

Bob sat in the back of the shuttle with several cargo containers. He did not wonder what was in them; that was not his concern. He had done his job, which was to load them up and get them home. Bob was the only member of Lightning Squad in the shuttle. Two *Impegi* crewmembers sat up front in the cockpit, and two were with him in the back, standing between containers.

The shuttle slammed to a halt in the cargo bay of the C-17. The shuttle's rear door opened; Bob began to climb out. When he looked up, he saw a man, who he instantly recognized to be a Vitahician, pointing a baby .380 at his face. Bob's first thought was 'why is this guy pointing a gun at me.' His second thought was 'is that a real gun.'

The man fired the weapon at point blank range. Bob wasn't afraid. He had been shot before, and by much larger weapons. Everything went black, and Bob was dead before he keeled over, face first into the hard metal deck.

What Bob would never know, was that Mike Evans, the Vitahician that killed him, was a scientist at the same lab where Bob had been born and raised. Mike knew that Bob's weakest point was his eyeball. Mike had shot Bob directly in his left eye, piercing his brain.

What Mike did not know, but it turned out in his favor, was that the jump shuttle had no other armor-clad soldiers in it. The four remaining on the shuttle were *Impegi* survivors, soft targets not expecting to be shot. In under a minute, all the shuttle occupants could no longer be classified as survivors.

Almost done. If I can get this cargo to the Ondagra, then maybe, just maybe, I can get Nakita back. Hopefully, the flight crew did not hear the shots. The flight crew. I must eliminate them next.

Mike knew that the giant fell where there were no security cameras, not that he could have moved him anyway. Mike only had two shots left in his small pistol, and three flight crew remained. Mike unsheathed the large combat knife strapped to the giant's leg, and concealed it under his jacket.

I must kill them all before any one of them radios Command. I need to get a head start before Command can dispatch interceptors.

Mike calmly walked up to the cockpit where the three pilots were sitting, paying no attention to him. Mike smiled. They had no idea what had just happened in the back. Mike fired twice in rapid succession. The first bullet struck the man to his right in the neck. He grabbed his throat, trying to stop the gurgling blood. The second bullet struck the other man in the face, just under the eye.

The pilot, realizing something was very wrong, tried to stand up and turn around. Mike lunged at the pilot with Bob's combat knife. The pilot was able to deflect the lunge, and Mike went toppling over the co-pilot's bloody body. The pilot pulled from his flight suit a Berretta pistol, but Mike had already recovered and grabbed the barrel of the pistol, pointing it toward the floor. The struggle continued until Mike plunged the knife into the pilot's chest, causing him to go limp. Mike pulled the three dead bodies from the cockpit and collapsed into the pilot's seat.

Mike had never flown a C-17 Globe Master. However, he had flown planes in the past. He helped design flight systems in the past, and had read the flight control manual. Not to mention the fact that the now dead crew had been so kind as to show him the flight controls on the long trip to Siberia.

Mike settled down into the pilot's seat, finding the perfect spot, before flipping the switch to engage the optical stealth, and changing course toward Antarctica. Mike turned off the Mission-Computer-Display and radio panel. He knew it would be a long flight to Antarctica. As he glanced over the gauges and four display screens, he remembered that fuel would be an issue. With a cargo this valuable, he was certain that the Ondagra would take care of the fuel, eventually.

CHAPTER FORTY-EIGHT

Major Tom had not slept since the *Impegi* went down. He stood next to General Stone Byrd in the rear of the command center on the Moon Base. Most of the officers were looking disheveled and tired, but Stone Byrd stood amongst the chaos like a chiseled statue with not a hair out of place or a wrinkle on his shirt.

Standing next to Stone Byrd, Major Tom thoughtfully recounted, more to himself than anyone else, "Magadan: The city that Jesus traveled to after he fed the five thousand."

Stone Byrd nodded his head, "Really?"

"Yes Sir. It was an ancient city on the Sea of Galilee. It's mentioned in both the Books of Matthew and Mark. Some say that Mary Magdalene was from there."

Stone Byrd was somewhat amused, "Well, aren't you a fountain of knowledge. Are you a Christian, Major?"

"My parents took me to Sunday School when I was a kid."

"You learn all that in Sunday School?" Byrd asked.

"Not really. I also read a lot. Some scholars believe that there may have been an ancient tower or fortress there."

"Anything else happen there?" General Byrd asked.

"Not that I can recall," Major Tom replied.

"Well, 2,000 years from now, they will be reading about how the events in Magadan Oblast changed the course of human history," Stone Byrd said, confidently.

One of the officers loudly announced, "All jump shuttles and cargo planes have cleared the crash site and are heading home,"

"Have all jump shuttles finished boarding the C-17s?" Stone Byrd asked.

"No. They are still trying to board, but there are no reports of problems," the officer reported. "Wait. No. I see one of the Russian crafts approaching a jump shuttle that has not yet boarded the C-17."

"Dammit. Fucking Russians," Stone Byrd muttered. "Keep me posted on that shuttle, let me know when it makes it to the cargo plane."

"Yes Sir."

Stone turned to another officer, "How much cargo did our boys leave at the site?"

"According to the last ground report and our sensor readings, it seems that we got about two thirds of the Element 115."

Stone shook his head in disgust, "So, the Russians and the Grays have a third of our Element 115. Damn. Major Tom, what are my options? Can we destroy that ship and all the remaining cargo?"

Major Tom responded slowly, "Yes Sir. I have four TEPNOS missiles left. One should do it."

Stone Byrd, sensing Major Tom's hesitation, asked, "But?"

"Well, Sir. It has been over a day since we launched six TEPNOS missiles at Russia. I'm certain they will have been trying to figure out what hit them, and with the incursion into Siberia, it's likely they have figured out what's going."

"Speak your mind, Major."

"Sir, two problems. Yesterday, they were not expecting a missile attack; so, they weren't looking for it, or trying to defend from it. Today, not only are they looking for it, but they may have figured out a way to defend. Second, yesterday we had the possibility of plausible deniability; today, they may be able to track these missiles right back to the Moon Base."

"I see your point, Major." Stone Byrd pressed his lips together so tightly that they began to turn white, then he clinched his fists. "Major, do we have any other options?"

"Not as I see it, Sir. Also, they have two off-world antigravity fighters in the area. So, it's possible that they could shoot down our missile."

"Have all of the jump shuttles and C-17s cleared the blast zone?"

"Yes Sir."

Stone Byrd took a deep breath, silently said a quick prayer to a God he didn't really believe in, and said, "Fire one TEPNOS missile at the *Impegi*."

CHAPTER FORTY-NINE

Nox felt at home behind the controls of his fighter. Despite having his weapons systems offline, and the *Impegi* crew escaping with the most valuable cargo, he knew there was still a victory to be found. The battle would be over soon, and he could get a full inventory of the remaining cargo aboard the disgraced interstellar ship. He knew there was no way that those little jump shuttles could carry away but so many resources.

Manpugna announced that he had just shot down one of the shuttles.

Even more precious cargo. No doubt, whatever is in that shuttle would be priceless. Why else would they have risked so much to recover it?

Nox piloted his craft toward the debris field that was once an escaping shuttle.

I will kill the survivors, if there are any, and then personally take inventory of the cargo. I wonder if Dale Matthews was on that shuttle. Stop thinking about him, it can't be him. He would be an old man now.

Visions of off-world technologies, equipment and gadgets that would soon be at his fingertips danced in his mind.

This could be a game changer. This cargo could shift the balance of power for centuries to come.

Nox's fantasies of finding a rare and precious cargo evaporated, when a familiar voice came through his COMM, "General, you have an incoming missile. We assume nuclear. Thirty seconds to impact."

"Target?" Nox asked, as sense of overwhelming dread washed over him.

"Crash Site Four," Popov reported.

Nox quickly turned the fighter toward the wreckage, while glancing at his display. Manpugna was out of position, too far away. Nox scanned the sky and his display panel. He spotted the missile arching down toward his prize. Instinctively, Nox lined up his weapons system and fired. Nothing happened.

Damn. I forgot my weapons are offline. The only way to stop that missile from destroying everything is to knock it out of the sky with my fighter.

Intuitively, Nox turned the fighter toward the incoming missile and pushed the antimatter reactor to maximum thrust. Nox had no doubt his fighter could outrun even the quickest American missile. What he didn't know, was what would happen upon impact. Seconds later, when Nox was absolutely certain that his AG fighter was on an irreversible intercept course with the missile; certain that his craft would slam into the missile that threatened his prize, he pulled the lever that would eject him from the cockpit, and into the dreary gray sky.

A second later, Nox was jetted into the atmosphere, and his parachute engaged, a human invention, he was glad that he had added to his craft decades ago. Large Gray's don't experience fear and anxiety quite like humans, but those would be the emotions closest to what Nox was feeling as his favorite fighter collided with the incoming missile.

What if the nuclear warhead detonates? Will my armor fail? Will it destroy the cargo ship? The answer is most certainly yes on both accounts.

The flash and explosion were deafening. Nox hurdled toward the ground, his parachute tangled and on fire. He tried to engage his personal energy shield. Failed. Failed. Failed. For a second, it crossed Nox's mind that the nuclear warhead did not detonate, but only for a second, as the frozen tundra raced up to meet him.

CHAPTER FIFTY

S nap opened his eyes. His head was pounding, and there was a spider web of cracks spreading across his vizor, impeding his vision. The shuttle was half buried in ice and snow, the fuselage ripped to pieces, leaving him exposed to the wind. Snap looked over at Furier; she lay still, slumped over the ship's controls. Snap release his harness and reached over to gently push her with his left hand. It was obvious that they would have been killed, if not for their advanced body armor.

Furier's arm twitched. She was alive. But for how long? Snap shifted closer to her and began to free her from the harness and tangled metal. Furier jerked awake and instinctively grabbed Snap by his shoulder.

"Whoa. Easy there. We are alive. For now," Snap said encouragingly, trying to calm her down.

"The crew. Did the crew make it?" Furier asked frantically.

Snap had not even thought of the other passengers that were in the back of the shuttle. Snap and Furier turned around to see that all the passengers were a mangled mess of blood and gore, smashed between the heavy cargo containers.

"Shit," Snap said. "Good thing we had on this armor, otherwise, that could have been us."

"Maybe, but also, maybe, they would have survived if we had not overloaded the ship with cargo," Furier said in an accusing tone.

"I'm sorry for the loss of your crew," Snap mumbled, as he finished freeing himself from the cockpit.

Snap climbed out of the shuttle and helped Furier to the ground.

"I'm surprised that fighter did not finish us off from the sky, or land to capture us. They just left," Furier said, as she surveyed the sky for enemy craft.

"Who knows why they left. But we need to get away from here before they return to finish the job," Snap said, scanning the horizon for any signs of enemy movements. "I'm going to see if Command can hear me."

"Won't that give away our position?" Furier asked.

"Pretty sure they know our position; they just shot us down. Besides, we have to let Command know we are alive."

"Slade to Command. Can you hear me?" Snap asked into his broken helmet.

"This is General Byrd. What is your situation?" The voice cackled over the broken COMM system.

"My shuttle craft was shot down by a Russian AG fighter. There is one other survivor besides me, a Vitahician officer. We need an extraction plan. There are two Russian AG fighters in the area, I'm sure they will return soon."

General Byrd responded, "Major Slade, there is only one AG fighter remaining, the other was destroyed. The remaining Russian fighter has diverted, it is unlikely he will return to your position anytime soon."

"Roger that, General. Do we have an extraction plan?"

"We can have an AG fighter to your position in a few hours. Until then, you need to hunker down."

"We can't stay here. This place will be crawling with Russians in a few hours," Snap said.

"It's hard to tell from our position, but it looks like there is an abandoned Cold War research outpost about 10 miles from your position. I'm sending GPS coordinates to you now. Consider that the extraction point."

"Roger that."

"Command out."

Furier had heard most of the conversation, but Snap filled her in on the parts she had missed. They took the emergency supply pack from the decimated shuttle and began walking east. The 10-mile hike would have been nearly impossible but for the exoskeleton armor they were wearing. Despite being damaged, the advanced armor still protected them from the weather and assisted with traversing rough terrain. In a short time, they arrived at the designated location.

"This is it," Snap said, while studying his forearm display.

"I don't see anything," Furier complained.

"Well, it's got to be here. It probably hasn't been used in 40 years. The entrance could be covered in snow, for all we know."

The landscape was flat and rocky, with an occasional small mound or hill. The snow was light and dry, almost giving the appearance of a barren planet or moon.

"Why would they have had a Cold War station out here?" Furier asked, as she studied her display monitor. "There's nothing here, no trees, no people, nothing."

"The Russians were very paranoid back then, still are, really. They could have been doing weather research, biological weapons, or it could have just been a listening post. Who knows, the outpost may have only had a dozen people stationed in it. But if we find it, it may be able to give us shelter and possibly supplies."

"Wait, I think I'm picking up something on my radar. Looks like a large underground cavern, directly below us."

"What are you looking at?"

"Oh, you don't have one? It's a ground penetrating radar, it allows me to see up to 100 feet below the surface," Furier bragged. "Definitely, a manmade structure. Too many square edges to be all natural."

"Well, this must be it. Now all we must do is find the door," Snap said, as he walked toward a ten-foot-high earthen mound that appeared to be too symmetrical.

"Where are you going?" Furier asked.

"This mound, it's too perfect, and it's larger than all other mounds for miles around. I bet its part of the structure."

A closer study of the earthen mound revealed a concrete entrance big enough for a single troop transport to enter. The metal doors were shut and locked; it appeared no one had been through these doors in many years.

"Look, the doors are just locked with a chain and pad lock. You can shoot it with your DE rifle," Furier said.

"Yeah, they were not terribly concerned with security when they locked this up, years ago. Probably figured no one would even find this place, much less care to enter."

Snap shot the lock off, and the doors slowly creaked open with little effort, revealing a dark tunnel leading underground. Furier turned on her helmet lamp; Snap's was broken. The walls and floor were smooth concrete, with dusty electric light bulbs hanging from the domed concrete ceiling. Snap shut the door behind him, as they began to make their way down into the Cold War base.

The manmade tunnel gave way to a more natural cave-like appearance, as it opened into a cavern with stalactites hanging from the cave ceiling. The stalagmites had been removed in favor of a flat concrete floor. The large cavern was littered with crates, equipment, machinery, and a few old trucks.

"Hey, at least it's not as cold down here," Snap said, as he removed his broken helmet.

"Still a bit chilly, but no wind and snow," Furier said, as she too removed her helmet revealing her long hair and blue eyes.

"Let's see if we can find anything of use," Snap said.

"Like what?"

"We got to sit tight for a few hours, maybe longer depending on weather and enemy troop movements. Maybe we could build a fire, find some blankets or a light source."

"I got a light source, Major," Furier said, as she flashed the helmet light toward Snap with a slight laugh.

After a cursory exploration of the cave, they found nothing of great interest, just forty-year-old equipment. They did find blankets and fuel to build a small fire for light and warmth.

Once the fire was built, Commander Furier began taking off her armor.

"What are you doing?" Snap asked.

"You don't expect me to rest in this armor, do you?"

"Well, yes, I suppose I did. What if the Russians show up in the middle of the night? We won't have time to armor up for battle," Snap pointed out.

"True. But, I imagine if they show up here, they will come with overwhelming force. We are not likely to prevail in a fire fight either way. Besides, I bet they have more important places to secure than an abandoned base."

Snap watched her take off her armor, revealing a dark blue, form fitting uniform. "I guess I need some sleep too," Snap said, as he stood to take off his armor.

In a few minutes, they were wrapped up in Cold War era blankets, gazing at a fire fueled by old wooden storage crates. The firelight danced among the stalactites on the ceiling making strange shadows as the two warriors tried to relax. Only now did Snap really have time to think about his fallen brothers.

Snap settled in on a mound of gray wool blankets that insulated him from the chilly concrete floor. Furier had stacked up several blankets into a make shift bed. Both sat on one side of the crackling fire, watching the light reflect off the run-down equipment from a bygone era.

"Do you think the Russians will find us here?" Furier asked as she ripped open a sealed package containing a dark green bar. She broke a piece off and offered it to Snap.

"Thank you," Snap said, taking the food from her hand. "No. I think Command will pick us up in a few hours, long before the Russians have time to look for us. The Russians will be too busy securing the crash site to worry about us."

"Why don't your people just destroy the *Impegi* with a missile?"

Snap shifted in his blankets, and said, "I don't really know, but I assume it has something to do with politics, and not starting World War Three."

"World War Three?"

"Yes. Some egg head probably calculated that Russia would not react to us nuking barren tundra, but a crashed ship is going too far. Way beyond my paygrade," Snap said with a smile. "You know I just found out last week that there are extraterrestrials, aliens if you will, on this planet. Now, I'm sitting in this Cold War bunker with one right next to me. Did you know that they keep your existence, your people, a secret from almost everyone on this planet?"

"Yes, I was aware that your leaders keep us a secret from the people of Earth. It is different on Vitahic, I grew up learning about Earth, humans and your cultures."

"Wow. How many inhabited planets do you know about?"

"Our space travel and exploration is limited to about twenty percent of the Milky Way Galaxy. We know of several planets that can, or do sustain some type of life. We have diplomatic relations, good and bad, with six different planets.

"As you can imagine, I have so many questions about you, your planet and your people. I hope you don't mind me asking," Snap said.

"No, I don't mind at all. Obviously, we have been trained not to disclose our identity to the general population on Earth; but, clearly, you are already aware of our existence. What would you like to know?"

"Everything, tell me everything about your world," Snap said, eagerly, mesmerized by the flickering fire light being reflected in her eyes.

"Well," she started out thoughtfully. "Being on Earth is like going back in time, several hundred, maybe a thousand years. It would be like you traveling back to your Renaissance Period. Back home we have all but eliminated sickness and starvation. We don't have governments and corporations, at least, not in the same sense that you do."

"How did you get rid of sickness and starvation?" Snap asked.

"Genetic engineering and managed population growth. The two go hand in hand. Our scientists developed a way to manipulate DNA prior to birth, so that we were born with absolutely no defects. We experienced rapid technological advancements in the fields of genetic engineering, and it wasn't long before everyone was born, not only defect free; but, also, immune from most common illnesses. Soon, we saw rapid population growth because people were living longer, putting additional strains on our resources."

"Our leaders tried everything from regulating birth rates among the population to outright euthanasia, nothing seemed to work. This was a dark time in our planet's past; there were resource wars, and millions were killed. Until the next scientific breakthrough in gene manipulation; they figured out how to custom design babies. But, not just eye and hair color; no, they were able to select skill sets and interests. At this point, we could basically order babies to fulfil specific needs. If we were projecting a shortage of medical professionals, we could order up a batch of babies that were predisposed to be interested in medicine and science."

With a confused look on his face, Snap asked, "How did that stop the wars and starvation?"

"It didn't. Not at first, anyway. It took a few hundred years; but, eventually, you had enough people that were genetically predisposed to being good administrators and planners that they were able to put mandates in place to regulate the population growth. Through certain factions yielding, education, and regulation; everyone agreed to the concept of limited reproduction. Now, every child born on Vitahic, is authorized by the governing body, and genetically predisposed to fulfil a projected future need. Of course, with this system in place, we never have too many people to feed; nor do we have unemployment."

Snap shook his head. "But, are your people happy?"

"Like I said, at first it was a very rough transition. But, now, after a few hundred years, most people understand that there is a tradeoff necessary when you are living over 300 years. When the life span of your average citizen grows from 80 to 325 years; that person consumes more than triple the resources. Something must give. Plus, they are genetically engineered to be, not only healthier; but, stronger and smarter. We are not producing dumb, or lazy people on our planet – why would we?"

"Wow. So, everyone on your planet is as smart as you, and the others I met today?"

"For the most part, yes. Everyone on Vitahic is born with a very high IQ, as humans call it; emotionally stable; an appropriate amount of personal drive; and, a predisposition to be interested in a needed skill set."

"So, you have people that are genetically engineered from birth to be garbage collectors?" Snap asked.

"There are very few menial jobs on Vitahic. Most of the labor-intensive or repetitive jobs have been taken over by automation. But, yes, we have certain jobs that require fewer skills and people are genetically designed for those jobs. It is not a problem, because, like I said, they are designed to enjoy that type of work. It's not so much that we can manipulate the DNA to create a person that will invent the next advance in a particular field of study; it more like, we can design person that will grow up to be a good scientist, or a good soldier, a good nurse, or an educator."

"Sounds to me like you are not giving your people the opportunity to choose who they will become," Snap countered.

"No different than here on Earth, you are a prisoner of your DNA. You did not get to choose your genetic makeup. The difference is, here on Earth, if too many teachers are born, then, you have teachers running around with no jobs; while there is shortage of nurses," Furier explained. "What caused you to go into the military?"

She had made a good point, without even realizing it. Snap immediately understood, and slowly responded, "My grandfather and father were both in the military."

Furier smiled, she saw that he got it. "See, it's not that much different on Earth. We just plan a little further ahead. Another problem we don't face is having narcissistic, egomaniacs managing the direction of our planet; and stumbling into wars that could kill millions of people."

"How do you avoid that?" Snap asked.

"Simple. One of our genetic templates is for an Administrator. Of course, we have thousands of Administrators, each with different responsibilities, but they all are cut from the same Administrator blank, if you will. They are predisposed to being fair, even tempered, empathetic and selfless. Of course, like everyone, some are better than others; but, when you have thousands of them across the planet, the better ones rise to the top and balance out the weaker ones."

"So, no individual nations, or wars?" Snap asked.

"Once genetic manipulation was widely accepted by the population, we have not had any warring nations on our planet. Once you realize that there are otherworldly enemies that threaten the very existence of your entire planet; trivial differences among yourselves become irrelevant. The people of Vitahic think of themselves as Vitahicians, and they all work together for the common good of the planet – not just their region."

"So, are you at war with other planets?"

"We are experiencing a moment of uneasy peace with another planet. But, we have engaged in interplanetary war in the past. That's one of the reasons we are reaching out to Earth; hopefully, to establish an ally."

"I can't even imagine what an interplanetary war would be like? Were you in it? Did you fight?" Snap asked.

"No. The war ended when I was just a child. Our planet sustained a tremendous amount of damage; entire cities were destroyed. I remember them rebuilding, well into my years at the Academy. No one on Vitahic wants to see that happen again. We try very hard to maintain diplomatic relations with the enemy; but, we also are building our defenses, just in case."

Snap could tell this was a touchy matter for her and decided to change the subject, "So, I know you are genetically designed for a purpose; but, are you raised by a mom and dad, a family unit?"

Furier paused for a moment, and stared at the fire, before saying, "Yes. I have a mom and dad, but it's not like human families. We are not as close. We don't have marriage anymore. We did, a long time ago. But, the government got rid of marriage after life expectancies increased. People could not stay together for hundreds of years, it just wasn't working. Now, some people mate for life, but it is rare. My mom and dad are no longer together, I see them when I can, but not really that often."

"Okay, Okay. I hope you don't mind me asking these questions?" Snap asked, not wanting to make her feel uncomfortable.

"No. It's okay. I am enjoying the conversation."

"So, what do people on your planet do? When they are not flying around the galaxy in a space ship?" Snap asked.

"A lot like your planet. Everyone works. They enjoy outdoor activities and entertainment. We have less crime, war, and strife, than you have on Earth. Some are raising children, while others are exploring hobbies and developing new technologies. A few still observe ancient religions, but not as many as do here on Earth."

"You said they don't have corporations, like we do. Where do people work?" Snap asked.

"Most of the means of production are managed by what you would call a government, those 'Administrators' I was telling you about."

Snap laughed, "Here, that's called 'socialism'. I can think of a few people that would have a problem with that."

"Yeah, another tough transition. There is no way we could have moved from capitalism to socialism without the technological advances in genetic manipulation. But, after a couple of hundred years, the people began to trust the Administrators, they saw that they were fair, competent, and not greedy. Once we established that level of trust between the people and the Administrators, it was easy to turn things over to them. After all, they really could manage things better than the rest of us; in the same way the Captain of a starship can chart a course more accurately than a supply officer."

"Well," Snap said, thoughtfully. "What about the bad administrators, you mentioned?"

"What? What do you mean?" Furier asked.

"You know, you said some of the Administrators were better than others; but, they were held in check by the good ones, and you alluded to the fact that maybe the best ones were promoted."

"I wouldn't say 'bad', they are just not as skilled as the others. They do cause small problems from time to time; after all, we are not cookie cutouts of one another. The problem occurs when one of these less skilled Administrators gets to another planet, and is isolated away from our culture and processes. We have seen them lose their way, and begin to regress back into the old ways. Of course, they still have their genetic predisposition to be a good

Administrator; but, without the constant reinforcement from the others, well, they slip. Genetic manipulation does not make us exactly the same, or perfect. It only predisposes certain attribute like intelligence, sex, physical features and general interests. Personal drive, ambition, and experiences play a part in the individuals development, an ultimately how useful they will become. You may be born a soldier, but you have to work hard to become a general."

"How so? I mean, how do they lose their way" Snap prodded.

"They could lose their way, especially over decades of being away from their home world. They lose sight of their directives, and start to put their personal ambitions and desires ahead of the mission. We have seen it happen before."

The conversation trailed off. Both were worn out from a hard day. Snap got up and rummaged around for some more wood to throw on the fire. Sparks raced up toward the stalactites when Snap dropped a piece of wood on the smoldering coals.

Even though he was exhausted, Snap's mind could not rest. "Wow. So, this is where humans could be in 500 years?"

"Maybe. Maybe sooner. With our help, we hope to speed up the process. Help you avoid some of the mistakes we made along the way."

"So, besides the genetic predisposition, what made you want to be the Quartermaster on an interstellar ship?" Snap asked with a weak chuckle as his eyes grew heavy.

"So, it doesn't really work that way. I was not genetically predisposed to be a Quartermaster; I was genetically predisposed to enjoying the study of science and math. From there, my personal interests and studies could have led me to any number of fields. As a child, I grew up hearing about all these exotic worlds, I just wanted to see them for myself. We have billions of people on my planet, but only a fraction of them can travel to space. It requires years of special training."

"I still can't get over how much you look like us. I mean if you evolved on another planet, what, hundreds of light years from here, why do you look like us?" Snap asked, as he pulled a blanket up around his chin and curled into a fetal position.

"Maybe a common ancestor? Who knows. Ancient forgotten civilization of space travelers, random chance, or God, as humans call him? People smarter than me have been trying to figure that out for generations, I'm not going to be the one to solve the mystery." Furier said, with a shrug.

"One more question; before I fall asleep. Please, don't take this the wrong way, but I must ask. Vitahicians look just like humans, can you have sex with a human?

Furier smiled and said with mock indignation, "Major, are you propositioning me?"

"No. No. I would never . . ." Snap stuttered.

"So, you don't find me attractive?" She said with a smile, clearly enjoying Snap's discomfort.

"No. I think you are beautiful, I mean attractive . . ." Snap's voice trailed off, trying not to dig a deeper hole for himself.

Furier laughed, "Human men are no different than Vitahician males. It's true the saying, 'men can only think with one head at a time.'"

"You have that saying on your planet, too?" Snap asked in surprise.

"No silly, it's part of the culture training we receive. I've watched hundreds of your movies."

"Now that I've had my fun with you, I will answer your question, Major. Yes, my kind has had sex with humans on many occasions."

Snap smiled, relieved that she had decided to stop putting him on the spot. "Has a Vitahician and a human ever had a child together?"

"No. It has never happened; but, not for a lack of trying. Our scientists have been trying to crossbreed humans and Vitahicians for years – with no success, I might add."

Snap laughed and said, "Wow. Just think of the lucky bastard that gets to repeatedly try to impregnate one of your kind."

"Yeah, but, I'm sure it gets old after a while. And they did try that method in the beginning, but now, I think it's all done in a research center, very mechanical."

"Not as fun," Snap sighed. "Why come here at all? I mean, after checking us out for curiosity's sake, why keep coming back, I'm sure it's not just to have sex with humans?"

Furier laughed, and then fell silent for a moment, thinking of what to say. "We need trading partners, we need to develop military alliances."

"Yes. You said that; you are looking for allies because your planet was attacked. But, how can we help, from a military stand point? What can we offer you in the way of protection?"

"You're right. As of now, your planet offers no strategic defense for us, but our goal is to develop your weapons systems to the point where you would be willing and able to form a long-term military alliance with us. That is why for the last 70 years we have been feeding you technology, and resources that you cannot get here on Earth. The anti-gravity fighters, the FALOS armor, the Micro Modular Fusion Reactors; all technology that you could not have developed on your own. One of the reasons for this supply ship was to bring you not only the Element 115, which is rare on your planet, but to bring the light elements needed for fusion reactors. With the loss of this cargo, it could be decades before we are able to be resupplied – setting back our plans to develop your planet, possibly by centuries."

Snap wanted to press for more information about interstellar politics but sensed she did not really want to discuss it further. In a few minutes, they were both asleep. Snap tossed and turned in the cave's darkness. He dreamed of unknown aliens competing for control of the Earth. His mind wandered back to the American Revolution; where France, England and Spain were all competing to settle the new-found Americas.

CHAPTER FIFTY-ONE

Nox's eyes fluttered open to the sound of his communication device squawking something unintelligible. His whole body was aching, and lightning rods of pain were streaking up his left leg. Breathing was difficult. He realized his helmet was off, and his face was freezing cold. He sucked in as much bitter cold air as he could muster.

I am alive.

A quick assessment of his situation led him to the conclusion that he had a broken leg and a collapsed lung.

No way I can walk out of here. That would be something. I travel through the stars, intentionally crash into a nuclear missile, only to die of a broken leg. Not the way I'm going out.

The communicator squawked again. A voice he recognized – almost. He gasped for another breath.

What happened to the ship? Did I save the ship? Of course, I saved the ship. If that nuke had gone off I would have been killed. I must have disabled the nuke before it detonated.

The communicator was in his helmet, which was several feet away. Nox crawled to the helmet and manually activated the communication device.

"This is Nox, can anyone hear me?"

No response. Nox initiated another transmission, "Can anyone hear me?"

"This is Manpugna. Nox where are you? I saw your fighter explode. I thought you may have . . ."

"I'm seriously injured. I need medical attention immediately," Nox gasped.

"I've fixed on your transmission. I'm en route."

"Manpugna, getting to me is your top priority."

"Yes Sir. I have some really good news."

"Are you going to make me guess?"

"Calidus just called."

"Calidus? What did he want?" Nox asked in an irritated tone.

"One of his Vitahician operatives contacted him a few minutes ago. Said he had hijacked a C-17 over Siberia full of alien cargo. Said he was heading toward the Antarctica base."

"This is very good. Send him a full escort and an IL-78 for refueling. We don't want the Americans to snatch him."

Nox collapsed, knowing that Manpugna would be there soon. Nox knew that he had just cheated death.

CHAPTER FIFTY-TWO

Mike Evans sat in the pilot's seat of the C-17. He thought he could feel the pilot's blood soaking through the seat of his pants. He knew it wasn't, though. Two Russian fighters had escorted him over the Pacific, and he had refueled midair several hours earlier. Mike had started to feel remorse for murdering the Vitahicians back in the jump shuttle. They did not choose to be in that shuttle, or even to align themselves with the Americans. They were simply crew on a cargo ship.

His mind drifted to the C-17's crew that he had murdered, their cold bodies lying not far behind him. He had spent hours talking to them on the flight to Siberia. There was Jason, a husband and father to three sons. There was Kirk, the pilot, a husband and grandfather who was only a few months from retirement; he would never spend time at his newly purchased vacation property in Hilton Head.

All this death just for him to escape the Americans. Had they really treated him that badly? Would the Ondagra really treat him better? Would he enjoy living in the desolation that was Antarctica?

Would Nakita really be there to meet him? His mind wandered to his vacation in Virginia Beach where he had met her. Was he romanticizing his time with her? Did he really love her? Would she forgive him for shooting her? Would she understand that all of this was for her? Would she care? It had been so long since he had spoken to her.

The flight from Russia to Antarctica was long and lonely. He had no one to whom he could talk. Occasionally, Calidus called for a status update. He had been over the ice shelf of Antarctica for a while. At over 5 million square miles, Antarctica is nearly twice the size of Australia, and it officially has less than 5,000 human inhabitants.

Mike flew the C-17 for hours over the snowy mountain ranges to the GPS coordinates he had received. The Russian escort had turned back because they lacked fuel for the entire journey. Except for the stiffening corpses behind him, he was alone, above one of the most remote places on Earth.

Mike's heart skipped a beat and he began to panic as he approached the location where he was supposed to begin his decent. He saw nothing but flat empty desert. No buildings. No runway. No people. No signs of life. He knew the Russians wanted the cargo; there was no way they would trick him into flying to the middle of nowhere, but, where were they?

His radio squawked to life for the first time in hours, "This is flight control. You are cleared for landing. Begin your decent now."

Mike followed instructions, but asked, "I don't see the runway, or anything for that matter."

"I know this is your first time landing here. You won't see anything, it will look like you are crashing to the ground, but you won't. Follow my instructions precisely, ignore what you are seeing, and you will be fine. The ground will open for you. You will need to come in faster than you would think."

Mike followed the instructions precisely. The ground was fast approaching, and the plane was not slowing down – not nearly enough. Seconds before the plane was about to smash into the ground, Mike clutched the flight controls, closed his eyes, and took a deep breath, expecting to die. His eyes opened; he had passed through the icy ground like it was a cloud, or an optical illusion. The plane continued its downward trajectory through two miles of ice and rock before it opened up again, and he was in clear sky – or so it seemed.

What the fuck? Where am I?

After a closer look, Mike realized that he was not flying above the earth, but below it. The gauges showed he was flying about a thousand feet above the rocky surface. Above him was a ceiling of rock and ice. There were mechanical devices above that funneled light from the sky into the huge cavern. Mike glanced to his right and left, it appeared there was at least 30 miles between him and the cave walls on either side. Ahead of him there appeared to be at least 100 miles of airspace, maybe more.

A closer look at the ground revealed tall buildings, factories, residential areas, warehouse districts, an airport, and a large lake. Mike navigated the large cargo plane toward the airport. The voice confirmed he was cleared for landing. The C-17 glided along the 3,000-foot-long smooth runway to a stop. Mike saw three people quickly walking toward the plane. He squinted to make out their features. There were two very large soldiers wearing body armor, Mike knew them to be Ondagra, the third person was much smaller, a woman.

Could it be Nikita? Was she here to greet him? Would she be happy that he was able to deliver this precious cargo?

As they approached, Mike's heart summersaulted as he saw that it was Nakita. He smiled. Everything was going to be okay. It was all worth it. He lowered the ramp so she could board. The two soldiers stayed back at the foot of the ramp. Mike ran to her and threw his arms around her.

"Thank you for being here. I'm so relieved to see you," Mike whispered.

Nakita returned the hug, but pushed him away after a few seconds.

Nakita stepped back and asked, "Remember that time you shot me in Virginia?"

Mike stuttered, "Yes, but I was forced to do that. Please don't hold that against me. Look what I have done for you. I did all of this for you. I killed my own people. I killed Americans. I stole this cargo."

Nakita smiled. "I'm a spy. That's what I do. The Ondagra thank you for your service."

Mike looked down at her right hand and saw a DE pistol.

"You are going to shoot me? After all we have been through? Are you kidding me? This is how it ends? Listen, you don't have to do this."

Still smiling, she said, "I know, Mike. I asked to do this." Nikita leveled the pistol at his chest, and said, "Consider us even."

The flash of light seared through his chest, burning flesh and sucking the air out of his lungs. He clutched his chest with both hands, staggered backwards, stumbled over some boxes and tumbled to the metal grating. He started shaking uncontrollably. The last thing he heard before darkness washed over him was Nikita yelling, "We need a medical team up here ASAP."

As he faded into oblivion, his last thought was, "Why would they need a medical team?"

CHAPTER FIFTY-THREE

It had been a week since Snap and Furier had been extracted from Siberia with the help of an American AG Fighter. The rescue went smoothly; it seemed like the Russians were too busy taking inventory of their newly found prize to even mount a search for the survivors of the fallen shuttle. There had been several debriefings since they returned. Top brass seemed very interested in the Russian soldier's battle armor. Snap was surprised that they didn't really ask that much about the Ondagra's capabilities; he guessed they were already familiar with those.

Snap sat alone in a conference room, several hundred feet below Dugway Proving Ground. He knew he was to meet with a VIP, but he wasn't sure who it would be. In walked General Benjamin Paxton, and with him a very distinguished looking Air Force General that Snap did not recognize at first.

General Paxton said, "At ease, Major Slade."

Snap stood to meet the Generals.

"This is General Stone Byrd of Space Command," General Paxton announced.

"It's an honor to meet you, Sir. We spoke a few times during the operation," Snap said.

"No. It's an honor to meet you, Major Slade. You and your men really saved the day by recovering so much of the Element 115."

"Thank you, Sir," Snap said. Snap had a million questions about the Moon Base, space aliens, and interstellar politics; but, he knew better than to ask. There was good chance he already knew more than he should.

"Major, I think it's time we read you in on a few things." The General paused and then emphasized, "highly classified things."

"Yes Sir."

"Let's have a seat," General Byrd said, as he pointed to the chairs at one end of the conference room table.

General Paxton started, "So, you already know there are two different species of aliens here on Earth, you have meet them both. You know that we have extensive diplomatic and strategic relations with the Vitahicians. The Russians have longstanding ties with the Ondagra, and there is a form of cold war going on between us."

"Yes Sir," Snap said.

General Stone Byrd interjected, "The problem, son, is that we, the humans, are the low man on the totem pole, so to speak. If either of these technologically advanced races were to suddenly decide that they don't need humans anymore, well, let's just say we would not have any meaningful way of defending ourselves."

"I thought both the Ondagra and Vitahicians prefer to control through diplomacy and political power?" Sap interrupted.

General Paxton said, "So they say. But we are in a tight spot if they change their minds. We are trying our best to catch up, as fast as we can. That's why we need the Element 115 and other off world elements, too. It's necessary to build AG Fighters and fusion reactors, and they can't be found here on Earth, at least in any kind of meaningful quantities. If we can't stand on our own, then we are subject to the whims of these aliens."

"Sir, I thought the Vitahicians were trying to help us?"

Stone Byrd answered, "They are, and they have. If it weren't for them, we would still be using rotary phones. But, they can only provide so much help. They are a long way away. If Earth were attacked, by the time they could get here, the war would have been over for years. Not to mention their weapons systems are still behind the Ondagra. If more Ondagra were to show up, well, I doubt we could survive even a month."

General Paxton added, "That's not even the most immediate problem. Mike Evans, one of our Vitahician scientists, someone who has been with us for decades, since the Eisenhower administration, defected. He killed all the crew on his C-17 and flew it to Antarctica with a load of Element 115."

This was the first time Snap was hearing this. "What? We lost a C-17? How? Who was on the plane he took?"

"None of your team. He killed the clone that was with you, the crew, the rest were survivors from the *Impegi*."

"He got Bob? How?"

"Bob?" Paxton asked.

"Bob is what they named the clone," Stone Byrd said. "I heard them referring to one of them as Bob; I was not sure which one they were referring to until now."

"You named the clone?" Paxton asked in surprise.

"Yes Sir. Was that wrong?"

"No. I suppose not. It's just never been done before. Anyway, Bob's dead. The problem is, we now know Mike Evans was not working alone. He had help. Help from within."

Snap asked, "How do we know he had help?"

The Generals glanced at one another; Stone Byrd nodded. General Paxton went on, "Shortly after we lost contact with the C-17, and we realized what had happened, we searched all of Mr. Evans personal belongings and found some of his communications.

It was clear that he was talking to other Vitahicians. Several of them."

"Do we know who they are?" Snap asked.

"No. Unfortunately, they used code names, and we cannot crack their encryption. Well, that's not entirely true. We don't even understand the technology they use to transmit data, much less how to break it down or track it."

There was a pause in the conversation, as if the Generals were wanting him to respond. Snap, not wanting to reveal too much of what he learned while in the Siberian cave, said, "So, what can I do, Sir?"

General Stone Byrd said, "Well, son, the dynamics of power are shifting now that the crew of the *Impegi* have arrived. You see, there were two commanders on that ship. Commander Furier and Forte are now among the top Vitahician leadership here on Earth. Forte has become a hero among the Vitahicians, based on him saving as many of them as he did that day. The others, the ones that have been here for so long, will be forced to confide in them. Forte and Furier will be forced to take sides."

"Take sides?" Snap asked. "Do you think the conspiracy that Mike was a part of is really that big, goes that deep?"

"Unfortunately, yes. We believe, based on the communications we could intercept, and the way he was able to execute his plan on such short notice, that he must have had substantial help," General Paxton replied.

General Byrd leaned forward in his chair and said, "Major, we don't know, but the conspiracy may lead all the way back to their home-world. We are concerned that the *Impegi's* crash landing in Russia may have been the work of sabotage."

"To what end? Couldn't that have killed the saboteur?"

"Maybe. But most of them escaped and survived the crash. It could have been planned to just drop the ship into the hands of the

Russians and Ondagra. If the *Impegi* was intentionally dropped, we need to know who ordered it. That's where you come in."

"I'm sorry, Sir. You lost me. How do I come in?" Snap asked, as he sat up straight in his chair.

"You spent the night with Commander Caliana Furier, down in that Russian bunker. We are assuming that you must have formed some sort of bond. Down there. Alone. For so long," General Paxton said with a weak smirk and raised eyebrow.

Snap shifted in his seat, more than a little uncomfortable, and said, "I assure both of you that nothing inappropriate happened."

"No. Major, you misunderstand. We are not accusing you of anything," General Paxton assured.

Stone Byrd laughed and said, "Not that we could blame you. She is one hell of a looker. If you know what I mean."

Snap smiled faintly and replied, "Yes Sir. She is."

"All we want you to do is to use your relationship with her to stay close and keep your ears open," Stone Byrd said.

"You want me to spy on Caliana?" Snap asked indignantly.

"No. Nothing like that, Major. Just keep an eye on her. If you see or hear anything out of the ordinary, let us know," General Paxton said firmly.

"How is that not spying?" Snap asked in the politest tone he could muster, trying to not be insubordinate.

General Paxton continued on in a firm tone, "Major, we don't expect her to side with the traitors. But we have no idea who they are, how many there are, or what their intentions may be. We must assume they have spies everywhere, and we have nothing. If she is contacted by the defectors, we need to know about it. Do you understand?"

General Stone Byrd added, "Do you agree to stay close to her and report back to us if she is contacted by any of Mike Evans' co-conspirators?"

Snap knew he had no choice, and why should he, if she was a traitor, then his loyalty was clearly with the military. Snap responded, "Yes Sir."

"Good. Thank you Major. And thank you again for the good work in Siberia," General Byrd said, as he stood.

"General, may I ask a question before you go?"

"Of course, Major."

"Sergeant Davis, the one that was hit by friendly . . . that I shot. He started acting funny, having premonitions of a sort. He could predict where the alien would attack next. Did we ever figure out what happened there?"

Stone Byrd stopped, frowned and replied quickly, "No, Major. We never did figure that one out. I guess there are just some things that happen in combat that can't be explained."

"Yes Sir," Snap replied. Snap knew the General was hiding something, but there was no point in pressing the issue.

CHAPTER FIFTY-FOUR

August 21, 1945

Dale Matthews wiped the sweat from his forehead as he walked into the mess hall. He had been at Alamogordo Army Air Field in New Mexico for several months. The Germans had surrendered, and the war was over. Dale shuffled over to where soldiers in olive drab uniforms were lining up for chow. The single story wooden structure had a few ceiling fans that helped with the dry heat. For months, Dale had been performing meaningless tasks, just biding time. It was clear that the Army had no idea what to do with him after he answered all their questions about the alien space craft he had seen in France.

Dale had been informed earlier that day that General Ryan Bartlett wanted to speak to him about an urgent matter. It had been months since he had been debriefed on the whole alien incident, and since then, the Army seemed to have forgotten about him. Clearly the meeting this afternoon would have something to do with the 'incident,' as they were calling it now. After lunch, he walked through the blistering summer heat to the office building where all the Army brass worked. It seemed a bit cooler in the nondescript, secretarial bullpen, as he sat waiting for the General to arrive.

A few minutes later, General Ryan Bartlett appeared from behind a closed door. Dale remembered him from Paris, France. The General appeared to be having a difficult day.

"Sergeant Matthews, Good to see you again. At ease."

Dale snapped to attention and saluted the General.

"At ease, Soldier. Come on back to my office, we have a lot to talk about."

Dale knew it had to be about the incident, but what could it be. He had already told them everything. What else could he say or do? "Yes Sir" Dale replied.

"Have a seat," General Bartlett said, holding his hand out to indicate Dale should sit in one of the chairs.

The office was small with peeling white paint on the walls. Behind the General was a window that looked out towards another plain wooden barracks. A heavy, metal desk stood between them. The General sat on a formidable, metal, rolling chair, trimmed out with green vinyl covering. His chair rolled back toward the window.

"Sergeant Matthews," the General said rhetorically, as he gathered his thoughts, "You know a lot more about these extraterrestrials than most soldiers."

Dale Matthews sat quietly, knowing the General was not seeking affirmation.

General Bartlett went on, "You see, you present a unique problem to the Army. We can't have you running around talking about space ships and aliens that have guns that shoot bolts of electricity."

"Sir, I have not said a word about the aliens. Not since we spoke of it in France."

"No. No. We know that, Sergeant. If you had . . . well, let's just say we would not be sitting here today. I think we have found a place for you, a place for you in our brand new, shall we say, military industrial complex," the General went on, choosing his words carefully.

Dale had never heard the phrase 'military industrial complex' before, but he fully understood the meaning. "Yes Sir," Dale said weakly.

"Since the war, the military brass has been divided over the extraterrestrial issue. After the war we discovered extraterrestrial equipment, planes, and weapons in several German laboratories. Hundreds of U.S. soldiers saw the equipment and figured out what it was. All were sworn to secrecy. Most of them will go to their graves never revealing what they saw. The few that break their oath will be discredited."

"That sounds right to me, Sir," Dale said, nodding his head in strong agreement.

"But, we still have a problem. You see, there are several very high-ranking Generals and Colonels that are grumbling about letting the American people know about the extraterrestrial nature of the Germans advances in weaponry and rockets. The problem is simple. If these high-ranking generals come forward and disclose what they know, the people will believe them. We will never be able to keep it quiet."

"Is that so bad. Why does it need to be kept quiet?" Dale asked.

"I'll tell you why it's so bad. The American people have just been through hell. Over 400,000 of their husbands and sons were killed. Worldwide, they are saying the death toll could be over 70 million. Americans need to rebuild; they need a rest. They need to sleep well at night. If they knew that there were beings from another world that possess weaponry so far superior to our own, beings we would have virtually no defenses against, well, there's no telling what they would do. It is imperative that we keep this secret."

"Yes Sir. But what can I do? I have already promised not to disclose what I saw."

"Yes, well, that brings us to you. You see we need people in the new, well, they are calling it the Air Force."

"Air Force, General?" Dale asked, pushing back in his wooden chair.

"Yes, soon a new branch of military will be formed; but it will break off from the Army and be a separate military force. They will call it the Air Force. It may be a few years before we can see it come about; but the central mission of the Air Force will be to defend against extraterrestrials."

"Wow. I'm willing to go where ever you send me, Sir."

"I'm glad to hear that because I need you to go to Germany," the General said.

"Germany?"

"Yes, there's an officer there that is threatening to tell the world about the extraterrestrial equipment he saw after the war. We need that to not happen."

"What would you have me do? Talk to him?"

"No. We have tried that. He won't listen."

"Then, what should I do?" Dale had a sinking feeling in is stomach, he knew the grim direction the conversation was heading.

"The only way to shut this guy up is to kill him. Otherwise he is going to let the world know."

"Can't we discredit him. Just like you said earlier?" Dale offered hopelessly.

"Nope, won't work for this guy. He's a national hero."

"What's his name?" Dale asked wearily.

"The target is 'Old Blood and Guts' himself."

Dale's heart skipped a beat. "No way. I can't kill The Old Man. That's treason. Not to mention just plain wrong."

"Dale, it's going to happen. This will remain a secret. There are only two ways this goes down. People are going to keep their secrets, or they are going to die. You are either with us or against us. You do this, or you end up on a list that you don't want to be on."

Dale sighed in defeat, he knew the General was serious and probably right about the list. "Yes Sir."

"So, you want to join the Air Force, son?"

"Sir, Yes Sir," Dale mustered, with false confidence.

"Good, Glad to hear it. In the meantime, I will make arrangements for you to be on a flight to Germany. Dismissed."

Dale went back to the barracks; it seemed even hotter now. Sweat poured from his brow as he sat before the small wooden desk near his rack. He opened his brand-new leather journal. The first clean, blank page stared at him. Dale began to write, his sweaty hand sticking to the papers.

THE END

POSTSCRIPT

Dear Reader,

Thank you for taking the time to read my first book. I hope you enjoyed it. As I am penning this final note, I have started working on a sequel to *Lost in Magadan*. The sequel begins only days after Snap and his team complete their mission and return home. The following is a brief excerpt from the upcoming sequel.

Respectfully,
William Lee

December 19, 1945
Bad Nauheim, Germany

Six months earlier, the Germans had surrendered to the allies. German cities were little more than hollow shells, and piles of rubble. The Americans, French, and Russians were overseeing the post-war reconstruction effort, and rounding up Nazi war criminals. Thousands of Germans were still homeless, hungry, and out of work. The Nuremberg trials had started at the end of the summer and were on going. Thousands of American troops still occupied the Germanic lands, while politicians and generals toured the remains of the former Nazi military machine.

The newly forming military-industrial-complex was circling the wagons and consolidating their power base. Secrecy was to be their weapon of choice. The alien technology discovered deep in the Nazi underground bunkers was alarming. Had the war gone on much longer, it was feared that Hitler may have been able to shift the tide in his favor with his quickly developing futuristic weapons. The newly discovered alien technology had to be kept a secret, and anyone threating that objective had to be eliminated.

Dale Matthews woke in in the early morning hours, the other men in the barracks were just now starting to get up. He was shivered from the cold, not wanting to begin his day, knowing it was even colder outside. It had been nearly a year since he came face-to-face with the large, gray alien in France. Feelings of guilt washed over him as he remembered how every other man in his squad was killed by the seven-foot-tall creatures. His feet touched the cold floor boards and he wanted to crawl back into bed.

Heading towards the showers, he thought of the terrible assignment he had been given. He had never murdered a person in cold blood. He had killed dozens of Nazis during the war, but that was different, they were pointing rifles at him. It was kill or be killed. Ever since he reported his encounter with the Large Grays, the Army had not known what to do with him. Until recently. The Army was coving its tracks, closing ranks. The Large Gray's involvement in the great war would remain a secret. Anyone brave enough to discuss alien technology with the public was to be silenced.

Dale Matthews was in a unique position, being the only person to ever survive hand-to-hand combat against a Large Gray, the Army would prefer not to silence him. But there was a steep price for his continued existence, he must help silence those that advocated for disclosure. Too many people witnessed the alien artifacts left by the fleeing Germans. Those that would not honor their confidentiality agreements would be dealt with harshly. That's where Dale came in.

The ice-cold water flowed over Dale's skin, he shivered. Others were slowly meandering into the open shower stall. Dale was assigned to the Army's 15th Battalion in Bad Nauheim, his role was to assist with documenting the reconstruction, a boring desk job. He wished that was his only job. Unfortunately, the desk job was only a cover for his real assignment, which was to eliminate those that may disclose secrets regarding alien technology. Those forming the new 'military industrial complex' as General Ryan Bartlett had called it, had a lot of power and influence.

As Dale dressed in his olive, drab uniform, he felt at ease, today was going to be uneventful, just passing time reviewing paperwork at his desk. No planning of assassinations or killing misguided loose-lipped soldiers. He was going to kill a VIP a few days earlier, it was supposed to look like a hunting accident. He was surprised by how deep the conspiracy went and how many people were involved, it was almost impressive. Dale had been given no time to plan or prepare, he was only given a few hours heads up.

Dale went to the location where the men were to be hunting, and waited in the freezing cold. The ground was wet and muddy, and snow was beginning to fall. Dale waited for the sixty-year-old General to arrive with his hunting party. When he asked his contact why he was given such short notice, the man said the hunting trip was just planned the night before. Dale waited on a ridge, among a stand of trees; he had no idea how they knew the General would stop here. Dale had an escape route planned, but he had no idea if it would work. He remembered that his stomach was turning over in knots, he threw up twice that morning. What if he failed to take the shot? What if he missed? Would he then be on that unenviable list?

Dale waited hours for the General to appear. His feet were wet and frozen. The time for them to arrive came and went. He waited another two hours, still no General. Eventually, a very relieved Dale got back on his Army motorcycle and drove back to headquarters.

Later that day, he found out that the General had been in a freak car accident and was paralyzed from the neck down. He felt bad that he was relieved the man had been injured in a car accident; for one more day, he would not carry the guilt of being a murderer.

A few days ago, his contact told him not to worry about killing the General because it looked like he was going to succumb to his injuries. Dale's spirts were rising, he hoped he could avoid murdering innocent people, maybe his bosses could find another task for him. He had been in Bad Nauheim for over a month now, planning the General's demise. During the last month, he had met an Army nurse, and they had hit it off. Elizabeth was from Bedford, Virginia and they had spent almost every evening talking about their futures. Of course, he had not mentioned his encounters with extraterritorial or his emerging career as a government hitman.

An hour before noon, Dale left his desk and stepped outside into the blistering cold to smoke a cigarette. Half-way through his smoke break, an officer, wearing a heavy trench coat, approached him. He did not recognize the officer as he walked directly towards him. Dale snapped to attention and gave a salute when he realized it was a Colonel that was standing before him.

"At ease soldier," the Colonel said, vapor forming in the air as he spoke. "Sergeant Matthews, I presume?" The Colonel was of average height with a muscular build, his face wore the signs of many sleepless nights. Dale suspected that he had earned his wings the hard way, and was capable of handling himself in any situation.

"Yes, Sir," Dale said as a knot started forming in his throat. He was certain that an unknown Colonel looking for him could only mean one thing.

"General Bartlett sent me," the Colonel said staring directly into eyes, looking for recognition. Apparently, Dale's countenance dropped, showing the Colonel what he needed to see. "It's time."

"I thought we were going to let nature take its course," Dale said weakly.

"That was the plan. Unfortunately, he showed signs of recovering today. The doctors said he could go home, soon. That we can't have."

"Damn," Dale muttered.

The Colonel continued, "I understand you have already familiarized yourself with the hospital, and you are ready?"

"Yes, Sir. I've been there several times, posing as a doctor. They have come to expect me from time to time. I have a good report with the guards," Dale said, somewhat proud of the work he had done. This was his first assignment as a spy, now to be an assassin.

The Colonel smiled and said, "Good work. Have you talked to the General?"

"I have. Not much though, only to introduce myself as one of his doctors, and small talk."

"That's good. You don't want to get too familiar with your victims. Remember that Sergeant."

Dale nodded his head, "yes sir."

The Colonel pulled from the right pocket of his trench coat a small canvas bag and handed it to Dale.

"What's this?" Dale asked, his voice cracking with surprise.

"What do you think it is, soldier? It's a hypodermic needle. How did you think you were going to kill the general? With a machine gun?"

"No. I figured I would strangle him or something," Dale said, trying not to sound stupid.

The Colonel shook his head, "Damn. You got a lot to learn, kid. This is special cocktail of drugs that were designed just for the General. They will cause his blood to clot, eventually he will die of a stroke or heart attack. Most likely, they will never detect the presence of the drug in his system."

"Most likely?" Dale asked.

"Yeah, you never know with these things. But I have been assured that the chances of detection are very slim. He will die slowly.

You will be long gone by the time the doctors even realize there is a problem."

"So, when do I administer the dose?" Dale asked, trying to not allow his voice to crack or tremble.

"Now. As soon as we end this conversation, you need to be on your way to Heidelberg. Matthews, did you really kill a Large Gray with your bare hands?"

"No. I used a knife," Matthews said as he made an upward hand gesture with an imaginary knife in it.

"No shit?" The battle-hardened Colonel looked impressed.

"I had help from my squad, another guy hit it with a carbine," Dale added.

"Well, Damn. Good for you, and the rest of your squad?"

"Didn't make it, Sir. I was the only survivor."

"Tough break, son."

"Colonel, what should I call you? I didn't catch your name."

"You shouldn't call me. Ever," the Colonel said as he turned and walked away, his boots crunching in the light snow fall.

ABOUT THE AUTHOR

William Lee is a life-long Virginia resident and student of history. After graduating with a degree in political science and philosophy, he worked on several congressional campaigns and remains interested in politics. He loves reading books about politics, American history, conspiracy theories, science fiction, and spy thrillers. He and his wife enjoy the outdoors, shooting sports, camping, hiking and kayaking. Please direct any correspondence with the author to: williamlee73@gmx.com or https://www.facebook.com/williamlee1973/

www.ingramcontent.com/pod-product-compliance
Lightning Source LLC
Chambersburg PA
CBHW061310170626
46817CB00001B/126